About *One Candle's Light*

My response to Fay Alexander's new book, *One Candle's Light,* is, Bravo! A great style of writing and a great way to draw people into history! Weaving the historic setting in such a way as to make the characters come alive brings the 16th and 17th centuries to life for the reader.

I highly recommend this book to readers who want to know the struggle of William Brewster in particular and the Pilgrim church in general in discerning whether they should separate from the Established Church of England.

The lessons learned in this work are not unrelated to our day. The commitment to truth as seen in Scripture, and the willingness to sacrifice when convinced it is the only way to preserve it, is embodied in the lives of the Pilgrims. It is also a lesson we might need more and more in the days in which we live.

May you be inspired as you see the Pilgrims in a fresh way through the eyes of William Brewster!

—PAUL JEHLE, Senior Pastor of the New Testament Church in Cedarville (South Plymouth, Massachusetts), Principal of the New Testament Christian School, author of *Plymouth in the Words of Her Founders: A Visitors Guide to America's Hometown*

ONE CANDLE'S
LIGHT

FAY ALEXANDER

OAKTARA

Waterford, Virginia

One Candle's Light

Published in the U.S. by:
OakTara Publishers
P.O. Box 8
Waterford, VA 20197

Visit OakTara at
www.oaktara.com

Cover design by Muses9 Design
Cover images: man, © Tony Alter; ship, © Christopher Schmidt; woman, © iStockphoto.com/ALiJA; Indian, © iStockphoto.com/Elerium Studios
Author photo © Olan Mills. Used by permission.

Scripture is taken from the King James Version of the Bible.

ISBN: 978-1-60290-221-3

TO MY HUSBAND, COMPANION,
AND CHIEF READER,
BILL

Who reflects the Lord's lovingkindness
and tender mercies
with grace and fervor
along this strenuous pilgrimage.

Acknowledgments

To those fellow seekers and writers in June Carlson's writing group—June, Orville Palmer, Mary Sessums, James Taylor, Linda Lassiter—I am grateful for many hours of concentration, encouragement, and kindly criticism.

I am deeply grateful to Smith Kirkpatrick, my professor of writing and mentor at UF, who nurtured my writing style from 19th Century excess to 21st Century economy. I wish he were here to critique this book.

For his perspective on American literature and firmly constructive criticism, I value Dr. Ben Pickard's expertise.

I much appreciate not only Dr. Corbin Carnell's excellent teaching of English literature but also his personal friendship and guidance to The Writer's Edge.

I am especially thankful to Dr. Paul Jehle, Senior Pastor of the New Testament Church of Cedarville, and Principal of the New Testament Christian School, for his valuable time spent reading the manuscript of *One Candle's Light*. He directed me to John Goodwin's *The Pilgrim Republic*, a rare book nearly fallen apart that the UF's library found hidden in a used bookstore in Tennessee.

To my husband and patient children who suffered late dinners and other delays during my pursuit of this novel, I express my gratitude and affection. I especially appreciate my son William's competence in computer technology and his patient tutoring without which I'd still be writing in longhand and typing on my cherished Olympic typewriter.

For their spiritual guidance and friendship I thank C.R. and Evelyn Smith, longtime pastor and first lady of Living Faith Fellowship.

To Gayle Roper, mentor at Blue Ridge Mountain Writers' Conferences, I am grateful for praise and encouragement for my work and a model of refreshing prose in her own.

Although I was privileged to consult the eminent libraries of the British Museum in London, and the Bodleian Library at Oxford University, I must heartily commend the George A. Smathers Library at the University of Florida, right in downtown Gainesville. I found a treasure of old books at Florida's library, some still unread as revealed by printed pages never separated. And to our great surprise and delight, my daughter, Beth, found in the Rare Book Room a collection of sermons written by Bishop Ezekial Hopkins of Londonderry, Ireland, a staunch Puritan and one of my husband's ancestors.

One

Cambridge

Young William Brewster peered over the gunwale of his skiff into the clear water of the River Ryton. His eel-pots on the bottom swarmed with flashing silver streaks, a good catch. But as he hauled the pots up, the eels' serpentine heads and thrusting lower jaws sent shudders through him, as if they might be offspring of the Serpent in Eden itself. He imagined that any one of them could rise up on its anal fins, lunge, and pierce him with razor teeth. He chuckled. He was grown up now, time to put away childish notions.

He dumped as many eels into the two baskets as they could hold, leaving the rest in the river to retrieve later. Gripping the handles firmly, he started off at a trot. He had gone only a few yards when he felt a sharp pain on his right wrist and glanced down at a large eel hanging onto his flesh, its teeth piercing like tiny needles. He stared at the creature, stunned that his nightmare had come true. He dropped the baskets, tore the eel from his wrist, and flung it into the basket with the other thrashing bodies.

As he watched the blood well on his wrist, he wondered: Had his very thought affected that fish? He recalled his Vicar warning against harboring bad thoughts, which gave ground to evil power. So, he was coming into manhood now. It was time to put away childish thoughts. Calmly, he wiped the blood on his breeks, snatched up the baskets, and ran halfway across the meadow, assured that the eels jostling in the basket could not possibly bite him.

Yet he might have to ask the Vicar about that power.

Nearing the Manor, he heard clamorous sounds wafting from the front courtyard and doubled his steps. The most exciting guests would lodge at the Manor tonight, another royal party visiting Scrooby en route to Edinburgh. Since the Archbishop of York had appointed his father manager of the post house in the village of Scrooby in the shire of Nottingham, William had been thrilled to host royal guests traveling between London and Edinburgh. Long before the Brewsters arrived, Margaret Tudor, sister of King Henry VIII, had stopped here on her way north to marry James V of Scotland. It was said that Henry himself had hunted in nearby Sherwood Forest.

Besides, William's father's position as agent to the Queen and manager of the post house carried prestige in the district, and Master Brewster intended that the good reputation of Scrooby Manor be properly upheld. Tonight the Manor would host these elegant royal persons with the best food and lodging in the land. Their bounty of river eels, among the fattest and tastiest in England, the cook's venison steaks, and the savory breads and sweets blooming in the bake house were sumptuous enough for Queen Elizabeth herself.

William dumped the baskets of eels on the kitchen table and ducked out before the cooks could nab him to clean them. He raced to the great hall, where a dozen or so men were doffing caps and jackets, stretching their legs, joyfully anticipating a feast after a long ride. William stopped abruptly in his headlong rush and shrank into the shadows against the wall. Though nearly a man himself at twelve years, he was suddenly shy of these lofty courtiers who not only stood in Her Majesty's royal presence but boldly offered her their sage advice. In turn she sent them on foreign missions to negotiate with kings.

"William!"

The sharp voice slapped his ears. "You're wanted in the kitchen, boy." Rob Douglas, his father's foreman, eagle-eyed and razor-tongued, caught the merest hint of any servant's shirking his duty, especially young ones. William scowled, turned sulkily, and dragged toward the doorway where Rob waited. Head down, he walked smack into a tall figure in plain leather and woolen riding britches. He stepped back. "Sorry, sir."

The figure did not stir. So William glanced up into the prettiest face he'd ever seen on a man, features lean and regular, almost as beautiful as a woman's.

Smiling, the Face asked, "In a hurry, son?"

William gazed into eyes as smoky-blue as afterglow. It took him a moment to recall his manners. "So sorry, sir."

The handsome head nodded toward William's wrist. "You've a bloody wound there, son. What happened?"

William glanced at his wrist and the crimson stain on his breeks. "Just a...." Could he admit to such an astute person that he'd been bitten by an eel?

The man took his hand. "Not a snake bite, I hope."

"Oh, no, sir. Only an eel." He blushed.

"An eel," the man said doubtfully.

"I catch them in the river, sir, the best eels in England."

The Face smiled. "And risk your own blood for our supper, I see."

William considered this astonishing thought. It made his effort sound almost...noble. "Well, sir, eels do look a bit like snakes. And they *can* bite. And..."

"What is your name, son?"

"William, sir. William Brewster."

"William, is it? Well, meet another of your ilk. I am William Davison."

"I am pleased to meet ye, sir."

"And I thee, Master Brewster. I take it you are the new host here?"

"My father is, sir."

"You should be proud, son. 'Tis a fine estate."

"Oh, I am proud indeed, sir." Amazed at such attention from a royal visitor, William nevertheless noticed the man's plain clothing. Only his silver belt buckle appeared to be of any value. "Are you a Queen's man, sir?" he asked abruptly.

"That I am, lad. A Queen's man to the death."

"Then why do you wear such—"

"William!" Rob suddenly loomed over William. "To the kitchen at once!'

Davison nodded at Rob, then looked down into William's eyes. "Such what?"

William swallowed. "Well, sir, if ye be a Queen's man, why do you dress so...so plain...sir?"

Davison broke into a grin. "Should we flaunt riches before the brigands waiting like vultures by the road?"

William took in a quick breath. "Oh no, indeed, sir."

Out of patience, Rob squeezed William's shoulder, yet spoke respectfully to Davison. "Forgive his manners, sir. He has not yet learned his proper place."

Davison nodded toward William's wrist. "Methinks so industrious a lad, willing to spill his blood for his work, knows his place well." He grinned down at William. "Yet your duty seems to be calling, son. Go along now."

William winced under Rob's grip, eyed him warily, then spoke boldly to the Queen's man. "We welcome thee to Scrooby Manor most heartily, sir." He wiggled out of Rob's grip, shot him a defiant glance, then scurried off to the kitchen. He paused at the doorway to glance back. The two men were chuckling amiably. He frowned. Were they laughing at him? Well, what did it matter? He had work to do.

That night, serving at supper, William hovered near Davison, hastening to refill his glass and to offer him special treats while he and his fellow envoys conducted lively discussion of political matters. These courtiers' elegant demeanor exuded that confidence of quality and privilege peculiar to gentry. Yet none fit so perfectly William's image of nobility as William Davison, truly a Queen's man!

❦

To William's delight, the next morning the royal party requested permission to hunt in the local forest. William begged his father to let him escort them to the hideaways of deer and foxes he knew so well. His father was curious. "Ye want to act as guide for the gentry, is it?"

"Should we not show them the best we have here at Scrooby, sir?"

"Son, gentry hunt the Queen's best preserves all over the land. They need no guidance from us."

"But we offer the best hunting, sir. And I know some secret spots."

Brewster eyed his eager son indulgently. "Laddie, ye have either the heart of a true servant or a canny diplomat, one."

Noting his father's puzzled brow, William guessed his thought. *If William is destined to manage a post house, he needs to learn early the skills and burdens of serving royalty. This extra service might well prove valuable.*

Brewster nodded. "Go on with ye, lad."

William trailed behind the hunting party gripping the leashes of four straining hounds while the hunters galloped ahead in pursuit of deer. His heart nearly burst with pride when Davison's arrow felled a buck with a shot clean through the neck. He could hardly wait to praise him for the expert kill.

His golden moment came later, as he hurried through the great hall that evening bearing a full tankard of ale and once again collided with the envoy, sloshing ale on Davison's breeks. Thunderstruck, he eyed the spreading stain with dismay.

Davison said calmly, "Still in a hurry, I see."

"So sorry, sir. Very sorry indeed."

"No harm done. Only my plain riding breeches." He winked.

William blurted out, "The buck was a beauty, sir!"

"Aye, I am proud of him. First buck I've downed all year."

"Tomorrow I can show you all the animals' lairs, sir. Everything! The deer, the foxes, the butterbumps' roosts. I know them well, sir."

"I am sorry, son. We lay over only one day for pleasure. Tomorrow we leave for Edinburgh." He glanced about the great hall. "God has given thee a fine place here to grow to manhood, William. Enjoy thy youth in this paradise while you may. Then if you travel about the world later, your home country will always rest securely in your heart."

"Aye, that I will, sir."

"How old are you, William?"

"Twelve, sir. Coming on to thirteen."

"Almost old enough for university."

"Me, sir? Oh, no, sir. I'm to manage the post house after my father."

"Perhaps. In a year or two, we'll see."

❧❧

When the envoys' party left the next morning, William approached Davison's mount and doffed his cap. "Godspeed t'ye, sir. May the wind blow fair for ye all the way to Edinburgh."

Davison smiled down upon him. "Why, I thank thee, lad, for that fine blessing." He reached into a pocket and held out a small object. "Here's a token for you in return. A memento of our first meeting, and a promise of others to come."

William took the object, then squinted up at Davison's figure silhouetted against the morning sun. The sun's dazzle behind him blotted out Davison's features, but William saw his hand rise to his brow in salute. The party gathered in column and rode out toward the North Road. When they had disappeared into the forest, William opened his fist and studied the object. It was an emblem bearing an Esquire's helmet over a shield inscribed *Gulielmi Davidsoni*. The crest of the shield bore an image of a stag's head cut off at the shoulders and winged. William took a deep breath. It was—it must be—Davison's family coat of arms.

He pressed the emblem to his heart. *A promise of meetings to come.* Yet Edinburgh was as many hundreds of miles north as London was south, weeks of journey by horseback. William Davison would come by Scrooby only once more this summer. Yet if William never saw him again he would cherish this crest all his life.

"Boy, stop dreaming and get to work!" Rob's voice pierced his daydream.

William stuffed the crest under his shirt and scooted off to finish his chores. Every now and then he raised his hand to touch his prize.

৵৽

Later that summer couriers brought stunning news of Mary Stewart's son, Prince James, who seemed to be a remarkable scholar. It was said that he could recite Scripture from the Bible in three languages. The Prince evoked much discussion among travelers at the Manor, for everyone knew that Elizabeth had birthed no natural heir, yet adamantly refused to name a successor. Mary's son greatly enhanced the Scottish Queen's chances to inherit her cousin's English throne.

William eagerly awaited Davison's return. Yet when his party appeared without him, William was both disappointed and yet proud to learn that Davison remained in Edinburgh as aide to Sir Henry Killegrew, Queen Elizabeth's special envoy to the Queen of Scotland.

The following year parties bound for Edinburgh passed through Scrooby often, but Davison was never among them. William inquired of each group until one aide told him that Davison had been sent to the Lowlands. "But wouldn't he have come by here? How could I have missed him?" William complained.

"Why, lad, he went by boat," the courier assured him, amused.

William consoled himself that Davison's status with Queen Elizabeth must have risen much higher, for everyone knew that the Lowlands were much more civilized than Scotland, known to be inhabited by savages.

William sometimes pondered Davison's suggestion that he attend university. His father had made it plain that he was to study diligently at the Vicar's school until he learned to read and write and do sums. A post house manager must be educated in such things. But the university? *Only gentry go to university,* he reminded himself. *People of the "commons" do not aspire beyond their station.*

William worked dutifully at the Manor the next year, and studied with the Vicar in the local grammar school. He learned to read and write English well, and began to parse Latin. His image of William Davison, risen high in the Queen's service, receded into a romantic figure of boyhood fantasy.

Then one day in the high summer of his fourteenth year his father called him aside and announced bluntly, "Son, the Vicar thinks ye bright enough to go to Peterhouse at Cambridge, his own college."

William was astonished. He had done well at school but could not imagine competing with the sons of gentry at Cambridge. Shaken, he grasped for an excuse not to go. "Will it not be very expensive, sir?"

"Vicar says it will be well worth our investment." His father's face, worn and creased with the toll of work, had never appeared more serious.

This heady prospect was at once thrilling and agonizing. In the midst of his chores he often forgot what he was doing and gazed off across the fields dreaming. Now he recalled more vividly William Davison, whose opinion counted even more than the Vicar's. If such scholars as these two recommended him, it just might be possible he could succeed at the university.

In September his father confronted him again. "When traffic on the Road slows for the winter you will leave for Cambridge."

A thrill shot through his stomach like an arrow. He actually was going to Cambridge, the finest university in the land!

⊱⋅⊰

As William and the post rider crossed the bridge over the river Cam and passed into the city proper, William absorbed the atmosphere of ancient buildings, rows of shops, and here and there the telltale round cap and long gown of an academic strolling by like any ordinary mortal.

After the post rider left him at the main gate of Peterhouse, William sat astride his horse, suddenly more frozen with doubt than winter's chill. Here he was, a country lad in this venerable city renowned for its prestigious intellect. How could he hope to compete? Yet, as he gazed at the gray walls and gates through which many hundreds of men had passed, calm drifted upon him. Many a country lad had matriculated here, and he was probably no more and no less competent than any of them, as deserving as any in the land. His Vicar and a Queen's man, both Cambridge graduates, had encouraged him. He need only do his best and persevere as he had done at Scrooby, and if it so pleased God to lead him through the academic maze to a degree, he could not fail.

He urged his mount forward, figuring that by the time he found the stables and the receiving office, he could muster enough courage to face the stern overseers who would admit him to these halls.

"Hail there, chap," a voice called out behind him. "Are ye bound for Peterhouse?"

He turned to face a lad as young as himself. "Aye, that I am. And you?"

"Aye. Fresh as a newborn lamb." The lad glanced up at the towers. "So this is the famed Old School. Looks a bit hoary to me."

William glanced at the lad's profile, a pleasant, not quite handsome face enlivened by flashing dark eyes and an amiable grin. A cheeky sort, apparently, showing no sign of anxiety.

They dismounted at the stables where two boys ran up to take their reins. The young man said, "Well, this is service fit for gentry. Now if the old graybeards treat us as kindly...." He thrust out his hand. "I'm John Penry from Cefnbrith, Breconshire, Wales."

William seized his hand. "William Brewster. Scrooby, Nottingham."

"Scrooby, you say?"

William nodded. "Aye."

Penry frowned. "I say, isn't that where Cardinal Woolsey spent his last days?"

William's eyes widened. "You heard of this in Wales?"

"Read about the old chap's change of heart there at the end." He struck a reverent pose, eyes toward Heaven, palm over his heart, and intoned, "If I had served my God as diligently as I have done the King, He would not have given me over in my gray hairs." He broke into a grin. "A splendid line, that. One to remember. Some bard will immortalize it one day."

So, William was thinking, *this lad is already a scholar.*

Behind the desk in the receiving office a clerk peered over half-rimmed glasses perched on his nose. "Welcome to Peterhouse, gentlemen. Names, if you please?"

"Brewster. William."

The clerk glanced down at his ledger. "Sign here, please."

While William entered his name, the clerk turned to Penry. "You, lad?"

"Penry. John."

The clerk turned the book to Penry.

"Can we be mates, then?" Penry asked eagerly.

The clerk frowned. "Sorry, sir. Brewster's on second floor, room ten." He glanced at the ledger. "And Penry, first floor, room three. You are assigned to different Fellows."

"Bother! This lad suits me well. Can we change the roster?"

The clerk raised one eyebrow. "A bit late for that, Mister Penry. Rooms are assigned by the Senior Fellow according to the placement of your guides." He squinted at Penry coolly. "Does that suit you, Mister

Penry?"

Penry flashed his amiable grin. "Of course, sir. Whatever you say."

As the two men went to their rooms, William asked wryly, "D'ye have it in mind to make a notable mark here, Mister Penry?"

"Aye, why not? If no one takes notice, one is lost in the crowd, is he not?"

William's room was only large enough for two students, for each a bed—one a trundle rolled under the high bed during the day—a plain wooden table for study, a shelf for books, a cupboard for personal belongings, and a jug and bowl. William stowed his stuff in the empty cupboard and looked about the room, then glanced out a small window facing the inner courtyard. So this was to be his home for the year. He took a deep breath. A country lad used to the wide-open fields of Nottinghamshire could scarcely breathe in such tight confines. Yet he had come to Peterhouse to develop his brain, not his lungs. And for that he supposed this room was adequate.

He discovered unhappily that he had just missed dinner, the first meal of the day served at eleven o'clock. But conveniently he fell in with a chap named Rogers, who directed him to Mr. Ramsey's lecture room. Fellows, who were senior students or graduates, tutored small groups of students and directed their studies. William sat through his first lecture in Rhetoric mystified by the unfamiliar terms and argument, but took hope that Ramsey, who seemed a congenial sort, would accept with patience his efforts to catch up.

He quickly learned the discipline. The first year of study for the Baccalaureate degree covered the study of Rhetoric, the second and third years Logic, and the fourth Philosophy. Students attended lectures in their own colleges as well as those in the larger University, and must pass two disputations in the public schools and two responses in their own colleges during four years' study.

His personal routine began with rousing out of bed at the ringing of the bell at five in the morning, then attending services and occasionally a short homily at Little St. Mary's Chapel. Then followed his personal studies interspersed with exercises and lectures, and public disputations. Without breakfast, he starved until eleven for dinner, a joint of beef, mutton, or veal, and fish on Fridays. During meals a Bible-clerk read passages from Scripture, and after dinner some declamation or dispute would follow.

Evening prayer in St. Mary's and supper at five o'clock ended the students' formal day, and the evening hours after supper were his own, with restrictions. He could not converse with fellow students in English, only Latin, French, Greek, or Hebrew. He could not leave the premises except by special leave in the company of a tutor or a Master of Arts. He could not attend the Sturbridge Fair, taverns, dice-houses, courts, boxing-matches, skittlegrounds, dances, bear-baitings, or cocking-mains, nor swim in the Cam. Penalties for infractions were severe: corporal punishment for the very young, fines for adults, or for the most serious offenses, to be "discommonsed," excluded from the dining hall, set in the college stocks, or—the worst—to be expelled.

For a while William missed the freedom of his fields, even catching eels in the Ryton. Yet soon he was too busy to look up John Penry in the same college. But one day he chanced upon the Welshman leaving the lecture hall. Delighted to see him, Penry whispered, "What do you say to a sojourn in the city Saturday?"

"It is forbidden."

"So they say. But I've been told that Fellows much prefer their own freedom on Saturdays and seldom check the students' rooms."

William shook his head. "Not for me. Cannot afford the risk."

"No risk. Chap tells me the boys go out by twos and threes and are rarely discovered missing."

"Rarely? Once is too much. No, I cannot," William said firmly.

Penry grinned. "Good lad. Full of noble convictions. Ye shall have no misspent youth to repent on Judgment Day."

Yet on Saturday next William was restless—and unusually bored with his studies. Despite his convictions, he was strongly tempted to seek out Penry. He considered a wayward dip in the chilly Cam, but that was no less a crime than sporting on the town. He found Penry's room empty, then trudged about all day, feeling morose, and worse, cheated, as if the reward of this exalted degree unfairly required the loss of all innocent, youthful pleasures.

Brewster awaited news of the students' reprimand but heard nothing. Neither Penry nor any other student was accused of scandal, nor were any penalties imposed. When he saw Penry again, he said, "I see that you accomplished your mission without mishap."

Penry was jubilant. "Superbly executed. Too bad you didn't join us. And how was your day?"

"Dismal. I confess that I pouted the day long."

"Spoken like a true suffering saint. Yet you might as well have suffered for the crime as coveted the pleasure of it. One sin is as bad as the other."

William waved off this comment. "What did you see?" he asked eagerly.

"Unbelievable wonders. I will tell you all about it after supper." His grin was jovial, infectious. He leaned closer to whisper, "In forbidden *English*."

Penry and his friends had taken in skittles, a boxing-match, and even gambled at a dice-house. William exclaimed irritably, "How many of you went?"

"Ten altogether. Two by two, one pair covering for another, then slipping out when each pair returned. One day, lad, before you leave here, you must sin a little, for your soul's sake. Else, how can you genuinely repent and save it?"

If by this reasoning, William had sinned no less than Penry and his clever cohorts, he consoled himself that at least he regretted it. The adventurers seemed to suffer not a jot of remorse for their breezy infraction of the rules.

William studied diligently through the winter and spring, quietly plodding from study to lecture to chapel and back to study, gaining ground in Latin and Rhetoric. So, on Commencement Day, the first Tuesday in July, when all students gathered to observe graduates "commence" in their degrees, he sat in the large hall with a comfortable sense of achievement. He must accomplish three more years before a degree could be conferred. Yet since December he had earned a place in this august body, gained confidence that his perseverance would prevail, and could believe at last that one day he would graduate.

How he welcomed, though, three months of freedom stretching before him! He sought Penry to say good-bye. "Are you back to Wales for the summer?"

"Aye, briefly. But soon to go to London."

William was aghast. "London in the summer? Why?"

Penry glanced about, then took William's arm and stepped away from the swarm of departing students. "I'll tell you this, Brewster, because I deem you trustworthy." He grinned. "One with your solid convictions won't betray me."

"Betray you! What have you done now?"

"A group of separatists meet underground in London under the bishops' very noses. They grow in numbers daily, and their sentiments are spreading to the shires. They were brave enough to meet under Mary Tudor and bred some inspired preachers. I want to know what they are about."

"Separatists! Surely you will not consort with such as that!"

"You've heard of Brown who stirred the pot here a few years ago?"

"Aye." Every student at Cambridge soon learned of Robert Brown, whose radical religious theories had disrupted the entire University. Brown believed that the Church of England was as apostate as the Roman Church and declared that true Christians could not dutifully worship in such churches without risk to their souls. He upheld Luther's thesis of justification by faith alone, a matter of brisk controversy among scholars, and anathema among Churchmen.

Penry said, "Their convictions are strongly biblical, my friend. Sooner or later the Church must acknowledge them."

William shook his head sadly. "Would you risk your future here to meddle with rebels? Whether right or wrong, they cannot overcome the Queen's law."

"Ah, but can the Queen's law overcome faith? Where lies our true loyalty? To the love of law or to the love of God?"

"You're treading dangerous waters, John. I'll pray for your safety."

Penry held out his hand, grinning. "Never fear, friend. I shall have much to tell you at autumn term. Meantime, enjoy your homecoming."

"Godspeed to you, John."

Riding the North Road homeward, William fretted for John Penry. His engaging cavalier spirit would doubtless sustain him through Cambridge where radicals were tolerated, but would surely make of him a target in the wider world.

Two

Penry

Arriving at Scrooby was like returning to Heaven, the serene countryside and lush flowers balm to William's senses. The village itself seemed hardly more than a bend in the road, but the Manor was more imposing for that. He looked upon it pridefully, grateful for his heritage. After the first flush of homecoming and sharing tales of his sojourn at Cambridge, he fell into his usual routine of chores, and found them, even catching eels, a surprising refreshment from the intensity of scholarly study.

Yet by the end of the second week home he lay abed one moonlit night and admitted to himself that he missed Peterhouse. The novelty of travelers at Scrooby did not compare with the intellectual stimulation at Cambridge. With a pang of nostalgia he realized that going to Peterhouse had been his rite of passage from childhood to youth. He would no longer be content at Scrooby.

Surely this was not what his father hoped for.

He would confess this change of heart to the Vicar who must have wrestled with the same dilemma after his sojourn at the University.

He studied the shadows on the ceiling, thinking of John Penry somewhere in London, no doubt pursuing new experience. He was not so different from Penry. He, too, longed to venture into a wider world, but not at the expense of his major ambition to serve the Crown, like William Davison.

To William's delight, Davison himself arrived at Scrooby within the month, bound again for Edinburgh. This time, as soon as William saw him striding into the great hall, he went boldly to greet him. Davison's face lit with pleasure. "Well, lad, 'tis a man you've become indeed."

14

William smiled. "A full term at Peterhouse behind me, sir."

"Splendid! So, did you find the Old School stimulating?"

"Very much so. I look forward to going back."

"Come tell me about it."

Davison listened to William's rapt account of his months of study, his teachers, and notable students. "And how is old Master Perne?" Davison asked.

"Old Turner? Some wags conjugated his name like a Latin verb—perno, pernare, pernavi-and so on, meaning of course, 'I change often.'" During the years of the Reformation Master Perne had served Kings Henry and Edward, and Queens Mary and Elizabeth, nimbly changing his religious position to Catholic or Protestant as the monarchs required. "Yet he is a good man, sir, strong for the college."

Davison agreed wryly. "To keep one's head in these times, one must develop a supple neck." Then he said seriously, "This will be my last mission to Edinburgh for awhile. I will be traveling to the Lowlands. Her Majesty's sympathies lie with the Protestants there, but she cannot support them openly. Delicate diplomacy is the requiried tactic."

William had heard much discussion at Peterhouse about Spanish aggression in Europe and England's obligation to support Protestant rebels there. Yet while the Queen pursued an official policy of conciliation with the Catholic governments of France and Spain, her usual *media via*, Protestant Englishmen naturally sympathized with Flemish and French "heretics."

Davison gazed at William levelly, a slight smile on his lips. "Would you be interested in joining me there, Will? I need a good steward."

William's eyes widened. "Are you serious, sir?"

"Very much so...eventually. But not yet. You must finish at least another year at Peterhouse. Then perhaps...."

So dazzling a prospect obliterated in one stroke William's desire for further study. He struggled to keep from blurting out, "But why not now, sir? I want to go now!"

"I did not join Sir Henry Killegrew until I had commenced my degree." Davison grinned. "Yet I admit, had he made the offer earlier, I would have swooned with delight." His gaze drifted past William's shoulder. "My first mission for the Queen was to accompany Sir Killegrew to Edinburgh to congratulate Mary Stewart on Prince James' birth. It should have been a joyous time for her, but she was disconsolate after her secretary Riccio's murder...in particular her husband's part in it."

William gasped. "You saw the Queen of Scots herself?"

"And a sight she was to behold. I was thrilled merely to breathe in such high company." Yet an expression of sadness crossed his face. "But I was very young, William. Such naivete is only possible in the innocence of youth." He smiled slightly. "Things are never as they seem."

William heard Davison's words faintly above his heart's clamoring. *Now! Why not now?*

Davison eyed him closely. "I see temptation in your face, son—that yearning for adventure. I know it well. I was heady with pride to be chosen aide to Sir Henry. Yet believe me, you will be wiser to finish your studies first." He reached out to pat William's shoulder. "You'll be better prepared for this wicked world."

William did not believe this for a minute. He swallowed. "If you say so, sir. I do thank you, sir."

⁂

William returned to Peterhouse in the fall resigned to Davison's advice and with renewed confidence in his own abilities. And he could hardly wait to impress Penry with Davison's offer. But Penry's mind was on more serious subjects. "You warned me of dangerous waters, friend. Those poor devils in London test those waters daily. They tolerate no taint of Romish influence in their worship. They declare that priests' paraphernalia is Satan's work and will cost them salvation." He wagged his head sadly. "True as that may be, methinks they spar with gnats."

William said offhandedly, "I say, let the bishops decide these matters—after all, that is their commission, to save the rest of us the trouble."

As they strode across the campus en route to a lecture, Penry nodded toward a young chap crossing the green. "Now here's a subject more to my taste. Note the gentleman approaching."

William saw a figure in a student's gown and round cap, yet bearing an air of aristocratic gentility. "Who is he?"

"Robert Devereaux, second Earl of Essex, who graces the halls of Trinity College, if you please. Have you ever seen a nobler figure of English manhood? Surely he is destined to catch Gloriana's eye."

William squinted for a better look. Devereauz nodded as he passed them, a slight smile on his chiseled face. His rank forebade the jocular greeting they might have tossed an ordinary student, and when he had passed, Penry said archly, "England's fortunes are made by such as he." He gave William a sly wink. "Oh, to be a mouse and follow that chap's capers about the Queen's court!"

William was impressed with other notable figures at Cambridge. William Perkins, graduate Fellow and lecturer to the prisoners at Cambridge Castle, spoke with magnificent power to mesmerize undergraduates and frustrate authorities with an innovative theology. And a quiet student named Christopher Marlowe was so proficient in English letters that some predicted fame for him in literary circles.

Not all was sober study at Peterhouse. As the last of autumn's fires set the countryside aglow, Penry and other boisterous lads planned illicit escapades to the forbidden Sturbridge Fair. The Queen's delight in bear and bull baiting seemed to justify their lust. But because everyone, including William, wanted to see this Fair, the students had to employ a bit more finesse to outwit their Fellows, who were reported to be especially vigilant during fairs. Penry refined his strategy so that the men departed in the usual twos and threes from different lodgings, staggering their absences so that the Fellows would not notice blocks of men missing at the same time.

His conscience somewhat strained, William at first demurred, then reconsidered. For him the sin was not so much indulgence in worldly behavior as willful breaking of University rules, which in good conscience he had sworn to uphold. Yet fairs were so integral a part of country life, such robust human pleasure, that stringent rules for students seemed more properly laws of men than God's. Besides, he decided somewhat guiltily, unless someone tattled, Penry's scheme was almost foolproof.

His turn came after dark when he joined Penry and a chap named John Greenwood from Corpus Christi College. The town was alive with country rowdies carousing along the streets, popping in and out of alehouses and mysterious closed doors from which lilting feminine giggles floated. This famed Fair presented a spectacle never beheld in Nottinghamshire.

Forced by their allotted time to be choosy, they decided to pass by games and dancing for a bit of dicing and animal baitings. Outside the cockpits the three men glanced at each other. Greenwood asked, "Will it be bears or cocks?"

Penry said, "We only have two hours 'til midnight. No time for both."

"Cocks it is then," said Greenwood.

They entered the pit, a mound of earth covered with sod and surrounded by seats in circular tiers crowded with eager bettors. They made their way to the top row. Soon the "setters-to" took two cocks armed with steel gaffles on their legs and placed them beak to beak. At a signal the cocks flew at each other, jabbing their vicious steel spurs and sending drifts of multicolored feathers aloft. The bloody fracus did not dismay William so much as the faces of the leering crowd, alight with bloodlust. After two such conflicts the three students glanced at each other and in tacit agreement quietly rose and made their way out of the pit.

"Well," murmured Greenwood, "so that's a cockfight."

"So," said Penry, "have we had enough?"

"Now we just have time for the bears," prompted Greenwood eagerly.

They had been gone from Peterhouse three hours, long enough to stretch their luck. A bit sickened by the cocks' contest, William warned, "It's late. Let's go back now before we're discovered."

"And miss the bears?"

"That would take another hour. Is it worth the risk?"

They hesitated, disappointment on all three faces. Penry spoke up. "Let's chance it. If we're caught, we'll have seen something worth the rebuke."

"Rebuke is one thing," muttered William. "Is it worth expulsion?"

18

"Ahh. They wouldn't boot us out for a mere bear fight," insisted Greenwood.

"All right, "Penry said with a chuckle. "Might as well be hanged for the goose as the gander."

Approaching the bear ring, they heard raucous shouts from the audience and the loud sporadic yapping of dogs. The three paid their fees and found seats high above the arena. At the center of the ring a large brown bear paced on four massive feet at the end of a heavy chain encircling its waist and tethered to a stake fixed in the ground. The creature was stunning in its enormity, now and then rearing up on hind legs and tossing its huge head about, trying to sniff its surroundings. In their locked box the dogs' yapping caught its attention. It dropped to its feet and growled toward the box, rousing the dogs to a frenzy.

At one side of the arena the bear ward took bets from an eager audience. Finally, the betting done, the ward unlocked the box and flung open the door. Five sleek grayhounds sprang out and streaked for the bear. It rose on its hind legs and gave forth a mighty bellow, then lashed out with huge paws bristling with claws. One swipe caught a dog full admidships and sent it sailing across the ring, and at once the other four backed off. The crowd sat forward in their seats, tense with anticipation.

Now the bear swung its head about as if to assess its position, then drew back to the stake so that its chain loosened and could not choke off its lunges. The dogs seemed to revise their strategy, too, obeying some pack instinct to spread in a circle and attack as a team. Their movement forced the bear to shift about trying to watch all of them at once.

Suddenly, one dog rushed the bear. The creature struck out, but the dog veered hastily out of its reach. At once the other dogs dashed from four directions, three biting into its haunches and back leg. The bear rose up roaring and shook them off. They streaked to safety. A cheer went up from the crowd at the first score.

The dogs resumed circling, poised for a second attack. This time the first dog rushed, but the bear feinted, then quickly swung to meet the others, catching one with claws like hooks that ripped its hide with deep bloody gashes. The dog limped away, yelping, to lick its wounds while the crowd lustily cheered the bear. Some jeered the whipped dog. This was the second score of the match.

For a moment William turned away, dreading the outcome.

The four dogs continued to circle the bear, now and then making short rushes within a safe distance just outside the reach of its paws. Suddenly, one dog streaked under the bear's paws and leapt for its throat. Instantly, the other dogs rushed the bear's back and legs. The bear reared, clutching the dog at its throat while the others held on. The bear dropped and rolled, dogs and bear snarling in a flurry of dust. Then three dogs scampered clear, and the bear stood up on four feet and shook itself, leaving one dog lying crushed and inert beneath it. The crowd applauded the draw, and the three students shouted out, unashamedly cheering on the bear.

Two dogs were down, but the bear was bleeding heavily from its back, legs, and neck. The arena reeked with the smell of animal blood and human sweat as the tension of combat to the death mesmerized the crowd. William wanted to turn away but could not move. Penry and Greenwood sat as riveted as himself, their eyes fixed on the wounded bear.

The three dogs remaining resumed pacing warily, their sharp teeth bared and eyes bursting with bloodlust, keeping the bear shifting and turning and lashing with futile effort. They moved in ever-closing circles, making dashes to a point just out of the bear's reach, then darting back. Then one dog dashed under the bear's front legs and charged its underbelly, tearing a long bloody gash in its abdomen. The bear reared up and screamed. At once the other two dogs attacked its legs and haunches. The bear dropped to all fours and batted the air as the dogs dashed to safety. The dog that had torn its belly swept in again, and the bear cuffed it and sent it sprawling. It did not rise, its back broken. The crowd stood up and roared as the bear reared its head and steadied itself. Now it was bleeding heavily from all its wounds.

The last two dogs approached, crouching like cats, stalking, closing for the kill. The weakened bear swung listlessly as each darted toward him, all three animals in continuous movement. William felt tears burning behind his eyes at the sight of that magnificent creature bravely holding on while the lean dogs, their tongues flapping, paced for the final attack.

As if at a signal both dogs rushed the bear, one charging its throat and the other its belly. The bear tore the dog from its throat and slammed it to the ground while the other dog clamped its teeth on the abdominal wound and jerked its head from side to side, tearing it open. The bear's intestines began to spill out, emitting a fearful stench. The bear staggered, still swiping at the lone dog which nimbly evaded the feeble sweep of its paws. At last the bear sagged to the ground made muddy with its own blood.

The crowd's roar rose to a crescendo while the dog tore again and again at the bear's abdomen. At last the great creature rolled over and lay still.

The three students sat in silence as the crowd continued to scream its approval and bettors scrambled to collect their winnings. A hollow pit of shame lay like ice in William's stomach. His companions sat in stony silence beside him, none daring to face each other lest each see his own chagrin mirrored in their faces. After a time the three rose without a word and left the arena.

Trudging back to Peterhouse they kept silence, each enduring the event they had witnessed, grimly realizing that if such a spectacle resulted in their expulsion from the University, it would be a worthless loss. At the gate where they would part, they paused and at last gazed guiltily into each other's eyes. "Well, lads," Penry said lightly, "what do you think?"

None answered for a moment. Then William said, "I wish the bear had won."

"Aye, me too," said Greenwood.

"And I," agreed Penry. "But what chance did he have, lads, five against one?"

They reflected a few moments. Then Greenwood said brightly, "Well, what chance do we have if the Fellows have tagged us?"

They snickered, shrugged, shook hands and parted.

None suspected that their generous guides, charged with their students' intellectual and spiritual welfare, and understanding full well the demanding thrusts of curious youth, had not once glanced into their study cubicles.

Though Penry was cavalier about breaking social rules, he was deeply serious about theological doctrine. He and Brewster argued frequently about the role of the Church in society, a topic of raging interest at Cambridge.

In the spring of 1570 Thomas Cartwright had astounded the Cambridge community with his interpretation of the first two books of Acts in which he contrasted the humble beginnings of the Apostles' church with the elaborate hierarchy of the Church of England. He claimed that Church authority so usurped God's power that it became the anti-Christ, authority in place of Christ, and boldly advocated the breakdown of the entire episcopate—the titles and offices of archbishops, deacons, deans, and chancellors. Flocks of students crowded his lectures, and according to the Archbishop Grindal, were thus "in danger to be poisoned by him with love of contention and liking of novelties."

Penry ardently agreed with Cartwright. "Think about this, Brewster," he urged, waving his hands as they walked. "We accepted that the Gospel of the Bible and the tradition of men were compatible, and now we find they are not. Which is more reliable, the word of men or the word of God?"

William squirmed when Penry criticized the Church. To demean the Anglican faith of the Queen and especially her servant William Davison, seemed to him to border on blasphemy. The shriveling thought struck him: Perhaps it *was* blasphemy!

Penry pressed on. "Do you realize that for centuries Churchmen actually kept the Scriptures hidden, dispensing rituals in Latin which illiterate men could neither understand nor question? The 'gospel' foisted on the people has been the word of priests, not the biblical message of Christ's atonement."

William bristled. "Priests are fallible men like any others. I do not believe that good men of the Church deliberately misled the people."

"Aha! That's my point. They did not need to mislead them, but only to keep them ignorant. Until Tyndale's Bible, the people could not read the truth, and therefore accepted as true, icons and artifacts which themselves became objects of worship. That is idolatry, worship of other gods, expressly forbidden in the Old Testament."

William frowned, shaking his head. "I prefer to believe that good men used visual symbols to inform illiterate people. How else could they teach them?"

"You have read Brown's works?"

"Aye, I have," William sighed, knowing where Penry was headed. While a student at Corpus Christi College, Robert Brown had been one of those "poisoned" by Cartwright's radical opinions. He went so far as to suggest that believers who disagreed with Church teaching should separate from it. The very word *separate* had since become poisoned, and anathema not only to the Church but also most of its ardent reformers who insisted that the Church be reformed by her members.

The two men paused where their paths diverged. Penry confronted William with a mischievous grin. "So, friend, where do you stand?"

William returned Penry's direct gaze, reluctantly admiring his friend's absolute conviction. Once Penry made up his mind, he never waffled, and gave short shrift to fence sitters. William answered, "They are both too extreme. I agree that the Church should be cleansed of Romish 'stuff,' but to dismantle its very structure, or to abandon it altogether...goes too far. The rebels will next demand that the Queen submit to presbyters!"

Penry grinned broadly and punched William's shoulder. "A capital idea! Bravo, Brewster!"

""Come, Penry, be sensible. Purists do more damage than repair with their nagging persistence. The Queen is Supreme Governor of the Church and Defender of the Faith. It is folly to expect she will reorder her government."

To William's surprise Penry conceded with a bright smile. "I agree, friend. I am not yet one of Brown's separatists. But if the authorities—including Her Majesty—refuse to change, we may come to that." He stuck out his hand. "Godspeed to you, friend, 'til we meet again." They shook hands and parted.

William suffered Penry's arguments because they were friends, but he avoided the hot debates surging in students' rooms and lecture halls.

Since Davison's last visit he was infused with ambition beyond earning his degree. He dared to hope that he might not only serve an apprenticeship with Davison, but one day might enter the Queen's service himself. He could hardly expect to endear himself to Davison, much less the Queen, by joining strident critics of their government.

One frigid day as he left the lecture hall, William Davison surprised him waiting in the foyer. The diplomat greeted him cheerily. "How goes it with thee, lad? You look well indeed."

William was overcome with gratitude. Davison was most favored among men, handsome of feature, fair and slim, and bore himself with easy grace. He looked every inch a servant to the sovereign. "Sir! I am delighted to see you."

"And I am eager to hear your accomplishments. Come, let us talk."

William looked about for Penry, hoping to introduce him to his mentor. But Penry did not appear, and William, keenly aware of students' admiring glances toward Davison's distinguished figure, succumbed to rank pride as they walked together to a local tavern, a rare treat for a student. Apparently accustomed to such attention, Davison seemed completely indifferent to admiring glances.

They sat in a quiet corner. Davison had been traveling between London and the Lowlands on a delicate political mission he could not discuss, and turned the subject to William. "Tell me what you are learning at this fount of wisdom."

William burst out, "Much! That is, when I can dodge ranting reformers."

Davison suppressed a smile. "I warned you. Great changes afoot."

"The radicals go too far. Some say that if the Church will not change they will separate. I cannot agree. I say we should comply with the Queen's law rather than disrupt the nation with bitter controversy. Why, if carried to extremes, this could become civil war!"

A few patrons nearby turned their heads at his voice, and William blushed, fearful he might embarrass Davison.

"Spoken like a true patriot," Davison said lightly, sprawling back in his chair. "But I remind you, son, that we Englishmen are free to discuss our differences. In Europe Protestants suffer persecution as heretics."

"Yet in England we profess to follow one faith. We jeopardize our unity haggling with our own brothers."

"I agree. The Queen's worst bugbear is anarchy. That is why she adheres strictly to her *media via*. Her cautious middle way balances extremes."

"Then I am bound in conscience to serve her loyally," William declared.

"With thy life, lad. With thy life."

Yet soon afterwards Penry informed William that he had decided to endorse Cartwright's call to replace the Church of England's episcopate with presbyters, elders selected by the congregation. "He is right, Brewster, don't you see? Leaders of the Church, like the earliest churchmen, should arise from the consenting will of the congregation, not the hierarchy of autocrats."

William protested. "Men of ambition will always drive to the top and dominate the ignorant not shrewd enough to choose wise leaders."

"Ignorant in worldly knowledge, perhaps, but men empowered by the Holy Ghost have the mind of Christ. They become 'new' men reformed by the love of God endowed with His holy wisdom. Only then can men's higher motives prevail over their base instincts."

William smiled. "My good Welsh brother, how the good Lord must esteem your faith and your optimism. Would there were more like you."

William did agree with Penry's premise. The essence of Christian faith held that a believer's submission to Christ transformed his human spirit through revelation by the Holy Ghost. Thus the "good news" message of the Gospel affirmed not only man's salvation in Heaven but also his regeneration in Christ's image on earth. If all men embraced that logic, Penry was right, men could govern themselves wisely. Yet as long as God apparently chose only monarchs and nobility to rule, men of the commons would never attain power. He feared that his dear friend Penry and his fellow zealots fought for a lost, perhaps disastrous, cause.

During his second year at Peterhouse conflict sharpened between radicals and conservatives when in 1583 the Queen appointed John Whitgift Archbishop of Canterbury and commissioned him to enforce uniformity of religion. Any criticism of the established Church, if only spirited debate among intellectuals, now became suspect of sedition. Even ministers supported by nobility, gentry, or Members of the House of Commons who dared to advocate presbyterianism within the established Church became targets of oppression. Whitgift prohibited all practices deviant from Church policy, allowing no unauthorized Bibles, services, or preachers, and no alterations in the Book of Common Prayer. His machine of enforcement was a High Commission endowed with wide powers of examination and censorship, while Whitgift himself and the Bishop of London censored all printed matter. Believers who reverenced biblical authority declared Whitgift's position as bishop to be unscriptural and his abuse of that office tyrannical. Not the least of their despair was that he performed with the full approval of Queen Elizabeth who referred to him affectionately as her "little black husband."

Absorbed in his studies, William was not personally affected by Whitgift's power until Penry and Greenwood appeared one night in his room and handed him a paper they had written damning all bishops and Whitgift in particular, daring to call him the Devil's advocate. William looked up from the tract shocked. "What do you intend to do with this?"

"Publish and circulate it," Penry said with a wry smile.

"You cannot be serious."

"Never more so, my dear brother. John here has found a publisher in London who will print it secretly, and we will broadcast it about the city. No one will suspect that its authors lurk in Cambridge." He grinned. "Unless our trusted confidants tattle on us." He gave William a broad wink and sprawled across his bed. Greenwood nodded, stationing himself against the doorframe from which point he could glance up and down the hall to see anyone coming.

"You are mad! You would flaunt this tract in Whitgift's face?'

"The man's zeal against true Christians is demonic. He must be exposed."

"Agreed," muttered Greenwood.

"But who will listen? No one dares cross him."

"The people of the commons will listen," Penry said to the ceiling. "They know the truth already but fear to speak it. Yet someone of courage must. One day men will rise up in their common strength and refuse the tyrant." Penry suddenly sat up, his smiling face turned serious. "Remember the bear baiting? I see us like that regal creature, which is only desecrated because it is chained and defenseless against Whitgift's snarling curs. We forget that our unity in the truth of the Gospel can make us strong."

Greenwood spoke up. "Or look at it another way. We are like dogs snapping at Whitgift the bear, yet he is free and we are muzzled. Like the dog pack, if we unite together in our common strength, we can overcome him."

"Both analogies are flawed," snapped William. "No unfettered bear in its natural habitat could be overcome by dogs. And Whitgift, the Queen's 'little husband,' is invincible in his own habitat, which is the very power she has given him." His eyes flashed with sudden insight. "Now there's the real bear!"

Penry and Greenwood burst out laughing, but William was stricken with shame. He waved them out of his room. "Go away. Your zeal corrupts me."

Penry tossed a parting remark gaily over his shoulder. "You know we are right, Brewster. Good men must never submit to tyranny. We will harass this bully with all our strength until we expose him. And one day you will join us." He tipped his brow in farewell. "You cannot help yourself. You are too honest a man."

When they had gone William sat depressed by the folly of their brash action. Whitgift's spies would not rest until they had searched them out. Could he stop them? He could tell William Davison, who might personally warn them of the dreadful consequences. Yet Davison as servant to the Queen might be honor-bound to report them to authorities. William shook his head sadly. *Lord, Lord, have mercy on these good men, my friends. Their hearts are pure, their intent is noble, but they know not what they do.*

❧❧

By the end of his second year at Peterhouse William felt confident that he could master the discipline required for the degree. Yet he was discouraged that Whitgift's zeal for religious conformity had changed the climate of free expression so highly valued at Cambridge. Even the best men inspired by the noblest intentions, keenly aware of the dangers of resistance, were forced to curb their tongues. And the subtle miasma of fear began to weigh upon William as well. He heard reasonable arguments on both sides of the conflict between reformers and the State, yet found himself growing restless in academia and eager to find his place in the real world. He began to think seriously of joining William Davison's staff.

One bitterly cold day after a lecture he and Penry found warm seclusion in a cubicle in the library, and William confessed his ambition. Penry was astonished. "Do you mean that Davison offered you a position?"

"Not officially. He said he needed a steward."

Penry exclaimed, "You will travel in high company indeed, my friend. Did you know that George Cranmer, the Archbishop's grandnephew, is already in Davison's employ?"

"Are you sure? How do you know that?"

"My sources of intelligence are infinite. Cranmer is an Oxford man. Traveled Europe with Sandys' son Edwin. Bishop Sandys of York, that is, your own landlord at Scrooby Manor!" He poked an emphatic finger at Brewster's chest. "Have you forgotten Scrooby already?"

William wondered. His position would surely be subordinate to George Cranmer's whose academic and social status far overreached his own. Could he fit into such high level society? Did he want to?

Penry was gazing at him with that wry smile, as if discerning his doubts. "Are you certain you want to give up taking your degree? You will be more valuable to him later."

William answered honestly. "It seems an opportunity too good to resist. I have heard much brilliant conjecture here, where we discuss ideas and theories but are not held to account for our decisions. I want to know how men of high station like Mr. Davison actually conduct the nation's business. How do such accountable men make decisions? Do they follow their consciences whatever the consequences, or do they merely justify convenient positions?"

For a moment the two gazed at each other, aware of an indefinable breach between them. Penry's earnest quest for truth drove him to demand change, while William, as curious as Penry, accepted the status quo as the safer route. How far would their quests separate them?

It was time for Evensong, and Penry held out his hand. "I wish thee Godspeed on thy journey, William Brewster." William saw amusement and yet affection in Penry's eyes, as if he regretted William's need to search for the truth he considered so obvious. Yet he would loyally encourage it. In turn, William was sorry that he could not support Penry's brave but reckless stand. The dangerous step he had taken in London would surely plunge the young Welshman into perilous waters he might not survive. For a moment William was touched with sorrow. "And I thee, John Penry. I want to say that I much value our adventures here at Peterhouse." He grinned. "Most particularly that bear-baiting."

Penry's eyebrows rose. "Ah, the bear-baiting. Methinks there will be many more baitings in our future, William Brewster. But at the end, whether bear or dogs, we who stand for truth are destined to win."

"Only God's truth will prevail, John. We have only to find it."

Three

Holland

Deafened by shouts of "God save the Queen!" William Brewster stepped carefully over wreaths of flowers strewn along the streets of Flushing to welcome the Earl of Leicester's entourage just arrived in the harbor. Walking ahead, the Earl returned greetings as radiantly exuberant as a crown prince hailing his subjects, tipping his cap from side to side, bowing and waving as if he were indeed the saviour these Lowlanders believed him to be. His rotund figure seemed to swell in stature absorbing their adulation. Apparently God himself had smiled at last upon Leicester's long-delayed mission to save the Netherlands from the King of Spain's iron grasp.

Yet William had been no less dazzled by the reception for his employer, William Davison, sent by Queen Elizabeth the previous year to administer England's treaty of Alliance with the Netherland States and to oversee the deployment of English troops to fortify Holland. The mayor of Flushing had presented Davison with the keys to the city, symbolizing England's protective custody of Zeeland and Holland. Davison had graciously turned them over to William for safekeeping. While the tokens reposed lumpily under his pillow that first night, he lay awake titillated by his sudden grandeur.

When William left Peterhouse in the summer of 1584 to join Davison's staff instead of going home to Scrooby, he did not foresee that his decision would bring him such thrilling adventure. Prince William of Orange, leader of the Protestant resistance to Catholic dominance in the Lowlands, had been assassinated in July, and the bereft citizens of Holland and Zeeland had begged Elizabeth for assistance. Her Privy Councillors, long apprehensive of King Phillip's intentions to invade England, finally convinced her that she would be safer from the

Spanish invader if she helped resist him in Europe rather than wait until he conquered the Lowlands and then rushed her emerald isle. After months of resistance, Elizabeth agreed to send Davison, one of her ablest diplomats, to support the Lowlanders.

The Queen's policy of *via media* had been sorely tested by Spanish dominance in the Netherlands. If she supported the Protestant cause in defiance of Phillip's armies, she would jeopardize England's tenuous relationship with Spain. Yet refusing to help the rebel states resist their Catholic oppressors would give Phillip license to sweep all of Europe. Her advisors argued both sides of the dilemma, but the critical reality prevailed: The Netherlands alone could not match Phillip's military power. If England did not help to contain his armies on the Continent, his fanatic mission to destroy all "heretics"—that is, all non-Catholics— would inevitably thrust across the Channel to invade Elizabeth's Protestant island.

Still she had vacillated, dreading to take the dangerous step of sending an English commander to the States. Robert Dudley, Earl of Leicester, stood by anxiously awaiting her appointment, yet when it finally came she instructed him to provide only protective management, strictly forbidding any assumption of executive supremacy over legally Spanish territory.

As members of Davison's staff, William and young George Cranmer had struck a friendship born of their intimacy with Davison's private affairs. George was grandnephew of William Cranmer, former Archbishop of Canterbury who had been martyred under Catholic Mary Tudor. As clerk and secretary he was privy to Davison's correspondence and frequently confided in William, who listened eagerly, realizing that he stood at the edge of history unfolding.

One day alone in Davison's office George spoke to William in strict confidence. "Mr. Davison thinks that Leicester's position here is at best precarious and can easily prove disastrous if the Queen does not fully support him. Yet he doubts she is committed to it. He wrote Lord Burghley that King Phillip is fanatic but not foolish. He sees our dilemma as clearly as we do, and is acutely aware that sooner or later we must act. He knows that Elizabeth despises the course he has set for her, and therefore must strike at least a pose of resistance." George's eyes sparkled with that secret knowledge only intimates can know. He glanced at the closed door, then leaned toward William to whisper, "Mr. Davison's real fear is that the States will offer Leicester the rank Prince William enjoyed, in effect, to become their new 'sovereign.'"

William gasped. "But he cannot. She has strictly forbidden that."

"Yet he is certain that is exactly what they will do—offer him supreme command. And he fears the Earl cannot resist it." George nodded with assurance.

"Then how will Mr. Davison advise him?"

George winked. "How do you think?"

William could not imagine.

George cast him a sly glance, then drew himself up in a pose imitative of Davison's regal style and proclaimed pontifically, "My son, that question poses a grave test of the art of diplomacy. Shall I advise him to overrule the Queen's edict and take full command, or to operate merely as manager, and therefore allow Phillip free access to Europe?"

George's mimicry was keen. The boys broke into chuckles. Then George said mischievously, "I told him to let the Earl rip."

"You did not."

"I did. And he laughed. He is not always the prig he appears to be. So, what would *you* advise him, Master Brewster?"

William lay awake pondering that question. In these months watching Davison and listening to George he had gained his own insights to the crucial choices that confronted statesmen, and he had come to appreciate that the arts of diplomacy and statesmanship required more than easy geniality and verbal finesse. They demanded of men their highest commitment to the nation's welfare, and sometimes wrenching decisions. He often remembered Penry and Greenwood and their scathing criticisms of authority. Now he would like to ask Penry some piercing questions. Until they faced such dilemmas themselves, how could ordinary men know the agonies of choosing between saving an oppressed people and sending the nation to war? Were ordinary men capable of such judgment? Did any men possess such wisdom?

Only the Lord God Almighty knew the perfect answers.

George's prediction proved accurate. On New Year's Day, 1586, three weeks after his arrival in December, Leicester received at his

32

lodgings at the Hague in Amsterdam a deputation from the States-General offering him the title of Governor General of the Netherlands. George reported that he gravely consulted his advisors, especially his liaison William Davison. "What do you think, lads? Do I go, or no?"

To a man, Leicester's staff urged him to accept, but Davison demurred. "I do not dispute your actual position, sir, but I think that a lesser title might be more acceptable to Her Majesty."

Leicester frowned. "What title would you suggest, Mr. Davison?"

"In view of her express restrictions, something less imposing. I think it wise not to risk antagonizing her beyond normal mischance."

Leicester replied, "Whatever my title, my responsibility is the same. They are asking me to command this expedition, and I am committed to do so."

"I only submit that a title suggestive of sovereignty may distress the Queen, sir, considering her instructions to you. You came here as Lieutenant General of English forces. Can you not perform your duties efficiently within that office?"

One of Leicester's men intervened. "I think Mr. Davison is suggesting a limitation on appearance, sir, rather than performance."

George quipped to William, "Speaking of appearance, the Earl's ample figure seems much less grand slumped in a chair thinking than when striding before cheering crowds."

Finally Leicester had declared, "I do not see that it matters much what they call me. I am here to rally our forces against the Spanish tyrant. If the job be done well someone must take command. And obviously I am the one expected to do it." His face brightened. "Methinks once these celebrations are done and our real work begins, Her Majesty will truly appreciate how royally we have been affirmed."

Leicester accepted the command and title of Governor General on January 14, was solemnly installed the next day, and at once commissioned William Davison to journey to London to inform the Queen of his motives and aspirations. Davison told his staff that they would sail as soon as weather permitted. William was delighted, yet could not fail to notice Davison's deep concern. One night before the envoy retired William told him, "Methinks something worries you, sir."

Davison sighed. "Aye, William. I regret that it falls to me to convince Her Majesty that his move was justified. He flies in the face of her great fear that Phillip will read this move as English defiance of his sovereignty in Europe. Worse, I dread that this news may reach her ears before I can convince her that the Earl had little choice but to accept the title."

Leicester's entry at Flushing proved to be only the beginning of a triumphant sojourn throughout the Hague, Rotterdam, Amsterdam, and Delft, each new welcome resounding with cannonades, fireworks, processions, elaborate masques and pageants. Though his stature as "messiah" was at first a bit embarrassing, it was nonetheless exalting and, gradually, dangerously convincing, not only to Leicester but many of his staff. He had come in the name of Protestant England to "deliver" his brethren from their Catholic oppressors, and borne on a tide of national gratitude, his elevation to "saviour" seemed inevitable.

Davison blurted out testily to William one night, "The man's pride will be his undoing. I dread the outcome."

That day Leicester had exploded in a fit of temper upon a ranking State official who deplored the lack of stout boots for the troops. The Earl was well aware of the miserable conditions his troops endured and blamed the lack of funds, the snail's pace of vital supplies, the incompetence of personnel, and not least the obstinate temperament of the Lowlanders—everything and everyone that hampered his efforts. Despite jubilant festivity in each Dutch town they visited, discord among his men was undermining morale. Their equipment was shabby and rapidly deteriorating, their clothing, food and lodging abysmal. Worst of all, they had received no pay since their arrival in December. Yet as Davison complained, "To humiliate this poor official shows gross misjudgment. These people have suffered persecution unlike anything we contend with in England, and they look to us for supplication." He wagged his head sadly. "An appalling lack of tact."

William said nothing, keenly aware that Davison was embarrassed as much by Leicester's overbearing management as his bloated pride. His mission to explain all this to the Queen would sorely test his diplomatic skills.

In the meantime the festivity accompanying Leicester's sojourn through the States offered his staff enticing opportunity for adventure.

George and William went out one night to sample local wares. Rowdies stampeded with joyous abandon along the streets, popping in and out of alehouses and mysterious closed doors, reminding William of Cambridge during the Sturbridge Fair. The boys steered clear of those doors, bound to serve William Davison with the highest integrity and honor. Davison was a generous and tolerant employer who trusted the judgment of his men and allowed them reasonable freedom. So while the boys swilled down jugs of ale and sang bawdy songs with gusto, they drew the line at excessive fleshly indulgence.

Then while singing boisterously in a tavern, William suddenly found himself enveloped by a voluptuous female on his lap and cooing in his ear. Dimly through a fog he sensed acute danger, bolted to his feet, and dumped the girl on the floor. He looked down upon her and bowed graciously. "Please forgive me, miss, but my duty calls. I must depart at once."

Picking herself up, the girl protested sweetly, "But you only just came in."

He groped through the fog. "Did I?" When *had* they come into this place? "George!" he bellowed. "George! Where are you?" Amid a sea of swimming heads across the crowded tavern he spotted George waving a mug in the air and singing. The girl smiled fetchingly. "Wot's yer hurry, lad? We've got all night." For a tavern lass to snare a rich Englishman was a prize catch.

William dodged around her to push his way through the crowd toward George, the girl trailing behind him clutching at his shirt. George blinked bleary eyes up at him. "'Allo, friend." He squinted. "Izzat you, Brewster?"

"It's late, George. We must report in."

George's head bobbled about, his brow furrowed. "Right. Mr. Davison would not approve thish most dishreputable place. Not befitting gentlemen."

"Come along, George." William hauled George to his feet, and the two plowed a path toward the door. The girl followed William, beseeching in a tiny voice no more enticing than a fretful bird darting at his head.

Outside it had begun to snow, and the cold smote them both with chilling reality. "Thish day is done," George muttered. "Lesh get to our beds."

"Aye, to our beds at once," William agreed.

But the narrow streets wound about canals and crossed bridges, and in the darkness strange buildings looked alike. "Where are we?" George growled.

"Somewhere in Delft. I think. Or perhaps Rotterdam."

"We were in Rotterdam yesterday."

"Aye. Then I think Delft."

"Right. Then where are we lodged in Delft?" Their situation was sobering. "Mayhapsh we should go back to the tavern. Hire beds there for the night."

"For the price of the women?" William asked.

George scowled. "No empty beds without women?"

"I much doubt it."

"You're sure of that?"

"Methinks 'twas more a brothel than a hostel," said William, a bit smug that George, usually the worldly sophisticate, had missed that message.

On these deserted streets only a dim light over a doorway nearby beckoned through the swirling snow. Above it swung a sign pronouncing *The Lion and the Lamb.* "What luck, a hostel!" William banged on the door. "Open up!"

No one answered. The two stood benumbed with cold and the dismal finale of their escapade. Then, abruptly, the door flung open. A little man in a priest's cassock stood before them. "What is it, lads?" he asked pleasantly.

"We're looking for lodgings for the night. Have you rooms to let?"

"You've come to the right place, boys. You may lie down at *The Lion and the Lamb* in perfect peace." Through his blurred vision William saw a small smiling face with snapping dark eyes and a bearded chin pointed like a ferret's.

He led them through a long dark hallway to a large room at the rear of the house where lumps of figures reposed on beds arranged around the walls. "Two to a bed," the ferret said amiably. "A luxury for the price."

"How much?" William asked.

"One pound apiece."

William gasped. "A pound!" His nose now picked up a stench pervading the room, a warning that neither the house nor the sleepers had recently known the touch of water. A pound apiece for this flophouse was outrageous.

Asleep on his feet, George suddenly sagged down upon the nearest bed already occupied by a sleeping body. William dug in his and George's pockets and found tuppence in one and two shillings in another, the last of their resources. Had they drunk that much? A sudden image of the girl at the tavern rose before his eyes.

He held out the money. "This is all I have. I will owe you the rest."

The hostlier peered into William's palm. "Oh, sorry, lad. That will not do. It's English coin. Have you no Dutch currency?"

"Perfectly good English coin. You can exchange it."

The man shook his head.

Indignation rose up in William's chest. "Would you turn us out to freeze?"

The man tilted his head as if to consider that option, then shrugged. William's alcoholic haze had begun to clear. "You're a priest. Have you no charity?"

The hostelier smiled. "I confess, I am no priest. This garment was left here one night in lieu of the owner's proper fee. It was all he had, poor man, and I found it nicely warm." One eyebrow rose. "Have you something else to offer?"

"Look here," William growled. "My friend and I are employed by the Earl of Leicester. You can trust us. I promise we will pay you in full tomorrow."

The hostelier closed one eye. "Ah, the English earl."

"I swear it. And he would be outraged at your poor show of hospitality."

The little man gave William a pained look. "The English earl indeed. Do you take me for a fool, laddie? Have you no other objects of value?"

"Nothing." William waved a hand toward the sleeping figures. "Which of these paid you a pound? Will they come back tomorrow with full payment?"

"Right, lad, they will not. That's why I charge the better sort like yourselves a bit more. I can see that you and your friend are gentlemen, out on a frolic." He grinned slyly. "Surely you can afford a bit of charity for some poor chaps less endowed than yourselves."

"This is robbery, not charity."

The hostelier looked thoughtful. "Have you a piece of jewelry, a watch perhaps?"

William glanced down at George deeply asleep, one arm flung across his unknown bedmate. And his eye fell on George's ring, a broad band of gold set with a ruby, an inheritance from his granduncle the Archbishop. Of course the ring had already caught the hostelier's practiced eye. He tried to shake George awake, calling his name. Dead asleep, George did not even grunt.

William assessed his options. George would be dead weight to carry through the snow, even if William knew where they were going. Both might be frozen by morning. Yet if they stayed here, how would they pay the hostelier?

He stared at George's ring. If he gave it up for collateral, would his host exchange it for only two pounds? Not likely. William tried tugging the ring but could not pull it past George's knuckle. A searing thought struck him—a horror story he had heard somewhere: the hostelier might cut off George's finger while they both slept. He glanced at the ferret's eyes watching him tug at the rich dark jewel. "'Tis worth about two pounds, I think, lad. A fair exchange." He reached toward the ring.

William clutched George's hand. "I can't give you this ring, but I swear I will return with the money."

The hostelier frowned, then tilted his head to one side, considering. Suddenly, William decided that if he could get the ring off George's finger he would wear it himself and stay awake all night guarding it. If it did not come off, he would stay awake all night guarding it on George's finger!

The hostelier said amiably, "You should have tried a brothel, lad. That ring would buy you a feast of flesh."

William growled, "Aye, pity we did not. Whores are more generous than hosteliers." He glared at his host. "And I warn you, I

38

awaken at a mere touch."

The hosteler shrugged. He had little to lose as he stood to gain either the ring or the money.

William dragged George to an empty bed and tugged again at the ring. He did not really believe that the hostelier would cut off George's finger, but worse things happened in this world, and he dared not risk the possibility. It was George's ring, after all, not his own, therefore a greater responsibility. Worse, it would take a year's wages to replace it, not even considering George's distress if he lost a finger!

He spit on George's finger to ease the ring off. At last it came free and fit his own thumb. He sighed, sniffing alcoholic fumes from the bodies snuffling and snoring about him. Outside in the night a bevy of banshees howled in the wind. He began to doze off, snapped awake at a sound at the door, perhaps the hostelier? Then for a while he would not close his eyes at all. Yet despite herculean efforts, he drifted off. Once again during the night he awoke with a start. This time he dreamed that his own finger had been cut off and ruby-dark blood dripped from his hand. He sat up, saw that his finger was intact, and fell back, disgusted. He lay awake awhile, dreading another nightmare. Worse, he dreaded what Mr. Davison would think of their absurd excursion. He sent up a prayer: *Lord, deliver me from this misery, and I promise it will never happen again!*

At last he fell sound asleep.

Near dawn his throbbing head awakened him. George awoke groggily, irritable as a stuck pig. "Where in Heaven's name are we?"

"We never made it home, George. We slept here."

"Then let's get out at once."

"Wait, George. We have a problem."

"What—besides my screaming head?"

"We owe our host two pounds."

George grimaced. "For what?"

"Our lodging for the night."

George glanced about the room. "For this? Preposterous!"

"He's charging us 'gentlemen' to compensate for these other poor blokes."

George's face drooped. "You have lost me somewhere in this tale."

"Rather than be turned out in the snow, I almost gave him your ring as collateral for our rent. Lest he decided to steal it, I wore it myself." He handed the ring to George.

George gazed at the gleaming ruby. Suddenly he grinned. "My father told me it would bless me. He warned me never to take it off." He frowned. "How did *you* get it off?"

William blushed, feeling foolish. "I thought he might actually cut off your finger to get it. So I promised to pay the two pounds we owe him."

George frowned, then chuckled. "Where is this unscrupulous creature?"

"He has not appeared yet this morning."

"Then let's be off before he arrives." George bounded up eagerly, stopped as suddenly, and seized his head. "Oh, Lord, bless me!"

As they staggered down the dark hallway, no brighter for daylight, the little hostelier appeared behind them. "Good morning, gentlemen. I trust you slept well."

"Splendid!" George exclaimed. "We thank you, and bid you good day, sir."

The hostelier peered at William.

"You have my word," William promised.

Outside George pulled a sour face. "Thank God that night's over. I hope Mr. Davison has not missed us yet. Let's hurry."

Ignorant of the city, they asked their way of passersby to the English lodgings. They wasted no time changing clothes and reported at once to Mr. Davison. He greeted them sternly. "From the look of you, I surmise you have been detained."

"Aye, sir. That we were," George responded.

Davison did not smile. "I realize you boys need diversion, but I disapprove of your disappearance in a strange city and your whereabouts unknown to us."

"Dreadfully sorry, sir," George said. "We ran into...ah...unexpected difficulty. We promise it will not happen again."

"You realize that we are here to help the Lowlanders, not to corrupt, nor be corrupted, by them."

The boys spoke in unison. "Yes, sir."

"We do not boast of our moral superiority, but neither do we add to their burdens by losing track of our own people."

"Aye, sir." William suddenly wondered if he had sent out searchers to find them.

"I expect more responsible behavior from my staff."

"Agreed, sir. Our apologies, sir."

"Now get yourselves properly dressed and report for duty. You have inconvenienced a number of people."

"Yes, sir. We do apologize, sir," George said, and turned to go. William hesitated, swallowed hard, then confessed, "There's another matter, sir, yet to be settled."

Davison's gaze fixed upon him. "Yes?"

"We owe money for our night's lodging."

"You did not sleep in your own rooms?"

"No, sir," William answered, ignoring George's warning frown. "We could not find our way home and had to spend the night at a hostel."

George closed his eyes, his lips pursed.

Davison sat back in his chair and folded his hands. "This venture grows more complex by the moment."

"Aye, sir," William replied doggedly. "We got lost when it began to snow. Nothing looked familiar. So we took refuge in a hostel."

George rocked on his heels, exasperated.

At sight of George's face, words failed William. Obviously, George was not going to help him explain. He stammered on. "We thought the proprietor was a priest and his hospitality charitable, but he was only a hostelier and charged us an outrageous price."

A quirk of a smile tilted one corner of Davison's mouth. "How much?"

William cast a glance at George who stood stoically silent. "Two pounds, sir, one pound apiece." It sounded to William like two hundred. Then to get the whole matter over with quickly, he blurted out, "We did not have one pound between us, sir. So I promised I'd come back today and pay him the full charge." He swallowed. "He's a scoundrel, sir, but he could have turned us out in the snow."

Davison nodded soberly. "I see."

"Sir, we don't have two pounds between us. So I am terribly embarrassed to have to ask you...for an advance on my wages."

"Umm. I do see the problem. Indeed." Davison stroked his brow. "Let us figure a bit. Two pounds would cover about...how much of your wages? Two months?"

"One month. We owe a pound apiece, sir."

"A month, then, discounting a day or two." He glanced from one boy to the other. "An expensive evening you two chose to indulge yourselves."

George spoke up at last. "I do not agree that we owe that much, sir."

"Oh? Why not?"

"The man took advantage of our predicament, and robbed us, sir."

"You think you owe him nothing for your lodging?"

George hesitated. "Perhaps a shilling or two. Nothing more. Cheap hostels like that never charge as much as pounds, sir."

"What do you say, William? You agreed to pay the price."

"Because I promised I would, sir. I saw no recourse at the time." He was beginning to resent George's obstinacy. Would he have slept so soundly in the snow? And what about his precious ring? The two pounds were beginning to seem a bargain compared to the alternatives.

Davison fingered his chin. "It seems fair that you pay something for your lodging. The question is, how much?"

The boys stood silently. Then William spoke. "He asked for two pounds, sir, and we had nothing of value to bargain with." The red ruby flashed in his mind.

"Why did he overcharge you?"

"He said he recognized we were 'gentlemen' and could afford to pay for some poorer clients who could not."

"Yet you had no such obligation."

"No, sir, but also no other options."

George suddenly spoke up. "William could have given up my ring, sir." He held out his hand. "This one my granduncle gave me is worth much more than two pounds. William feared this hostelier might try to steal it and wore the ring himself to keep it safe."

A range of expressions flickered across Davison's face—

amusement, sympathy, understanding, and finally, a bit of pride. He smiled broadly. "Well, now, I think you boys have behaved rather admirably. You found yourselves in a sorry predicament of your own making but took the wisest way out of it. Some of our most honorable statesmen have not done as well."

Both boys' eyes flashed with surprise. They stared at Davison, who merely raised his brows. "As to the matter of the two pounds, I think you two might earn those with a bit of extra duty, say, relieving local servants of duties they perform for us. And your hostelier deserves his wages, too, does he not?"

"But not two pounds, sir!" George persisted.

"His fair price as he saw it, son. And wisely or not, William agreed to pay it. Would you have him back down now on his word? What sort of example does that present to our allies?"

George shot an amused glance at William, then smirked. And William's heart warmed for William Davison, master diplomat in any situation.

"Thank you, sir," they breathed, and hurried away to fulfill all required duties with buoyant energy.

கைக்

Their journey to London was delayed by various interruptions and minor crises that demanded Davison's delicate touch. Then while they awaited passage from Brill, a season of bad winds caused them further delay and Davison much agitation. As time dragged on, he grew more convinced that the Queen would learn of Leicester's command via the diplomatic grapevine well before he arrived to explain it. William and George tried to encourage him. "You could only advise him, sir. She cannot hold you responsible for the Earl's decision."

Davison shook his head sadly. "Understand, lads, that in the best sense of the word I represent Robert Dudley, both the man and his position. I must convince the Queen of his integrity, for it is she who bears the ultimate responsibility for the success of his expedition. If I cannot convince her of Dudley's sound judgment, she will distrust both of us and perhaps the entire Netherland States. And all our effort here may be lost."

William lay awake once again listening to the north winds blustering against his window, and for the first time wondered if he wanted to live the sort of stressful life Davison endured. Perhaps he was not cut out for the high order of statesmanship after all. He had neither the social nor verbal skills of diplomats like Davison, nor the clever wit and style of gentlemen like George Cranmer. If he were in William Davison's boots, what would he say to convince the Queen that Dudley's course was wise? He hadn't the foggiest notion. He would rather face the teeth of eels in the River Ryton than the fierce countenance of Queen Elizabeth at Windsor in one of her tempers. His stomach quailed at the thought.

Actually, when they arrived in London, Davison had no opportunity to explain Leicester's action because the Queen adamantly refused to receive him. She had already learned of Leicester's acceptance of supreme command, and everyone within the confines of Windsor cowered before her monumental rage at his audacity. Davison's party encountered an atmosphere of violent censure against the Earl, this "creature of our own" whom she thought she could trust implicitly. She rebuffed with contempt Davison's repeated petitions for an audience, while the women attendants slipped in and out of her quarters in hushed silence, their eyes wide with horror at the outrageous epithets loosed in that royal inner sanctum.

Davison fell unnaturally silent, his face grim, his appetite spare. He spoke little to his staff and confided only in Lords Burghley and Walsingham, who best understood his precarious position. William told George, "He warned the Earl not to take that title, but he refused to listen."

George thought that Davison had long ago lost confidence in Leicester's competence. "'Tis not only the title Dudley covets but the power. The Queen and everyone knows of his ambitions, yet Davison is obliged to defend him. Still, methinks she will eventually relent and listen to Mister Davison's buttered words spoken into her delicate ear."

William wished that he or George had sufficient status to defend Davison's efforts to the Queen. But never could they reveal to anyone the envoy's private confidences to them.

At last she received Davison, only to rail at him with terms "most bitter and hard." George wrote down Davison's report of her blistering words, and William could see Davison's keen humiliation in his despairing countenance. He had effected no change in Her Majesty's opinion. In fact, news was scuttling about that on February tenth, three days before Davison's party arrived in London, she had already commissioned Sir Thomas Heneage to deliver a stinging rebuke to Leicester in Holland, demanding his resignation.

Yet the crowning insult to Her Majesty's ego were rumors running rampant that Leicester's wife, Lettice Knollys, the Queen's perennial rival for his affections, was about to embark for the Netherlands to take her place as the esteemed leader's "queen." She would be accompanied by a grand retinue said to surpass Elizabeth's. The rumors proved to be false, but the Queen's outrage exploded into vengeance. She insisted that Heneage command Leicester's resignation without mercy.

In London Davison called his staff together to tell them that their mission had failed and that they would soon depart for Antwerp to settle affairs there. "She will neither hear me, nor any account of the tragedy we now face in Holland."

After Sir Heneage's official demand that Leicester resign, in Holland Davison was even more morose. "By God," he told the boys, "never have I seen such chagrin on a man's face, as broken as a child's betrayal by his mother. She has done him in."

Despite the Council of State's strong protests against Leicester's demotion and their assurance that the will of the Dutch people had conferred the title of commander upon him, the Queen did not soften. Burghley and her Council warned that the success of the mission was badly undermined, that without her support the Dutch would distrust Leicester's authority. Burghley complained that "this matter hath been more cumbersome and more severe to me than any whatsoever since I was a Councillor." Only his threat to resign finally softened the Queen's stand, and by summer she relented and allowed Leicester to retain his title. Yet by then conditions in the Lowlands had so deteriorated that the end of his expedition was predictable. His soldiers were ill-trained and half-starved, his officers thieving and incompetent, his English and Dutch advisors constantly quarreling, and his Queen stringently guarding both her power and her purse. At last Leicester admitted defeat. In November he accepted Elizabeth's invitation to come home to England, gratefully enjoyed the Queen's royal reception, then hastened to the waters of Bath to recover.

Davison and his staff wound up affairs in Antwerp in December, then departed to celebrate Christmas at home. In London before they parted ways, George and William made a last foray on the town's taverns.

"I'm sorry to see this venture end badly," George said. "In particular I fear that Her Majesty may hold Mr. Davison responsible for Leicester's failure."

William was aghast. "Why? He could not have served the Earl better."

"You know our Gloriana. She holds grudges like a burr sticks to fur."

"But what could he have done differently?"

"Threaten to resign unless Leicester refused to accept the title of Governor General." His look was grim. "As Burghley had to do to move her."

"So drastic a step? It was Leicester's responsibility."

"William, I share your affection for Mr. Davison, but do not be deceived. If the Queen perceives that anyone is contrary to her interests, he is suspect. A marked man. And, unlike Burghley and Walsingham, Davison is not indispensable to her."

William's stomach chilled. "You mean, he has not their influence on her."

George sighed. "I've been reminded of my granduncle's trials all my life. At the end he stood on principle, and paid his life for it. My father used to quote a favorite expression: 'One who would survive takes off his slippers and trods lightly by the monarch's door.'"

Four

Davison

Davison's party returned from Antwerp only to be at once immersed in the current crisis confronting the Queen: What to do about Mary Stewart.

Mary had been convicted in October of compliance in the Babington plot in which Anthony Babington and six Catholic accomplices proposed to assassinate Elizabeth, free Mary, and claim the English throne. Yet despite irrefutable evidence that Mary endorsed the plot, Elizabeth loathed to pronounce her death sentence because she was an anointed prince set above the mundane rudiments of judicial trial and execution. To subject monarchs to codes of human justice was to tempt the wrath of Providence. Far better to poison a prince at his dinner or to smother him in his bed than to subject him to public spectacle.

On September 20th Babington and his cohorts had been executed in the most tortuous manner, and reports of their excruciating sufferings had shocked Leicester's party in Antwerp. Enraged at the plotters' arrogance, Elizabeth had requested extreme punishment for their treason, and their executioners complied by cutting them down before death could numb their senses and then disemboweling them while still alive. Elizabeth's thrust for vengeance went too far. Such barbaric cruelty horrified the populace, the more so since Mary Stewart had as yet suffered no punishment for her part in the plot.

Elizabeth's advisors pleaded with her to sign Mary's death warrant. Failure of the campaign in the Lowlands and Phillip's increasing dominance in Europe confirmed their fears that as long as Mary lived, there would be no end to Catholic threats to their English Queen and her domain. Wild stories of Spanish troops invading Wales, arsonists scheming in London, Mary Stewart's escape from prison, and Elizabeth's imminent assassination kept the people in continual tension.

"Despite all this, she cannot bring herself to do it," Davison told William one night. "Some overpowering threat must move her to take that final step."

"What sort of threat, sir?"

"God alone knows, son. This Babington affair should have been enough to convince her, but mayhaps only Phillip's armada in the Channel will sufficiently startle her heart to action. By then the Stewart may be waiting at the quay for Phillip's ships." He gave William a mirthless smile.

"But the strategy to intercept her letters at Fotheringay was very clever, sir. Wouldn't that catch any other plotter?"

"My son, if a wolf paced before your door, would you simply throw the latch and hide inside?"

"I think not, sir."

"Of course you would not. You would shoot him and be done with it." Davison sighed and poured himself a draught. "Any zealot committed to the Queen's death, and as willing to forfeit his life, might easily ambush her as she strolled in her garden or lolled in her bath. No strategy will deter an assassin willing to die for his cause."

Later William puzzled over this, then asked George, "What do you think she should do about Mary?"

George winked. "Send her to Heaven." He grinned. "That is, in fact, the blessing she claims to desire. To free at last her poor abused soul of all torment."

"But she is Catholic!"

"And so, you think, will go to hell instead?"

William frowned. He was never quite sure who would or would not go to hell. "She has done great evil."

George shrugged. "Do you see any pure saints about you? Mr. Davison comes closest, but I'll wager there is a sin or two in his past."

William scowled at George's joke. Though the grandnephew of an archbishop, sometimes he could be annoyingly worldly. He still begrudged the two pounds William had agreed to pay the hostelier at Delft, insisting that the man did not deserve the money. Yet William would be forever grateful to Mr. Davison for defending his promise to pay the hostelier's outrageous fee.

All that was past, however, and now that Leicester's sorry sojourn in the Lowlands had ended, all attention in London focused on Mary Stewart's fate and the Queen's reluctance to order her execution.

Elizabeth's dread of ordering the execution of a monarch, and as well a kinsman, was painfully obvious to her intimates. Some suspected that the orphaned child within the adult queen's person perceived a disturbing parallel to her own mother's execution that festered still, like a wound. Her more objective Councillors sensed that her reluctance to dispatch Mary was more a matter of method than conviction. She could not bear the full responsibility for so final a judgment upon a fellow prince, though her reluctance may cost her own life.

Then a trusted advisor, Lord Howard of Effingham, the Lord Admiral, a commissioner at Mary Stewart's trial, told her frankly that her procrastination not only angered her Councillors but dismayed her people, for it exposed her to extreme and unpredictable danger. His remarks apparently pierced her paralysis, for that very day, February 1, she sent for William Davison while he walked in Greenwich Park in unusually fine weather. When summoned, he hurried to his room.

William looked up, startled, from brushing his boots. "What is it, sir?"

"I've been summoned by the Queen." Davison's face was flushed.

William took a breath. "Does that mean...?"

"Whatever it means, son, I am ready." He seized a sheaf of papers piled on his desk, among them the warrant for Mary's execution, and hastily left the room. William stared at the empty desktop that he and George had eyed frequently, giving it a wide berth, as if the dreaded document might spring to life and somehow implicate them. Was she actually going to sign it? He wished he had studied it more carefully, and fixed its image and its words in his mind for posterity.

Of course the summons may mean nothing. The Queen called her Councillors for many odd and sundry reasons, yet a sense of impending crisis had rushed in with Davison and now pervaded his rooms. Not ten minutes later George burst into the room. "She's called for him!"

"Yes, he was here. Do you know why?"

"Lord Howard sent for him immediately after he left the Queen's chamber. I followed Mr. Davison to her door, but the guard brushed me aside. 'A mere clerk,' he said, 'out of his proper place.' Would I were a mouse within that room!"

"We will know when he comes back."

George frowned and paced about the room. "Mayhap. Everyone's so touchy here of late—even Mr. Davison—afraid to speak, dreading to annoy the Queen. He may tell us nothing."

But William knew better. Mr. Davison indulged him in little confidences even George did not share, personal grievances and confessions that a man revealed only to a trusted servant. Mr. Davison did trust George, but the bond between Davison and himself was closer spiritually, a brotherhood based on their shared faith. William could not speak of it to George, nor in fact to Mr. Davison, but he was acutely aware of its presence, as intangible yet as real as filial love.

In later years long after Mr. Davison had gone and William lived thousands of miles from England on another continent, he would vividly remember that day, for it effected a climactic change in both Davison's and William's lives. Soon the Privy Council, the entire court, and eventually the whole world would realize the significance of Mr. Davison's summons from Greenwich Park.

∾∾

Seated at her desk in her Privy Chamber, the Queen received Davison genially, commenting on the fine weather and commending his enjoyment of it. She urged him to use early morning exercise oftener, as she was wont to do. Then she glanced at the papers in his hand and asked what they were. He answered, "Divers things to be signed that concerned your service, Madam."

"Did Lord Howard mention the warrant?"

"He did, your Majesty." Davison held out the warrant to her, then presented her with a pen. She took it and signed the warrant, then dropped it on the floor. She looked up at him. "Are you not heartily sorry, Mr. Davison, to see it done?"

Davison gazed into her face. She returned his gaze coolly, and yet, he thought, a touch poignantly, as if she sought his approval. "I am heartily sorry that it is necessary, Madam. Seeing how the life of that Queen threatened your own Majesty's death, this act was of that justice and necessity that you could not defer it."

She smiled, he thought, agreeably. "What else have you to sign?"

He laid other papers before her. She signed them and he took them up. Then she said, "Take this warrant to the Lord Chancellor to use as secretly as possible, lest the divulging thereof before the execution might increase my danger." She smiled faintly. "And on your way to the Chancellor, stop at Walsingham's house and tell him. The grief thereof will go near to kill him outright."

Her humor was an effort to lighten the somber deed, for they both knew Walsingham would be overjoyed that she had finally signed the warrant. Yet, a bit uncertain of her mood, Davison merely bowed and did not reply.

Then as he retreated toward the door she said brightly, "I would there were a better way to settle this matter. One that did not cast the entire burden on myself."

He did not mistake her implication. She had hinted earlier that someone might "have eased her of this burden," meaning that someone else should dispose of Mary Stewart, quietly, behind the public scene.

"What of Mr. Paulet?" she asked. "He signed the Bond to preserve my life. Would he not indulge his Queen this small request?"

Davison paused. She was asking forthrightly that someone murder Mary to spare her that dreaded responsibility, so that her scalding signature would not sear that warrant down through the ages.

"Madam," he said quietly," it would be so much labor lost, knowing the wisdom and integrity of the gentleman who would not do so unlawful an act for any respect in the world."

"Nevertheless, you will ask him!" she spat out. "And now you have it. Let me be troubled no more with it."

Davison bowed again and backed out. "As you request, Madam."

51

When Davison had not reappeared in his rooms by suppertime, William and George went to the kitchen for their meal, and by bedtime William asked George, "What do you think has happened?"

"Who can tell? I saw him go into that chamber, but I did not see him come out. He may be there still."

William could not always tell if George were joking, and said peevishly, "'Tis no matter for jest, George."

George shrugged and went to bed, but William waited up until Davison returned at midnight, his countenance tight and brow drawn. William helped him undress, thinking it best to ask no questions while Davison remained silent. As he turned down Davison's bed he asked, "Is there anything more I can do for you, sir?"

Davison lay back on the pillows and sighed. "Aye, William. Pour me some wine, and when you say your prayers tonight petition the Lord for my soul."

"Surely you are in no danger, sir."

"Perhaps not, son. But I am not wholly convinced I am not."

William hesitated, reluctant to probe, but bursting with curiosity. "What happened today, sir?"

Davison gestured toward the carafe of wine on his sideboard, and William sprang to pour some, hopeful of confidences to come. "You will know soon enough, son. I hope the news has not already leaked out." He smiled sadly. "Servants uncannily discover the most dire secrets before they are done."

"Sir, I know nothing, but I admit that George and I are very curious. He saw you go into the Queen's chamber after Lord Howard came out."

"Ah, yes, clever George. He did follow me." He sat up to take the wineglass and drew deeply from it. "I feel greatly burdened tonight, William. This day's events have been most disturbing." He glanced into William's eyes, then blurted out, "She signed the warrant."

William drew a sharp breath.

"This morning she summoned me to her chamber." He spoke dully, his tone betraying distress rather than joy, and a tiny chill brushed William's breast. "I swear you to secrecy on pain of your life, William. My words must not leave this room." He set down the wineglass. "She signed it, told me to take it to the Lord Chancellor to have it sealed, and to tell Sir Walsingham. Then she asked me to write Sir Paulet and have him see to the deed himself."

William waited, hearing nothing significant so far.

"Sir Paulet is Mary Stewart's jailor," Davison added.

William nodded. "Yes, I know, sir."

"Of course he will not consider it."

Consider what? William wondered. Paulet was responsible for the Queen of Scots' person at Fotheringay.

"She signed the warrant," Davison muttered. "She, and only she, must take full responsibility for sending it out."

"Yes, sir."

Davison took up the wineglass and finished it in one gulp. "Chancellor sealed it this afternooon at five. She made a cruel joke that the grief thereof would near kill Walsingham outright."

William frowned. He was missing something here.

"Grieved as he is, Walsingham will send the letter to Paulet tomorrow."

William said, "I don't understand, sir. What letter?"

Davison set down the glass again, stood up and paced across the room. He spoke in a low voice. "Despite her signature, she is not firmly resolved. As she did with Norfolk, she may rescind it. And Paulet will not be enticed to do the deed for her. Yet we are obliged to put her case before him because she demands it. That will sorely test his conscience."

His meaning suddenly came clear to William. "You mean..."

"One can never be sure of one's ground with her. She shifts precariously when one least expects it."

William thought, *She wants Paulet, or somebody, to dispatch Mary Stewart.* It's that simple, and she expects it. He recalled George's warning from his granduncle: *"One who would survive takes off his slippers and trods lightly by the Queen's door."*

Yet Davison had walked right through that door into her chamber, like a fly blundering into a spider's net.

Davison dragged back to his bed. "Sufficient unto the day is the evil thereof," he murmured. "Tomorrow's evil will descend soon enough."

William probed his brain for some consoling comment to ease his master's anxiety, but could think of nothing. Mr. Davison had only done as she ordered, to dispatch the warrant. She had not asked him to dispatch Mary Stewart.

Davison turned his head into his pillow and closed his eyes. As he always did before sleeping, he would pray. He had asked William to pray for him, too. That he could do, with confidence.

Davison slept fitfully and rose at dawn. From his bed in an adjoining alcove, William had awakened occasionally in the night and heard him tossing, and rose early to serve him. Davison looked no better for a night's rest, poor as it was.

William sighed. Until this business with Mary Stewart was settled, no one at court or in the whole country would rest easily.

⁂

The Queen's first question to Davison that morning was whether or not the Lord Chancellor had sealed the warrant. "Yes, your Majesty," he replied, "in the afternoon, as you directed."

Her eyes flashed. "What needeth that haste?" she asked, her words like darts flung into Davison's chest. She signed his papers irritably, her face a mask.

Alarmed, afterwards he hastened to Sir Christopher Hatton who agreed that the signs she was radiating were ominous. The two decided to consult Burghley who sent out an urgent summons to members of the Privy Council and told them, "Gentlemen, we have a matter of some urgency before us. Her Majesty has signed the warrant for the Queen of Scots' execution in Mr. Davison's presence, but now indicates that she may change her mind. She had instructed him to have the warrant sealed with the utmost secrecy lest her life be further endangered when the news is known. Yet this morning she questioned his haste in sealing the document, which arouses our suspicions that she may, as she has done before, rescind the order at any moment. We beg your support of Mr. Davison's action. He cannot take sole responsibility for effecting this warrant."

The group murmured their approval.

"Moreover," Burghley went on, "I propose that we send the warrant to the Lord Lieutenant of Northamptonshire at once for execution as Mr. Davison insists that she declared she wanted to hear no more about it until the deed was done. We have waited long for this moment, gentlemen, and must seize our opportunity."

All approved grimly, and agreed to send Robert Beale, secretary to the Council, on his way at once to Fotheringay to deliver the warrant. Hearing this tale that night, William heaved a great sigh of relief. With the full support of the Council behind him, Mr. Davison was truly safe.

Yet on the morning of February fourth the Queen greeted Davison with jolting news. She had dreamed the night before that Mary Stewart had been executed, which had awakened her with such anger that she "would have run him through with a sword."

Though spoken with a smile, Davison was nonetheless unnerved and answered lightly, "It is good for me that I was not near you then, Madam, so long as that humor lasted." Yet her remarks stirred more unsettling doubts in his mind. "Your Majesty, since you have proceeded so far, do you still intend to carry out the execution?"

"Yes, by God," she answered tartly. "Yet I think it might have received a better form. This throws all the responsibility upon myself. For mine own life, I would not touch her. I should prefer that she be strictly incarcerated. I think that the country can expect no more of me, lest I be accused of personal vindictiveness."

"Majesty," Davison soothed, "you have acted as the law requires, and that law cannot be altered without honesty, justice, or surety. You can take no other course but that which stands with law and justice."

She seemed mollified, until Paulet's letter arrived next day on February fifth. Paulet wrote that he was:

so unhappy to have lived to see this unhappy day in which I am required by my most gracious sovereign to do an act which both God and the law forbiddeth. My good livings and life are at her Majesty's disposition, but God forbid that I should make so foul a shipwreck of my conscience, or leave so great a blot on my poor posterity as to shed blood without law or warrant.

Elizabeth exploded. Flinging the letter aside, she screeched, "Ah, the niceness of these precise fellows who in words would do great things for my surety, but in deed perform nothing." She flounced about her chamber, vibrating with frustration. Hotly she declared, "I could have it well enough done without them. There is one by name Wingfield..."

"Majesty," Davison prevailed upon her, "in my poor opinion such a course would be most dishonorable."

She flashed about, her teeth gritted, cheeks enflamed, sure signs of the volcano seething within her.

Davison crept away to withdraw to his rooms, his face grim. William noticed but said nothing, his stomach cold. He longed to confide in George, hoping for his friend's light touch, but thought better of it. The least spark set in this inflammatory atmosphere might set off a conflagration.

❧❦

The next morning when Davison appeared as usual in the Queen's chamber, he noted at once her extreme agitation. Overnight she had worked herself into a lather, her wild imagination devising schemes to relieve her of this action. She greeted him coldly. "This danger to myself I live in daily is intolerable. It is more than time this matter were dispatched." She swung on him. "By God's breath, you will have another letter written to Mr. Paulet for the dispatch thereof, because the longer it is deferred, the more my danger is increased."

Davison quailed. The Council had decided not to tell her that the warrant had already gone to Fotheringay since she had wanted not to be further troubled with it until the deed was done. "Madam," he said, a slight quaver in his deep voice, "I think there is no necessity for such a letter, the warrant being so general and sufficient as it was."

She said tartly, "Yet I am not certain of that dainty fellow. No, Mr. Paulet will look for it."

There was a clatter at the door. The Queen's ladies had come to hear her Majesty's pleasure for dinner.

Davison withdrew, and outside the chamber leaned against the wall and closed his eyes. Today was February eighth, 1587, the morning the Council had ordered for the execution of the Queen of Scots at Fotheringay.

☙❧

The goblet sailed from Elizabeth's hand through the air to skim Lord Burghley's head, and instinctively the other Councillors' heads twitched aside to avoid the blow. Her face purple with fury, neck veins standing out taut as bellcords, the Queen's towering rage was powered as usual by her constant soulless fear of her own untimely death.

"Madam...," Burghley began.

"Be quiet!" she rasped.

All ten of her Privy Councillors stood fixed, not daring to move, dreading that her wrath might wreak its most insidious damage within her skull. What irony! That after all their careful work to contain the threat of the Scottish Queen's conspiracies, Elizabeth would accomplish her enemies' end by means of her own apoplectic fit.

Yet Mary Stewart was dead by official warrant bearing Elizabeth's own signature, and nothing under God's sun could change it now.

Elizabeth twirled about the Presence Chamber, fuming in a guttural voice, "By God's passion! Someone's head will roll for this!" Suddenly she halted to face them. "I would hang all of you in a twinkling, every single one, do you hear me?"

"Perfectly, Madam," Burghley murmured calmly.

She thrust out her arm, her forefinger an arrow aimed at his heart. "You as well, Burghley. You have fostered this, dreamed, and schemed it. Don't deny it!"

"I do not deny it, dear Madam. Your safety required it."

"My safety indeed! Am I the safer now? What dainties you are, swearing by Bond to protect your prince and yet too timid to rid me of a rat in my cupboard!"

They had no recourse but to hear her out. During such ventings her men had learned to pray the Almighty to cool her fevers, calm her humors, and to blot from her brain her vengeful threats of annihilation of "traitors" who thwarted her.

Suddenly she whirled on William Davison and hissed, "You, sir, have deceived me most grievously."

Davison, the color of wood-ash, declared in sonorous tones, "Never, Madam, I swear."

"You took that warrant directly to the Lord Chancellor to seal it. Yet I told you to wait and keep it secret."

Davison stammered, "Madam, I...I did only as you bade me." His voice surged up from his chest. "You said you did not want to be further troubled with it."

Her voice was a screech. "You numbskull! How could I *not* be troubled?"

Davison shuddered.

At once Burghley said in consoling tones, "Madam, Mr. Davison took great care to consult with your Council, and we all agreed the warrant should be sent without delay. He is to blame no more than the rest of us."

"Then by God I will hang every one of you!" She swung in a full circle, her skirts swirling, ropes of pearls swinging. Yet the strident note in her voice denoted the merest crack in her resolve. While all prayed that the worst of this diatribe may soon be over, for her frail body could hardly contain it, none would take an easy breath until her hysteria was spent. "I have had enough of numbskulls!" she screamed, and stomped from the room.

While the Queen's outburst at her Councillors deafened any ear within fifty yards of the Presence Chamber, the news of Mary Stewart's execution roared across the continent,.

❧❦

William finished setting Davison's clothes and papers in order, and briefly at leisure, gazed out the window at grimly overcast skies. On the day of Mary Stewart's execution four days ago, the weather had been brilliant, a sign that some interpreted as favor from Heaven for the deed to be done. Now in the dismal aftermath Heaven seemed to reflect instead a profound dismay. While William thought she should be grateful that her men had so carefully prepared the case against Mary so that no one could question the punishment required by law, the Queen had sunk into a tortuous display of grief.

The door swung open and Davison came in, his face drained. One look and William knew something drastic had happened. "What is it, sir? You look unwell," he said softly, moving to take Davison's jacket.

With a great sigh, Davison murmured, "Only pray for me, William."

Oh, yes, he had already done that. But how to pray that the Lord somehow justify what man's folly had wrought? "What is wrong, sir?"

Davison glanced at William with despairing eyes. "I have never seen her look with more contempt upon any man than she did upon me today. Her ferocity fair wilted me."

William held the jacket, still warm with his master's presence, imagining the scene in the Presence Chamber. "Sir, you know how violent her storms can be, but when they blow over, all is clear again."

"I feel a chill wind, William, laden with ice, and none to stay the bite of it."

George slipped in with papers Davison would take to the Queen tomorrow, if she permitted him into her presence. He scowled at William, warning him of dire trouble. He had already learned that the Queen had spared none of her Councillors, not even Burghley, and threatened all with banishment or ruin, but that only Mr. Davison had taken the warrant from her hand. His look confirmed William's worst fears, that all did not bode well for Mr. Davison.

George beckoned him outside the chamber door, then whispered, "Sir Hatton told Mr. Davison to steer clear of her until the storm abated."

William nodded. Thank God for Sir Hatton.

Word of the Queen's inconsolable grief reached the populace and within two days the celebratory bells were stilled and bonfires smothered. Outraged letters from heads of state began to arrive at the Palace. Mary's death had transformed her into a heroic martyr, especially in Scotland, where cries went up for vengeance among those who hated her most. Her son James declared that he would not condemn Elizabeth unheard till further trial, whether she had yet satisfied the world to her honor or not. This sly suggestion only intensified the Queen's determination to deflect the blame anywhere but to herself.

Davison secluded himself in his quarters, speaking little and eating not at all, occasionally sorting through his papers and fitfully napping. William and George began to despair of his health and, God forbid, perhaps his sanity. When once again Davison refused his dinner, George whispered to William, "He cannot go on like this."

William's heart fluttered. "I know, I know! What can we do for him?"

George sighed. "Alas, my friend, I fear the die is cast. She is determined to absolve herself of blame before the world. Even Burghley has been banished from her presence and lies abed, mourning." He flopped down in a chair, more distraught than William had ever seen him. "My worst fear is that our dear Mr. Davison is destined to receive the full brunt of her vengeance."

William hissed with alarm, "How dare she? He did exactly as she bid him."

George nodded sagely. "So he claims."

William was aghast. "You do not believe him?"

"Aye, I do. That is the rub. We all know him well, that he could not lie for his life, yet I fear this time the truth itself will condemn him."

As if emblazoned by a shaft of light from Heaven, William saw that the Queen would take no blame for the execution and therefore must find a scapegoat. She had accused her entire Council but must demonstrate its incompetence through one sacrificial member. His stomach turned icy cold. If only one was chosen, it must be Mr. Davison.

❧

In the next days Elizabeth's wrath intensified rather than abated, and tales of her dire threats and grieving fits wafted from her private chambers throughout the palace. Then on February tenth, Lord Buckhurst came to Davison's door, his face grim.

William stammered, "Good day, sir. Mr. Davison is not yet dressed, but I will tell him you are here."

"Only let me in, lad. I will tell him myself."

William hesitated. Mr. Davison had not slept well that night, had arisen early, but had not yet dressed for the day. Then behind him he heard Davison say, "Come in, sir." Davison approached Buckhurst and held out his hand.

Buckhurst's face flushed. "My dear William, how goes it with you?"

Davison shrugged. "As might be expected." He waved Buckhurst to a seat.

Buckhurst sat down gingerly on the edge of the chair. Davison gestured to William to serve tea, but Buckhurst raised a hand to decline. "I come strictly on business, good sir."

Davison eyed Buckhurst coolly.

Buckhurst straightened, composed himself, and looked Davison fully in the eye. "My orders are to escort you to the Tower."

Davison's expression did not change. "So it has come to that." He took a deep breath. "I cannot say I did not expect it. Yet I hoped that she..." He faltered, put a hand to his brow, and leaned forward.

Lord Buckhurst said, "I understand, of course. I shall inform her Majesty that you are unwell and cannot be moved today."

Davison made a gesture of futility, and Buckhurst addressed William. "Put him to bed and tend him carefully. I will insist that he cannot be moved."

"Aye, sir. Thank you, sir."

Buckhurst patted Davison's shoulder, nodded to William, and left the room.

Davison shook his head. "I will not spend my days abed, William. Please bring my clothes to me."

William snatched up his shirt and held it before him. Davison put one arm through a sleeve, drew a deep breath, and extended the other arm. As William pulled the shirt over his head, a wracking sound came from under the shirt. Yet Davison's face emerging from the shirt was calm, set in the same stoic mask he had worn since Mary's execution. He looked directly into William's eyes. "You heard what he said. I have been summoned to the Tower."

The deeply sonorous tones of Davison's voice drifted on the air above William's head, surrounding him with melliflous sound, like the tones of a churchbell rung far away. Yet the meaning of his words was insufferable.

The Tower. All the anxiety of the past days centered on those two terrible words—the ultimate punishment for traitorous guilt. He dared not repeat it, so scathing was its meaning. "I did hear, sir, but I do not understand why."

Davison sat down suddenly on the edge of his bed. "Because...she has ordered it. Only God can judge her motive, but she has done it. She has chosen me to bear her guilt." He shook his head slowly. "I have suspected this since she told me of her dream. I do believe the Lord forewarned me that day of what was to come."

William stammered, "But the Council stood by you, sir. They agreed to send the warrant."

"Yes, and she knows it. I believe she would hang us all if she could conveniently do so. But even she knows that is nonsense. She needs only one scapegoat to display before the world."

At just that moment George burst in and demanded, "Why was Lord Buckhurst here?"

Davison stood up and held out his arm toward George. "Good lads, come here to me."

George hastened to Davison, who put an arm about each boy. "You have been a blessing to me, lads, friends, and confidants, as dear as sons. I will never forget you."

George flashed William a look of alarm. William bit his lip as a flood of tears threatened his eyes. *I will not cry. I will not.*

Davison said. "I'm off to the Tower, lad."

George's eyes widened. "No! She cannot!"

"Ah, but she can," Davison said quietly. Then he drew himself up and smiled brightly. "Come now, do not despair. This is a logical move, quite appropriate, to convince the world that she is innocent of crime. It may be nothing more than that, a mere gesture, and I will be free in a fortnight."

The boys stared at each other in a paralysis of fear. No one ever escaped the judgment of the Tower. If not beheaded, at least they suffered disgrace. Yet no one knew that better than William Davison, whose genius in times of crisis was always to put forward his best face. They stared at this man who had so richly tutored them, then at each other. Neither could make a sound.

Three days later Lord Buckhurst returned to wait while Davison calmly adjusted his clothing and arranged his person in full court dress for the sojourn before him. At last he stood ready and faced his two stewards. "I may be allowed one of you to serve me, but not both. Therefore, I will need William to attend my daily toilette, and will request that you, George, be allowed occasional visits to conduct my affairs." He smiled. "Do not despair, lads. Despite appearances, the Queen is not heartless. She knows the truth and will honor it in due time."

He held out his hand and shook each of theirs, then turned to the door where Lord Buckhurst and an escort of two guards awaited. William glanced about quickly for the personal belongings Davison would need, but when Davison stepped outside, one guard barred William's way. Flanking Davison and Buckhurst, the guards escorted them down the hallway and disappeared.

William rounded on George. "God help him! She cannot do this!"

George's scoffing bark sounded like a shot in the room.

Five

Trial

Davison walked stoically beside Lord Buckhurst between the guards escorting him to the Tower, and held himself erect while riding in the cart and ascending the stairways to his room high in Beauchamp Tower. After Buckhurst departed and the door locked behind him, "Beefeaters" stationed themselves outside it, and Davison collapsed on the hard bed, utterly spent.

❧

As soon as Davison disappeared from their sight, George rushed to beg Sir Hatton to petition the Queen to send some of Davison's staff to attend him.

The next day a guard escorted William and George to Beauchamp, where they found Davison shivering under a thin woolen coverlet in a dark room with no fire on the hearth. The boys were appalled.

"Mr. Davison, sir," George explained cheerily, "Lord Hatton had us sent here. He will seek better quarters for you."

Davison moved his head feebly from side to side. "All of them—the Council—begged her on their knees to spare me. They can do no more."

William said eagerly, "But they will see you are well treated, sir."

Davison lifted his hand limply in a gesture of futility. The boys looked at each other, confirming in their glance the same thought—he was giving up in despair.

George at once protested Davison's dismal provisions, declaring them an insult to one of his stature, and demanded of the guard that he be allowed to fetch proper comforts for his master. The guard smirked but rather admired George's pluck and agreed to let him go.

When Davison had been in his room two days, Sir Christofer Hatton appeared at his door. Yet it was soon apparent from Sir Hatton's demeanor that he had come not to console Davison, but to interrogate him. His mission was to confirm the Queen's stand, not Davison's. William slunk to a far corner of the room, out of their sight but within earshot, wishing that George were here to eavesdrop with him.

"My friend," Hatton said kindly, "you know how much I regret the necessity for this."

Davison nodded. "I appreciate your concern, good sir, and as well your delicate position."

"I am directed to put to you some questions." Hatton waited for Davison to install himself comfortably in a chair by the lone table, then sat down opposite and spread his papers. Hatton was young and handsome and the Queen's current favorite, and to his surprise William felt sudden fearful concern for him. The fates of the Queen's favorites were always precarious. He wondered if Mr. Davison was thinking the same.

Hatton began. "When Elizabeth signed the warrant, did she not order you to keep it secret and not to mention it to anyone?"

"No, sir. She gave me no such command."

"Did she not order that when the warrant was sealed, you were not on your life to let it out of your hands until you knew her further pleasure?"

"No, sir. She ordered me to carry it to the Lord Chancellor to be sealed, and then forthwith dispatched."

"Did she not tell you later in the gallery that she had a better way of proceeding in the affair?"

"I repeat what I have said before, that the Lord Admiral sent for me and told me to bring the warrant for her signature as she intended to carry the sentence into execution. When I brought it to her, she signed it and commanded me to carry it to the Lord Chancellor for the great seal and to be forthwith dispatched. She had told the Lord Admiral herself, of necessity the Lord Chancellor must learn of it, and she directed me to tell Mr. Secretary Walsingham abed in his house. I swear before my Creator, sir, that I speak the truth."

Hatton cleared his throat, his face studiously impassive. "Let us consider Her Majesty's dilemma. She signed the warrant authorizing the Queen of Scots' execution, knowing that her reputation, her very life, may be greatly endangered if this action were known. Is it not possible that you misunderstood her command to wait and acted in undue haste to seal and dispatch it?"

"No, sir. It is not possible. She urged me to have it sealed and, I assumed, to be dispatched with the utmost care and secrecy such action required." Davison eyed Hatton levelly. "May I ask a question of you, sir? Did the Queen mention that she commanded that I write a letter to Amyas Paulet to effect Mary Stewart's demise by some other means? That was, to her mind, 'a better way of proceeding in the affair.'"

Hatton gazed at Davison somberly. "I think it unwise to arouse that issue, sir, unless in your own defense you deem it feasible to accuse her."

"Paulet made his defense clear enough. He declined to shipwreck his conscience and blot his posterity by acts which God and the law forbid."

Hatton bit his lip thoughtfully. Then he lowered his voice and spoke more softly. William, straining to hear from his corner, heard him say, "For God's sake, man, give her a bit of room to wiggle. It will go better for you."

Davison's voice came forth boldly. "Would you have me shipwreck my conscience as well, Hatton? I did as she directed and swear by it. Nor will I sully her name further by telling the whole truth of it."

For the first time William heard a bitter note in Davison's tone. To reveal to Hatton the Queen's intent to have Mary assassinated must nearly choke him. Yet obviously his safer tactic was to be compliant, not defiant.

When Hatton had gone William offered Davison his dinner, which he refused. "You must keep up your strength, sir, in faith that you will not be here long."

Davison passed a hand across his brow. "Do you remember, William, when first we met at Scrooby Manor? You asked me about Beggars and Huguenots, and I wondered how to explain to so young a lad the magnitude of their struggle. Now I begin to comprehend what sacrifice for one's conscience truly requires."

"History will redeem you, sir."

Davison sighed. "If so, I doubt I will live to enjoy it. Yet you will remember this affair, my son, and can advise your grandchildren how we suffered for conscience."

Davison was put to two more interrogations, asking essentially the same questions in slightly different phrasing favoring the Queen's position. He maintained a steadfastly consistent defense. After the last interrogation on March sixteenth, a hearing by the Star Chamber was set for March twenty-fifth, and Davison and the boys resigned themselves to a dreary wait.

One day, on his daily visit with papers and letters and the latest news, George told William worriedly that everyone at the Palace was gossiping that the Queen had found a judge willing to support her imperial authority to hang any of her subjects at will without conviction by law. It was said that Lord Burghley near fainted when he heard of it.

Terror struck William like a blow to his stomach, and for a moment cut off his breath.

"She has gone mad," George growled, shaking his head. "She declares that she may hang all of her Council." He glowered at William. "You know who that means."

"God help him," William moaned.

"Lord Burghley has warned all other judges whom she may consult to consider the dire consequences of such advice."

They glanced at Mr. Davison dozing by the fire. He had seemed to age ten years since his arrival in the Tower, all his noble hopes dashed by the very Majesty he had served so devotedly.

A consuming rage stirred in William, squelching his fear. "By God," he muttered, "she will suffer one day for this."

"Indeed," George agreed. "Before she is done, she will drive all of us mad."

That night William felt the cold void in his stomach take form, twist into a knot, and seem to harden into stone. *I have come to hate her,* he thought, and was at once deeply ashamed. He began to pray fervently, repenting for his sins for the first time since Mary's execution.

On March twenty-eighth, Davison was brought before the Star Chamber. Silently, the Commissioners watched him enter, one arm weakened by an attack of palsy and supported in a sling. During a long harangue, Counsel for the Crown charged him with "misprision and contempt," contending that although Her Majesty had condemned the Queen of Scots, it had never been her intention to execute the sentence. Rather, she wanted the warrant held in abeyance as a threat to other plotters, or until some unforeseen dire necessity required its execution.

Davison did not alter his defense and reiterated his conviction that the Queen fully intended to execute the sentence for all the pressing reasons it was necessary, and because she had said so directly when he asked her, declaring she would no more be troubled with it. He spoke clearly with all the resonance of his baritone voice. "It is not usual at Court for the Queen to be troubled with any particulars attending the execution of such warrants, and after giving her consent, the time, place, and manner of execution were always left to the Privy Council. The Council concurred unanimously that the warrant for the Queen of Scots' execution should be activated at once without further 'troubling' the Queen, as she requested."

Thomas Edgeton, Solicitor-general, read excerpts from Davison's previous confession, challenging the credibility of his statements, to which Davison answered that he would rather suppress it entirely than contend with the Queen by divulging any private conversation or commands he had received that might cause her embarrassment.

After Davison's defense, the Commissioners delivered their opinions. Sir Walter Mildmay declared harshly, "In my judgment Mr. Davison's negligence has been amply demonstrated by his obvious attempts to cast the Queen's comments in light of his own opinions. As she has declared openly, she had no intention of carrying out the execution of her royal kinswoman, an anathema to her keen sensibilities, but only to hold in abeyance the threat of execution intended to deter traitors. It is reprehensible that Mr. Davison's obvious zeal for the Scottish Queen's demise, and the opportunity thereof to dispatch her, colored his interpretation of the Queen's commands. I call for the imposition of a fine of ten thousand marks and his imprisonment in the Tower during the Queen's pleasure."

Lord Gray countered with a brisk defense of Davison's motives. "Mr. Davison has done no more than his duty in discharging the warrant and preserving its secrecy. Had not the warrant been forwarded, any ill that may have befallen the Queen would have denounced him as a traitor. Yet I am content that the punishment mentioned by Sir Mildmay should be laid upon him, desiring that it might please the mighty God to put it into Her Majesty's heart to remit his punishment, so that all good subjects, by his example, may be encouraged to perform their duty."

The Chancellor of the Exchequer praised Davison's service but qualified his performance in this case. "I am heartily sorry that he was not in this so good a servant as in all other things."

The Earl of Lincoln, touting Davison's usual competence, observed, "The deed was negligently done but not contemptuously. I agree with Lord Gray that the punishment is too severe, but, knowing the Queen's penchant for mercy, do commit to her generous heart his due reward."

In succession, the others declared for the proposed punishment. Finally, the Lord Chief Justice, presiding, delivered the sentence of the Court. "He should pay a fine of ten thousand marks and be imprisoned in the Tower during the Queen's pleasure. These proceedings prove the integrity of Her Majesty's conduct toward the Queen of Scots, and as she thought the Council had been deceived by Mr. Davison, she imputes no blame to any of the others."

Davison raised a hand. "Sir, I would ask a question."

Mildmay snapped, "It is not permitted in this Court to ask any question after judgment is passed. It is permitted only to petition."

The Lord Privy Seal sang out, "I concur."

Davison insisted, "I would say nothing offensive to this Court."

"Then speak," said Mildmay irritably.

"I ask whether, if the Queen had been injured and the warrant was found in my hands, ready signed and sealed, what course...."

Mildmay broke in. "That point has already been discussed by Lord Gray."

Davison gathered himself together and stood erect. "Then, gentlemen, I say to you in all humility that I accept the will of God in this matter. I care not for the loss of my situation, my disgrace, the fine or the imprisonment, which my illness makes especially hard to bear. All that gives me concern is Her Majesty's displeasure. I beg each of you to plead for me, for if I could again obtain her gracious favor, I would be indifferent to the situation in which I am placed."

He fell silent and they waited for him to continue. But he dropped his head, finished.

The Lord Chief Justice dismissed the court. One by one the Commissioners approached Davison, shook his hand, complimented him on his petition, and promised him they would inform the Queen of it.

In the Tower George and William glumly awaited Davison's return. "I would give ten years of my life to have heard that trial," George said. "I would give twenty to have testified to our man's integrity."

"Soon enough we will hear every detail of it."

The boys sat sullenly. *Surely,* William was thinking, *she will lift his sentence. No prince anointed of God could in conscience blame him for what she has done.*

"It will never be the same," George muttered.

William looked down from the slit of a window high above fields glazed with snow and resigned himself to a long winter. He would serve his master as devotedly as possible in this damp, stone edifice whose underground chambers of torture and vile instruments of destruction lay hidden, and where victims of English justice had languished, suffered, or died. He would pray that Davison be spared so cruel an end and send up petitions of gratitude to be allowed to serve him in this cold drafty apartment, offering only bleak comfort against the bitter howling winds of fate.

Six

Tower

T he despair of that winter of 1587 in the Tower chilled William's heart more thoroughly than the weather stiffened his bones as two of his dearest friends endured the indifference of the tyrant Elizabeth. One was John Penry, who in the same month that Mary Stewart was executed, boldly petitioned Parliament to dispatch preachers of the Christian faith to his native Wales, an act certain to agitate Bishop Whitgift, the Queen's iron hand of conformity. Now the concern William had felt for John at Cambridge bloomed into a grim forboding. Henceforth, John would be a marked man, and fear for him compounded the despair William suffered for his master, Davison.

Davison's apartment was meagerly but adequately furnished and his simple needs supplied. Yet, the reality of his master's fall, his person so demeaned, his brilliant conciliatory talent stifled while he sat writing or reading at his table, and most grievous of all, his spirits so crushed, settled in William's heart like a stone. He could not forgive Elizabeth for Davison's betrayal. Though it could not be spoken, her intimates had suspected the Queen's desire to dispatch Mary Stewart secretly. Yet now to blame her most honorable men for exposing her perfectly legal "crime" while declaring herself innocent of malice, was for William hypocrisy beyond bearing. Especially as she made so good a show of it, railing at her Council and even banishing Lord Burghley from her presence.

Moreover, William was angry with God. How could he designate such a hypocrite to rule his people! William had beseeched his Lord in prayer for insight to this injustice, had found none, and felt that stone of bitterness turn into acid to poison his breast like a rotting tumor.

On one fiercely windy day, as the north wind moaned at the walls and sleet slashed the window, he stood shivering before the fire and suddenly blurted out, "May that witch be damned to hell!"

Davison looked up from his desk. "How so, Master Brewster?" he asked mildly.

William blushed. "I am sorry, sir." Yet in his heart he was not sorry at all and thereby compounded his sin of unforgiveness with a lie. He felt his gorge rising as his oath released a suppressed torrent of hatred.

Davison regarded him silently a long moment while William hung his head, rubbing his hands for heat and glancing up at his mentor several times with contrition. He choked out, "Forgive me, sir. I *am* sorry."

Davison put down his pen, a slight frown nicking his brow. "My son, I am sorry too, but I do readily forgive you."

William could force no further sound past his burning throat.

"Moreover, my son, I do sympathize. I have had such dire thoughts myself."

The burn in his throat rushed up to fill William's eyes, and he swung his head away, lest Davison see his futile tears. The possibility that this virtuous man had thoughts as bitter as his own pierced his heart with pity, and he feared he would burst into unmanly sobs.

Davison suddenly went lax, his shoulders sagged, and his head dropped to his chest.

William blinked back his tears. "Sir, forgive me. I know not what possessed me to speak so."

Davison raised a hand to quiet him, then shook his head sadly. "I know well what possessed you, lad." He sat silently a long moment, then asked, "Have we something warm to drink? The damp is piercing today."

William reached for the jug of ale set to warm by the fire. "Yes, sir, at once."

As William poured the ale, Davison said, "Sit down here with me, son. I have something to say to you."

"I would rather stand, sir, if you please."

"No, son. Sit down with me. I would speak with you as a friend, not a servant." As William sat, Davison gazed across the table into his eyes. "We have been friends a long time, lad."

"Aye, we have, sir."

"And I hope will be friends, and comrades, forever, into eternity."

"Yes, indeed, sir."

"But now you are very young and must discover a new life for yourself."

"I am happy to serve you here, sir."

"No, William, it is time for you to leave me and serve someone else."

"Never, sir."

"Now hear me out, son. I have accepted my fate as God's will. One day He may soften the Queen's heart and restore her favor to me. I pray for that but do not expect it. It may be that I was born to this end."

"Oh, surely not, sir. Never!"

"We do not know the heart of God, lad. His purposes are higher than ours."

"Of course, sir, but surely he would not sacrifice one so good." He stopped, blushing with embarassment.

"Whatever his intentions, we must cope with life as we find it. I would not have you spend your youth in this prison. It is time for you to move on."

"I could not leave you, sir."

"I will find you other employment here in London. I have already spoken for George to Henry Killegrew, who will take him on as secretary, and I have been thinking who best you can serve."

"I beg to stay with you here, sir. It will not be forever."

Davison smiled sadly. "It may be exactly that, son." He sat forward. "Now I do have someone in mind, a good, honest fellow coming up at court."

"Please, sir. If I cannot serve you, I will go home to Scrooby." William's words surprised himself. He had made no such conscious decision.

"Scrooby? Surely after your experience here you would find Scrooby—" he paused for the appropriate word—"to say the least, subdued."

"I believe that is exactly what I want, sir. I do not think court life is for me."

Davison sat back and regarded William solemnly. "Nor, apparently, any longer for me." They smiled at the gentle irony. "Did I ever tell you that once I gave up court to play at squire at Stepney?" His eyes softened. "I was married then to my young Scottish bride, who was not welcome at court. She was such a lively lass that 'quiet' country life seemed much more enjoyable than the turmoil of Whitehall." He sighed. "And my father had most soberly warned me of the perils of serving royalty." His eyes clouded. "Dear father, how wise he was."

"You never spoke of a Scottish bride, sir."

"So long ago. We met in Edinburgh while I served Henry Killegrew at the birth of Prince James. Her father forbade our marriage, preferring that she marry a Scottish nobleman." His eyes brightened. "Now there's an irony for you. Jean was lady to Mary Stewart when Henry Darnley was murdered, before she married Bothwell." He took a deep breath. "I have not thought of these things in years."

William was astonished. "You married a lady to Mary Stewart?"

Davison nodded. "And twenty years later I am blamed for causing Mary's death." He chuckled. "Jean would be amused."

William stammered, "But your wife, sir. Does Lady Davison know of her?"

"Oh, yes. Jean died, you see, in childbirth. I married Katherine two years later." Suddenly his forehead crumpled in a frown. "I have a daughter somewhere in Scotland with Jean's family. I have not seen her in years, yet I think of her, sharply, whenever I see a lass with flaming bronze hair. When I think of her, I see her looking exactly like her mother."

William sat silently, wondering at the complexity of this man he served. He had met Lady Davison occasionally, a charming Englishwoman whose family served royalty and whose position had probably enhanced Davison's career at court. Only now, reminiscing, had Davison revealed anything of his early life. William asked timidly, "Why did you leave country life, sir?"

Davison glanced up from his reverie, blinking as if awakened. "When Jean died, I could not stay on at Stepney, to watch her daughter—her image—unfold before my eyes. Before I met Jean, I was certain that God ordained that I serve the state. In fact, Sir Henry

Killegrew tried to convince me she was a distraction from my destiny." He gave out a sharp burst of sardonic laughter. "So also, it has been a short, happy departure from my 'destiny' to end in this Tower."

William said nothing, watching a play of memory suffuse Davison's face. Suddenly he recalled his own first impressions of Davison's visits to Scrooby en route between London and Edinburgh. This drama of Davison's early life must have happened soon after William was born, before his father had been appointed postmaster at Scrooby. Yet Davison's marriage to Lady Katherine seemed a happy one, his four children a blessing. How many knew in that distinguished English court that he had once lived a completely different life with a Scottish bride and a child deeply buried in his memory?

They sat silently awhile, each in his private reverie, while the wind and sleet outside buffeted the Tower walls, sometimes wailing through a crack as if mourning. At last William, shivering, noted Davison's brew grown cold, and asked, "More ale, sir?"

Davison glanced up. "Yes, if you please, son. 'Tis a devil wind be-seiges us today."

William stirred the fire whose hottest blaze never warmed the damp walls of these high Tower rooms. On blustery days like this every Englishman in the realm, the Queen as well, huddled before his hearth. He scowled, thinking of that evil woman basking in warmth and comfort, her every whim lavishly served by countless devoted servants whom she would betray in a moment if it pleased her. Abruptly, he cut off the thought. Perhaps it was time he left London. With the Queen's presence lurking over the city like a miasma, he could never be certain that the same sorry fate would not befall any other royal counselor Davison found for him to serve.

Davison sipped his hot brew. "Would you be happy at Scrooby, William?"

"I think so, sir. I've been long away."

"And I think much changed from the lad who left home. After seeing London and Antwerp, will he be satisfied merely to serve travelers at his post house?"

"I truly do not know, sir. I shall have to try it and see."

"You are sure you would not want to serve here? With Sidney, perhaps even Hatton? Hatton is always looking for good men, and honors my recommendations."

"Especially not Sir Hatton, sir. I fear for him."

"Why so?"

"I fear for all the Queen's favorites, sir. The less-noticed men fare better." William thought suddenly of John Penry, who was of no social importance, but surely destined to command royal notice.

Davison frowned. "An astute observation, that. My father gave me such a warning long ago. God is the master of men's fates, not monarchs, he said. Always seek His will and serve Him first, and He will, like Wolsey said, not give you over in your gray hairs."

"Cardinal Wolsey, sir?"

"Aye. He returned to York before he died, you know, after Henry had banished him from court. In his last days he served the people of Scrooby in penance for his sins against the country." He added thoughtfully, "When I learned this, I prayed he had not been penitent too late."

He set aside his mug, then looked intently at William. "You cannot leave until spring, son. I remember well my first trip to Edinburgh in December for Prince James' baptism. 'Twas the worst of seasons. We lost a horse and almost the rider fording one rushing stream. Yet I was elated, thrilled to be Killegrew's aide, to be attending the baptism of a Scottish prince perhaps to be our Queen's successor. And most delightful of all, seeing the notorious Mary Stewart in the flesh. Despite all weathers, the world was quite magnificent then!"

Enthralled, William sat down to listen intently to Davison's memories, enjoying this brief respite from his grim fate while transporting himself to another happier world beyond the Tower. Yet later that evening as he stoked the fire for the night, William was surprised to realize that his plans for his own future had settled upon him. He had blurted out the truth. He would return home to Scrooby.

&oc&

That winter William was determined to find John Penry somewhere in the city. He confided this intention to George. Soon afterwards George, who as steward to Sir Hatton was privy to many avenues of secret intelligence, revealed that Penry lodged in a small warren buried in the maze of London streets where a quick exit could be made easily. And such an exit would inevitably be required. Whitgift would surely declare Penry's strident criticisms of Church practice in Wales derogatory of the Queen herself.

William made sure no one was near on the street when he knocked at Penry's door. No one answered, but as he waited, a voice behind the door snapped, "Who is it?"

William whispered to the thick door, "An old friend from Cambridge. Perno, Pernare."

The door opened a crack, an eye peered out. Then the door swung wide. "Brewster!" In one quick move Penry seized William's arm while his head swung about, peering both ways down the street. He yanked William through the doorway. "How good to see you, old man! Ha! Perno, Pernare indeed!"

They embraced, then stood back to gaze into each other's faces, Penry's grin as eager as a child's. "You look splendid, my lad." His eyes raked William's fine attire with amused admiration. "And I must say, adversity gives you not only status but the patina of maturity." Penry pulled up two chairs. The tiny room was cluttered with papers arranged in stacks about the walls.

"You know about Mr. Davison," William said.

"Of course. 'Tis the shame of the decade. She has outdone herself in malice, a monstrous feat, even for her. So how fares the gentleman?"

"I marvel at his courage. Though broken-hearted he goes on gamely, believing she will change her mind. He claimed at his trial that he only regretted displeasing her, and I believe he means it."

"The witch! She should be boiled in oil!"

William put a quick finger to his lips. "Ye dare not speak so, John."

"My lad, I shall speak and speak and *speak* until they cut out my tongue."

William winced. "Do not be foolish, John. You tempt fate."

John brushed the remark aside. "Have you read my *Aequity* paper? It's for sale in Paul's Church-yard at the sign of the Tygerhead, Toby Cooke's business house."

"By Heaven, man! Whitgift cannot ignore that."

"Someone must expose his tyranny. Many feel as I do, yet have too much to lose. I have the least—only my head." He barked a mirthless laugth, shrugged at William's frown, and furrowed his brow. "Ah, well, there is someone whose welfare I do value. I have a wife now, you know, but I can let nothing interfere with my mission."

"What exactly is your mission, John?"

Penry's eyes brightened. "We plan to print anonymously a series of papers to enlighten the people. And I have found a reliable printer."

William glanced about the tiny room. "But what of all this? If you are surprised here, this very evidence will condemn you."

"We tread carefully, lad, senses alert to all comers. I peered at you through a slit in my door. And we are armed with clever informers in high places. We can move in a twinkling if we must." He sat forward. "Brewster, why not join us? You can do nothing now to help Davison."

William said sullenly, "I will continue to serve him until...well, when I am dismissed, I am going back to Scrooby. I have had enough of royal service."

Penry's eyes popped. "Scrooby! Dear Lord, what will you do in Scrooby?"

"Live a quietly peaceful life without fear of treachery." He leaned toward Penry as if a spring wound within him was about to uncoil. "John, have you any idea what she has done to him? Ruined his future! Someone should expose the sham of his trial. All the Councillors, his closest colleagues and friends, agreed to convict him, full knowing his innocence, yet terrified of her wrath."

Penry grinned. "You write the story, Brewster. We will print it."

The boldness of his own statements, even to trustworthy Penry, suddenly struck William with dismay. Exposure of Davison's betrayal might rather doom than free him. "I dare not. She had spoken of executing him without a trial. Each day I dread that guards will appear unannounced to take him to the scaffold." He shook his head. "I can well believe now the horror stories told about her."

Penry got up to pour them mugs of ale, handed one to William, then sat down. "Now listen to me, friend. I plan to write a series of lampoons against the bishops, telling the truth with humor to amuse the people. We must do it on the run, but I find that strangely stimulating. It adds a certain pique to our mission."

William scowled. "This is no game you play, John."

Penry nodded. "I know that well, and I do not speak in jest. Remember the bear baiting? The poor doomed beast fought bravely to the last. If it is my destiny to die for this cause, despite all odds I must persevere to the end."

"But is it your destiny, John?"

Penry shrugged. "If my God does not direct me, then my efforts are wasted anyway. I offer this crusade to His glory."

They sat awhile, sipping ale, retelling old tales of Cambridge days. When William left, saddened, he grieved for himself and the friends he was powerless to help.

Not a week later George informed him that the copies of Penry's *Aequity* still left at Toby Cooke's were seized by Whitgift's men and that John Penry was now lodged in the Gatehouse at Westminster. George predicted grimly, "Whitgift accuses him of slander of Her Majesty's government, flat treason and heresy, nothing less."

William groaned. "I tried to warn him."

"He is a zealot bound to his cause. Zealots never listen to reason."

The sorrow William felt at Penry's lodging plunged him into a miasma like a fog from the sea. He mourned both good friends, Davison in the Tower and Penry in Westminster, and as much as these, his "Christian" homeland persecuting her own best people.

Seven

Brewster at Scrooby

Nothing had changed at Scrooby, but its peace offered Brewster little solace. Elizabeth's treachery had cut short not only Davison's luminous career but Brewster's own shining dreams of high service to his God and country. The doubt that he could ever trust authority again festered in his heart like a sore scabbed over by practiced obligation to his family and duty to his country.

His aging father now needed constant help at the Manor, which left the son little time for brooding upon his fate. Yet having grown intellectually well beyond the confines of his village, he was keenly alert to the news that couriers and travelers brought along the North Road from London.

Foremost that summer of 1588 was the menace of the Spanish fleet hovering off England's southern coast, threatening to launch the invasion she had so long dreaded. Brewster could imagine Davison peering down at the Thames through the slot of his Tower window, expecting to see a fleet of Spanish galleons sailing inland. He wondered how George Cranmer was faring with Sir Henry Killegrew, and about the fates of John Penry and John Greenwood, and others he had known and held dear in Cambridge and London.

He knew that George was in London, but he had lost track of Penry and Greenwood. After his confinement at Westminster, Penry had been released for lack of formal charges, and then simply disappeared. Before leaving London William heard speculation that Penry might be the anonymous author of the notorious Martin Marprelate Tracts, whose ridicule of the bishops much amused the people but infuriated the archbishop. Recalling Penry's and Greenwood's bold tracts circulated at Cambridge, Brewster could well believe that they might have written the Marprelate papers. Yet whether or not they were guilty, if Whitgift's pursuivants searched them out, no power on earth could save them.

Then stunning news of the naval battle between the Spanish Armada and the English fleet in the Channel swept across the land. Apparently the Lord God Almighty had reinforced English naval strategy with a violent storm, scattering the Armada across the northern seas. Yet not until coastal towns reported flotsam, bodies, and near-drowned Spanish sailors cast upon their shores could the English believe they had actually repelled their formidable enemy. The nation rejoiced.

Yet in September of that year the execution of the Earl of Essex, Brewster's noble contemporary at Cambridge and once-esteemed favorite of Elizabeth, overshadowed for William the nation's triumphant victory at sea and confirmed his contempt for the Queen's duplicity. Despite his noble lineage and renowned position, the elegant Essex could not escape a traitor's fate when the Queen was convinced he threatened her power.

News of neither event had much effect on the northern shires.

こめ

After William's father died, he was appointed to succeed him at Scrooby Manor, a position secure enough for him to consider taking a wife. Soon after returning home he had noticed at St. Alfred's Church Mary Wentworth, a woman of good family and fine character, and found himself gazing often at her handsome profile each Sunday. Her calm and devout demeanor pleased him the more he beheld her. Yet for all his cosmopolitan experience among the high courts of England and Europe he was reduced to an inept, awkward country dolt when attempting the small talk expected of a suitor. Finally, after several false starts at which he nodded and smiled at her but could find nothing to say, he found his voice at a harvest fair. Mary had entered a savory eel pie in a baking contest, the pie a variation of a baked eel dish long a specialty from the kitchen at Scrooby Manor.

William stood over the dish, inhaling its luscious aroma, and said,

"Miss Wentworth, the aroma arising from that dish would enthrall visitors at the Manor's dining hall."

Mary smiled. "Would you like a taste, Mr. Brewster?"

"Indeed I would. Even without tasting, I would buy the whole pie for the aroma alone."

"Oh, 'tis not for sale yet, sir. Only when the winner is announced."

"Would I were a judge then."

Mary whipped another pie from under the table. "This one is for tasting."

William gazed at the steaming crust. "Have you more under there?"

Mary blushed. "Several, sir. Methinks if this one wins the contest, the others kept warm will surely sell quickly."

So the girl had a keen eye for trade. And at once the thought struck him that he needed just such a manager in the kitchen at Scrooby Manor. And as well perhaps he needed a manager for the Manor itself. With sudden confidence, he grinned. "Whether you win or not, you have sold me the lot."

She frowned slightly. "That would not be proper, Mr. Brewster. If this be a champion dish, it should be shared with our community."

"True, but if I serve it at the Manor, your fame and mine will spread along the Road and increase our trade." He said this with a sly grin so that, if she were offended by so crass a remark, he could quickly claim to be joking. Instead she gazed into his eyes seriously, frowned a bit chewing her lip, seeming to turn over in her mind his proposition. He watched her, ready to retract the proposal at once.

Suddenly her face brightened with a smile. "A capital idea, Mr. Brewster. I will supply your kitchen with my best pies, and you may pay me a commission on your increased revenue."

He was struck speechless. Thus began a congenial relationship much enhanced by the success of their venture. Mary's talents extended well beyond eel pies to an instinct for pleasing customers with dishes of fine quality and variety. Travelers on the North Road extolled the cuisine and the hospitality of Scrooby Manor from London to Edinburgh. Inevitably, their partnership bloomed into friendship.

One day Mary came to his office to tell him that a stranger

claiming he had known Brewster in London awaited him in the great hall. He had not given his name. Brewster put his books aside and went down to the hall where the visitor, his back turned, was gazing at tapestries on the wall. He wore a felt hat pulled well down on his head and was swathed in a great cloak of a dark heavy cloth.

"Sir, may I help you?" Brewster asked.

The figure swung round to face him. He appeared middle-aged, gray-bearded, and stooped. Brewster did not recognize him.

"Brewster, you old dog. Do you not know your former colleague in crime?"

Brewster blinked, mystified.

"I canna' believe it. This guise is better than I thought."

The saucy voice struck a bell in Brewster's memory, but the face escaped him. Brewster stared at him.

The man raised his hat brim and grinned. "Of course, I have aged a *bit*."

It was John Penry! "God be praised, you look a complete stranger."

Brewster embraced his old friend, at once aware of his slight body, a mere rail of a figure concealed under the cloak. He stepped back and peered into Penry's eyes. Of course, how could he miss those snapping eyes? "What are you doing in Scrooby, my dear John?"

"Quite literally hiding out."

"In Scrooby?"

"On my way to Edinburgh. Constables on my heels. Dinna' worry, friend. I'll be gone before they find me here. I could not resist stopping by."

Could Penry be in danger even here in Nottingham? Brewster took his arm. "Come up to my room. No one there to listen."

Moving up the staircase, Penry chirped, "Who is that charming hostess, old chap? I say, you should bind her up and seal her tight. Why haven't you married her?"

"I will," Brewster muttered. "I've been planning to ask her."

"Planning as usual, not doing. Why waste precious time?"

They moved into Brewster's office. "I'll have some food sent up for you, John. Tell me why you are going to Edinburgh."

Penry collapsed into a chair, opened his cloak, and took off his hat.

His face sagged with exhaustion. "Tiresome, this constant running."

"From whom are you running?"

"You've heard of the Marprelate Tracts? Umm, maybe not up here yet. Better you know nothing. If anyone asks it will be true, for I will tell you nothing."

"What are these...tracts?"

"A masterpiece of satire about our beloved archbishop and his ilk. I wish I *had* written them. I do know the printer, which association arouses their suspicion of *me* as the author. He has just been arrested, and God help his soul, no doubt his bones are being racked this moment for the name of that author."

"And no doubt you are next on the archbishop's list."

"Better than that, I head the list. Unfortunately for my printer, they found him first." Penry heaved a sigh. "He printed some of my work as well."

Brewster shook his head. "Oh, John, how I wish you would settle down somewhere, and raise a family. Leave reform to the zealots."

Penry grinned. "I *am* raising a family, two daughters already. And despite that I am still a zealot."

Brewster shook his head. "Where is your family? Do they know where you are?"

"I'll send for them as soon as I settle in Scotland. Eleanor is God's gift to me. She supports me and my work, God bless her soul." He sat forward. "Brewster, we are making headway. The people love the Marprelate papers, which devastate those bishops. Whatever it costs me, I am proud of our people. They are doing God's work."

Brewster eyed him skeptically. "But you didn't write the papers."

"I will never admit to it. Certainly not to friends who might suffer for it. To convert my Welshmen and to expose Whitgift and his ilk is *my* mission, William, not yours."

A knock sounded on the door. Brewster stood up and opened it. Mary said, "Did you find your visitor? Will he stay for dinner?"

"I did indeed. And yes, he will stay the night."

Penry bounced up. "No, friend, I cannot. I must be off."

Brewster pulled Mary inside. "This is my old Cambridge friend, John Penry. You have heard me speak of him."

Mary smiled. "Most pleased to meet you, Mr. Penry."

Penry bobbed his head. "Brewster, she is irresistible. And has convinced me to accept your offer of dinner. But then I must be off. Time never waits for Penry."

"Mary, bring up our dinner. We'll eat it here."

Mary's gaze lingered on Brewster's face, reading there his message of caution. Then she said briskly, "Of course. I'll bring it myself." She slipped out the door and closed it firmly.

"You must sleep somewhere, John. Why not here?"

"Too public. I do not frequent inns or post houses. And yours is touted along the Road as a fine establishment. If I were seen here I could cause you trouble."

"In that disguise? I didn't recognize you myself."

"Good. I have grown adept at disguise. Perhaps I should give up this mission and become a traveling actor."

Mary brought dinner for both men, then discreetly disappeared.

They talked late, Brewster determined that Penry gain a good night's rest whatever the risk. Food and rest were the very least he could do for him.

Since Brewster left Peterhouse, Penry had taken a Master's degree and preached at several churches but also continued writing anonymous exposés of Church bishops. Soon after the Armada's defeat the Marprelate tracts had been published, arousing Whitgift's raging obsession to find the author. Actually, Penry hinted, the tracts obscured his own, and for a time occupied Whitgift's total attention. But when the printer was discovered, Penry's implication by association redirected the archbishop's focus. "Now it is time for me to hide among the Prebyterians in Scotland. I will be safe there."

Brewster plied Penry with food and ale until he was so relaxed, Brewster could lead him to bed, where he fell soundly asleep. Brewster knew he would sneak out before dawn, so aroused himself early to serve him breakfast and food for traveling. But Penry had already risen, bribed the stableboy for his horse, and departed before Brewster could catch him. Gazing along the North Road as the sun rose, Brewster spoke to the Lord, whom Penry so staunchly defended. "Lord God our Father, bless John Penry, deliver him from evil, Lord. Bring him home safely."

Mary and William married in 1590. William had never been so content. His and Mary's post house thrived, and he reveled in their success. He reflected occasionally that all went better for him now than when he exulted in serving Davison, once the height of his ambition. He heard that Davison had been released from the Tower and gone back to Stepney, and now assured that Penry was safe in Scotland, he thanked God for both his friends' well-being.

Then one day in late summer of 1592 Mary came to him to say, "Your friend is here again." Brewster eyed her closely. "I hid him in the bake house." She smiled broadly. "And gave him some eel pie."

Brewster found Penry perched on a stool chewing one of Mary's butter rolls. This time his beard was brown, his cheeks rosy, his figure ample, almost plump.

"The Scots have been good to you."

"Aye, a capital people. I canna' praise them enough."

"You even sound like a Scot. Then why are you leaving?"

"Things are deteriorating in London. And nothing has been done for Wales. I must plead again that the Church send preachers to insure their salvation."

"You have a family now, John. You must think of them."

"Eleanor understands my mission, William. They will be taken care of."

"Methinks if you go back this time they will find you. If they have not found the actual author of the Marprelate tracts, they will settle for you."

Penry grinned. "I would be proud of it."

"And your family? What of them?"

"An old married man sees the world from a different plane, does he not? Some men's mission is their family. Mine is to expose the Queen's deceptive bishops to her good heart and to convince her to send preachers to save Wales."

"John, I pray that God will preserve you."

"He will. And I predict that one day you, William Brewster, will be called to such a mission. You will not resist, your heart is too true, though you do not yet see it. You thought you would serve our God through Davison, and through him the Queen. Methinks our Lord has something different for you."

"I have found my niche here, my mission, if you will. I will stay in Scrooby, run my post house, and God willing, raise my family. I am content. My cup runneth over."

Penry wiped his mouth of the butter roll and shot out a hand. "Friends forever, wherever He leads us."

Brewster took his hand. "Friends forever."

Penry left before dawn.

જ્જ્જ

The Brewsters' first son was born August 12, 1593. They chose the name Jonathan to honor King David's loyal friend, and in a subtle way, William Davison.

News of conflict between puritans and Churchmen drifted into Scrooby Manor via travelers from London. One day a party from London breezed in full of chatty news of the clash of puritan dissenters with Whitgift's constables now ranging throughout the realm. Listening with his usual curiosity, Brewster heard one of them say, "A shame about that Welshman gutted at St. Thomas a Watering. He was a good chap, preached the bitter truth, that's a fact. Even old Burghley couldn't save 'im."

Brewster burst out, "What Welshman?"

The traveler glanced up. "Name was Penry. Connected with that bloke Barrow in London, a 'separatist' wanting to get out of the Church. Barrow and Greenwood were hanged a few weeks ago at Tyburn. I tell ye, lads, whatever ye think of the blasted bishops, ye keep your lip buttoned these days." He lanced around the great dining hall. "Even here, you don't know who's listening." He suddenly noticed William's stricken face, raised his mug, and grinned. "Here's to ye, sir. Fine house ye have here."

Brewster left the dining hall, walked through the kitchen and set down his tankard, and went out the door. Crossing the fields to the

River Ryton, there he sat down on the riverbank, paralyzed with grief. *God be with you, old friend.* For a moment the horror of Penry's death—hanged, drawn, and quartered—flashed across his mind: hanged by the neck, then cut down and disemboweled before he died, the ultimate punishment for treason. He shut off the image. Treason! A travesty as foul as Davison's betrayal! This man trying desperately to save his country died the martyr's death. When England's best men devoted to her welfare and anxious for her "soul" were sacrificed so callously, what hope for justice was left to the people?

He collapsed into wrenching tears. Mary found him at midnight and brought him home.

ℛ∞

In the next few years as turmoil among churchmen swirled throughout the shires, Brewster compared his comfortable and serene life as manager of Scrooby and respected citizen with Penry's years of flight from tyranny. To prosper, Brewster needed only to live humbly with his God and conform gracefully to the limitations of the law. Yet the shock of his friends' betrayals had fanned in his heart those embers of rebellion first stirred at Cambridge. He remembered Henry Brown whose despised name, "Brownist," now branded all who favored separation from the Church. He recalled William Perkins' brilliant orations on ecclesiastical order, and Thomas Cartwright's radical proposals to ban bishops and allow congregations to elect their own presbyters. He recalled, too, a sermon by Laurence Chaderton slandering the church as "a huge mass of old and stinking works." Their words surged up from his memory like a fish rising for air in a putrid pond. He recalled his arguments with Penry and his defense of Church authorities as good men dedicated to preserving order for the welfare of the state. Now he faced the reality that half a century after Tyndale's Bible had been revealed to Englishmen, their pleas for reasonable change within the Church of England had all been denied. The populace still starved for illumination of God's truth, yet their mildest protest risked persecution and death.

William was living an easy, comfortable life, but his conscience began to torment him. He spoke of this only to Mary and occasionally to his cousin, the Vicar, who told him of a preacher by name, Richard Clyfton, a Cambridge man, preaching at the tiny church at Babworth only a few miles from Scrooby. Clyfton did not limit his subject to the prescribed homilies decreed by Elizabeth to be read in the parish Churches but preached the Gospel from a Bible translated by English dissenters in Geneva during Mary Tudor's reign. William was intrigued.

One Sunday he sent Mary and Jonathan to St. Alfred's and walked the six miles to Babworth alone. Mary had been wary. "What if the constable asks me where you are?"

"Tell him you don't know."

"But I do know."

He smiled, tongue-in-cheek. "You cannot know exactly where I am every moment of the journey, my dear."

Mary sighed. "I wish the Vicar had not told you of this man. He must know you would go to hear him at great risk to himself as well as you."

"We are all Cambridge men, my dear. There is brotherhood among us."

William was not worried. He served the Queen faithfully in his position as "post," held respect in his community, and caused no local trouble. Yet he could not deny that Mary's caution was reasonable. After all, he had served William Davison, also a Cambridge man and known in London to be a "purist" wanting to reform the Church. If the long arm of Archbishop Whitgift had reached to the northern shires to search out John Penry, the catchpoles in Nottingham must certainly be alert for other dissidents. His strategy would be to accompany Mary to the parish Church on alternate Sundays and be ready with claims of "official business" on the Sundays he walked the six miles from Scrooby to Babworth.

So began Brewster's Sabbath routine. Much to Mary's relief, his "business" serving Scrooby Manor and its various visitors was irregular enough to safely screen his activities. If anyone occasionally noted his absence from St. Alfred's, he conveniently "happened" to be hosting official travelers passing on the North Road.

One Sunday Brewster sat contentedly listening to Clyfton explain the meaning of Jesus' parable of the persistent widow, advising that seekers ask and keep on asking for answers to their prayers, not from priests but the Saviour himself. Two young men stole into the back of the church and sat quietly in the last row. One boy seemed vaguely familiar, though Brewster could not place him, and when he next returned to Babworth, the same lad was present. He thought he recognized in the boy the same eagerness for knowledge in himself when he had first met William Davison. He asked Reverend Clyfton who the lad was.

"Bradford. Namesake of his father, William, who died soon after the boy's birth. Related to the Bradfords of Austerfield, a prosperous family." Clyfton paused. "Why do you ask, sir?"

"Reminds me of myself at his age. Has that searching, wondering look about him."

"A strange young lad, something of a misfit in that diligent family. Sickly, methinks probably lonely. Mother remarried, placed him with his grandfather 'til the old man died. Now he's ward of his uncles, Robert and Thomas, the practical sort, no nonsense. They don't approve his coming here."

"How do you know?"

"He told me straight out. They're good industrious people who want no trouble with authority, distrust us 'forward' preachers." Clyfton looked levelly into Brewster's eyes. "And you, sir. Coming here is a bit risky for yourself, is it not?"

"Listening to you preach, sir, I am reminded of my mentors at Cambridge, and find myself thinking more deeply on their preaching now than I did then."

"Ah, Cambridge! No doubt some seeds of rebellion sprouting deep inside you somewhere. When an honest man hears God's truth, sooner or later he must confront it."

"I'd like to meet young Bradford."

"He'll be back." Clyfton grinned. "And he'll welcome your interest in him. He needs a confidant."

At their next encounter Brewster introduced himself to young Bradford, a boy of slight build, fine-featured but pale, apparently not given to heavy work. Bradford suggested, "Since I come from Scrooby, and you from Austerfield two miles beyond, let's meet and walk together."

"Yes, sir. I'd be pleased, sir." The boy paused. "But is it safe to meet, sir?"

"Why not? Only two friends having a pleasant Sunday trek from Austerfield to Babworth."

"Yet we are missing official Church at that time, sir."

"Aye, but worth the risk, no? What brings you here, lad?"

"Well, to speak plainly, Mr. Clyfton says things here I never hear at Church."

"Such as?"

"He says that the Bible never mentions bishops and creeds and ceremonies and such like they have at Church. He says that the Apostles walked and talked with the Saviour as if he were an ordinary man, though they saw that he did extraordinary things. No priest explains Jesus' miracles, or even the parables, but reads only homilies we hear over and over, explaining nothing."

"You realize, lad, that expressing this sort of opinion may cause you great trouble."

Bradford cast him a sidelong look. "So my uncles keep insisting."

"They don't approve?"

Bradford shook his head vigorously. "They say if I listen to these preachers they call schismatics, I may cause the family to lose everything we have—our land, our reputation, even our souls!"

Brewster sighed. "They are right, William. I have lost some dear friends who protested Church authority."

Bradford's eyes widened. "How so, sir?"

"Did you ever hear of William Davison or John Penry?"

"No, sir."

"I served Mr. Davison, the Queen's loyal servant, only to see him ruined by her treachery. And two friends at Cambridge, Penry and Greenwood, were hanged in London for treason. Treason!" He scowled. "Penry was the bravest man I knew, daring to speak against the archbishop's violence, no matter the odds."

Bradford watched Brewster's face, somberly waiting for him to continue.

"I tell you this because your family is rightfully trying to warn you. Defying authority may cost everything that your family and you value. 'Tis dangerous business…and likely to get worse."

"But, sir, if the Lord gives me to see the truth I have to accept it, whatever it may cost me. And I believe He has done that, sir."

They walked on silently awhile. Then Brewster held out his hand. "Let us seek His truth together, son." Bradford grinned.

Clyfton's congregation continued to grow, with seekers coming from all over the shire. Brewster learned from travelers at the Manor that congregations eager to hear preaching from the Geneva Bible were gathering in other villages as well: one at Worksop on the Ryton and another at Gainesborough east of Scrooby in Lincolnshire. Despite the contempt the Church held for those they called "puritans" wanting to reform the Church, the people of East Anglian communities flocked to hear them.

Then one day a courier stopped at Scrooby en route to Edinburgh with stunning news: Queen Elizabeth had died, and he was on his way to inform James of Scotland, son of Mary Stewart, that he would succeed her.

A week later, couriers in advance of James' entourage arrived at Scrooby to inform Brewster that Scrooby Manor would not be adequate accommodations for the king's party, and that he would progress south to Southwell. Brewster was much relieved. Years before while his father was postmaster, the Bishop of York had intervened to prevent Elizabeth from seizing the Manor as a hunting lodge. Brewster had secretly dreaded that James might also discover the delights of Nottingham's lush forests, and appoint his own Scottish postmaster to the Manor.

Bristling with curiosity, the people came from miles around to line the road for a glimpse of their new monarch. Local folklore held that Scotsmen in the flesh were wily, barbaric creatures, hardly more than savages. So when the little King appeared resplendent on his horse surrounded by burly Scotsmen in rough sheepskins, they thought he must be the King's harlequin and giggled at his puny figure. Undaunted, James accepted their gaiety as grateful adulation, convinced this was his rightful due, granted by God's gracious will. Ecstatic to be King of

England at last, he rode triumphantly down the North Road, bowing and basking in the people's boundless affection and reverence.

Mary and William stood by the road watching the royal parade. At least James' attendants adorned with blazing tartans and animal skins fulfilled their expectations of Scottish natives. "Well, what do you think of him?" Mary asked.

Brewster cocked his head. "He's a strange royal breed for us, hardly the majestic cut of Elizabeth. But I have hope in him. He's been schooled by true Scottish believers keen on the Bible." He grinned. "Let's just hope his heart is as big as his grin."

Eight

Robinson

That Sunday morning as Mr. Laurence Chaderton, Master of Emmanuel College at Cambridge, ended his speech and his audience began to stir, John Robinson remained quietly seated. The Scripture that Chaderton had just explicated from the Gospel of Matthew, "Tell it to the church," shimmered in his brain; Chaderton insisted that "church" meant "the whole Church and not some part only."

The words flashed in Robinson's head like a lighthouse beam. "What is it, Lord?" he whispered. "What are You trying to tell me?"

The answers to the question, "What is it, Lord?" solicited many times in his life, were not always immediate. He had learned to wait patiently for revelation of nuggets of wisdom hidden in Scripture, usually prompted by a deeper look into familiar concepts.

Chaderton's assertion was not new to Robinson. King James VI's obstinate resistance to the least reform had driven many despairing puritans to consider separation from the Church. Yet Robinson could not go that far, believing that Mother Church must be cleansed of Romish attributes by the faithful within her bounds. Now a new level of meaning in Chaderton's words unfolded in his mind like the petals of a flower. Was this the clarity of vision and refreshment of spirit he had returned to Cambridge to find?

James' Scottish Presbyterian upbringing had given English reformers high hopes of change in the Anglican Church, which James I of England now headed. They did not suspect that he had been more embittered than enlightened by his Calvinist mentors, and that any taint of democratic intrusion into Church policy was to him anathema. He ardently preferred the episcopal structure of the English Church

94

wherein the monarch and his bishops held absolute authority to determine procedure and pronounce doctrine. No cleric or lay person was permitted to interpret, much less protest this supremacy. James' response, therefore, to the puritans' Millenary Petition for reform was a blast of invective against the poison of presbyterianism "where Jack and Tom and Will and Dick shall meet, and at their pleasure censure me and my Council and all their proceedings." He dismissed the petition with a grim promise: "I will make them conform or I will harry them out of the land, or else do worse."

While a student at Cambridge, Robinson had sat under mentors who railed against the Church's man-centered doctrines unsupported by biblical principle, but their intent was to reform the Church, never to disengage from her hallowed halls. Yet James' intolerance of any reform was so inflexible that some of the most devoted Anglicans had begun to waver in their resolve to stay within Church bounds. Besides unbiblical doctrine, they detested gross corruption in ecclesiastical courts, negligence of magistrates to enforce the law, and contempt and indignity heaped upon "good and learned" preachers while ignorant laymen were appointed to conduct services. At St. Andrew's at Norwich in August after James' ascension to the throne in April of 1603, Robinson himself had dared to criticize the imposition of "dumb dogs" to instruct congregations seeking biblical wisdom.

Because his power for preaching and explication of the Bible drew hundreds to his sermons at St. Andrew's, for awhile Robinson had been tolerated by his bishop despite his "somewhat factious" attitude, but at last the bishop was forced to suspend him from formal preaching. Robinson continued to address his considerable local following of the failings of the Church, hoping to arouse enough support for reform among the people to impress the King. Yet despite her ills and injustices, he had not been able to make a permanent break from his spiritual "mother."

Suddenly today, Robinson's entire perspective on reform was shaken.

In the afternoon he attended the lecture of Mr. Paul Baynes who quoted Ephesians, chapter five, to show the unlawfulness of familiar conversation between the servants of God and the wicked. Robinson listened closely, taking careful notes on Baynes' points: (1) That the former are light and the other darkness between which God hath separated, (2) That the godly hereby are endangered to be leavened with the other's wickedness, (3) That the wicked are hereby hardened in receiving such approbation from the godly, and (4) That others are hereby offended, and occasioned to think them all alike, and as birds of a feather which so flock together.

He had not noticed before how perfectly these Scriptures meshed. Here was the essential locus of difference between the Church of England and her reformers, that the faithful living in the same parish must separate themselves from the unfaithful lest they become "birds of a feather" in danger of being leavened with wickedness.

Robinson returned to St. Andrew's grim but resolute to follow his conscience. He handed his wife, Bridget, his notations on the two Scriptures. She read them, laid them aside, and gazed at him wistfully. "What does this mean for us, John?"

"I know not certainly yet. Our Lord will clear a way for us." He gazed out the window at green fields rolling to the horizon, the lushly fertile landscape of East Anglia, his homeland. Would this decision finally cost him its peace and serenity? He had a family to support. How much further could he discredit the Church to which he had sworn allegiance and devoted his life?

"I have been thinking that we might move to Sturton to stay with your family awhile. Separatist groups are meeting secretly throughout Lincoln and Nottingham. There's a congregation at Babworth under Richard Clyfton and another at Gainsborough under John Smyth. Still another at Worksop."

"Do their Vicars retain their livings?"

"So far, yes. Clyfton's following is considerable, and as more people listen and protest, sooner or later the King must recognize our discontent."

"But how are we to live, John?"

"By faith, Bridget, as always. The Lord will provide."

Bridget sighed. That retort was often slim consolation to a young wife nurturing two babies, but she had learned to rely on God's often mysterious provisions. And she knew that her husband could not compromise his convictions. Thank God they were not alone; there were others like him, staunch in the faith, devoted to reform of the Church. Her family was sympathetic, well established in Nottinghamshire, and would be willing to sustain them for a time. Perhaps this was God's direction for John.

They moved to Sturton within the month, and John lost no time contacting Richard Clyfton. He was delighted with the robust congregation at Babworth, and particularly with William Brewster, postmaster of Scrooby Manor, a post house on the North Road. Brewster was a solid citizen in the community, above reproach, who trekked six miles to Babworth every other Sunday to hear Clyfton preach. There were other good men in the area, John Smyth of Gainsborough and Richard Bernard of Worksop, in whom John found kindred spirits. He told Bridget eagerly that if men of this integrity joined their cause, God surely must be moving among them. And eventually the King must listen.

Robinson bonded most closely with the Cambridge men at Babworth, Clyfton and Brewster, and as an ordained Anglican minister, he became the natural choice for Clyfton's assistant. The Robinsons breathed more easily; they had found a home.

Yet news from London was growing ominous. Bishop Bancroft's Book of Canons introduced to the Lower House of Parliament on May 2, 1603 soon after James took the throne, held the force of law by the King's "hand and seal" but without the sanction of Parliament. Yet after James' rejection of the Millenary Petition at Hampton Court, Bancroft demanded that all clergy observe the prescribed Church ceremonies to the letter. That meant that the Archbishop of York and the Bishop of Lincoln could no longer ignore but were obliged to censure illicit "gatherings" springing up throughout their shires. The only hope puritan ministers now held to convince the King and his bishops to acknowledge their movement lay in the force of their growing numbers.

Then Richard Clyfton and Richard Bernard were notified that they would be deprived of their positions at Babworth and Worksop. William Bradford ran all the way to Sturton to tell Robinson the news. Robinson took one look at Bradford's flushed face. "What is it, lad?"

"Sir, 'tis Mr. Clyfton. He's been deprived of his living by the Bishop at York."

"Come in, lad. Tell me."

Bradford poured out the story. A courier had come from the Bishop to inform Mr. Clyfton that he was no longer rector at Babworth and was forbidden to speak to any public gathering in matters concerning the Church. The notice bore the Bishop's official seal. "And Mr. Bernard was deprived at Worksop, too, sir," Bradford gasped out.

Bridget appeared at the parlor door. She gazed at the two men as John laid his hand on Bradford's shoulder. "So. Our trial begins in earnest," he said, glancing at Bridget.

Bradford nodded. "Mr. Brewster asked if you could come to the Manor House today, sir. He's called everyone to a meeting there."

"That I will. Bridget, my dear, can you refresh this boy with some of your excellent eel soup? He is badly in need of sustenance."

Bridget silently turned from the doorway toward the kitchen.

After they had eaten Bradford waited outside while Robinson spoke quietly to his wife. "Do not worry, my dear. We will be careful."

Her fair face, usually brightly cheerful, was lined with strain. "Surely the constables will be watching the Manor."

"Brewster knows the dangers. He's had practice." John put his arms about her and caressed her hair under his chin. "The Lord has prepared us for this, and He will provide for us. You must not lose faith, Bridget."

She nodded against his shoulder.

Robinson and Bradford found Brewster and Clyfton waiting in a small room upstairs at the Manor. Clyfton began with a prayer for protection, guidance, and above all, wisdom, then produced the Bishop's notice of his deprivation of living adorned with his official seal. It passed from hand to hand, each man reading the cryptic words carefully. Brewster said, "I have just learned that Hugh Bromehead of North Wheatley has lost his living as well."

Clyfton raised his head. "Well, gentlemen, how are we to greet this news?"

Robinson spoke up at once. "I have been thinking long on this. Our strength lies in numbers. We should solicit every Vicar in the district to join us. Since Bancroft is as determined to purge our disruptive

presence as we are resolute to defy his Canons, we must stand united."
He took a breath, then said solemnly, "He wields the King's power, but
we wield God's. What say you, gentlemen?"

They answered together, "Aye."

Brewster said, "There may be a brighter side to this. Bancroft
realizes our influence is growing among the people. We threaten his
power, so he must take a firm stand to maintain it."

"I cannot find it in my heart to sympathize with his plight,"
Robinson said wryly. "Any cleric worth his salt knows that we mean
only to improve the Church, not destroy her. For the sake of their own
future they should acknowledge us."

Clyfton said, "I think Brewster is suggesting that the Bishop's bark
may be more fierce than his bite. The Bishops may not so diligently
enforce the Canons as Bancroft threatens. If so, we may gain time to
reach more people."

Brewster said, "I have had good dealings with York in the post. I
think he may even sympathize with our cause."

"But his bread is buttered by Bancroft," reminded Robinson.

After a moment Clyfton said firmly, "Brothers, we are at a
crossroads. Those of us deprived of our livings face a clear choice,
conform or separate. Your 'living' is safe, Brewster, but I know your
heart. You will stand with us however we go." He looked warmly upon
Bradford. "And so does our faithful lad here. But the time for dreaming
is past; we must be practical. We conform to the Church individually or
separate to unite with our brothers. Which shall it be?" He glanced at
each man, then grinned through his white beard, vivid evidence of his
age and experience. "No condemnation either way, lads."

Young Bradford cleared his throat. "May I speak?"

Clyfton nodded. "Of course, son."

"I see only one course for any of us. We must stand together for
reform. If we surrender now and obey the Canons, we will lose all the
momentum for change we have gained, and the people will desert us. Is
this not a sign that God is with us? Are we as brave as Joshua and Caleb
to invade the Promised Land? We must believe that our God hears our
pleas and will change the King's heart."

The men sat silently. Young Bradford, only seventeen and

unencumbered by responsibility, had stated their dilemma clearly enough, but without the obligations of family or community to consider. After a moment Clyfton smiled at him. "Methinks you speak the Lord's wisdom, lad. He's confronting us with the choice to sink or to swim. Now we must each seek His will in the matter, and then decide."

When Robinson returned home from that meeting, Bridget handed him a letter from Bishop Jegon. It was his own letter of dismissal.

ॐ∽

After Clyfton's loss of living at Babworth, Brewster opened the third floor of Scrooby Manor to the congregation for meetings for worship. The house was large enough to accommodate the group without attracting undue attention among travelers. Brewster ushered them singly up a back stairway, keeping alert for any strangers looking on who might be bishops' spies disguised as travelers.

Yet nothing deterred Bancroft's intent to crush the purist movement. John Smyth lost his lectureship at Lincoln, and one by one Vicars throughout the shires who ignored the Canons were suspended from preaching. Ironically, more and more of the commons, desperate for any spiritual guidance, began to risk meetings for worship in private homes or taverns, even in wooded dens. Puritan leaders realized that a wider strategy for meeting this crisis must be devised, or else half the population would be persecuted.

Two prominent leaders, Arthur Hildersham and John Dod, called for a meeting with men of Yorkshire, Lincolnshire, and Nottinghamshire at the home of Lady Bowes at Coventry to discuss that strategy. None of these were as yet ready to renounce the Church until John Smyth announced, "I thank God, gentlemen, that He has given me my mission and I am bound to follow it. The Church of England is beyond hope of reform, and we are apostate to remain in her fold."

Hildersham heaved a sigh. "That, John, is our great dilemma. We pray God to change her because we so dread to leave her."

"But Mother Church is corrupt, Arthur, poisoned with the deceptions of anti-Christ. We can no longer hope to revive her."

100

Smyth's voice rose. "We offer her the real meat of the Gospel and she cannot digest it. That is the work of anti-Christ. Their stand against it is proof of it."

After a moment Dod asked, "Yet if the Lord has not abandoned her, how can we?"

All sat silently. Then Robinson cleared his throat. "Gentlemen, we know well the tenacity of our Enemy. He has rendered the King and his authorities deaf to our pleas. Therefore we must take some kind of definite action."

Hildersham said, "What action have we not tried, John, short of actual separation? We may be forced to take that step only if the Spirit, like Ichabod, has deserted her." He wagged his head sadly. "Because if the Spirit has gone, she is truly lost."

Again they fell silent, each sunk in his own thoughts. Then Bernard said gravely, "Well, I will return home and preach as I have done, and say as Naaman did, the Lord be merciful unto me in this thing."

Hildersham asked, "Have we a consensus to separate?" He glanced about the group. No one replied. "I think not yet. Meditate on this, men, and seek the Lord earnestly as never before."

They parted brothers and allies of one heart, but not as yet of one mind.

Riding home to Scrooby, Brewster, Robinson, Clyfton, and Bradford meditated on the exchange at Coventry, then solemnly met together upstairs in the Manor's meeting room. Brewster sent for food and ale and lighted a fire on the hearth. When they had refreshed themselves, he asked, "Well, men, what is our next move?"

Robinson took a long swig of ale. "I am with my brother Clyfton here. My living is gone. I have decided to leave Mother Church."

Bradford stirred in his chair, eager to speak, but as the youngest, did not want to appear presumptuous.

Brewster said, "It is a hard thing we ask of these men, to leave the Church. It is their life and their community. We have no right to press them. Only the Lord can guide them."

Robinson asked, "Are we agreed among ourselves then, that we will separate?"

All but Brewster answered, "Aye." They waited for his reply. He looked at each in turn. "I am of a mind to agree, but I cannot take that step until I have considered my position here, and of course, consulted with Mary. She knows my heart, but I have not put the final decision to her sharply."

"You take the greatest risk, William," said Clyfton kindly, "because you have the most to lose. We honor and bless you for your sympathy, but do not bind you to it."

Brewster nodded. "This I suggest we do. Like the Apostles, we free people will join ourselves together in covenant with the Lord into a church estate. In the fellowship of the Gospel, we agree to walk in all His ways made known, or to be made known unto us, according to our best endeavors, whatsoever it should cost us." He looked at each man in turn. "Are we agreed?"

"Agreed," they answered.

And Bradford repeated eagerly, "Agreed!"

The following Sunday upstairs in Scrooby Manor Clyfton's congregation met to hear the results of the Coventry conference and Brewster's suggestion that they join in covenant. In Gainsborough John Smyth was making the same proposal. One by one the people stood to declare their commitment to the Lord and His people, making clear by this action their separation from the Church of England. They further committed themselves to meet every Sabbath at one place or another as convenient.

❧❦

Separatists were now flourishing in the shires, enabled by sympathetic patrons and disaffected parishioners who had not abandoned the Church but earnestly desired her reform. Despite the watchful presence of constables alert for puritan preaching, Robinson and others were often asked and frequently agreed to address numerous small gatherings in the area, thereby drawing many lay converts from the established Church. This practice was duly reported to the new Archbishop of York, Toby Matthew, who in a sermon at Bawtry near Scrooby roundly denounced all "Brownists" and made clear his intention to purge pockets of puritan sentiment within his diocese. His net at once began to encircle the Scrooby group.

His tactics were to cite "patrons" of the deprived preachers for various offenses and summon them to appear at court. One Gervase Neville of John Smyth's congregation and grandson of the High Sheriff of Nottinghamshire was accused as a dangerous Brownist for making "contemptuous and scandalous speeches and frequenting conventicles." In response he openly criticized the "Antichristian Hierarchie" of the Archbishop and was subsequently imprisoned at York Castle. Richard Jackson, Robert Rochester, and Francis Jessop, brother-in-law of John and Bridget Robinson, were cited for religious "disobedience."

John Smyth of Gainsborough came to Robinson one morning early. "It is time for me to go, John. I have arranged for passage to Holland the week next."

Robinson had seen it coming. Usually quick to make decisions, Smyth had confessed at Coventry that he had doubted "nine months" the issue of separation, but once decided, had never wavered on his stand, which now was confirmed by the wave of widespread persecution. "'Tis no good here, John. And will get worse. You should get out before they cast you into prison to rot of jail-fever."

"Aye, friend. 'Tis a matter for grave reflection."

"Reflection! While you reflect you will rot."

"I must think of my family, John, and no less the congregation. They know no other home but rural England. How would they live on the continent? Only God, not I, can convince them to leave."

"We are their leaders, John. He speaks through you as He does through me. He has entrusted their care to us. Who else will take responsibility? Not the Church. Your future here is dead."

Bridget came into the room, and Smyth stood up to greet her. Without pretense he said, "I hope to see ye soon in Amsterdam, my dear. I've been telling your dear husband 'tis the only choice you have now."

A flash of anxiety crossed Bridget's face as she glanced at her husband, fearful that he had made a commitment to Smyth. But he smiled congenially. "You know John, dear. He lets no grass grow under his feet."

"Are you leaving us, John?"

"Aye, the week next."

"And your people?"

"Many of them will leave. Not all, of course. 'Tis a hard choice for each one of us." He dropped his chin to his chest for a moment and took a deep breath, a rare show of sentiment.

Bridget cast a desperate look at her husband, who put his hand on Symth's shoulder. "John is going ahead to pave a way for us, Bridget. He is our wise and courageous elder. We wish thee Godspeed, John."

When Smyth had left, Bridget asked, "Is he serious?"

"Never more so."

"What did he tell you?"

"That we should join him soon." He looked into her eyes. "I made no commitment to him, dear. But he is right. Our future here is bleak."

Bridget sat down and dropped her face into her hands.

As soon as Clyfton learned of Smyth's decision he called the Scrooby congregation together at the Manor to inform them of the Gainsborough group's intent to emigrate. A chorus of questions assailed him: "How are they going?" "What is it costing?" "How will they pass the constables?" "Is everyone going?"

"Please, people. One at a time." The chorus quieted to a murmur.

"I have called you together to inform you of this action, and to seek your feelings about going ourselves. Others have gone before us to Amsterdam. One, a congregation from London, the Ancient Brethren, is well established there. We would have friends to help us settle. Please tell us what you are thinking."

Someone called out, "Are you asking us to make a decision now?"

Clyfton waited a moment before answering. "Those of us who have lost our livings cannot live on charity indefinitely. We must decide soon." He stroked his beard. "Yes, I am asking you to decide as soon as possible."

Another voice asked, "Did you all know that Francis Jessop has been taken ill with jail fever at York?"

"Jail fever!" Gasps and whispers rounded the room. "God help him!"

Clyfton said gravely, "I do believe that the Lord is sending us fair warning of what will befall us if we tarry. Gather yourselves together now, each family, pray earnestly, and make your decision." He glanced at Brewster. "I say we shall meet again here in three days and consider our plans. All agreed, friends?"

"Aye," all agreed.

⁂

Bridget's family, the Whites, her sisters and their husbands, had taken in the Robinsons gladly at Sturton, understanding the significance of John's suspension from St. Andrew's. They had even spoken of emigrating themselves one day "when things became desperate," but none had yet seriously confronted the prospect of leaving their homeland. When soon after the Scrooby meeting, a soft knock sounded on Robinson's door, Bridget opened to her brother-in-law, John Carver. Her face crumpled. "Oh, John, do come in and talk to us."

He nodded at Bridget. "I would speak with your John alone, sister. Will you leave us?"

Bridget glanced between the two men. "Of course." She left the room.

Carver said, "John, I have foreseen this since you came to Sturton."

"Yes, brother, I have, too. Yet I have dreaded the moment."

"Is there no hope of change?"

Robinson shook his head slowly. "I see none. The only good thing to come of our petition is the King's commission to revise the Bible. That is a good move, but will take years to finish." He looked into Carver's eyes. "Will you join us, John?"

Carver dropped his head. "I do not know. Can any of us stand by while you and Bridget abandon us, perhaps never to return?"

Robinson said at once, "But you must not merely follow us, brother. You must seek the Lord's will for yourself and your family. I do not think He presses everyone to take the same path."

Carver sighed. "I have thought long on it. We manage well here at Catherine's farm. Our living is assured. And my conscience does not compel me as yours compels you, John."

Robinson said nothing, aware that this confession was difficult for

Carver.

"I have watched you struggle, yet envied your strength of faith." Carver gazed into Robinson's eyes. "Not all of us have such faith, John."

Robinson nodded agreement. "I know, I know."

"Though I know the source of your strength, I fear for Bridget and the children, and what high price this move will cost you. To leave all behind to begin anew in a strange land...such a choice asks much of any man, John."

"Your obligation is only to follow the path the Lord sets before you, brother. And no other! If you are convinced He is telling you to stay, by all means, do it gladly, without guilt!"

Carver lowered his head, and heaved a sigh.

"What does Catherine think?"

"She leaves it to me, of course."

"But what does she *think?*"

Carver hesitated. "I'm not certain. We have talked occasionally, but never faced a decision. Perhaps the women have shared their feelings with each other. Is Bridget eager to go?"

"I can not say 'eager,'" Robinson said with a wry smile. "But she certainly knows our situation and does her best to accept it."

Carver sat frowning. "I have talked with Roger and Francis." He looked at Robinson with a wisp of smile. "They seem to expect the inevitable. But the women...I do not know."

Robinson nodded. "Find out, brother. Ask her directly. And soon."

Nine

Scrooby

Huddled against the bitter November wind, the men clustered together on the quay in the dark, their fears as black as the water sloshing against the seawall at their feet. They took some comfort that after their long journey from Scrooby to Boston their families were sheltered at inns in the city, but their own fatigue and the gloom of midnight threatened to weaken their resolve.

Their ship should have put into port today, but had not arrived on the evening tide. Now they must wait out the long night until morning, skulking in doorways and behind cargo to evade constables alert for residents trying to leave the city illegally.

Since the conference at Coventry each man had faced the grim alternatives given him and his family in England if they persisted in their biblical faith. They must submit to Church authority, go to prison for "disobedience," or try to leave the country. Jail fever in the cesspools of England's prisons amounted to suicide. Yet to leave one's home for an alien land was as wrenching as death—was *actually* death to the only life and homeland each one had known.

William Brewster shuddered in the frigid wind moving in from the sea, a portent of bad weather, but counted it only another of those unforeseen obstacles certain to hinder their way. If God favored their exodus, He could provide fair weather.

Young Bradford edged up to Brewster. "Sir," he whispered, "I think Mister Rigsby is faint of heart and in need of encouragement."

Brewster glanced about. "As are we all. Why so?"

"He quarreled with his wife when we left them, and I heard him just now...weeping."

"Weeping!"

"Aye, sir." Bradford hesitated. "Methinks his wife objects to going, sir. I overheard the women speaking of her reluctance."

Brewster was annoyed. "And we heard none of this? She had every chance to object openly. He assured me they were ready."

"Methinks she agreed to go in wifely submission to her husband's authority, but not in the desire of her heart."

Brewster snapped, "That is no good. She must commit herself willingly. I thank you for this observation, William. I will speak with him before we depart."

Brewster gritted his teeth. After all their careful planning, every grievance aired to exhaustion, it was essential to their success that every one of this congregation be committed to each other and to their mission. While some had elected to stay home, others had never wavered. He and Mary could count on Bradford, Pastor Clyfton, the Whites, the Robinsons, the Mortons, and Francis Cooke, all firmly convinced from the beginning. And John Rigsby had seemed as eager as the others. Yet now Brewster recalled sharply that Rigsby's wife, Agnes, had kept silent. He should have suspected that her silence might have been evidence of resistance. He hunched his shoulders against the damp and sighed deeply. Apparently they would be bedeviled with new uncertainties all the way to Zeeland.

Even after Clyfton and Bernard were deprived of their livings at Babworth and Worksop, only John Smyth had been ready to abandon all hope for reform and leave the country. Not until Richard Jackson, Robert Rochester, Francis Jessop, and Brewster himself had been imprisoned for the "disobedience" of missing regular Church services, was the congregation convinced it was time to go. Brewster resigned his postmaster's position, paid his twenty-pound fine for not attending Church, and heaved a sigh of relief to have escaped so easily. By now all of them could have been dying of jail rot.

All their hopes now centered on the English sea captain who had agreed to pick up their group near Boston. His fee seemed outrageous but was probably reasonable considering he put his ship and himself at risk of treason. This adventure was costing everyone dearly.

He must be firm with Rigsby.

Brewster found Rigsby leaning in the shadow of a warehouse door and asked him bluntly, "My brother, are you certain you want to hazard this journey?"

Rigsby's eyes flashed at Brewster, then glanced away. "Yes, indeed, Mr. Brewster, I surely am. Do you doubt me?"

"Methinks perhaps you waver between loyalty to your wife and to our mission." He paused. "How say you, John?"

Rigsby swallowed. "Well, my wife...does dread...leaving home. That is only natural...we all do." He glanced at Brewster with anxious eyes. "Is that not so?"

Brewster nodded but stiffened against any appeal for sympathy. "So she prefers to stay here in England."

"Aye, but I told her, this is our only chance. If we do not leave now with good friends we can trust, what hope have we of escape later? Few of us are bold enough to leave home, even for God!"

"You did not convince her, did you?"

Rigsby's eyes cast down. "Her fears overwhelm her, sir. She dreads the unknown world in Holland more than tyranny at home."

Brewster's voice softened. "Then go home, brother, before our ship departs. There will be others leaving, I assure you. England's trial has only begun. You must both be convinced in your hearts that God wills you to leave now."

Rigsby's voice flared with resolve. "But I *am* convinced, Mr. Brewster. And it is her wifely duty to follow me."

"Not unwillingly, friend. Even our Lord does not *command* loyalty. It must come from the heart."

The torment roiling in Rigsby's breast crumpled his brow, yet at sight of it Brewster's own resolve rose like a banner. This small band of believers facing unforeseeable hazards could ill afford bickering spouses. He put a comforting hand on Rigsby's shoulder. "Retrieve your family, John, now, before the ship arrives. You will still be innocent of illegal departure and can return home unhindered." He leaned closer to whisper, "I am truly sorry, John. We will sorely miss you."

Rigsby sighed, lifting agonized eyes to Brewster's. "Forgive me, sir. I grieve to trouble you like this, at the last."

"Strive not to grieve our Lord, my brother. He will direct you."

Despite the pain of departure, Brewster was grateful that so far their plan was going well. The families had come down from the village of Scrooby on several small boats by the rivers Ryton and Idle, to Gainesborough on the Trent, then continued upriver to Torksey by Foss Dyke, an old Roman canal, then across to Lincoln and by the river Witham to Boston. When their ship did not appear at the rendezvous, they waited anxiously for signs of her arrival, and by nightfall the women and children were growing weary and fretful. Though some sympathizers in town might have risked sheltering them, strangers were always noticed and suspect, so they decided it was safer to put their families into proper inns while the men kept vigil on the quays.

They waited all night and another day. Well after dark the second day the ship anchored in the bay and put out dinghys to pick them up at the quays. The men hastily rounded up their families and rushed them to the quays and into the boats. Greatly relieved to be aboard, they gathered on the foredeck to hear Clyfton offer a prayer of thanksgiving. Suddenly, shouts went up from the water where a troop of catchpoles appeared swiftly out of the darkness yelling, "You're under arrest! The lot o' ye!"

The people reeled with shock. Robinson confronted the captain. "We bargained in good faith for this passage, sir."

The captain smirked. "Good faith, is it, to break the King's law? Count yerself lucky, fellow, to keep your head!"

The port officials rowed them ashore in the dinghys, ransacked their belongings and money, embarrassed the women patting and jostling their clothing for hidden treasures, then hauled them off to the local jail.

Dismayed, the group sat dumbly in prison like lambs before the shearer, only young Bradford pacing the floor, now and then bursting with bitterness. "How did this happen? Did no one suspect this man would betray us?"

Brewster had searched his brain for any signal he might have missed. "We took him at his word. And paid his price."

Robinson said, "Don't despair, son. The Lord is testing our faith by teaching us discernment. We shall be wiser next time."

Brewster was thinking how like John Robinson it was to put the best face on things no matter how grim, and to thank God for it.

Otherwise, they would all sink into despair. The others seemed resigned to their fate, hopeful but without illusions or expectations.

Yet young Bradford was livid. By God, he would have taken them all on, sailors and catchpoles alike one by one, had any of his brethren moved to help him, but the men had been too surprised to react quickly. Besides, once aboard ship they could have done nothing without jeopardizing the women and children.

Their ordeal had only begun.

Since the magistrates could not act without word from the Privy Council in London, they jailed the group a month, sending the littlest ones out to live with sympathetic families. At last, hearing nothing from the Council, they released the women and children and held seven of the men for trial. Beset with more pressing problems of state, the Council continued to ignore the matter until the magistrates grew weary of the lot and released them all to survive however they could in the dead of winter.

Having cashed their assets for the journey, they had nothing left in Scrooby. Only the kindness of strangers in Boston kept them alive, leading some quite naturally to wonder why the Lord had allowed them to fail so miserably. Had they completely misread His directions?

Even Bradford nursed doubts. "Mr. Brewster," he said one day," it does not appear to me that the Lord is blessing this mission."

To Bradford's surprise, Brewster agreed. "I am sometimes hard put to convince myself, lad."

"Do Mr. Clyfton and Mr. Robinson still think we should go?"

"I confess I have not confronted them. We are forced to accept charity for the winter, but we cannot impose on sympathy indefinitely. The truth is, methinks we have more to gain leaving than staying, however impossible it appears at the moment."

Bradford thought awhile, then asked the unanswerable question: "Sir, if the Lord really wants us to go to Amsterdam, why does He allow so much hindrance against us?"

Brewster smiled grimly. "Men have been searching the Lord's will for centuries, lad. And few find the answers. We can only pray and fast, and humble ourselves, and walk in faith as we are given strength for it."

"What should we do now?"

Brewster was silent awhile. "Nothing has changed our situation, William. We have only found our venture more bitter than we expected. Methinks Mr. Robinson is right. There may be much worse than this to come, and the Lord is teaching us to persevere." He paused gravely. "And I think there is another more basic reason."

"What is that, sir?"

"Only the strongest of us will succeed, son. Any weakness will break us, and many will fail. The Lord winnows his people, then blows away the chaff. Those who are called must count the terrible cost, and decide if they are willing to pay it."

Over the dismal winter this discussion surfaced among both the dissenters pressed to depart and those sympathizers reluctant to leave home, each person testing his answer for himself against the witness of others. The problem was simple: What does the Lord say? Should they go or stay? Those who felt "called" away must be convinced of that call beyond doubt. Those who were reluctant had better stay home. Some were newly persuaded to leave; more decided to stay home.

⌀⊷⌀

Seven months later in the dim predawn light under an overcast sky a column of men trudged along the deserted East Anglian shore of the North Sea between Hull and Grimsby. Young Bradford lagged at the rear of the column, glancing frequently back toward the town of Hull from whence they came, squinting at suspicious movements in the tall marshgrass bordering the shore. So far, the movements had been only seabirds rustling for fish. Relieved, he turned to catch up with the column.

Brewster and Francis Cooke headed the line, pausing now and then to study the labyrinth of marshes and swamps stretching inland, and to peer at the sea's horizon. Brewster muttered, "How far have we come now?"

Cooke glanced backwards. "About one league. We should see them soon."

"I see nothing yet. No barque. No ship. Nothing."

"It's too early, William. The ship will arrive on the noon tide."

They walked in silence, one combing the sea, the other glaring across the watery fens.

Brewster breathed heavily. "Where are they? They should have been here yesterday. And where is the ship? If this captain proves as treacherous as the last one...."

"This one is Dutch, William. He understands our purpose."

Brewster suddenly stopped and pointed ahead. "Look there, in that dry creek. It looks like...is it the barque?"

They ran forward through the grass toward a creekbed running to the sea but almost dry now at low tide. On the far side, stuck on a sandbar, a small barque held a dozen women and children, three men, and four crewmen. The women looked up, saw the men approaching and shouted with joy. "Thank God you're here at last! We've been here all night! We're freezing! Come get us out!"

The men crowded at the edge of the hard sand, but saw at once that they were blocked by a bog, which sucked at their feet like quicksand, impossible to cross on foot to reach the barque.

John Robinson aboard the barque called out, "Don't try to reach us. Wait for the tide!"

Brewster raised a hand to acknowledge Robinson's warning as Bradford rushed up beside him. "The coast is clear so far, sir. But do we dare wait long enough for the tide to float them free?"

Cooke said solemnly, "Methinks we dare not test that bog."

Bradford asked, "Have they a rope aboard? We could try pulling them over."

Brewster shook his head. "No. We will wait. They are safe in the barque." He grinned wryly. "But we may pray the Lord to hasten the tide a bit."

Charged with frustration, Bradford paced the edge of the bog. Kindly, Brewster told him, "Go out to the beach, lad, and watch for the ship. You can do nothing here."

The rising dawn brightened the eastern sky, but the sun had not yet broken through the scudding overcast, and a gale briskly chopped the sea. Studying the horizon, Bradford heard behind him women's voices pleading, "Canst thou not save us?" and the men calling out reassurances: "Be patient, ladies. The tide is rising swiftly."

It was not in Bradford's nature to wait; he must do *something*. Yet all he could do was pace the shore while his mind raced. A week ago the group had left Scrooby by boat to sail down the Idle River to the Trent. There they split at West Stockwith and hired the barque to sail their two pastors, Robinson and Clyfton, the women, children, and baggage down the Trent to the Humber River sweeping to the seacoast. The men had then trudged forty miles across the fens, taking shelter on farms and in barns, toward this deserted stretch of shore between the towns of Hull and Great Grimsby. Mr. Robinson had arranged for a Dutch sea captain to meet them here and take them across the English Channel to Amsterdam.

Bradford ground his teeth. As if their journey were not risky enough breaking the King's law and dodging his constables, Satan's minions, even more determined to stop them, had roused up a gale at sea that drove the barque into that sheltering creek during the night. By daylight the ebbing tide had stranded the little boat, and across that formidable bog only high tide could float it free.

Waiting was most vexing of all, for they half-expected constables to come roaring down the beach intent on their capture. The men walking cross-country had hidden themselves wherever possible, approaching a few farms for food and shelter where some of their brethren knew sympathizers. But they knew others must have seen them, and now it was urgent that they board their ship before anyone reported them to the authorities.

Of course they had eaten all their food, and Bradford was starving!

Well, he consoled himself, he was no more so than the others, especially the children aboard the barque. He took a deep breath. No matter how carefully they planned, some unforeseen hindrance always rose up to strain their faith almost to breaking.

He slumped into a pit of self-pity. What had their mother England come to when honest God-fearing men were persecuted by men of their own faith in their own country, branded as criminals by the King's laws, and tormented by bishops condemning them as "heretics"?

"Bradford! Look there!" a voice called behind him.

He squinted at the horizon. A mere speck had appeared on the sea. God be praised, a ship! He shouted, running back and forth, leaping like a child. "Ship coming! Ship coming!"

He kept his eyes glued to her progress, achingly slow, then watched to make certain she was coming toward them and not turning upriver toward town. Then he rushed through the marshgrass to the men awaiting the barque, shouting, "She's here, she's here!"

Squeals and shrieks of delight rose from the families. Running down to the surf again, he noted a rogue wave, larger than the others, rolling inshore to rush across the creekbed, almost reaching the barque. The tide was rising!

Some men came down to the water's edge to watch the ship anchor, anxiously studying the tide. Bradford climbed the highest point on the dunes to peer back toward town, relieved that only seabirds rustled the grass. Thank God no one was chasing them yet!

On the beach the men watched the anchor drop down, then a dinghy pull away, and only then erupted with shouts of joy and relief. Brewster came down to the water to tell Bradford, "William, you go with the first load; make sure they know we are all here and ready to come aboard."

Bradford beamed with delight to be put in charge. "Aye, sir!"

Brewster addressed Cooke. "Francis, you stay with me. We'll see everyone off and go with the last load."

Cooke winked at Bradford, grinning encouragement.

The men greeted the dinghy sailors warmly, pointing to the stranded barque. The sailors checked the angle of the tide, still not high enough to float the barque, then decided to begin loading the dinghy with the men onshore. Suddenly a shriek of delight rang out from one of the children on the barque. The rogue wave had surrounded the boat and tilted it sideways, almost floating it free. A cheer went up from the occupants. Another half-hour and she would float.

Bradford shoved the dinghy off, then leapt aboard. They crested several breakers, then stroked strongly for the ship. The breeze in his face was delightful, a promise of freedom. Oh, praise God for merciful deliverance!

Aboard the ship, peering down from the rail, the leathered face of the captain scowled at this ragamuffin party he took on. They looked to be an ignorant lot of seedy crofters full of passion and pathos, as innocent of the world as lambs. Well, so be it. They had paid him enough to cross to Amsterdam and back.

Bradford scaled the ladder last in line, then swung over the rail and approached the captain. "Good morrow, sir. How glad we are to see you!"

The captain's eyes narrowed. "Your people appear to be stuck, lad. And we've no time to waste."

"Aye, sir. They were grounded by the storm and await the noon tide."

The captain grunted, then called down to the men manning the dinghy, "Be off at once, lads. Quickly now!" He addressed Bradford. "You in charge here, son?"

"No, sir. Mr. Brewster sent me on the first load to assure you we were all ready."

"How many more are coming?"

"A dozen or so, counting children."

The captain twisted his lips. "Two more boatloads at least." His brow beetled, calculating. By the time they got the first load aboard, the tide should float the barque. He peered through his glass at the stranded boat, its keel still dragging on the sandbar. Then he swung his glass to check the rise of surf farther up the beach.

Suddenly he made a quick adjustment on his glass, peered into it, and growled, *"Sacremente!"*

"What is it, sir?"

"Look there, lad!" He pointed far up the shore.

Bradford shaded his eyes to look and caught his breath. A horde was sweeping down the beach from whence they had come, some on horseback, others running on foot bearing guns and staves, straight toward their people.

The captain bellowed, "Anchors aweigh, men! And be quick about it!"

The Scrooby men groaned. "No, no! Our wives, our children—we cannot abandon them. For God's sake, leave us off!"

Bradford seized the captain's arm. "Sir, I beg you, send us back. We cannot leave them!"

The captain ignored the men, shouting at his crew, "Aweigh, I say, at once!"

Bradford clutched the captain's sleeve. "Sir, please, I beg you. Our people will be massacred!"

The captain growled, "I will not have my ship seized by English dogs. We made no bargain for that."

Bradford ran to the rail with the other men to watch the horde bear down on the barque, at last floating free on the tide. Bradford cried aloud, "Merciful God, spare them!"

As the sails billowed and the ship began to move, Bradford stared down at the water, measuring the distance to shore. With a sudden movement he leaped upon the rail. One of his brethren seized his shirt. "No, lad. Dinna' do it. 'Tis too late. You canna' save them!"

Bradford hovered on the rail, knowing with dreadful certainty in his heart it was true. Though he could swim like a fish and knew he could reach shore, he could do nothing. Only God Almighty could prevent that mob from capturing their people. *My Lord, my Lord, why have You forsaken us?*

తించ

On shore the men helping the families disembark heard the mob approaching, and for a few moments were paralyzed with shock. One of the older children shrieked that the ship was moving off, and a mob was sweeping down the beach!

The men quickly gathered to stand between their families and the mob while the women screamed at the sight of horsemen galloping upon them brandishing weapons. Brewster called out to the Constable, "Call off your men, sir! These little ones are defenseless innocents."

Caught up short at the sight of terrified children, the guards held back their weapons while glaring with contempt at the men. The Constable growled at Brewster, "What have we here? Have ye the King's permission to leave the country? Come peaceably now, or it will go hard with ye."

Brewster said calmly, "We will come with you peaceably, sir. But spare the women and children, I beg you."

The Constable bellowed so all could hear. "By the King's law, you're all guilty. Come along quiet now, and ye'll not be harmed." He rode to one side and waved the cowering women and children into a column. "Move along, children. Obey yer elders!" He smiled down upon one tearful boy shrinking against his mother's skirts. "There's a good lad. Don't cry. We won't hurt ye." Under his breath he growled, "Ingrates! Scum! Draggin' little ones about like dogs!"

Francis Cooke nodded toward the sea. "They're going." The Scrooby people looked sadly seaward at the departing ship carrying a third of their men.

❧

The guards herded the group along the beach to town, then hauled them before the Magistrate, who glowered at sight of the children. "How now, what's this? What's the charge?"

The Constable answered, "Attempting to leave the country without license, sir."

The Magistrate's eyes ranged over the men. "Who's your spokesman?"

Richard Clyfton stepped forward. "Sir, I am the pastor of this congregation."

"How do ye plead?"

"Guilty of assembly, sir."

"Assembly? On a deserted beach in a gale? What ails ye, man? To put these little ones to such torment!"

Clyfton replied calmly, "None here has been coerced, sir. Each family chooses his way freely."

The Magistrate snorted. "Chooses freely to break the law, do they?"

"Sir, the King's law forbids us to worship our God as our highest law, the Bible, commands us to do."

"The King's law commands ye to worship God properly in the Church of England, sir, not as ye please in a bog by the sea."

The Constable spoke up. "Their ship left without them, sir. She's a

Dutchman. We think she had already taken some aboard." The Constable added contemptuously, "A group like this one tried to leave a year ago from Boston...even though they know we are bound by law to detain them."

The Magistrate sneered. "God is not mocked, then, is He? They are guilty of illegal departure. Lock them up."

John Robinson stepped forward. "Sir, if it please thee, let me speak."

"Who are you?"

"Assistant pastor to this congregation, sir."

"Be quick about it."

"As our pastor says, those of us here only gathered on the shore. We did not board the ship. We did not leave the country."

The Magistrate studied Robinson, considering whether he was clever or only impudent. "Do not spar with me, fellow. 'Tis clear ye intended to leave the country."

"Yet we carried out no such intentions and therefore cannot be called guilty of illegal departure. You see that we are all here. Thus, we are guilty only of unlawful assembly."

The Magistrate scowled. "Do not beset me with quibble, fellow. You rebels suffer no more restriction than the rest of us. Why can ye not quietly tend to your work, obey the law, and give us peace?"

"We regret any inconvenience to you, sir. We seek only freedom to worship our God as the Bible and our consciences command."

Exasperated, the Magistrate lowered his voice and spoke each word deliberately. "Do your dainty consciences also command ye to vex your betters? You do that well enough." He looked about the court. "Is anyone in town willing to shelter these impoverished children?"

The Constable answered, "Aye, there are purists here who sympathize with this sort, God forgive them. Some will take pity on the children."

"What folly!" the Magistrate growled. "A man should provide for his children, not drag them starving about the countryside defying the law!" He smote his desk. "We shall confine the elders until the Privy Council decides their fate." He focused his gaze on Clyfton and Robinson. "Since you people persist in defying the law, causing us much trouble, we are required to detain ye. Yet ye do none of us any good in jail, least of all your poor children. So, I warn ye, when ye are released, go back to your homes, tend to your proper business, and thank God and our good Sovereign for the laws that protect our motherland from her enemies." He waved a hand at the Constable. "Off with them now, and good riddance!"

The Constable's guards surrounded the group and herded them off to the jailhouse.

The Magistrate grumbled, "A sorry lot, these ingrates! Have they never heard of Queen Mary's gibbets? She would have twisted their necks! They should praise God for King James, who lets them live."

❧❦

Meanwhile, far out in the North Sea the Dutch ship bound for Amsterdam only twenty miles across the Channel had been caught in a ferocious storm that drove them north far off course, and beat them near to foundering in a mountainous sea. Only the captain and the helmsman dared stay on deck to man the wheel and try to keep the ship from broaching. Below decks, the terrified countrymen and crew huddled together, the Scrooby men praying fervently. Suddenly, a great wave heeled the ship over sharply, hurling the men against her bulkheads while seawater cascaded down her hatches. The sailors cried out, "We sink! We sink!"

"Yea, Lord," the Scrooby men pleaded, "Thou canst save us! Thou only canst save us!"

Under tempestuous water the ship lay nearly level on her beam end, teetering on the brink of rolling over and going under. Belowdecks, above the clamor of crashing debris, men's voices cried out for mercy. "Save us! Save us, Lord!" The ship hovered, her decks awash, tossing among furious waves. "Save us, oh, save us, Lord!" came the frail cries up from her bilge again and again.

Slowly, miraculously, the ship began to right itself, straining upwards like a sick cow dragging herself to her feet. Among the debris sloshing about, the men, soaked in watery despair, scrambled for holds on anything secure, clinging to hope the ship would survive.

At last she rode almost upright, still tossing in vicious seas, but afloat. The Scrooby men continued to praise God for their salvation. While equally grateful for survival, the sailors eyed them suspiciously, half-scoffing, half-believing that the desperate prayers of such unlikely lubbers had seemed to convince the Almighty to save them all.

The storm at last abated, and during all four hundred miles back to Amsterdam from the coast of Norway these poor countrymen sang a refrain: "We thank Thee, Lord, that Ye have heard us. We thank Thee, we thank Thee, Master!"

Two weeks out from the shores of the Humber where she had abandoned the rebels, the Dutchman put in to Amsterdam and dispatched her bedraggled, penniless passengers in a strange land. Possessing only the clothes on their backs, having no benefactors to greet them save a few immigrant Englishmen like themselves, all of them were poor as church mice. None of their brethren in England would know their fate until young Bradford appeared one day at Hull to tell the remarkable story of the ship's survival in the storm.

❧❧

It was obvious now to those in England that after two failed attempts to escape together, each family must find its own way across the Channel. Some gave up the effort, convinced it was not God's will that they go, and elected to stay and worship in the Church of England. Yet a hard core of believers remained faithful to their mission. The Brewsters, the Robinsons, the Jessops, the Cookes, the Mortons, Pastor Clyfton, and Bradford held to their plan and devised various passages for their people determined to go.

Having seen their charges off one by one, Brewster and Clyfton were last to leave. "God willing, William, we will meet soon again in Amsterdam," said Clyfton, shaking Brewster's hand in farewell. "Methinks God asks too much of this old man. I pray that He preserve you young ones through this great adventure."

"God keep you with us, Reverend. We need your wisdom."

Clyfton stroked his white beard. "Not mine, son. Only His."

Ten

Amsterdam

Amsterdam! City of Freedom!

Brewster gazed down the street at the tall narrow houses arrayed together facing the canal like palisades. He was no less overwhelmed than he had been years ago as William Davison's aide. The city bustled with commerce and dazzled the eyes with material wealth.

Robinson asked, "So does it look the same to you, William?"

"Yes, and yet no. 'Tis much more grand than I remember." Indeed, the city abounded in grandeur: tall buildings festooned with fretwork and flowers, the cobbled streets laid in precise geometric patterns, majestic full-masted ships bobbing at the docks, and shops boasting rare treasures brought from all over the world. Yet Brewster's awe was tainted with searing memories of Davison twenty-two years ago, that excellent Queen's man whose loyalty and integrity so richly deserved her reward rather than betrayal. He had gloried in his service to Davison, a man openly recognized by all the court as one of Elizabeth's noblest servants. Old resentment flared anew in Brewster's breast. He had not forgiven her after all but had only buried deep the rancid hostility festering in his soul. Sadly, he looked into Robinson's kindly face. "I have not forgiven her. I did not know the depths of my sinful heart."

Robinson drew his brow gravely. "We all have much to forgive, William. The greater sin is to deny it when the Lord brings to mind need for repentance."

Brewster nodded. "Yet now I wonder if my motives for coming here are as pure as I thought. Did I want to serve my Lord or only escape royal tyranny?"

"Perhaps it is the same motive with two faces. Had the Church been more tolerant of our faith, all of us would have rejoiced to stay home."

The urgent business of the new residents was to find employment while they settled in with other brethren who had preceded them. Yet the realities posed to simple yeomen trying to earn a living in Amsterdam were formidible. Members of the Brethren of the Separation of the First English Church at Amsterdam, known as the Ancient Brethren, indoctrinated them soberly. "The guilds control all skilled labor, and without industrial skills, you are limited to work as laborers, most likely in the cloth industry. There is always need for fullers, combers, carders, felters, tailors, drapers, and the like. And shops and taverns and all manner of merchants also need workers. Do not despair, friends, there is hope."

Young Jonathan Brewster asked, "What do fullers do?"

"Aye, and carders?" asked another. A murmur went round the group, and the Gainsborough elder answered genially, "Fullers cleanse and thicken cloth. Carders pull the long fibers together before they are spun. 'Tis much like combing your own hair. Simple work, and you will learn the language quickly."

"Ach, the language!" Someone groaned. "Like spitting phlegm!"

A ripple of laughter rounded the group.

"Methinks butchering in a shop is my meat," joked Jonathan.

Gradually as the men found work, each family found lodgings clustered together in adjoining houses. Yet it was soon apparent to the Scrooby group that all was not as well as it appeared among the three English churches already established in the city. The Brethren bickered among themselves continually, usually about fine points of doctrinal difference, but also they were quick to criticize individual behavior they considered "ungodly." Most embarrassing was the personal animosity between brothers Francis and George Johnson concerning Francis's wife, Thomasine. George stridently resented his sister-in-law's gaudy personal dress, and continually chided Francis for allowing it. To the Scrooby group this sort of contention did not enhance the separatists' reputation for godly living among the Dutch.

Yet reluctant to complain of their benefactors, they made no comment until one day, while kneading dough for bread, Bridget commented to her husband John, "Methinks there is trouble brewing. Some of our women are puzzled by the liberties Francis allows his group."

"Do they speak of this openly?"

Bridget pursed her lips. "Only when speaking of...certain persons."

"Which persons?"

Bridget's lips curved in a sly smile. "You cannot guess?"

Robinson cocked his head. "Thomasine?"

Bridget nodded. "She is a topic of lively interest among the women."

Robinson frowned. "Surely my dear wife does not indulge in idle gossip."

Bridget cast him a pert look of injured innocence. "We only observe the obvious, husband. Certain flamboyance among women cannot be ignored."

He sighed. "We have heard clamor enough about Thomasine's ruffs and laces. What more is there to say about it?"

Bridget floured her hands, then resumed kneading the ball of dough. "That Francis not only indulges her but allows other strange beliefs among his people."

Robinson burst out scornfully, "Thomasine is the least of my concerns. 'Tis some of Francis's own doctrines that disturb me."

Bridget's eyes widened. "I'm glad you speak of it at last, John. And not only Francis's doctrines. Does John Smyth seriously intend to baptize himself?"

Robinson shook his head sadly. "Yes, I believe he does."

Bridget slapped the dough. "I think he is quite ridiculous. We will all be a laughing stock in this city." Dusting her hands, she glared at her husband. "What does he mean by claiming that none of us are 'true' Christians, and that our English Bible is a false translation?"

Robinson sighed. "Are the women discussing this as well?"

"Not to outsiders, of course, but among ourselves. It is quite normal, John, for women to talk intimately while they work together. We are not dumb oxen unable to think or speak. And we do not accept every whim of thought without question." Her eyes flashed and her lips pursed.

John Robinson smiled at his wife's spirited outburst. Not even their worst enemies would call these resilient Scrooby women "dumb." Rather than scold her, he thought suddenly, he should praise a wife who alerted him to hidden currents among the brethren. "I think it is time we Scrooby men speak forthrightly to Smyth and Johnson. We dread to criticize because we owe them our very subsistence here. Yet this perpetual dissension among them does not honor our Lord. It must be exposed."

Bridget sighed with relief. Thomasine had been causing much dissension throughout the community. "I agree, John. The sooner the better."

Robinson spoke first with Pastor Clyfton. "Richard, I would speak frankly with you. Bridget tells me that the women are unsettled about—" he cleared his throat—"some inordinate behavior among the brethren. They are aware that such talk verges on gossip, but I think their concerns merit our attention."

Clyfton smiled. "Do they object to Thomasine's whalebone stays?"

"If that were their only concern, I should not speak of it to you."

"Ah, there you err, John. The Lord often gifts women with fine discernment we men lack. What seems frivolous to us may obscure deeper spiritual error."

"Then let us be candid with one another. I suspect that few of us approve of Smyth's capricious turns of belief—his claims that we are not true Christians, that our English Bible translation is erroneous. Did our Lord speak in only one tongue? Then Hebrew and Greek versions are false as well. And his intention to baptize himself...that is idiocy!"

Clyfton patted the air as if to soothe Robinson's ire. "Judge not so harshly, son. Perhaps he touches truths we should hear."

"And having heard, can make no sense of it. You know well, Pastor, that no man receives revelation perfectly. We should have no clear doctrine at all if we did not temper revelation with reason."

"Methinks we should wait and see. We have been here only a few months. Amsterdam is still new and strange to us. I am convinced that, despite our differences, we brethren agree on the fundamentals of our faith."

"I do pray so, sir. Yet I have grave doubts of it."

Robinson's doubts proved prophetic. By winter of the Scrooby group's first year in Amsterdam, dissension among the factious Ancient Brethren and the Gainsborough group had degenerated into open conflict. No tempering advice from the Scooby group seemed to calm the contending forces. At last Brewster and Robinson agreed that eventually their own people would be drawn into controversy. They began to seriously consider withdrawing from the Brethren. Still advising patience, Clyfton did not agree.

"Pastor," Brewster addressed him kindly, "did we abandon our homeland and our mother Church only to be buffeted here by capricious doctrine? We barely have a toehold here. Our situation is too precarious to weather conflict among ourselves."

Clyfton protested. "Remember what trials the Brethren weathered in London. They are faithful believers. Henry Ainsworth, for example, is a man of great and constant faith."

"That is so," agreed Brewster. "I have no complaint of Ainsworth, nor of Fuller or Cushman or others of the Brethren. But I fear that this community's contentious spirit will infect us all. A little leaven can indeed spoil the whole loaf."

Clyfton shook his head sadly. "Have patience, brothers, I beg you. Wait awhile longer and see, wait and see."

Brewster suggested that they consult the other Scrooby men who had faithfully followed them to Amsterdam. Having endured harrowing attempts to leave England and just now beginning to get settled in this city, would they have the heart to start again in another location?

As was customary, only the men gathered at Robinson's lodgings, their women's sentiments reflected in their husbands' concerns. Pastor Clyfton deferred to Robinson to expose the controversy. "My brothers, I will come right to the point. We are disturbed by the dissension we observe among our English brethren, and fear that it will taint our own people. Our pastor Mister Clyfton, Mister Brewster, and I want to hear your sincere expression on this matter. Please feel free to be candid."

The men sat silently for some moments. Then Francis Cooke spoke. "I am glad to bring this into the open, brother. Petty squabbling demeans not only our mission to witness for Christ but our gracious Lord Himself. I do not believe that He called us to abandon all that was dear to us in our homeland only to covenant here with contentious men. We should carefully consider whether or not we want to join their congregation."

Roger White added, "Aye, I heartily agree and am glad to declare it. I am already embarrassed. Do ye hear how the Dutch speak of us? We separatists have become the butt of jesting among them. Already we have been tainted by association with the Brethren's reputation."

Young Bradford spoke up. "May I speak?"

Robinson nodded.

"I am yet single and without family obligation, but I think we cannot long withstand this sort of contagion. I have noticed that our children are especially prone to willfulness and argument over the slightest differences. I say we should soon look for a more congenial environment."

The men sat silently thoughtful. Robinson asked, "Does anyone object?"

"Aye," said Degory Priest. "I dread to begin again. I have just found gainful work as a hatter, and was hoping soon to settle my family in better lodgings."

Pastor Clyfton spoke. "My dear brothers, I beg you to be patient with the Brethren. They have overcome much to survive here. Be not too quick to judge."

Brewster said, "We leave judgment to God, sir. Did not God send us to Amsterdam to find our own proper place? I beg you mark what young Bradford has said. What is our profit if we squander all that we have sacrificed to get here among those who dishonor the very faith we strive to uphold?"

Several voices spoke up at once. Robinson gestured for quiet. "We will hear every voice and every objection in turn. Be patient and speak one by one."

They wrestled far into the night airing pros and cons to leaving the Brethren and possibly even the city. Yet having exhausted alternatives, they reached no consensus except to agree that something must be done to improve their situation. A majority favored relocating as the only solution, but the objections of those wanting to stay could not be dismissed casually.

Robinson finally closed the meeting with advice "to pray ceaselessly, men, and listen to your wives. They and your children are most strongly affected."

That winter Robinson was further troubled by a letter he received from Rector Joseph Hall of Halstead in Essex deploring the separatists' betrayal of their mother Church of England and lamenting their act of separation:

> You could not do a greater injury to your mother, than to flee from her. Say she were poor, ragged, weak; say she were deformed, yet she is not infectious. Or if she were, yet she is yours. This were cause enough for you to lament her, to pray for her, not to avoid her.... The God of Heaven open your eyes...otherwise, your souls shall find too late, that it had been a thousand times better to swallow a ceremonie, than to rend a Church.

Robinson toiled over his reply, yearning to make clear to the Church his position. He firmly believed that separation from the world "is the first step to our communion with God, and angels, and good men." For if "your church be deeply drenched in apostasy, and you cry Peace, Peace, when sudden and certain desolation is at hand, it is you who do wrong." He further declared that "as Christ shall be our judge, we are bold...to proclaim to all the world separation from whatsoever rises up rebelliously, against the sceptre of his kingdom, as we are undoubtedly persuaded (are) the Communion, government, ministry, and worship of the Church of England."

Ironically, his words to Rector Hall clarified the situation they faced in Amsterdam. Much as they loved the Brethren, as they had loved the Church of England, this church's behavior was also "drenched in apostasy." Robinson was convinced that to maintain communion with their God the Scooby group must again take the first step of separation.

Reading Hall's letter, Bridget moaned, "Oh, John, his words do grieve me. The Church is our mother, and we have abandoned her."

"No, Bridget, she has abandoned the Gospel of Christ in favor of men's doctrines. We are sworn to obey Christ's word, not the bishops.'"

"But here we are so far from home, from all that is familiar to us, yet find no constancy among these brethren all following their own doctrines. At least our Churchmen at home hold true to their belief."

"Bridget, hear me, my dear. You know how we agonized over this decision in England. None of us wanted to abandon our home. Yet we must hold to our conviction that God directed us to this path, and we cannot lose heart now we have chosen to follow it. Neither can we become embroiled in the controversy we find here. We must find a more congenial home where we can observe our true faith. Do not lose heart, wife. The Lord will sustain us."

Yet alone in the dark of night, John's own doubts and fears assailed him. During the previous century in England men like himself devoted to the biblical Gospel contested Church doctrine, hoping to change the Church from within. Yet for their tireless effort they were branded with the condescending epithet "puritan." They saw no recourse but to separate. Yet their piercing dilemma persisted. Was separation God's choice, or did these idealistic "puritans" only indulge their own self-serving desires? How did one know beyond all doubt that he truly heard the Lord's voice? Only by the fruits of his obedience. Robinson dreaded to admit that so far the fruits of the Scrooby people's experience had been sparse indeed.

And yet, and yet... The families from Scrooby were still firmly bonded together in spirit. They owed gratitude to their brethren in Amsterdam but not obligation. Despite Clyfton's reluctance to break away, the longer they waited, the more ensnared in controversy they would become.

A sudden insight struck him. Perhaps they could explore other places—Leyden, for example, where the academic atmosphere of the University was familiar to him and Brewster and Clyfton. Why not investigate? If the officials of Leyden permitted them to immigrate, that may be a sign that God directed them there.

So, in February, 1609, one "Jan Robarthsen" went to Leyden to officially petition the burgomasters on behalf of one hundred persons or thereabouts of the Christian Reformed Religion in Amsterdam for the right to come to live in that city.

But Richard Clyfton could not bring himself to leave Amsterdam and the Brethren. He told Robinson, "Methinks, son, that you search for a Paradise that does not exist. These, our brethren in spirit, desire the same communion with God that we do, and are struggling to find their way. We must be patient with them. They need us to enlighten and nurture them in godly ways."

"Sir, forgive me, but our Dutch hosts snicker at their worldly ways. What sort of witness is that to our faith? The great temptation we faced leaving our Church was to follow men instead of God, and thereby to fragment into individual desires and doctrines. If we do not cling to the standards of the Gospel, continually testing our capricious whims, we will utterly fail."

Clyfton sighed. "Go then, my brother, if you must. Only beware that this betrayal of your brethren may be your own desire, not the Lord's."

His words stung Robinson at the core. Betrayal? Yes, he did anticipate a personal association with the University, believing that Clyfton and Brewster, as well as himself, could better serve their small community there, both spiritually and financially. Yet he must honestly search his conscience. Was Clyfton's warning God's will for the Scrooby group, or only his own for himself?

Thank God he need not make the decision alone. He was confident that while he followed his deepest convictions, so would Clyfton, Brewster, Cooke, and the others. As they had done in England deciding to leave or stay, each member of the congregation would search his own soul and try to discern God's will for himself.

Then one day John opened his door to Samuel Fuller, a stalwart member of the Ancient Brethren. Sam was a steady fellow, much interested in medicine and healing, and especially sensitive to men's consciences. Usually congenial, today his face was grim. "May I speak with you candidly, John?"

"Come in, Samuel. Come in."

"I have heard that you men of Scrooby are considering leaving Amsterdam."

"We have discussed it, yes."

"Because of us and our fractious membership." Fuller stated his suspicions bluntly.

"Yes, we do find the Brethren excessively contentious. All of us suffer for it."

Fuller sighed deeply. "Our brethren seem deaf to all complaint. I do not blame you for going; in fact, I urge you to." He took a breath. "And if you go I will join you."

They gazed into each other's eyes, Robinson feeling keen empathy for the other man. "I can imagine what this decision will cost you, Samuel. We all know the agony of breaking ties with friends."

"I am not the only one disturbed, John. Cushman and I agree. If the Johnsons would only listen to us! But they hear only their own voices. I cannot understand it. They have suffered mightily for the faith, have been the most 'godly' of men. What devils possess them?"

Robinson thought suddenly, perhaps Bridget's womanly intuition was more accurate than they knew. When men left the security of a structured organization, whether family or Church or nation, alone they were especially vulnerable to strange concepts, their ears easily "tickled" to hear only what they wanted to hear. This was surely evidence of the tyrannical fleshly "self" asserting dominance over the minds and spirits of even the best of men.

"Only God knows men's hearts, Samuel. And only He can deliver them." He smiled. "We would be pleased to have you join us."

Fuller nodded solemnly, for John's welcome brought no joy to his countenance. As any separatist knew well, to leave "home" for a principle is the most painful of decisions. Worse, to claim that Almighty God commands his decision must not only compensate for the loss of attachment to human kin but must sustain all aspects of his spiritual life.

Not long afterward, Robert Cushman of the Brethren approached Brewster. "Many among us are unhappy here but cannot afford to break away. They are bound by work or family."

"We solicit no one to join us, Robert. We of Scrooby always decide only for ourselves."

"Some of us will join you, John, others not. We, too, decide for ourselves."

"I will rejoice if you join us, Robert. God will forge a strong bond between us."

Cushman extended his hand. "I feel that, too, John. Yet I must appeal to Francis one more time. We have been deeply allied. He may yet listen to me."

"I wish you Godspeed, brother."

Eleven

A Goodly and Pleasant City

Leyden! More beautiful than Amsterdam!

The Scrooby group set sail in the spring of 1609 across the Zuyder Zee out to the coast, down to the mouth of the old Rhine, then upriver to the quays of the city. Leyden's fine houses, wide brick streets, stone bridges arching over blue canals lined with fine linden trees, and green-shaded squares were kept spotlessly clean and everywhere adorned with brilliant flowers. Coming up the river, Bradford told Brewster eagerly. "Sir, I do believe that the Lord has at last directed us to our Promised Land."

"Aye, lad, we all do fervently pray so."

The whole group was energized with hope. Young Bradford and the children paced about the deck exclaiming at sights passing along the river—vast green fields, herds of cattle and sheep, towering windmills turning in the breeze. The air seemed fresher and the flowers brighter away from the oppression of their quarreling brethren in Amsterdam. No less happy a prospect were the opportunities for peaceful employment offered by the new treaty between the Spanish and the Dutch, permitting Dutch independence and the right to trade to the Indies for twelve years. After years of tyranny, the fortunes of both the Dutch and the small band from Scrooby could not have looked more promising.

They settled in the area of the Pieterskerk, St. Peter's, once a Catholic cathedral, near a complex of buildings formerly a convent and now occupied by students of the University of Leyden. The network of alleys and closes surrounding Pieterskerk was located central to the University and the business of the city.

Those first months were a time of settling in once again, finding work, and adjusting to the language and customs of the citizens of Leyden, a hospitable and generously tolerant people. Yet especially after their brief experience in Amsterdam, the Scrooby group's primary motivation, to establish a habitation devoted to biblical worship of their God, took precedence over all other necessities.

As they had not done so in Amsterdam, they now established a new church based on the practice of early Christians, declaring one by one their covenant with one another and with the congregation, and choosing their own officers. Since Richard Clyfton had chosen to remain with the Brethren in Amsterdam, they elected John Robinson pastor and William Brewster ruling elder.

This organization of a body of believers declaring covenant together and selecting its own leaders followed the simple structure of the early Christian church. Tyndale's Bible had revealed no precedent for the doctrinal complexities required by law in England's traditional Church inherited from the Roman. By contrast, the Lowland States' official position was that "the design of the States undoubtedly is, that none should be persecuted on account of their religion...Force will not make Christians, but could only fill the world with hypocrites under the name of Christians." As early as 1564, William of Orange had declared before the Council of State: "Although attached to the Roman Catholic faith, I cannot possibly approve that princes should wish to rule the consciences of their subjects and deprive them of their liberty of faith and worship of God." James I of England, however, devoted to the principle of the Divine Right of Kings, upheld the authority of the monarch as head of both State and Church and dictated civil and ecclesiastical law.

The Scrooby group was also discovering that the influence of Dutch society on all aspects of living was profound. Holland was an oasis of learning, scientific development, commercial enterprise, and theological discourse. Brewster and Robinson, both Cambridge men, soon found access to the University, Brewster teaching English to students, and Robinson engaging the professors on theological doctrine. At this time the major controversy between Calvinism and Arminianism was generating among intellectuals a debate that raged across Europe. Some thought the resolution of this debate would instigate the radical reform of Protestantism in Europe.

During that year the Scrooby group learned of further troubles among their brethren in Amsterdam, and though grieved, rejoiced all the more in the freedom of their Sabbath service and the companionship of their intimate society. Particularly did they relish the hours of "prophesying" on Sunday afternoons. After formal songs and sermon Sunday morning, the group convened again after noon hour to share their common concerns and successes, and to integrate their daily trials with biblical wisdom. Ironically, without the support of devices like worship of the Cross, holy water, incense, candles and the like, this "freedom" of expression required the believer to pursue a more intimate, more personal relationship with his Lord. Robinson was particularly zealous to simplify his people's faith, and to clear away any hindrances to their reliance upon divine wisdom.

In the spring of their second year in Leyden Bridget Robinson rushed home from market one day calling, "John! John! Come quickly. I have found us a house!"

John glanced up from his studies. "A house," he replied absently, his mind preoccupied with Arminian concepts he had been invited to debate.

"An ideal house just down the street. It has everything we need."

John put down his pen. His study of Arminian "free will" would have to wait.

Bridget was bursting with joy. "Mary agrees with me it is ideal. There is a large house in front facing the street and a garden adjoining at the back. There is a spacious lot behind the garden, room for at least a dozen small lodgings."

John nodded soberly. "At *least* a dozen. Remarkable."

They had been searching for proper lodgings for months, wanting space enough to house a number of the group who could not afford single abodes. They had prayed diligently for this favor.

Bridget prattled on. "It is on Bell Lane right across from St. Peter's. John, you must see it at once. Come, come! Set your books aside and come look."

It was exactly as she described, ideal for their needs. All in the Scrooby group were overjoyed. On January 11, 1611, Robinson,

William Jepson, Henry Wood, and Jane White, as representatives, officially agreed to purchase the Groenepoort, or Green Gate, an estate belonging to Johann de Lalaing, for eight thousand gilders—two thousand outright and five hundred to be paid per annum until the sum be fulfilled. So large an obligation taken on by so impoverished a group was a profound expression of faith that they would be able to fulfill the contract.

Robinson and Bridget moved into the house fronting the street, which provided room enough for the congregation to meet on Sundays for service and prophesying. Soon they would take in other members of the congregation to live on the grounds. At last it seemed they had truly found their Promised Land.

❧◆❧

Young Bradford knocked at Robinson's green door and waited for Mrs. Robinson to usher him in. "Good day, Madam," he said wearily.

"You're late, William," she said brightly.

"Aye, Madam. We finished extra bales from England today."

Bridget smiled. "Then you have missed your supper. And we are about to dine."

"I am sorry to intrude, ma'am. I will wait until Mister Robinson has finished."

She looked at him askance. "You must eat with us, William. Or you will have no strength to study."

He was not often late for Robinson's lessons in Latin and Greek, but though he gained extra pay for longer hours at the corduroy processor's, the extra working time cut his valuable study time with Robinson. He was determined to master Latin quickly so that one day he could tutor students as Mr. Brewster did, a better living than working with corduroy. He was thinking to marry and needed to earn enough to support a family.

Robinson came out from his study. "Another long day, William?"

"Aye, sir."

Robinson led the boy to the kitchen. "Then the Lord granted us both extra favor today. While I waited for you, He clarified for me another argument against Arminian 'free will.'"

Bradford sighed. Much as he yearned to learn, he scarcely understood and had little time to investigate the theological discourse that preoccupied Mr. Robinson. "And what is that exactly, sir?" He stifled a yawn.

"Sit down, son. We will dine first; then I shall explain it to you."

Robinson had made contacts at the University of Leyden soon after his congregation arrived in the city. His credentials from Cambridge and his status as ordained minister of the Church of England gained him access to academic circles, but it was his sharp intellect and keen intuition that endeared him to professors and students alike. Unlike many brilliant men who often found it difficult to impart their special knowledge to lesser minds, Robinson's talent for interpretation of Scripture into laymen's language illuminated biblical teachings as few others could do. At Leyden he followed intently the argument raging between professors Jacob Arminius and Gomerus on the merits of Calvinism, John Calvin's strict interpretation of the Bible embraced by most Reformers.

After supper, in Robinson's study Bradford took out his Latin grammar. "I think I have finally grasped the declensions, sir. I see the logic of them now."

Robinson smiled. "You're progressing well, William. But let us put that aside for a moment. I want to test your thinking on another matter."

William closed the book. "Gladly, sir."

"I am devising arguments against Arminius' teaching to present to a student debating group. I would like to test my presentation on you."

"I am honored, sir."

"First, do you understand Calvin's concept of predestination?"

"Well...ah...I think so, sir."

"Tell me what you think it is."

Bradford swallowed, uncertain how to express abstract thought into words. "I believe that if one accepts that God created the world and its creatures and set all life into motion, it follows that He must have known how things...especially man...would turn out. That is, He must have known that some men would believe in Him, and some not. Those who do believe are thus predestined to accept the Savior sent to redeem us." Hearing his words, he grinned uncertainly at Robinson. "Is that too simple, sir?"

"Not at all. I want to express this concept in the simplest, clearest language."

"Is that all of it, sir?"

"There is a bit more to predestination than that."

"Then I'd be pleased to understand it fully, sir."

Robinson measured his own words, hoping to explain the concept to academicians in language only slightly more sophisticated than Bradford's, so that even the most resistant mind could comprehend it clearly. "Calvin claims that God ordained salvation only for certain select men, making no allowance for man's 'free will,' as Arminius called it, to choose salvation or not as each man saw fit." He paused as William listened intently. "Calvin further insists that the Bible declares that man is born to evil and his mind is enslaved from birth by Satan. In that state he cannot possibly make a choice for salvation until he has first forsaken Satan's kingdom of darkness and is reborn in the Holy Spirit."

Bradford nodded. "That seems reasonable to me, sir. Did not our Lord explain this to Nicodemus in John, chapter three?"

"He did. But the point Calvin makes is that man can only choose under the impetus of God's Grace, His unmerited favor, and not by man's own finite enslaved mind."

Bradford frowned, pondering the gravity of Robinson's words. He did not consider his intelligence to compare with Mr. Robinson's, but after a long day of work, he could hardly think at all.

Robinson continued. "However, Arminius declared that God has given man 'free will' to choose his own salvation—or not—while still in the darkness of his mind."

"How can a man do that, sir?"

"That is the question being hotly debated among theologians. How can he do that? By Grace, or by his own evil intelligence?"

"How does Arminius support his thesis?"

"He claimed that Jesus of Nazareth did not die for only those few that the Almighty ordained to follow him but for all men. Hence, all

138

men have 'free will' to choose to live in eternity. Or not."

Bradford said thoughtfully, "If Jesus died for all, yet many do not choose to follow Him, are they not consigned to the Lake of Fire?"

"Precisely. So we are taught. But think on this. If Jesus died for all men, yet they do not all choose to follow Him, then God is neither omniscient nor omnipotent, for man has power to defy Him."

Bradford shook his head to clear it. "I do not quite follow that reasoning, sir. I should like to meditate on that further."

Robinson sat forward. "The Bible teaches that God's will shall prevail, that nothing can thwart it. His purposes shall be achieved. Therefore, can it be His purpose to save all men? And if it is, how can man resist it?"

Bradford's brow furrowed. "Only if God gives men power to resist Him. This 'free will' you speak of. If man has it, God must have given him permission to use it."

Robinson grinned. "You follow the argument exactly."

Bradford's eyes held Robinson's. "But which is true, sir?"

Robinson sat back. "That is always the highest question, Will. What is true? The Bible teaches that Jesus Christ is 'truth.' I accept the teaching as I understand it, that God predestined some men for salvation, but not all. If I am wrong, I pray God will enlighten me. My concern with the Arminian argument is that it is a grave deception to propose that man's will can thwart the will of God, that he has power to deny Him. Men thinking they are free to choose, even those destined to be saved, may carelessly live their lives in dissipation, believing that at the end they need only recant of their sin before death and still escape it. Yet we see all about us how Satan's grip upon men's thinking never relents but binds them more severely the longer they submit to him."

"But if men are destined for hell, does it matter how they live?"

"That is the most troubling question of all. How can we judge at any moment which men are chosen or not except by the fruits of their lives? God's Grace gives us the desire to please Him. Therefore, if men live in degradation against His will, we assume they are not saved. Yet, with God, all things are possible. So, is it not possible that the worst of sinners can still repent and be saved at the end, if God meant him to be saved? Our God is a loving, gracious Sovereign, desiring the best for all men."

Bradford sat silently awhile, struggling not to offend Robinson with his weariness. "This seems a very weighty subject to me, sir."

Robinson sat back, smiling. "Agreed. Perhaps we have done enough for one night."

"But you have tweaked my brain, sir. I shall think on it seriously."

Robinson saw Bradford's weariness in his lean face and felt a moment of chagrin. He had been carried away by his own pursuits, forgetting that working men had little time to ponder theology. Yet Bradford was eager and quick to learn and needed to broaden his mind beyond the demands of labor.

Robinson stood up abruptly. "Forgive me, son. We have indeed done enough for one night."

Bradford rose slowly, then paused. "But, sir, how do any of us know our fate for certain?"

Robinson gazed into Bradford's young face, always so eager for the truth. "No man knows the complete Mind of God, son. We walk in faith as we are given to understand it. And as the Bible says, 'We see through a glass only darkly.'" He smiled. "Your questions tweak my brain as well, William. I will continue to seek God's wisdom on this 'weighty' subject." He patted Bradford's shoulder. "Now go home and sleep."

It was well past Bradford's usual time to leave, but he stood as if still pondering the gravity of their discussion. "There is something else, sir, I would discuss with you. If the hour is not too late."

"Of course not. My time is yours, William."

"I am thinking of marrying, sir." The young man's face flushed.

Robinson was startled. His own mind full of theology, he had expected another intellectual question. "I am surprised. Who is the girl?"

"That is a bit of a problem, sir. She is one of the Brethren in Amsterdam."

"Ah." Robinson's mind traced swiftly over the young women he could recall in Amsterdam. He prided himself on sensing his people's needs, yet had no idea which girl it might be.

"She is Dorothy May, sir."

"Dorothy!" After a moment a face flashed before him: the daughter of Elder Henry May of the Ancient Brethren. Very young, he remembered, hardly more than a child. Pretty, of course, as are all young girls, but ready for marriage? He expected Bradford to choose an older, more mature wife.

"How have you managed this courtship, William, so far removed from the city?"

"We were friends in Amsterdam, sir, and I have written to her. I have set some money aside and now would like to visit her. But I wanted to share my intentions with you first, for your approval." He paused. "I have only shared this with Mr. Brewster. No one else."

Robinson's mind turned over the prospect of such a match. "You have tweaked my brain indeed, son. I will meditate on this match, and pray for God's wisdom for you."

Later, lying awake listening to the nightbirds' call, he thought seriously about Dorothy May. A modest girl, quiet, apparently even-tempered, possibly to become a handsome woman, but her character was still amorphous, unformed, probably quite pliable. And unfortunately, she had been nurtured among the Ancient Brethren in an atmosphere of perpetual contention, overly exposed during her formative years to negative influences of vanity, worldliness, and malicious gossip. How would she complement a brash young buck like Bradford devoted to attaining righteousness? So young, she would probably receive him submissively, flattered by his attention. The Brethren were keen to observe form. But underneath...? Perhaps he was shortsighted, for if Bradford found her appealing she may already have developed character enough to weather unscathed the climate in Amsterdam. Yet he felt uneasy about this match. It would bear watching.

He would put it before Bridget, whose womanly insights he could trust. They were after all "one flesh," and Bradford had not sworn him to absolute secrecy. He reached out to touch his wife's shoulder, but she slept soundly and he would not waken her. Tomorrow was time enough.

Yet by morning his thoughts were full of his discourse and

eagerness to run his arguments by Brewster as soon as convenient. At breakfast Bridget greeted him. "Young Bradford looked unusually weary last night. He works so hard. Is all well with him?"

An image of Dorothy May flashed before him. "Ah, yes, Bradford. I might as well tell you now. He wants to court Dorothy May."

Bridget looked up from her kneading. "Henry's daughter?"

"The same."

"So this has been brewing awhile."

"It seems so."

Bridget said nothing.

"What do you think?" he asked.

"Too young," she replied at once.

He nodded. "My thought as well."

"Not in years, but in maturity."

"Well, she is hardly...what? Fourteen, fifteen?"

"Is he only beginning his suit, or already planning to propose?"

"He has been thinking about it since Amsterdam. Yet the distance from here to there is formidable for a working lad. He cannot have progressed far."

"Advise him to wait awhile. I've seen some lovely girls here in Leyden."

"Now, wife," he scolded, "you are not thinking of making a match?"

"Why not? I am being practical. He is thinking of marriage, and I think Dorothy not quite ready. If he is in a hurry, there are others more suitable."

Robinson exclaimed, "Dear wife, you are forgetting true love! He is seeking a wife, not merely a woman." He smiled mischievously.

She said pertly, "Mary Brewster will certainly agree with me."

"Speak not yet to Mary, my dear. He has told only Brewster and me in confidence."

"If William Brewster knows, it's no secret from Mary. And if young Bradford is in love, neither of them missed it." She dusted her hands, as if the matter were settled.

Robinson sat silently eating his porridge. So *he* had missed it. And as pastor he should have sensed it. Definitely, he must get his head out of the clouds and observe his people more closely.

He met with William Brewster that afternoon. "William, my brother, I need your advice on an important matter."

Brewster smiled. "And so was I about to solicit yours, friend."

"Nothing of grave concern, I hope."

"No. A plan I have been hatching."

"Well, tell me."

"It can wait. How can I help you?

"I have been asked to address a student's debating group on Calvinism. I am expected to rebut Jacob's challenge to the doctrine of predestination."

"Aye. How will you approach it?"

"By refuting his blasphemous 'free will.' Of course it is an enticing concept, an appeal to the masses to indulge the luxury of choosing salvation anytime they decide to take it. I do not want our people to be tainted by this."

"They are well grounded in the faith, John."

"I do thank God for that. Yet the great price we pay for freedom in this liberal country is the danger of these new temptations. Our brethren would be less than human if they did not wonder and question what we have taught them."

Brewster nodded. "Aye. Young Jon asked me the other day why we do not frolic on the Sabbath as the Dutch do."

"We will have to contend with that worldliness as long as we live here. That is why I want to set forth our doctrinal position to these young students reasonably and clearly."

"So what do you ask of me?"

"This morning young Bradford gave me his definition of predestination, amounting to the idea that if God created the world and its creatures He must have known how it would turn out, that some men would accept Him and some not, the latter to be consigned to Fire." He leaned forward. "In simple language this is very close to the essential meaning. Yet the idea that a loving God would lay down so absolute a condition for the lost mankind He professes to love arouses suspicion in many...even resentment. Would not the natural man consider it more 'loving' for God to allow him to make his own choice?"

"And thereby deny God's sovereignty."

"Exactly my thought. God cannot be omnipotent and omniscient if He allows His own will to be thwarted by man's random 'free will.'"

"Then what is your problem, John?"

"How to set forth this doctrine as a loving God's most benign will to save mankind enslaved by Satan at birth."

"You have Scripture to uphold your words: Christ's words in the books of John, 'You have not chosen Me, but I have chosen you' and Ephesians, 'He hath chosen us before the foundation of the world,' and many more."

Robinson's grave face revealed his deepest concern. "William, I am dismayed that we have found a haven here, accepted the hospitality of this generous country, only to contend with deceptive teaching among the most elite minds of the land."

Brewster sympathized but did not share his worry. "Be assured, John, our own people are too busy surviving each day to be swayed by the argument of theologians. They are content to let you define the fine points of faith. As for the students, they have come here to question, to learn from diverse opinions." He put his hand on John's arm. "You need only clarify our religion. Those whom God has chosen to hear will listen."

Robinson shook his head in chagrin. "You are right to scold me. I did impose on young Bradford last evening, belaying him with deep questions of faith, the poor lad, after a long day of combing corduroy. I stand rebuked."

"I mean no chastisement, friend, but rather encouragement. Your role is to inspire and uplift us. For these verbal conflicts, of which we know little, the Lord will give you proper words. And if any of these intellectual elite are among the Chosen, they will hear you."

"Speaking of Bradford," Brewster began. "I seek advice for the lad."

John nodded. "He has already told me. He wants to marry Dorothy May."

"Aye. What do you think of it?"

Robinson frowned. "She is very young. I do not like that she has been bred in so contentious an environment."

"Agreed. Should we discourage the match?"

144

"Bridget thinks yes, for the moment."

"As does Mary."

"Bridget said she and Mary would agree." John sat back in his chair. "I see great potential in this young lad. But he needs the proper wife."

"Well, he is thoroughly smitten with Dorothy. Apparently for the first time."

"Ach, that compelling first love. Yet he works a long day and often late hours. The situation may take care of itself. Let us wait and see."

Brewster nodded agreement.

Robinson asked, "And what plan are you 'hatching,' my brother?"

Brewster's eyes brightened. "I am thinking of setting up a printing press."

"A press!"

"Aye. You will be my first author. We will distribute *Justification for Separation* throughout England."

Robinson frowned. "We dare not press our fortune, friend. Some are already there."

"Why not broaden our audience? You speak better than anyone for our cause. What have we to lose? And much to gain."

"Our good King James will pop his buttons."

"Indeed. He pops already. Give him good reason."

Robinson leveled his gaze at his friend. "You are serious about this?"

"Remember John Penry, my Welsh friend at Peterhouse?"

"Of course." Robinson knew it was still a painful memory for Brewster to recall Penry's and Greenwood's martyrdom so long ago in 1593.

"I railed against his broadcasting tracts in London under Whitgift's evil eye. Now I understand his zeal. I feel an urgency I've never known before." He gazed into Robinson's eyes. "And perhaps I can make some small retribution for his death."

"A noble but expensive venture, William. Have you the funds?"

"Not yet, but I think I may have a supporter. I received a letter from a Mr. Thomas Brewer of Kent. He has read a copy of your *Justification* and suggests it would be well received in England."

"Indeed. It must certainly command the King's notice."

"His interest aroused my own. Since some copies printed here found their way to England, why don't we reprint it and send it abroad?"

Robinson felt a flurry of excitement. "If we could broadcast our effort here, it might well encourage our separatist brothers to throw off James' yoke and join us."

Brewster chuckled. "I can see him now, popping about his throne crying out, 'I will harry them out of the land!'"

"He needs some strong Gospel meat to chew on."

They laughed.

Robinson said thoughtfully, "An intriguing idea, William. Let us think on it and see what the Lord provides."

☙◦❧

William Bradford consulted his calendar. In two weeks he would have saved enough to travel to Amsterdam to see Dorothy. Probably he should send a letter telling her he was coming, but he would much rather see the delighted surprise on her face. Yet, if she had other suitors by now—and what male could resist so adorable a girl as Dorothy—his sudden appearance might prove embarrassing to both of them. He would think about that.

One small thing that disturbed him was Mr. Robinson's hesitation when he mentioned Dorothy's name; he was not overjoyed. William had long observed Mr. Robinson's subtle expressions of emotion. He was always discreet and kindly, but sometimes, William noted, contrived to appear forgetful or confused while he assessed his comments so not to offend. Probably Mr. Robinson thought Dorothy was too young, not mature enough yet for marriage. Yet that was exactly what he wanted in a girl—innocence, simplicity, no flirtatious affectation. He had seen the worldly behavior of the Brethren pastor's wife and wondered how it might affect Dorothy. Yet he saw, too, that Thomasine Johnson apparently considered such vanity merely normal feminine behavior and was not ashamed of it. In fact, he had observed that most girls seemed to like clothes with ruffles and flourishes and

146

wanted to look their best. Certainly the girls of Leyden did. Yet he had not seen such display of vanity in Dorothy. Like most girls in their congregations, Dorothy chose clothing in good taste, never extreme or fancy, and always behaved like a perfect lady.

He sighed. He had had little experience with women, because most did not appeal to him. Dorothy's shy smile and her wide eyes intent on his face when he told her of his ambitions sometimes caught his breath. She seemed to understand his deepest thoughts and absorbed his every word. True, she did not show much enthusiasm for his plans, merely listened to them. He put that down to her innocence of worldly things, of money and property, and achieving something important in one's life, like taking the Gospel of Jesus Christ to a suffering world. Why, she had never even been to Leyden.

Which was what he had specifically in mind on this next trip to Amsterdam: to ask her father's permission to bring her to Leyden to visit the congregation, particularly the Brewsters and the Robinsons, and to see how happy they were all together. That visit would open the way for his proposal when it was time.

かき

Bradford did write her he was coming, and she did smile prettily when he arrived at her door. She ushered him to dinner and listened intently to his tales of the beautiful city of Leyden. Her parents seemed just as interested in Leyden as Dorothy did, perhaps more so. Little comments they made during dinner indicated that conflict among the Brethren was no less than before and may actually have increased since the Scrooby group left for Leyden.

Encouraged, Bradford decided that when they were alone, he would hint to Dorothy of their future together, to see how she responded. It was too early for a betrothal, but it could not hurt to lay the groundwork for a match in the future. When the parents retired, he elaborated on the pleasures of living in Leyden, the spotless streets and gorgeous flowers adorning elegant houses, and their congregation's tidy complex at the Green Gate. At last he asked, "Do you think you would like to live there, Dorothy?"

She smiled. "It sounds lovely, William."

"But do you think you might like it as well as Amsterdam?"

"Oh, I couldn't say. I have not seen it."

He sat forward eagerly. "I've been thinking of taking you there."

"That would be lovely." Her smile dazzled him.

"As soon as your parents will let you go. Sometime soon."

"Oh, that is not likely."

"Why not?"

"Well, they would not allow me to go alone with you. And it would be very expensive for them to go with me."

"You would stay with the Brewsters. They can trust them."

She shook her head. "I know. But you see, well, Father is looking ahead...to my marriage. He has someone in mind he wants me to consider."

Bradford's heart flipped.

"He says this young man is ambitious and will be prosperous," Dorothy added. "It would be a good match for me."

His heart felt as if a cold knife had pierced it. "Who is it?"

"His name is Joseph. He is a garment worker, but wants to open his own shop."

"Do you like him?"

"Oh, yes. He is very pleasant."

"But do you want to marry him?"

She laughed. "No, not yet."

"But some day? Do you like him well enough to..." His voice failed. He'd had no intention of going this far, of pressing her so soon, and now suddenly he was boldly confronted with a serious suitor. He stammered, "Dorothy, I wanted to say...I thought it was too soon, but now, if you are thinking of marriage..."

"Oh, *I* am not. Father is just looking ahead for me. Isn't that what fathers do? Plan ahead for their daughters? Of course he wants me to marry within our group and is looking there first." She laughed merrily. "I feel like a prize cow at a fair. Or standing for sale at market to the highest bidder."

Bradford almost burst into tears. There was nothing for it now but to declare himself. If her father was considering suitors as husbands already, he must be one of them. "Dorothy," he said soberly, "since we lived in Amsterdam and you were a little girl I have admired you. I knew you would grow up to be a fine woman. And you have. I want you to know..." She was gazing at him intently. He swallowed. "I love you, Dorothy," he burst out.

She smiled sweetly.

"I didn't want to say that so soon, until we got to know each other better. That's why I wanted you to see Leyden first. I couldn't ask you to leave your home if you didn't like it."

Her steady gaze unnerved him. Yet he could not read her face, could not tell if she was pleased or not. He heard himself prattling on about Leyden. She had to choose *him*, not the city of Leyden, he thought irritably. Why was he rambling on so?

At once he stopped dead and simply looked into her eyes. They gazed at each other for a few moments, then burst into laughter. How silly! How juvenile they were! There was nothing more appropriate to do than laugh.

Then at last he said, "Well, Dorothy, here I am. And here are you. What do you think?"

She took a deep breath. "I think you are a fine man, William Bradford, and I am honored that you care for me. If the good Lord ordains that we marry, then so be it."

Ah, yes, he thought suddenly. *It is the Lord's choice! It is His work, after all, to make matches in Heaven, and ordain them on Earth.* How presumptuous of himself to think *he* had to arrange it!

He thought of speaking to her father before he left for Leyden but decided it was too soon. Surely, the Lord would favor his suit. When he returned to Leyden he wrote her at once, lavish in his appreciation of her family's hospitality and eagerly anticipating their joint visit to Leyden.

Twelve

Choir Alley Press

I n his first year at Leyden Robinson had printed his *Justification of Separation* wherein he claimed that the apostles of Jesus Christ demonstrated the ideal model for a church in the New Testament. Like other separatists he believed that a "true" church consisted of members who covenant with one another to follow the teachings of Christ, and choose their own leaders among that body irrespective of the authority of bishops, presbyters, and elders. The Church of England instead embraced all citizens within legal districts called parishes as members whether they were believers or not. The primary distinction, then, between a "true" church and a church organization binding residents of a parish, was the professed faith of the believer in Jesus Christ and his commitment to covenant with other believers under Christ's lordship.

Robinson explained his position to Richard Bernard, a former contemporary at Cambridge, and later minister at Worksop near Scrooby. Bernard had tried to lure Robinson back into the Church fold, but Robinson assured him, "If your eyes had but seen the brethren's sober and modest carriage toward one another, their humble, and willing submission unto their guides, in the Lord, their tender compassion towards the weak, their fervent zeal against scandalous offenders, and their longsuffering towards all, you would (I am persuaded) change your mind."

Puritans from England, loyal to the Church but impressed with Robinson's arguments in *Justification*, came to visit him in Leyden, curious to see how his independent congregation fared. William Ames, Robert Parker, and Henry Jacob were among those leaders of the movement for reform in the English Church who sympathized with the principles underlying the Scrooby "experiment." Their visits instigated lively discussion of policies and principles fomenting among churchmen and Parliamentarians in England whose growing interest in religious independence was threatening the stability of the English Church-State. This activity greatly distressed His Majesty King James and his hierarchy of bishops.

Much encouraged by their visionary compatriots who foresaw the spiritual awakening destined to alter England's history, Robinson and Brewster were imbued with missionary fervor to expand their press. The Scrooby experience could at least inspire reformers within the Church to continue to press for reform when they could not succeed in changing her structure. While such intellectual pursuits energized Robinson, mundane practical affairs absorbed most of his daily attention. His and Brewster's mission was to nurture and inspire a young and energetic congregation coming of age and acquiring responsibilities of work and family. Meanwhile, new members drifted in from Amsterdam and England seeking spiritual support and material sustenance.

Years later Bradford would write: "I know not how it may be spoken to the honour of God and without prejudice to any, that such was the true piety, the humble zeal and fervent love of this people (whilst they thus lived together) towards God and His ways, and the singleheartedness and sincere affection one towards another, that they came as near the primitive pattern of the first churches as any other church of these later times have done, according to their rank and quality."

And he would remember about John Robinson: "Yea, such was the mutual love and reciprocal respect that this worthy man had to his flock, and his flock to him, that it might be said of them...that it was hard to judge whether he delighted more in having such a people, or they in having such a pastor. His love was great toward them, and his care was always bent for their best good, both for soul and body. For besides his singular abilities in divine things (wherein he excelled) he was also very able to give directions in civil affairs and to foresee dangers and inconveniences, by which means he was very helpful to their outward estates and so was every way as a common father unto them."

These busy years saw many marriages and births and an influx of new members. Brewster's daughter, Love, was born in 1611, the same year that William Bradford turned twenty-one and inherited his great-great-grandfather's estate at Bentley-cum-Arksey, nine-and-a-half acres with a house, cottage, garden, and orchard in Yorkshire. He regretted that his ancestor would have grieved at his sale of property passed down from son to son, for yeomen of England prized productive use and ownership of land above all other wealth. Yet this inheritance opened the way for several bold moves Bradford planned. He applied for citizenship in Leyden so he might join a guild, required by all workers in Holland. He bought a small house on the Achtergracht, and he set up his own loom. Other plans he had for the inheritance would soon be evident.

Despite Bridget's efforts to interest him in other young women, his heart was set on Dorothy May. Soon after his declaration of intention to marry her, he made the twenty-five mile journey to Amsterdam again to ask permission of her father to court her. He assumed that Elder May would guess his purpose, so he promptly launched into his rehearsed speech. "Mr, May," he began, "I have come to ask permission to court Dorothy."

"Aye," said May, nodding.

"I am employed in Leyden as a worker of fustian, which you may know is highly specialized. And I am good at it. I have set up my own loom and will work independently for the mills."

May nodded.

Bradford took a breath. "I have a house of my own bought with my inheritance so that I am free of debt and can support a wife."

May nodded.

Bradford suddenly realized he had told his tale. Should he say that he loved Dorothy? Was that not obvious? Why else would he be here? May sat silently. Bradford's brain spun around for something more impressive to say. "I am studying Latin with Mr. Robinson, hoping one day to improve my lot by teaching."

Elder May's eyebrows rose, but he said nothing.

At last Bradford stammered out, "I have loved Dorothy since she was a little girl while we lived here in Amsterdam. I looked forward to the time when she would be old enough to marry." He looked directly into May's eyes. "Sir, what more can I tell you? Have you any questions to ask me?"

May cleared his throat. "Have you spoken to Dorothy?"

"Yes, sir."

"And does she want to live in Leyden?"

"I am eager to show her the city, sir. With your permission."

"She is only fourteen. She cannot travel alone with a man."

"I realize that, sir. But the distance is only twenty-five miles by boat. And she could stay with the Brewsters in Leyden."

May took out his pipe, then leisurely probed and lighted it. After his first puff he said, "I would prefer that she marry and live in Amsterdam. This is her home, and she has grown up in the Brethren."

"I know that well, sir. But you know our congregation's commitment to the Lord."

"Aye, I thought we agreed, but your elders did not choose to stay here with us."

Bradford swallowed to relieve his tight throat. "No, sir. They felt—that is, I believe that Mr. Robinson and Mr. Clyfton felt, and the others agreed—that there were...problems here, sir. Issues of doctrine and practice." He thought desperately, must he defend his church to get his bride? "Sir," he said boldly, "are these things important between Dorothy and me? She is my first concern, sir."

"Shared belief matters between spouses, son. Dorothy is used to friends and family about her. I believe she would be happier married and living among her Brethren."

"We in Leyden believe the same Gospel as do the Brethren, sir. And surely, if we care for each other, small practical differences can be overcome."

May put his pipe down on the table next to his chair. "Son, my daughter is only fourteen, and you are not much older. Marriage does not survive on passion alone. Those emotions wane. 'Tis the burdens of daily living, hardship, and children, that strain marriage. She will have to adjust to a wedded state, a strange church, and a stranger city."

Bradford gritted his teeth. "Well, sir, I am asking permission to court Dorothy, not yet to marry her. If she does not want to marry me and live in Leyden, I will accept that. I will even consider..." He caught himself. He was not yet willing to move back to Amsterdam, not even for Dorothy. But, he wanted to shout, *I want her to make that decision!*

Elder May took up his pipe and puffed it. After awhile he nodded again. "You have my permission to court her. But I forbid her to marry before she is sixteen. I insist on that."

"Yes, sir. Thank you, sir. I accept that."

He went home disgruntled. Yet what had he expected? Elder May was only protecting his daughter as he should. And much could change in two years. He vowed to make the most of them. He would establish his own business; he would become proficient in Latin. He would become Dorothy's most eligible suitor in both Amsterdam and Leyden.

Sometime later, May agreed to allow Dorothy to visit Leyden, on condition that her married older sister Jacqueline accompany her and Bradford. The girls were welcomed by the Leyden group as warmly as if they were already members. Jacqueline told Dorothy, "How sweetly they treat each other. I hear not one harsh word among them."

Dorothy replied, "And the women speak quietly and dress modestly."

They giggled. "Not like our Thomasine," Jacqueline whispered.

"Shhh. Do not speak ill of her where anyone can hear."

"I wonder if they know about Elder Studley," Jacqueline mused.

"How could they not? They lived among us in Amsterdam half a year." Dorothy frowned. "Methinks they were more disturbed by Elder Smyth and his 'impure' Bible than Thomasine's ruffles. William is so serious about such things."

Jacqueline cast Dorothy a sly look. "And what do you think of Mr. Bradford, dear sister? He dotes on you."

Dorothy sighed. "He is so...intense. He tells me all his hopes for the future. Sometimes I wonder..."

"What?"

"He is never content. Always planning ahead for something better." Her face took on a sober cast. "I sometimes think, when he tires of me, what else will he do?"

"Tires of you! You don't mean..."

154

"Oh, he will not betray me. He is too righteous for that. He will pursue some other interest, like teaching Latin or learniug Hebrew, and leave me to manage the household and—" she blushed—"whatever children we have."

Jacqueling pursed her lips. "What else would you expect? Men are only romantic during courtship, aren't they? They do not need to pursue *wives.*"

They looked at each other. Then Jacqueline burst out, "Except Mr. Studley!"

"Aye! He pursues *every*body's wife!"

Their merry laughter rang through the Brewster house.

The girls made no mention of Studley or other distractions among the brethren at Leyden. Such "gossip" would be deemed worldly, if not downright sinful. And though the Robinsons had indeed wondered at Studley's flamboyant fornications, now such rash activity distressed them more for the effect it might have on William Bradford's bride-to-be, Dorothy May.

Bridget told John, "She has grown into a pretty and pleasant girl, docile and devoted to William. I think she will make him a good wife."

John studied Bridget's impassive face. "But..."

She said soberly, "When they are married, there can be no 'buts.'"

"But you have one now."

Bridget frowned. "Methinks she is not quite hardy enough for one as ambitious as William."

"Hardy? What mean you by 'hardy'?"

"I wonder how well she will endure here. You know how hard life is for the young people. They struggle merely to survive, with little hope that the future holds better. She is used to comfort and security."

"William will do well enough. He is setting up his own loom."

"Aye. But there will be children to come, and they will not be...can never be...English." She sighed. "None of our children will be truly English."

John saw in her eyes that unspoken grief seen from time to time in all those who had come from Scrooby. Despite their relatively pleasant situation in Leyden, freedom from restriction, and the natives' congenial hospitality, Holland was not *home.* He said gently, "There is talk abroad that Commons has put great pressure on the King to cease persecution of reformers. He is overwhelmed by petitions sent to court for redress of grievances."

Bridget muttered, "That merciless Scot! I wonder if even the Lord Himself could soften such an iron heart!"

Robinson agreed but saw no harm in offering his wife hope. "My dear, you know that with the Lord, anything is possible, even mellowing James Stewart."

She glowered.

James' solution to Commons' pleas was simple. Alarmed by the force of resistance to his restrictive policies, he simply found an excuse to dismiss Parliament and not call another session for seven years, thereby ruling unhindered as absolute monarch by "Divine Right."

❧❦

In 1613 Dorothy May turned sixteen. Bradford's steady courtship had convinced Elder May of his devotion to her, and she blended well into the Leyden congregation, whose congenial fellowship charmed and reassured her about leaving the Brethren. She told her father, "They are so kind to each other, Father. I hear no backbiting or criticism among them. If they find fault, they speak to each other kindly."

Elder May nodded. "Aye, that is the biblical way."

"Then why are not our Brethren like that?"

"The great danger of anarchy, my daughter, is that freedom may become license. Men set free from authority often become gods to themselves. They think they can do no wrong, or that what they do must be right because they do it."

"I do not understand it."

"You have not yet been tempted, my dear. Humanity is prey to worldly desires, which require great discipline to resist. This is why the Lord gave us commandments."

"Will I be tempted?"

May nodded sagely. "All come short of the glory of God."

"Is my love for William a temptation?"

"Only if you indulge it out of order, that is, without marriage."

She blushed. "Oh, I would not think of that."

"Then have you decided to marry him?"

"Only if you approve, sir."

"He has proved himself to me. He is a worthy young man and will provide well for you. You have my blessing, Dorothy. Now the decision is yours."

Suddenly she trembled, realizing her father's approval removed all barriers. "I think I love William but am not certain I am ready to marry. Am I ready to put my husband's needs first?" Her cheeks reddened. "...perhaps to have a child?"

He nodded. "Aye."

The prospect of committing her youthful self, her individuality, to another person was frightening. She confided in her sister Jacqueline who had married Jean de l'Ecluse three years ago. Jacqueline answered light-heartedly, "Oh, you will find it fun, little sister. Sometimes, any-way." She gave Dorothy a wise, old-married woman look.

Dorothy took a breath. "Should we speak of such things?"

"Why not? Love between men and women is perfectly natural."

"What advice did Mother give you?"

"Submit to whatever your husband requires. 'Tis as simple as that."

Dorothy felt her cheeks warm. She had lived among the Brethren long enough to know exactly what that meant: men ruled, women obeyed. Yet such advice confused her. Francis Johnson defended his wife Thomasine against her critics, which indicated that either he approved of her behavior, or that she somehow deceived him. Therefore, if a wife persuaded her husband of her point of view and they agreed, they stood in unity. She eyed Jacqueline sharply. "If you and Jean disagree, do you submit to him in everything?"

Jacqueline laughed. "Of course not. When we disagree, I simply keep quiet, and do as I please. Within reason, of course. The trick is, unless the issue is critical, he need never know you disagree. Do not worry, dear child. Bradford is absorbed in his own interests and will leave you to yours. He will not make unreasonable demands of you. Praise God, plunge in, and enjoy it."

Bradford and Dorothy, accompanied by Elder May, appeared in Amsterdam on November ninth, 1613, to declare their intention to marry. Bradford arranged for the banns to be published in Leyden, and on December tenth they were wed in Amsterdam by the magistrate in a civil service. The Brethren feasted the newlyweds but held no religious ritual for them. The English had adopted the Dutch custom of contracting marriage as they would a business, as a binding legal agreement between parties. The newlyweds went home to the little house on the Achtergracht to embark on a honeymoon full of promise of an exultant life together.

Delighted in her new home and new friends, Dorothy did plunge into the responsibilities of making a home and joining other young couples for fellowship and corporate worship. Her "sweete and delightfull societe" included William and Susanna Fuller White, the four White sisters, Bridget, Catherine, Jane and Frances, and their husbands John Carver, Ralph Tickens, and Frances Jessop. She soon formed a close bond with Susanna, nearest her age, who had married William White the year before the Bradfords married. The girls going to daily market enjoyed ogling the myriad exotic items shipped from Asia, which revealed a material world of astonishing wealth they could not hope to possess but found fascinating to behold. Their English husbands, countrymen unskilled in urban work and limited to labor in mills and shops, were paid barely subsistence wages for long, exhausting workdays. Their status offered little hope of improvement, and as the colony's children grew older and joined the workforce, the same destiny lay before them. So the girls' expeditions were more an exciting entertainment than anticipation of reality.

Then one day Susanna stood at Dorothy's door beaming. "Why are you smiling? Has something happened?" Dorothy asked.

Susanna giggled. "Yes. Something indeed." Susanna's face shone like a lantern lit from within. "I'm getting fat!"

Dorothy glanced at Susanna's slim girth. "You look no different to me."

Susanna thrust out her stomach. "Look at that!"

No change was visible, but the light in Susanna's face struck Dorothy. "You are expecting?"

"Yes!" Susanna screeched.

They fell together, shrieking for joy. This day, inspired, they would inspect the shops offering items for babies and children, not with intention to buy, but merely to dream. Essential household items for families circulated about the congregation as needed, mended, patched, and rejuvenated until they fell apart and must be replaced. Then some artist in the colony would craft the new item. Yet, in addition to hand-me-downs, every new baby was given something new to celebrate the arrival of a precious child unique among all children, a blessing offered by God.

Between them the girls had suspected several pregnancies that had come to nothing and had begun to worry that they were barren. Now Dorothy was as thrilled for Susanna as she would be for herself. "Have you told William?"

"Aye. He is proud."

And so would be her William, Dorothy thought with a touch of envy.

The next months as they focused on the Whites' child, Dorothy found herself feeling anxious. Most young women of the congregation bore children regularly, rapidly filling their family "quivers" with "arrows" the Bible recommended.

Susanna consoled her, "Be patient, Dority, your time is coming. Be content just to enjoy your husband now. You will never have this time alone again." She threw up her hands. "A child changes your life forever!"

Then, before Susanna delivered, Dorothy began to suffer assorted strange discomforts, mostly a distaste for food. She complained to Susanna, but not to William, that she was eating so little she felt weak. Susanna burst out, "Of course, you're with child!"

"Do you think so?"

"Just wait. The answer will soon be evident." Susanna shook her finger, grinning.

Dorothy would not tell William until she was absolutely certain. She consulted Mary Brewster. "What do you think?"

"Your symptoms sound hopeful, Dorothy." Mary looked at her closely. "Are you happy about this?"

"Oh, yes, mum. William will be overjoyed."

Mary smiled. "He will be if you are."

"Oh, I am, I am!"

⤜⤛

As they did with all new babies, the congregation welcomed John Bradford as a gift only God could provide. For his father. this gift was especially dear: John was the family he had never known. For Dorothy, he was literally the "fruit of her womb," which changed her from a child to a woman. In the year 1615 the Bradfords' cup runneth over.

⤜⤛

During the next years many more exiles came to Leyden to be embraced within the congregation. Thomas Brewer, the gentleman from Kent who had written Brewster, came to Leyden to matriculate at the University. Later he bought the Groenehuis on Bell Alley near Robinson's Green Gate, where he housed three young students, all sympathetic to the separatist cause.

Soon after Brewer's purchase, Brewster came eagerly to Robinson's Green Gate. "Good news, John. The Lord has indeed sent us a benefactor."

"Tell me!"

"Thomas Brewer. He tells me that his original motive for coming to Leyden was to set up a printing press to publish our work. He proposes to finance our project." Brewster paced about, hardly able to contain his excitement. "He has already suggested a name for it: the Choir Alley Press. We will set up in my garret." He sank into a chair and took a deep breath. "Forgive my running on like this. I am overcome."

Robinson grinned with delight at his friend's uncharacteristic outburst. "This is an answer to our prayers, William."

"Listen to this. He proposes that at first we will publish 'safe' books like the *Tenne Commandments,* then others in Latin and Dutch, and bearing our own imprints, but nothing that King James can object to. Then as our reputation grows, we will do some of our own work. What a blessing is this Dutch free press! What great potential here for reaching our people in England."

160

Robinson leveled his gaze at Brewster. "I see more clearly than ever, William, why the Lord sent us to Leyden. Where else could we find such an opportunity?"

Brewster beamed. "I have already designed my own imprint. Remember the bear baiting I saw at Scarborough Fair?"

"Aye, with Penry and Greenwood."

"Remember our discussions about its symbolism? Was Whitgift the trapped bear and we 'rebels' the attack dogs, or were we the bear hopelessly bound at the mercy of Whitgift's dogs?" He grinned. "I have decided that my imprint will be a small woodcut figure of the wounded but defiant bear symbolic of our oppression."

Robinson had matriculated as a student himself at the University of Leyden and continued to impress the scholars with his clarity of vision and interpretive gifts. Now he began to hear subtle invitations to associate officially with the academic staff. He consulted Bridget. "I think Professor Polyander is serious about this. How should I respond, do you think?"

"It would be recognition hard to refuse, John. Yet it would surely agitate the King."

"Yes, I've thought of that. The University has been so generous to me, to all of us here, I would not want to cause a diplomatic incident. These good people cannot afford to alienate James. They may need his help badly in a few years."

Rarely did Robinson or any of the Scrooby group acknowledge openly the unspoken threat that hovered silently over Leyden like gathering storm clouds. The official truce between the Dutch and Spain would end in 1621, and while diplomatic relations were currently stable, most Dutchman expected that when the treaty expired, Spain would renew her aggression in the Lowlands. The Spanish were more determined to scourge heretics now than they had ever been, and since Elizabeth's time England had been the Lowlands' chief defender.

After discussion with Brewster, and Deacons Fuller and Carver, Robinson decided to politely decline official association with the University. Yet he saw no risk in responding to Polyander's request to publicly debate Arminianism, a subject that had become his particular grievance.

Meanwhile, Brewster's home on the Stincksteeg, "Stink Alley" for obvious reasons, became a hive of activity. He and Brewer chose the title *Vicus Chorali*, Latin for "Choir Alley," as their address, and began to publish in Latin and Dutch the "safe" books readily acceptable in England. Their first book, *Tenne Commandments*, by Dod and Cleaver, bore the legend *Tot Leyden, voor Guiliaem Brewster, Boeckdrucker, Anno, 1517.* The next two publications bore the legend in Latin, *Apud Guiljelmum Brewsterum, In vico Choralii.* Ten books later printed in English and distributed in England did not bear Brewster's name but only the tiny emblem of a bear.

One day two young men recently from London appeared at Brewster's door and addressed Mary. "Madam, we have come to see Master Brewster on a matter of business, if he is willing."

Mary appraised them cautiously. They were pleasantly polite, new to the congregation, obviously English, but one could never be sure that engaging strangers might not be King's men seeking evidence against them. "I will tell him you are here," she said and seated them in the parlor. At her call Brewster came down from the garret. "Be careful," Mary whispered, a finger to her lips.

As they stood to greet him, Brewster recognized them, for they had recently attended the Leydeners' meetings for worship. "Yes, gentlemen? How can I help you?"

"Sir, I am John Reynolds, and this is my apprentice, Edward Winslow. We are printers from London. We have read your imprints, and are interested in your press. We hope that we can serve you."

Brewster gazed into each face before answering. "In what way?"

Reynolds and Winslow exchanged glances. "May we take your time to talk?"

"Of course."

They sat down and Reynolds spoke directly. "We are sympathetic to the separatist cause, and when we learned of your congregation here in Leyden, we determined to print tracts that you might distribute in England."

Brewster considered carefully. So direct an offer could easily be a trick of the King's men to trap him into admission of printing books critical of the English Church. "As you must know, gentlemen, we are

162

free to print anything we like here and have ready access to printers. There is no restriction on the Dutch press."

Reynolds said, "We do know that. But our hope is to promote the separatist cause in England. We have access to marketers there who can distribute tracts widely."

Brewster's eyes narrowed. "And how exactly will they do that, sir, without arousing the King's ire?"

Winslow spoke up. "Mr. Brewster, your group has become a model for Englishmen like yourselves who chafe under Church restriction. We want to advertise your success here."

Advertise their success? Brewster was amused. Flattering words, and only partly true. Yet to those still languishing under repression at home, perhaps the Scrooby group had been successful merely to survive in Leyden. He felt a surge of excitement. If these men were sincere, the influence of his books may be profound among Englishmen. Until these two had proved themselves, however, he must be cautious. "I thank you, gentlemen, for your offer, and will take it under advisement with my pastor and elders."

Winslow's eyes brightened. "Your pastor John Robinson? I much admire this man, an inspiring preacher and esteemed scholar. And a most congenial host."

Brewster nodded. "And genuinely receptive to our brethren from home."

Reynolds rose. "We thank you, sir, for your time. Please do consider this seriously. We are most sincere."

Brewster sought out Robinson at once. "What do you think? Is it a trick?"

"Ask Brewer. He may know something about them we don't know."

Brewer knew nothing but suggested, "We can inquire in London about their credentials. Yet that would take some time."

"We have the Lord's time," said John. "Let us make no quick agreement, but simply welcome them to our community, take their measure, and in due time give them something safe to print. Unless these two have been sent by the King to harass us, we will consider they have come to fulfill the Lord's particular purposes."

Soon afterwards, Brewer reported that Winslow was a gentleman of "qualitie" from a good family, had been trained as a printer, and worked with Reynolds in London. Both seemed genuinely devoted to the separatist cause and eager to print Robinson's works. Within a few months they had printed in Dutch *A Plaine and Familiar Exposition of the Tenne Commandments, with a Methodical short Catechisme*, and two books in Latin, one by Thomas Cartwright, former fellow at Brewster's Peterhouse College. These were "safe" books, not written in English and not controversial, therefore unlikely to arouse suspicion among English authorities. The Choir Alley Press had been safely launched, and its sponsors rejoiced in its future.

Thirteen

Perth Assembly

While Brewster enthusiastically began printing, John Robinson had begun to spend many hours in fervent prayer for wisdom to direct his colony's future in Leyden. Despite Brewster's hopeful enterprise, ominous signs told Robinson that their group, heavily oppressed financially and socially, was facing an uncertain, perhaps dangerous future. Their purpose for migrating to the Lowlands—to escape persecution at home and to live productively in a godly community without fear—had always been limited by their meager resources. Now, after ten years away from home, few of their congregation earned more than a bare living wage gleaned at backbreaking cost in good health and well-being. While their elders were aging, their children were spending their youth in arduous labor with little reward beyond survival. Worse, they were becoming more susceptible to the enticing freedoms of Dutch youth. Though the permissiveness of their adopted country gave them a haven from ecclesiastical tyranny, that very tolerance also allowed licentious behavior abhorrent to the people's Christian values. Robinson saw little hope of achieving a comfortable security, much less converting their neighbors to a virtuous lifestyle. Only their own dedication to their biblical mode of life sustained them.

Glowering overall was the impending end in 1621 of the truce between Holland and Spain. If Catholic Spain resumed its oppression of the Protestant Lowlands, as all of Europe expected, what possible hope had the "heretic" Leyden group of surviving war in a besieged land?

Robinson kept his fears to himself, not wanting to burden his people beyond their daily trials, but it became clearer to him each day that something must be done to improve their status. Then one day when his brother-in-law, Deacon John Carver, came by to discuss church business, Carver said morosely, "I've heard from my cousin at Doncaster. He has decided not to join us."

Robinson studied Carver's drawn brow. "I know you are disappointed."

Carver sighed. "His family would have been a great blessing to us here." Carver glanced dourly at Robinson. "We are in great need of blessing, John."

Robinson nodded. "Always. Why are they not coming?"

"He feels it would deprive his family too severely. I confess I spoke honestly of our hardship here, perhaps too honestly. 'Hardship' he says he can bear but cannot subject his children to the 'frivolity' of Dutch youth."

Robinson was suddenly prompted to reveal his fears to Carver, whom he could trust implicitly. Carver had not left England with the Scrooby people but later had given up security in England to join them in Leyden. His good judgment and practical business sense had been a great benefit to the community and to Robinson personally. Robinson said gravely, "John, I think we must face a grim reality. Knowing our hardship, few will be inspired to join us here. Some among us are even thinking of returning to England." An expression of pain crossed his face. "To England! And the King more rabid than ever to crush any opposition."

Carver nodded, surprised at this unusual show of emotion in his pastor.

Robinson went on, "I think we may have to consider leaving Leyden."

The possibility did not astonish Carver. It had occurred to him as well, for despite their spiritual stability he had seen poverty steal much joy from the younger generation. After a moment, he asked, "When?"

"Not at once; perhaps not for a year or two. I have been contemplating this for some time but did not want to alarm any of you with my fears." He smiled faintly. "The prospect of uprooting, moving again...few could bear it. Yet your cousin's decision moves me to share with you. We may not have as much time as I thought."

Carver leaned back in his chair. "You do not suffer alone, John. I think all of us are keenly aware of our limitations here. And Philip of Spain looms over us like a spectre of doom."

Robinson felt immense relief sharing this burden. He thought suddenly of Proverbs eleven, verse fourteen, warning that where there was no counsel the people fell, but in the multitude of counselors there was safety. May the Lord forgive him for pride, thinking he alone should bear responsibility for the colony's welfare.

He went to his desk, took out two books, and handed them to Carver. "I have done some research. Here are John Smith's *Description of New England* and Raleigh's *Discovery of Guiana.* You will find them most interesting."

Carver glanced at each cover. "So you are well ahead of us!"

"Read first of Guiana. The description is rhapsodic. Warm climate, abundant food, a virtual Paradise."

Carver said doubtfully, "Yet also wild creatures and tropical disease."

Robinson chuckled. "You have researched some yourself. Then read Smith's *New England,* a climate more familiar to us. But say nothing yet, not even to Catherine. I have told Bridget nothing of my fears." He smiled wryly. "And yet, I would not be stunned out of my senses if she already suspects what I am thinking."

After Carver read the books, he advised Robinson to open discussion with the elders and deacons about the prospects of leaving Leyden. No one seemed surprised; some were already resigned. Reassured, Robinson urged them to share the prospect with their wives. When he and Carver presented the idea to their own wives, Catherine said archly, "We wondered when you were going to tell us your big secret."

Said Bridget, "You've been brewing some plan for months now."

Carver winked at Robinson. "So we need not be stunned out of our senses." He grinned at the sisters. "What do you women think of the idea?"

"We are stricken," retorted Catherine sharply. "We thought we had found a home here. And we dread moving again."

Robinson said soothingly, "We are only facing realities, my dears, and searching out possibilities. We've decided nothing yet."

Bridget said, "To leave Leyden seems a drastic move. Were we not certain that God directed us here? Why would He send us away?"

The women's firm resistance sobered their men. "Yes, we do believe the Lord sent us here," Carver answered. "But our circumstances have not improved in ten years, and soon may become much worse. We think He may be warning us now of trials to come, and urging us to reassess our position."

"But must we leave Leyden?" Catherine asked plaintively. "Many of us will not want to begin again. Where would we go?"

Carver said, "We are considering that very problem." He glanced for support at Robinson, who answered, "We have several places in mind. Perhaps it is time to put this before all our people."

The women sat silently. Then Catherine said in a tentative voice, "Methinks much will depend on where we can settle. Will ye heed the voices of us women?"

Carver glanced at Robinson, who smiled. "My dear, we are listening now."

When Robinson presented the proposal to leave Leyden to the congregation, they received it in profound silence. "We will hear everyone's opinion on this matter, my good people. Do not hesitate to speak. We will make no decisions until we reach consensus."

"John," one voice spoke up, "do you consider this move urgent?"

"No, not this year, nor even next. But the Spanish treaty expires three years from now. We must look ahead."

One who had joined the group in Amsterdam stood up. "I cannot abide another move. It cost my family too much. We English have no quarrel with Spain. Surely we need not abandon our homes here."

Another voice called out, "And the Dutch have sheltered us! Surely they will not persecute us. Can we not trust them?"

Said another, "'Tis the Spaniard hates all heretics. They will not spare us."

"I'm for Guiana. Somewhere warm!"

Obviously, the people were far from agreement. After much argument, all realized that they could only come together after earnest congregate prayer for the Lord's will to be revealed to them.

Brewster's first publications after the *Tenne Commandments* were Thomas Cartwright's commentary on the Proverbs and a theological attack by William Ames, both in Latin. The books caused no furor in England. Now Brewster took a further step with Robinson's *The People's Plea for the Exercising of Prophecy,* presenting an argument for lay preaching within the congregation, certain to antagonize Anglican authorities. With this bolder effort, he decided not to adorn the book with his impress. The Choir Alley Press had established itself and was cautiously expanding.

Then one day Brewster told Robinson, "I have received a manuscript begging for publication, but I am not certain we are ready to print it."

"Received from whom?"

"Calderwood on the Press Assembly."

Robinson let out a long sigh. "Ahhhh, Calderwood."

In the city of Perth, Scotland, in August of 1618, King James, determined to impose an episcopate on the Presbyterians, had called an assembly to propose five articles defining Anglican ceremonies meant to quench Scottish resistance. While the leadership at the Assembly had nominally accepted the articles, the Scottish people violently objected and refused to practice them. David Calderwood, a fiery minister of the Scottish Kirk, had gone into hiding to write a treatise "with much scorn and reproach" of His Majesty James, and no printer in Scotland dared publish it.

The Choir Alley Press had by now issued a number of theses setting forth their own religious philosophies more or less in sympathy with the Presbyterians but had not directly attacked James and his English Church. Could they afford to risk publishing Calderwood's blatant condemnation of the Perth Assembly? Brewster handed the manuscript to Robinson. "Tell me what you think of this."

After Robinson and the printers Brewer, Reynolds, and young Winslow read the manuscript, they met with Brewster. Thomas Brewer gave voice to the danger obvious to all. "Printing this tirade, my brothers, will certainly invite the King's wrath upon us."

Winslow said, "Yet Calderwood speaks for our own sentiments exactly. Can we in good conscience refuse to support him?"

Reynolds suggested that they print it anonymously, revealing neither author nor printer. This seemed the safest option but aroused other questions. Should they consult the congregation? Their body shared a common fate and made communal decisions. Should not they approve of the risk their elders were taking on their behalf? Yet the more persons aware of the printers' identity, the greater the danger of their discovery. What should be the elders' course here?

At last they agreed that the issue must be put before the body despite the risk of discovery. Robinson addressed the group. "My dear brothers, you are aware that we are printing books that King James finds distasteful." Smiles broke out here and there. "Now a Scottish brother speaking for his people who are defiant of the King's policies against their Kirk, a cause most congenial with our own, asks us to print his book. No printer in Scotland will do it. We want to make clear to you that if we undertake this work, our welfare as a congregation may be threatened. We need your approval to proceed."

No one spoke for a few moments. Then a cacaphony of voices rang out. Brewster rose and gestured for silence. "Brothers, we will hear all your concerns. But first, let me emphasize that if we do print this book, we shall not advertise our part in it. We will print it anonymously."

A voice called out, "Mr. Brewster, have you already agreed to print it and now ask us to approve your decision?"

"No, we have agreed to nothing yet. We want your approval first."

An older member stood up. "We survive here in Leyden by the good graces of the Dutch people. Will this book threaten them?"

Brewster answered, "We think not. But we are always mindful that we do not want to jeopardize the States' relationship with King James."

A young voice piped, "Then let's just give that canny Scot a bit of a jolt."

A titter rounded the room. Robinson raised a hand and smiled tolerantly. "We understand your zeal, young friend, but this is no frivolous matter."

Silence fell across the room. Then Samuel Fuller, a transfer from the Ancient Brethren, stood up to speak. "We are a united body, which does not mean that we always agree." A murmur of assent rippled about. "I propose that we seek the Lord both separately and together, praying for unity. If there is none, then we will reconsider."

A week later the body met again. Several voices spoke out, and it was clear that no unity had been reached. Then Francis Cooke of the original Scrooby group spoke. "Having sought the Lord fervently in this matter, still we find that we do not all hear His voice in the same way. I suggest that we trust our elders and deacons to use their best discernment of His will and to proceed accordingly."

Robinson said, "What say you, people?" Some heads nodded assent.

"How go the rest of you? We must reach agreement on this matter."

Degory Priest, once of the Brethren, said, "How do we recognize agreement? When there is no disagreement?"

Brewster glanced at the elders. "Methinks 'agreement' means 'consensus.' If a majority are in favor, and there is no firm objection, we have reached consensus."

"I object," said Priest at once.

"That means you will not agree to print *Perth Assembly*."

"That means I am not convinced that the Lord directs us to print it."

Brewster sighed. "Here is our great dilemma. Who hears the Lord's voice perfectly? How then do we decide?"

Cooke declared, "Why do we elect elders and deacons? Are they not called to make decisions for us who cannot always agree? I say, leave it to the elders."

Robinson called out, "What say you to that, people? Let the elders decide. Do you agree? How many do not?"

Most raised their hands to agree. A few did not, one Degory Priest.

"How say you, Degory? Agreed or not. Resigned, or not."

Priest replied, "I think the Lord did not tell me to print that book, but if He has told others in the body, I will submit to their witness."

Others nodded agreement with Priest, but the final decision to print or not was deferred to the elders.

When the people had gone, Robinson asked, "Well, Mr. Brewster, do we do it?"

The elders and printers glanced among themselves. Winslow grinned. "I say, indeed, let's give our Scottish sovereign, the wisest fool in Christendom, a jolt of English mettle."

They laughed.

❧❧

During the following weeks, the prospect of leaving Leyden arose again. Trudging to work, no one could fail to notice increasing Dutch activity in preparation for war. The children found this exciting and eagerly inquired of their parents about the soldiers and military reinforcements bristling about the city. The adults were wary. How much of their own fears should they reveal?

Bridget opened her door one day to Dorothy Bradford and her infant son. She saw at once that Dorothy was distraught. "What is it, my dear?"

"They are reinforcing the dikes by the Zee."

"Why, yes, they do every spring."

"But now they are building outposts."

Bridget thought a moment. "Ah, they are fortifying against the—"

"Spanish!" Dorothy spat out the word. "Oh, mother, I cannot bear to think of what may come to us here."

"Aye, my heart aches for you young ones. We have been through this, you see."

"Not war! You did not fear Spanish invasion in England."

Bridget sighed. Dorothy was too young to recall England's continual fears of Spanish invasion. "We dreaded not only the Spanish, my dear, but our own countrymen. The spectre of the dread jailhouse loomed over us. Most imprisoned there soon die of fever."

Dorothy's eyes brimmed with tears. "How dreadful to live in constant fear!"

Bridget sat the girl down, patted her golden hair, and said, "Since Adam's Fall in the Garden men have lived in fear, my girl. Yet the Lord takes care of us who trust Him. Think of the millions in their misery who never know His generous love."

Dorothy shook her head. "I have not your measure of faith, Mistress Robinson. I dread leaving Leyden for some unknown wilderness. My son never to see his family again in Amsterdam."

Little John, seeing his mother's tears, frowned as if puzzled.

"Believe me, I understand, child. I dreaded leaving my English home." Bridget drifted into a moment's reverie. "How lovely it is now, in springtime. The fields greening, flowers budding. Yes, it is lovely here, too, but it is not...home." She fell silent.

Dorothy looked up into her face. "That's what William remembers best. Springtime in Yorkshire. I hardly remember England at all."

John's bright eyes spied a fresh loaf on the table and stirred in Dorothy's arms. He lost interest in her tears and reached out for the fragrant bread.

Bridget said, "He's hungry. May I give him a bit of bread?"

Dorothy nodded, smiling wanly. Bridget picked the boy up and dandled him on her lap while he munched the bread.

Dorothy was not cheered. "I want to confess something," she said softly.

"Of course, dear."

"When I agreed to marry Will, he talked of moving back to Amsterdam because there is more work there. I expected to return."

The women looked into each other's eyes. "Did he promise that?" Bridget asked.

"No, he did not. But I thought that at least we would visit often. Yet he works so hard at his loom, there is no time to visit. I rarely see my family."

"He is an ambitious young man. You are fortunate."

"But now he says we may leave Leyden." She looked desperately into Bridget's eyes. "Not for Amsterdam but some unknown country we have never heard of. I do not want to go!" Her eyes were wide with distress.

Bridget assured her, "We have not decided to leave Leyden."

"But William has. He says we must go *somewhere*. It will be too dangerous here when the Spanish return."

Bridget took a deep breath and clutched John to her breast. How could she console this young wife? She felt much the same herself. She put wriggling John down on the floor to scramble about. "Dorothy, do not despair. No decision has been made. And if we do go, it will be somewhere the Lord has chosen for us. Better than Leyden, as Leyden was better than Amsterdam, and Amsterdam better than—" she choked on this—"England. No, I take that back. Nowhere is better than home." At once she realized she had misspoken, for Dorothy's home was Amsterdam. "I mean, one always misses one's homeland; it is part of our heritage wherever we go. I regret that none of our children here will grow up 'English.'" A pang of deep sadness washed over her.

Dorothy brushed back her flaxen hair. Her pretty, petulant face was masked with sorrow; her blue eyes glittered with tears. "I cannot go. I *cannot*."

Bridget recalled her doubts when Bradford chose Dorothy as wife: the girl was so young, not "hardy" enough for William. With an acute sense of disloyalty, she recalled that she had encouraged William to find another girl in Leyden. Yet now that Dorothy was his wife, Bridget must not only sympathize but also sustain her. "My dear, you must put your trust in the Lord, and He will guide your husband. Wherever we go, He is our strength."

Dorothy's brimming eyes gazed at Bridget, her cheeks turning pink, her chin trembling.

Bridget said, "There is talk of our going to Guiana, a tropical land sounding most luscious indeed. Think of it! No cold winters, balmy winds, abundant fruits. Little John here would love it." She scooped John up in her arms but felt herself to be an utter hypocrite. Guiana was not their most likely choice of habitation, but at the moment she wanted to give the girl hope of something, anything that might compare with Leyden.

Dorothy sighed, then managed a fragile smile. "You have been good to me. I am sorry to trouble you. William's need for adventure and high optimism do distress me sometimes. I want only my home and son."

Bridget looked upon the girl sadly. She seemed hardly more than a lovely child. Bridget wiped John's buttery mouth and held him out to his mother. "Do not let fear possess you, my girl. Fear is the devil's torment. We have nothing to fear. And much to hope for."

They embraced and Dorothy departed. Bridget decided not to burden her husband with this episode. He and Brewster and the printers had more serious business to occupy their minds.

∽∾

An unknown burly figure appeared at Mary Brewster's door, and when he asked for her husband, Mary knew at once by his speech who he must be. "Missus, I would speak wit' yer master, if he be at home."

"Come in, sir."

He doffed his woolen tam. "Ye be Missus Brewster, I take it."

"I am. And I can guess who you are. Mr. David Calderwood of Scotland."

His florid face brightened. "Ye've heard o' me, then."

"Indeed I have. Is my husband expecting you?"

"I doubt it. I can ill afford to announce my intended presence anywhere."

Mary could not help smiling. He was a sight to behold in heavy sheepskin breeks and coat and leather boots, bearded and beaming. Probably no disguise could hide the Celtic bulk of him. He could only be a Scot.

Brewster, Mr. Brewer, and Calderwood disappeared upstairs into the garret while Mary prepared a robust dinner. When the men came down to eat, their enthusiasm was evident, not only for food. Mary did not need to ask if the Press would publish Calderwood's book. The men were as eager as schoolboys on a holiday.

∽∾

Some months later the Collector of the Customs at Burntisland, Scotland, denied a request of the Minister of the parish to inspect some wine vats recently delivered by ship. The vats were taken from Burntisland to Leith and deposited on the landing with other French imports. There the Archbishop of St. Andrews, John Spottiswood, noted the vats, a usual French import, and did not ask to inspect them. From there the intoxicating contents were shipped about the country to titillate the population well beyond the usual alcoholic effects. The vats contained tightly packed copies of Calderwood's condemnation of the Perth Assembly.

Their effect was inflammatory. When reports reached London, James and his bishops denounced the work as atrocious and seditious libel and undertook an intense search for the contemptible author. Hunted from house to house and town to town by the King's men, Calderwood was spirited to Holland by the women of Edinburgh who raised funds to send him there. No one yet suspected that the Choir Alley Press had printed his pamphlet. Instead, suspicion focused on a more likely Scottish bookseller named James Cathkin, whom James summoned for interrogation in June of 1619.

"Where were ye born?" bellowed James.

"In the city of Edinburgh," answered Cathkin.

"What religion are ye of?"

"Of the religion your Majesty professes."

"The devil take ye away, both body and soul," James spouted. "For you are none of my religion. You are a recusant. You go not to Church."

Kneeling before the king, Cathkin endured silently and did not flinch while James railed about the holiness of attending Church. At last the King vented, "Ye are worse than Turks and Jews!" He rounded on his watching courtiers and proclaimed, "I can never get order of these people of Edinburgh! The devil rive their souls and bodies all in collops and cast them into hell!"

Now James launched into a sharp inquiry about Calderwood's pamphlet. Had Cathkin published it? And if not, did he know who did? Had Calderwood resorted to Cathkin's house while lurking about Edinburgh? Cathkin denied all knowledge of the offensive treatise but confessed that Calderwood had in fact slept at his house within the last fifteen days.

"Aha!" cried James in triumph. "We have found the taed! Let us hold us here, forsooth!" But he could pry no further information from stubborn Cathkin, charged him with having declared the Assembly unlawful, and in a final fit of pique berated him for kneeling. "See, their people will kneel to me, and will not kneel to GOD!" This remark referred to Presbyterians' refusal to kneel for Communion, which they considered a Papist ritual. In frustration James consigned Cathkin to prison for further interrogation where he was kept three weeks, then dismissed.

∫∫

Meanwhile, a clerk serving Sir Dudley Carleton, English ambassador to the Hague, received an official note from Secretary of State Naunton's office in London. He read it carefully, put it in his pocket, and set out on a round of local booksellers' shops. He soon found a number of copies of *Perth Assembly*, none of which named either author or printer. Curious, he inquired about other such "puritan" books, and was directed to publications of the local Choir Alley Press, whose design and typescript seemed remarkably similar to that of the *Assembly*. On a hunch, he took his copy of Calderwood's book to the ambassador. "Sir, I have made an interesting discovery methinks you will appreciate."

Sir Carleton peered over his half-glasses at the clerk. "Eh? What?"

The clerk gave the book to the ambassador, who inspected the title and title page, then glanced up at the clerk. "What is it?"

"A treatise sharply critical of His Majesty's Assembly at Perth. Mr. Naunton's office requested our attention to this publication and its authors. Therefore, I took the trouble to look for it here." His eyes glittered with expectation.

Sir Carleton flipped through the pages. "No names here."

"Quite right, sir. But its type matches that of a number of publications done locally by a press known as the Choir Alley Press, a shop operated by a known Brownist. Methinks the King will reward thee well for his name."

Sir Carleton studied the book, then nodded. "Thank you, good sir. I will attend to it."

Vaguely disappointed, the clerk bowed out. Yet he consoled himself. When the ambassador realized the importance of his find, he would surely express more generous gratitude.

On July 17, 1619, Sir Carleton composed a letter to Sir Robert Naunton, Secretary of State in London:

I have seen at the Hague within these two days, a certain Scottish book, called *Perth Assembly*, written with much scorn and reproach of the proceedings in that Kingdom concerning the affairs of the Church. It is without name, either of Author or Printer, but I am informed it is printed by a certain English Brownist of Leyden, as are most of the Puritan books sent over, of late days, into England.

Which being directly against an express edict of the States General, which was published in December last (1618): I intend when I have more particular knowledge of the Printer, to make complaint thereof; concerning that His Majesty will not dislike I should do so.

Five days later he reported:

A William Brewster, a Brownist, hath been for some years an inhabitant and printer at Leyden, but is now within three weeks removed from thence, and gone back to dwell in London, where he may be found out and examined.

🙞🙜

Sir Carleton did not know that the bookseller recognized the Ambassador's clerk at his first visit, and had at once alerted Brewster. "He appeared more curious about the printer than the book itself."

When Brewster told Robinson he sat thoughtfully for awhile. "William, I suggest you remove yourself from the premises for a few days. Your printers can manage without you. Tell them you have urgent business out of town."

"I cannot abandon them to face my danger, John."

"You will not. You are the 'Brownist' the Ambassador looks for, and your 'urgent business' of the moment is to remain elusive."

Brewster frowned. "I wonder, should I tell Mary where I am?"

"I think it wiser not to. Then she can honestly say she doesn't know where you are. 'Tis not a lie. Just not the whole truth."

Brewster looked doubtful.

Robinson spoke slyly, a slight smile on his lips. "I recall you once told me that when you hiked to Babworth Church eight miles of a Sunday, so Mary would not know exactly where you were at any given moment and could truthfully say you were somewhere on 'business' for Scrooby Manor."

Brewster grinned. "You have speared me with my own dirk."

But when he told Mary he must leave Leyden "for a short while," the anxious query in her eyes unmasked him, and he confessed, "Sir Carleton is inquiring about the author and printer of *Assembly*. John thinks it best I disappear for a few days."

Mary caught her breath. "Where will you go?"

"The less you know the better, dear Mary. I will send you word of my health."

Brewster removed himself only as far as Thomas Brewer's house. Reynolds and Winslow operated the Press in his garret as usual. The bookseller reported to Brewer Sir Carleton's persistent inquiries about Brewster's whereabouts, which only Robinson and Brewer knew. Yet when suspicious figures were seen lurking about the street near Brewster's press, Robinson sensed that the time for decision had come. The congregation must begin to plan for their exodus. Leyden did not seem so safe a haven as before.

Fourteen

Flight

When news reached Leyden that Cathkin had been questioned by the King and imprisoned, Brewster met with Robinson and the elders Carver, Fuller, and Cushman in Brewer's house and told them, "He will not rest until he finds me."

The men nodded. "We agreed to take that risk."

"One day soon they will come looking for this press. I do not want to impose any further risk on our people."

"What will you do, William?" Robinson asked.

"I think it best I return to England. They will not think to look for me there."

The men exchanged ironic smiles. Robinson said, "Perhaps this is the Lord's timing. While you are there you can contact the Virginia Company for a patent."

With Brewster forced into hiding, the quest for a new home became more urgent. Discussion among the brethren had focused on a destination in Virginia, territory under English jurisdiction. The Leyden people were eager to restore ties to their mother country, and one small Anglican Church at the struggling colony at Jamestown did not seem to pose a dire threat.

Deacons Robert Cushman and John Carver were chosen to seek a patent through Sir Edwin Sandys, son of the Archbishop of York, Brewster's former patron at Scrooby. Sandys took their petition to Sir Robert Naunton, who presented it to the King. Always intrigued by schemes to make money, James asked, "What profits may arise in the parts to which they intend to go?"

"Fishing," said Naunton, tongue-in-cheek.

"So God have my soul, 'tis an honest trade! It was the Apostles' own calling."

Yet for political reasons James refused to grant the patent, declaring, however, that if they chose to go without it, he "would connive at them and not molest them, provided they carried themselves peaceably."

This news met with keen disappointment in Leyden. Without the King's approval, the Leydeners had no legal sanction to establish a colony. Despite the elders' assurance that the King's permission was not reliable, for it could be cancelled any time at his whim, many began to lose heart for the project. Cushman and Carver continued to negotiate but could not affirm promises with the Virginia Company because now the company itself was insolvent and verging on bankruptcy.

Cushman sent other discouraging news back to Leyden. Francis Johnson's Ancient Brethren, their former colleagues in Amsterdam, led by their elder, Francis Blackwell, had sailed to Virginia under great duress, only to meet with devastating storms, illness, and ultimate disaster at Jamestown on the Chesapeake. Cushman lamented the Brethren's debacle. "Heavy news it is, and I would be glad to hear how far it will discourage."

Indeed, by now many of the Leyden congregation gravely doubted that God was directing them to the New World. Even if He were, their situation in Leyden seemed preferable to tropical plague in Guiana, savages in Virginia, or tempest on the high seas. More and more grew reticent, and some withdrew.

Then came a surprising apparent breakthrough. Taking the advice of friends in London to hide their identity, Cushman secured a patent for land between the Delaware and Hudson rivers in the name of John Wincomb, a "forward" preacher who served the household of Elizabeth de Clinton, Duchess of Lincoln. Yet Wincomb suddenly changed his mind and allowed the patent to lapse.

As the Leydeners' spirits flagged again, another surprising offer arose from an unexpected quarter. The New Netherlands Company, inspired by "a preacher well-versed in the Dutch language who expected to entice over four hundred families to join their expedition," agreed to settle a colony at the Company's trading post on the Hudson. The Company offered to provide free transportation and cattle for each family, freedom of religious practice as they had in Leyden, and two warships to protect the colonists en route and during settlement from violence from other "potentates," namely King James. At long last, this offer seemed to be the answer to their prayers.

"What do you think, Bridget?" Robinson asked his wife.

"Perhaps it is our Lord's answer at last," she replied. "Except...we will be pledged as citizens to another country. We cannot maintain our English heritage."

"Aye, my first thought. Perhaps the Lord means to broaden our experience. There are no nations in His Kingdom."

Bridget frowned. "But here we are natives of another country. We have learned that well enough."

Robinson reflected awhile. Throughout this venture, breaking ties to England had always been the keenest loss to bear. In each person's heart hope still flickered that a venture into the wilderness might at least afford the comfort of English administration. And yet, could they expect less oppression in a new English colony than they had endured in their homeland? Robinson decided, "We shall put it before the people to consider once again."

The Netherlands connection provoked much discussion and argument among the people. As the Robinsons had guessed, the issue of Dutch alliance was the major hindrance to accepting the offer. Samuel Fuller, always among the most steadfast and patient of their group, pleaded, "Wait a bit, good people. God is with us. He will sort it out."

One man apparently sent to help "sort it out" was a newcomer to the congregation, an English soldier who had served the Dutch against the Spanish. He appeared at Robinson's door one day, a short, ramrod-straight figure whose speech was as terse as his stature. He wasted no time on amenities. "Mr. Robinson, sir, I am very much interested in your venture to the Americas."

"And so, Mister Standish?"

"Captain Standish, sir."

"Captain. Do you have it in mind to join our expedition?"

"I do, sir, if it pleases you. Yet I am not a member of your group."

"So I am well aware, sir. Yet we rejoice that you worship with us."

"I am Catholic, sir, and will remain so until death. I mean no offence to you, but want to make my position clear."

Robinson smiled. "Sir, we welcome all true believers, whatever their manner of worship. Of course, you realize that we hope to 'convert' you to our ways."

"I do, sir. That is why I make clear my affiliation. Yet I see no reason why this difference should hinder your mission. We believe in the same Saviour, and I believe my experience will stand you in good stead in the colony."

Robinson sat back leisurely. "Then tell me, friend, how can we help you?"

Standish told Robinson that he had been drawn to the Leyden meeting by the reputation of its people frequently commended by local Dutch merchants and citizens. As a military man devoted to the service of his country, he believed that he and the Leyden group held in common the virtues of loyalty, honesty, and diligence as the core of their character. He had served the English army during the Spanish oppression of Holland, and his observations of Spanish cruelty to Dutch "heretics" had not only confirmed his loyalty to England but reinforced his faith in the gentle Saviour who came to free men, not to enslave them.

Robinson said, "You astonish me, sir. Yet I rejoice that you wish to join us. I do not doubt that we will need military guidance in our 'wilderness.'"

"Yet I see that your venture is far from assured, Mr. Robinson. I simply want to make plain my intention to accompany you when that is accomplished."

"You have my heartfelt gratitude, Captain Standish. I do value any firm support the Lord offers me."

Suddenly, amidst the turmoil of doubt in their mission, a Mr. Thomas Weston from London appeared at the Green Gate with a startling pronouncement. "Ye can expect nothing from the Virginia Company," he announced flatly. "They're insolvent and split within themselves, soon to be bankrupt."

"We suspected that, sir," said Robinson. "We are currently considering an offer from the New Netherlands Company. A fine, generous offer."

"Which will force ye to raise your progeny as Dutchmen. Have ye thought of that? Ye might as well stay here in Leyden."

Weston had touched the raw nerve. Deacon Fuller fixed the merchant with his piercing physician's eye as if assessing a patient. "Have ye something better to propose, Mr. Weston?"

An ironmonger by trade but a born entrepreneur, Weston saw in this small group an opportunity for both adventure and profit. A colony of impoverished but religiously motivated, industrious workers desperate for any means to establish their way of life was exactly the sort of enterprise that promised stable profits. Unlike colonists seeking only material gain, this group was driven by high principle, moral integrity, and willingness to endure deprivation for the good of the community. To an investor, men such as these and their families were prospects most likely to establish profitable trading posts in the New World.

Intense discussion resumed at Leyden. The primary appeal of Weston's proposal was the backing of English investors in an area under English jurisdiction. He urged them to go as soon as possible, promising that they should "neither fear want of shipping nor money." The principals soon drew up a contract of conditions mutually agreeable to all parties, and Weston returned to London at once to set about recruiting investors willing to underwrite the project. In Leyden, energized by renewed hope, those intending to go began busily to make preparations. No one imagined that the following weeks would be marked by radical changes, sharp disagreements, wrangling, and even bitterness among their own people.

Weston convinced his investors with praise for the brethren at Leyden. He told them that the group was "as industrious and frugal as any company of people in the world...well weaned from the delicate milk of our mother country...not as with other men, whom small things can discourage, or small discontentments cause to wish themselves at home again."

It was decided that only the youngest, strongest, and most eager would undertake this initial venture, and the majority would follow. Robinson would stay with the larger group and Elder Brewster would accompany the colonists, and all would be considered one body and

184

members of the same church. If the expedition failed, the Leyden congregation would help the colonists to return to the Lowlands.

Meanwhile, the Adventurers in London, who had little interest in the colonists' religious convictions or general welfare, reconsidered their financial positions. They deleted two clauses of special interest to the congregation: Houses, and lands improved, especially gardens and home lots, would not belong to the colonists as originally agreed but should remain undivided wholly to the planters at the end of seven years. Accordingly, the colonists would not be allowed two days a week for their own private enterprise. The Leydeners were incensed. Not to be allowed two days to develop their own resources, and not to claim any part of their labor or possessions after seven years' struggle was an insult more fit for "thieves and bondslaves than honest men."

So began weeks of wrangling and dissension between the Adventurers and the sojourners who sharply criticized Cushman for agreeing to the altered terms without support from the home group. He and Carver had been charged only to deliver the draft of the articles of government to London, there to receive moneys and make provisions both for shipping and other necessities for the journey. Cushman insisted he had saved the project from "shipwreck." Unless he agreed to the new terms, some investors threatened to withdraw their money. What other course could he have taken? Did they think he had no brains?

The elders jointly replied he might have better exercised his brains than to submit to such rash terms. Even Robinson chastized him. He wrote Carver that Cushman was "a good man, and of special abilities in his kind, yet most unfit to deal for other men."

Bridget was appalled by these harsh exchanges among the leaders. "Robert is one with us, John. Surely you cannot think he meant to betray us."

"In matters of business, my dear, one must stand fast on his principles, or be overcome by opponents. Our Adventurers care much more for their money than our mission."

Bridget retorted crisply, "What would you expect? They are *investors.*"

Cushman defended his action sharply. "If we will not go, they are content to keep their moneys. Our purpose of good and fair houses is not our primary mission. Our purpose is to build for the present such houses as we may with little grief set afire and run away by the light; our riches shall employ them to provide more men, ships, munitions, etc. You may see it among the best politics that a commonweal is readier to ebb than to flow when once fine houses and gay clothes come in." The colonists raised their brows at this defense, thinking it at best a lame excuse.

The Virginia Company, split by insolvency, now petitioned the Crown to obtain clear and undisputed title to the northern half of the original Virginia grant and to rename it "New England." And Weston insisted that the Leyden company establish in this area because no Anglican Church dominated there, and greater profit could be made by the fishing found in that country.

On both sides the project languished in serious jeopardy. Weary of the colonists' carping, Weston almost abandoned the venture himself, relenting only because his friends would lose all their money. Just as weary in Leyden, Robinson informed Carver in Southampton that, "You do thoroughly understand by our general letters the estate of things here, which indeed is very pitiful, especially by want of shipping and not seeing means likely, much less certain, of having it provided." Several of the Leyden investors would not commit their moneys until shipping was guaranteed, leading Robinson to lament, "Neither do I think there is a man here would pay anything, if he had again his money in his purse."

So many withdrew at this point that not enough Leydeners were willing to go to maintain the minimum strength needed to settle a colony in the wilderness. Some suggested that they invite members of Ainsworth's church in Amsterdam and remnants of the Brethren to join their venture. Cushman commented, "I had thought that they would as soon have gone to Rome as with us, for our liberty is to them as rat's bane, and their rigor as bad to us as the Spanish Inquisition."

While the colonists fretted, the Merchants, fearful that all would be lost, took a drastic step and opened the venture to Londoners willing to settle the New World without religious or moral motivation. They chose a third agent, Christopher Martin, to represent these "strangers" in organizing the venture. Martin's attitude was high-handed and dictatorial and only antagonized the two agents and Weston by scorning their advice and buying supplies where he pleased. Weston lost patience, refused to give them any more money, and declared that this venture would never get underway with three agents "going up and down, wrangling and expostulating."

Cushman lamented that "there is fallen amongst us a flat schism."

Throughout this turmoil, those devoted to the expedition held fast, believing that eventually God would provide the proper means to their end. After all, their motives were pure and their mission holy. Would not the Devil do his best to hinder them?

William Bradford was among those so committed. One day as he paced the kitchen floor denouncing the rank hypocrisy of men, he was brought up short by Dorothy's sudden burst of tears. Surprised, he went to her and gathered her into his arms. "Ah, forgive me, pet. It is sinful of me to rail on so. Sometimes I cannot abide the deceit, the duplicity of men, and vent hostile words. I *am* sorry."

Dorothy sobbed on, inconsolable, as if within her a dam had broken. It dawned on him slowly that his words, though shameful, were not at the heart of her distress. "What is it, my dear? What troubles you?"

She gasped out, "'Tis not what you have said. 'Tis what you will *do.*"

He was mystified. "Do?"

She flung herself from his arms. "You will go on this voyage, however it is done, whether well or ill. And you will drag John and me along." She whirled to cast him a furious glare. *"And I do not want to go!"*

He stood a moment, struck. "You do not want to go...to Virginia?"

"Oh, dear Heaven," she wailed. "Canst ye not see? 'Tis a hopeless venture. All things go wrong. How can ye believe it is God's will for us to leave Leyden?" She bit her tongue, too late to hold back the unspeakable words that had choked her all these months. Was she the only woman in this congregation to speak out?

Bradford stared at his wife, for the first time perceiving her deep despair. He had thought her apathy had come from so many keen disappointments. He had observed that women were not by nature adventurers, were always more distressed than men by change, indecision, uprooting of the home nest. His courtship of Dorothy, to entice her from her comfortable home in Amsterdam, had taken all the tact and promise he could muster. Yet he had made good all his promises of a good life with him. Now she was revealing a bitter, hidden resentment. He said at last, lamely, "I thought you wanted to go," knowing the moment he heard his words that he had been certain of no such thing.

"Never," she moaned. *"Never!"*

He waited awhile, knowing that since this impasse had reared its ugly head, they could not ignore it. It was already summer. Their journey must begin soon if they would cross the sea and establish shelter before winter. He took her hand and sat her down on the settee. "Dorothy, you know well why we decided to go. We cannot stay here in Leyden."

"Why not?" she flung back. "Why not? You have a good business here. We have done well. Why must we leave?"

"Because..." What more could he say that had not been said many times over? Every argument for or against the venture had been aired to exhaustion. Each member of the congregation was well aware of the dangers looming over Holland. True, some could not find the courage to break away from the relative comfort of this city. Yet most believed that to find another home in the New World was their only hope of survival as a community.

She said in a leaden voice, "I will never see my family again. They will never see John grow up."

"No, no," he countered eagerly. "They will join us. As soon as we are well settled, we will come back to visit. Have faith, Dorothy. God does not send us out to die but to live!"

Dorothy shook her head. The pent-up tempest in her breast was spent. And in its place a frail hope arose again, not that the voyage would be accomplished, but that God would allow it to fail.

The strongest barrier now to the voyage was the sum of a mere four hundred pounds sterling. Cushman complained that for 150 persons there could not be found more than 1200 pounds and odd monies, some cloth, stockings, and shoes. Some other monies must come from somewhere.

Realizing the voyage must begin now or never, the Adventurers chartered the *Mayflower*, "a fine ship" of 180 tons, and a pilot, one Mr. Clarke, who had gone to Virginia the year before. The colonists bought a smaller ship of sixty tons, the *Speedwell*, which would convey part of the group across the seas and stay with the colonists' company to be available for fishing and other uses as needed. Yet the *Speedwell* needed a larger mast and new sail—expensive but essential repairs. Much was still unresolved, supplies were woefully short, and their dispute with Weston over terms had not been settled. Yet each person knew that if they were going at all, they must go now in mid-summer of the year 1620.

Bradford mustered his courage and told Dorothy, "We can delay no longer, my love."

She sat quietly watching little John on the floor and did not raise her head to look at him. Little John sat stacking blocks, now and then glancing from one parent to the other. Bradford walked over to Dorothy and lifted her chin. "Are you with me?"

Dorothy swallowed. "I have thought...could we not wait and go on the second trip? John will be older and..."

He shook his head. "No, Dorothy, I am called to go with the youngest, the hardiest. We will need the strongest hands to build shelter, plant gardens. And I will need you with me."

She glanced away, then back at him with flashing eyes. "Then we must leave John with my family in Amsterdam. He is too young to face such danger. I refuse to take him with us." Her eyes squinted with steady resolve.

Bradford's heart sank. Some families were leaving their young children behind, and some were separating, husbands going without wives and older children, taking only servants. Perhaps it was best to leave the weakest behind. Yet to leave this dear son, his only blood relative, was a wrenching choice. Years may pass—he dreaded to think of it—before they could reunite. He sent up a quick prayer, the same he had prayed so often before: *Lord, what shall I do?*

Dorothy's voice broke the silence. "I will not take him with us."

Was that His answer? He waited. So be it. "All right, Dorothy, I will agree to leave him here. But I will not leave you."

She thought suddenly, she could simply refuse to go. He would not dare to carry her kicking and screaming aboard the ship. Yet she had been well-schooled in wifely obedience. God would honor her decision to abandon her child for his best welfare, but not to deprive her husband merely because she wished to. Obviously, her arguments with God about their family's welfare did not coincide with William's. She said through clenched lips. "All right, William. If John stays here, I will go with you."

He nodded as if resigned. Yet she knew she must go before the Lord and beg forgiveness. For bitterness in her heart would give room to the Enemy, who would use it to find new ways to curse this voyage.

Bradford saw her pursed lips and suddenly remembered Rigsby weeping on the quay at Boston. Mr. Brewster had advised him to stay home with his wife. Would he now advise him to stay with Dorothy? Mr. Brewster was hiding from the King's men somewhere in England. As soon as he returned, William must seek his advice.

Bridget and her sister Catherine visited Mary Brewster. "Have you any word from William?" asked Bridget.

"None. But Robert sent word that 'Mr. B.' might be in the north of England. He knew not for sure. Perhaps he means to meet us in London." Mary would take her two sons, Wrestling and Love, six and nine years old, but leave behind her two daughters, Fear and Patience, and her son Jonathan, who had not recovered from the recent loss of his wife and only child. She missed her husband's counsel desperately.

Bridget said, "William has asked me to keep John."

Mary and Catherine exclaimed together, "Does Dorothy know?"

"I know not. Dorothy would have him stay with his grandparents in Amsterdam, but William is wary of that connection. We promised we will take John to visit them often. It is the least we can do for her, dear girl." Bridget bit her lip. "How miserable she is."

Catherine frowned. "Perhaps it is best she not know you will keep him."

"I begged John to tell William to leave her behind. She is not well with this venture. But John says that William is committed to the voyage and will not go without her."

"My sisters, let us pray God that we do the right thing in His sight. There is little joy among us for this voyage."

Fifteen

Departure

The moment came when the tide had to turn. The day of departure was at hand. Dissension and disappointment had to be set aside to make final preparations for the journey. Robinson proclaimed a day of humiliation before the Lord and gathered his flock together. He told them in a firm voice, "I charge you before God and His blessed Angels to follow me no further than I follow Christ, and if God shall reveal anything to you by any other instrument of His, be as ready to receive it as ever you were to receive any truth by my ministry." He urged them to be alert for new light to come from the Gospel, for "it is not possible the Christian world should come so lately out of such thick antichristian darkness...that the full perfection of knowledge should break through at once."

Amid copious tears, song, and professions of devotion, those staying behind in Leyden celebrated a feast for the voyagers. To the younger ones born and matured in Leyden, that "goodly and pleasant" city was a dearer home than England. Some reluctant ones, like Dorothy Bradford, tried desperately to lift their fears to Heaven, praying for courage and the faith to endure unknown trials to come.

The voyagers and their well-wishers in two canal boats left Leyden from the Nuns Bridge on the Rapenburg at sunrise on July 21, bound for Delfthaven fourteen miles south. They traveled along the Vliet and the Schie on canals so full they ran level with lush green fields abundant with tulips, grazing cattle, elaborately fretted and decorated farmhouses, white shell walkways, and gardens, the bounty of Holland. Even the stoutest hearts suffered pangs of profound grief to be leaving this rich countryside, appearing so peaceful and calm.

As they approached the quay at Delft they saw awaiting them the

Speedwell, a trim sixty-ton pinnace fitted out in her new rigging. She would be their workhorse in the New World, providing their chief means of livelihood—fishing for the plentiful cod offshore—and also their lifeline between their new colony and England.

The party feasted into the night, with only some children sleeping. As the dawn light rose, though, tears were shed and expressions of anguish revealed, for the unspoken dread that few would see each other again in this world. Robinson fell to his knees, his congregation following, to pronounce a final blessing. Then the voyagers filed up the gangway.

One most piercing farewell was the Bradfords'. As his parents boarded the ship, little John, held in Bridget Robinson's arms on the quay, stretched out his arms toward them with a shriek as if to protest that they had forgotten him. Then, suddenly realizing they were going without him, he gave way to anguished wails, twisting in Bridget's arms to be let down. Standing on deck, Dorothy drooped as if she would faint. William held her tightly while the wind lifted the *Speedwell's* bright new sails and moved her slowly out into the canal. John's cries lifted on the breeze, a frantic sound echoing in every voyager's tormented heart.

The sailors fired a salvo from her cannon that was answered by a blast of small-arms fire from the onlookers ashore. As the smoke cleared, in salute to their shared community, all persons ashore and aboard ship raised their arms toward each other in a final farewell gesture, and with one accord lifted their hands toward Heaven. Years later Bradford wrote of this parting:

> So they left that goodly and pleasant city which had been their resting-place near twelve years; but they knew they were pilgrims, and looked not much on those things, but lifted up their eyes to the heavens, their dearest country, and quieted their spirits.

A prosperous wind carried them past the hook of Holland and out into the North Sea, bound for Dover and Southampton, flying the white and red-crossed flag of St. George at the stern and the Union Jack at the masthead. Most passengers were too blinded by tears to notice that in this moderate breeze the *Speedwell* heeled over too far and shipped water. But Captain Reynolds and his crew, while pleased with their rapid progress, keenly noted her strange behavior.

Now it was time for those aboard, having wrenched themselves from Leyden, to reflect on the voyage facing them. Only a small part of the congregation had finally chosen to go. Forty-six adults, including sixteen men, eleven women, and nineteen children comprised the Leyden company aboard the *Speedwell*. John Carver, William Brewster, and Robert Cushman were expected to join them at Southampton, where the *Mayflower* waited with additional colonists recruited by Weston. These the Leydeners thought of as "strangers," English countrymen Anglican or Catholic, but not of their congregation of "saints" according to the biblical definition—those committed to follow Jesus of Nazareth as Saviour and Son of God.

At Southampton the *Mayflower* bobbed at her dock taking on supplies. The long-standing dissension among agents Cushman, Carver, and Martin had not diminished. Cushman complained that Martin obstinately refused to make any accounting to anyone else, thus forcing each agent to operate on his own without mutual consultation, which caused wasteful duplication and expenditure.

Much irritated by this arrogance, yet with no authority to interfere, Bradford longed for Brewster to reappear and put in his place this presumptuous puritan, Martin, who usurped command and dominated their expedition. Bradford had noted one sturdy, red-haired fellow who appeared capable of taking charge, a Captain Myles Standish, who had joined the Leyden group only recently, and whose military bearing suggested he would not suffer imperious tyrants easily. Bradford had not had time to develop a friendship with this man in Leyden, and now with characteristic confidence, he introduced himself. "Sir, I am interested in why you joined this venture. You do not appear to be a typical colonist."

Standish eyed him coolly. "And who, pray, is a typical colonist?"

Bradford grinned. "Methinks a yeoman or planter, perhaps a tradesman or craftsman."

"I am none of these. I am a soldier."

"Your bearing testifies to that, sir. Do you expect to fight in the

New World?"

Standish hesitated, taking Bradford's measure, obviously a bold yet amiable young man, not so much presumptuous as curious. "God forbid, lad. I am weary of war, weary of strife among nations and peoples. I long for a quiet life, perhaps even a prosperous one, as the Lord provides."

Bradford smiled brightly. "As do we all, sir. So, if I may ask your opinion, if this party seeks community, how is it that this Mr. Martin takes so high-handed a position with the rest of us?"

Standish smiled wryly. "I am merely a passenger, sir, not appointed to authority." He glanced about. "Where is your leader?"

"Our Pastor remains behind in Leyden, sir, with our larger congregation, and our Elder has not yet arrived. When he does, he will set things right."

Standish bowed his head slightly. "Then I, too, shall welcome his appearance."

Bradford was thinking that this Captain Standish seemed forthright enough but might be a disguised agent of the King. Brewster had been in hiding for weeks, and may still be in jeopardy. He decided that he dare not reveal anything to anyone of Brewster.

As the two groups made tentative acquaintance aboard ship, Mr. Thomas Weston suddenly appeared on the quay and marched up the *Speedwell's* gangway with a brisk and determined air. As he came aboard, Deacon Fuller, and the Misters Winslow, Cooke, and Allerton came forward to speak for their absent leaders, Brewster and Robinson, and greeted him amiably.

Weston merely nodded and announced, "I will not sanction your departure until we have settled this business between us. You must agree to our terms."

Deacon Fuller replied calmly, "We regret that Mr. Cushman acceded to your terms without our consent, Mr. Weston. We have not changed our minds."

Weston seemed to hold his breath, glancing from one man to another while his cheeks blazed red. "Does he speak for all of you?"

They nodded.

He scowled. "By God and the King, then I will advance thee not one more penny. Henceforth, ye will stand on your own legs." He whirled about, strode to the gangway, and stomped down to the dock. There he stopped, stood defiantly glaring at the group, and shouted. "Not one more penny. Do ye hear me?"

All four men nodded assent, and answered nothing. Winslow even gave him a friendly smile. Weston charged across the quay and departed for London. Now the four leaders gathered the colonists together on the main deck to take stock of their dismal situation. They were desperately short of funds, and worse, they faced another delay of departure, which greatly increased their risk of seasonal storms at sea. Almost certainly now they would not arrive in the New World before winter. How to make the best of this precarious situation?

They went into an interlude of prayer. Then each in turn spoke his opinion. No lightning wisdom had struck anyone's head. So after a discussion, Dr. Fuller suggested they make one final plea to the Adventurers, to which all readily agreed. Winslow wrote a congenial letter, expressing hope for profit for their investors as well as themselves, but would not concede that all material goods they might attain in seven years be equally divided among the investors. They promised, however, that if the Adventurers were not satisfied with profits after the seven-year limit, they would agree to extend their terms beyond it.

Winslow wrote:

We are in such a strait at present, as we are forced to sell away sixty pounds' worth of our provisions to clear the Haven, and withal to put ourselves upon great extremities, scarce having any butter, no oil, not a sole to mend a shoe, nor every man a sword to his side, wanting many muskets, such armour, etc. And yet we are willing to expose ourselves to such eminent dangers as are like to ensue, and trust to the good providence of God, rather than His name and truth should be evil spoken of, for us.

Almost all the colonists signed this letter dated August 3, 1620.

The day set for departure, Bradford arose before sunrise to stretch on deck, and leaning upon the rail, saw a familiar figure approaching on the quay. He caught his breath, then dashed to the gangway to greet him. "Mr. Brewster, thank God you are here at last!"

They clasped hands. "William, lad. How goes it here?"

"Oh, sir," Bradford began, then caught himself. "Many troubles, sir, but now you are here, you can put all to rights straightaway."

"First, lad, where is my wife?"

"Belowdecks, sir. Comfort is hard to come by, but we are doing our best."

At sight of her husband, Mary simply rushed into his arms and stood silently while their two sons clasped their arms about them chirping with joy. The sight heartened the company as well, so badly were they in need of encouragement.

The next day a letter arrived from John Robinson, cheering them more.

...first, you are many of you strangers...to the infirmities one of another, and so stand in need of more watchfulness this way, lest when such things fall out in men and women as you suspected not, you be inordinately affected with them; which doth require at your hands much wisdom and charity...your intended course...will minister continual occasion of offense and will be as fuel for that fire, except you diligently quench it with brotherly forbearance...And as men are careful not to have a new house shaken with any violence before it be well settled and the parts firmly knit, so be you, I beseech you, brethren, much more careful that the house of God which you are and are to be, be not shaken with unnecessary novelties or other oppositions at the first settling thereof. Lastly, whereas you are become a body politic, using among yourselves civil government, and are not furnished with any persons of special eminency above the rest, to be chosen by you into office of government; let your wisdom and godliness appear, not only in choosing such persons as do entirely love and will promote the common good, but also in yielding unto them all due honor and obedience in their lawful administration, not beholding in them the ordinariness of their persons but God's ordinance for your good...And this duty you may both the more willingly and ought the more conscionably to perform, because you are at least for the present to have only them for your ordinary governors, which yourselves shall make choice of for that work.

An unfeigned welwisher of your happy success in this hopeful voyage. John Robinson.

❧

Passengers were divided into two groups: Leydeners on the *Speedwell*, supervised by Cushman, and Londoners on the *Mayflower* under Martin. These two men were assigned to organize and store provisions, and allot space to families. The two ships departed that day on a fair wind, yet had hardly cleared land when Captain Reynolds of the *Speedwell* hailed Captain Jones of the *Mayflower* to announce that his ship was leaking and should put in at Dartmouth to be searched and mended.

The saints' leaders considered this new problem. "What do you think, William?" asked Winslow of Brewster. "It cost us a sweet penny to refit her at Leyden. What could be wrong?"

"Methinks he finds much trouble about his ship," Brewster muttered.

"My thoughts exactly," charged Bradford. "But why?"

Fuller and Allerton agreed. "I heard him complain of her in the Channel," said Allerton. "That she seemed to be overmasted and prey to a brisk gale."

Brewster said, "The captain is supreme authority aboard his ship, lads. If he wills it, we have no choice but to go to Dartmouth."

❧

The women and children struggling to adjust to life belowdecks welcomed this respite ashore. Dartmouth was a charming village set among high Devon hills looking to sea through a narrow strait. The sun shone benignly, the wind blew softly, the hills glowed in high summer green dotted with sheep, a scene to strike each breast with intense nostalgia. Oh, that they could stop here and settle down, home at last!

Hovering over the leaders' sentiment, however, no less anguished than their passengers,' was a cloud of anxiety as each day's delay meant reduction of their valuable stores for the New World, and another day nearer winter.

Dorothy Bradford moved next to Mary Brewster at the rail. "Dear Mistress, will we have anything left to eat in our new home?"

Mary said soothingly, "God will provide for us, my dear. Have faith."

Have faith, have faith, have faith, ran Dorothy's thoughts like a ticking clock. Answers to all questions required only faith. She gazed at the Devon hills and nursed some comfort that her tiny son was safe in beautiful Leyden with Bridget Robinson. Yet her own heart felt heavy with guilt, though she would utter not a word of it, for she dared to hope that perhaps if God did not bless this voyage, that it would fail after all, and they could all go home.

๛

The *Speedwell* was pronounced sound, only some minor leaks needing repair, and again they departed English shores, this time no less wrenching than the first two. Then a hundred miles west of Land's End, Captain Reynolds proclaimed once again that his ship was leaking and they must put back to Plimoth for repairs.

"This is quite provoking," growled Winslow. "Do we sail a ship or a sieve?"

"Mr. Brewster, sir," asked Bradford, "I have seen them use the pumps below. Does that mean we are sinking, too?"

Brewster said, "Call our men together. We must address our captain."

They spoke with Captain Jones, who had already questioned Captain Reynolds. Reynolds agreed that the *Speedwell's* problems seemed mysterious, but he was adamant that only the pump running full tilt kept his ship afloat. He would not risk an Atlantic crossing facing autumn storms dependent only on the pump. He claimed that the ship suffered "general weakness," probably due to her faulty trim, which in heavy seas worked her timbers loose and popped leaks. As the colonists considered this dire news, Cushman spoke up to say he had seen on the *Speedwell* a board a man might have pulled off with his finger where the water came in as at a mole hole. "So," Brewster announced, "Reynolds is our captain. We have no recourse but to accept his account."

❧∽❦

At Plimoth, while the ship was inspected once again, the colonists enjoyed another respite, wandering about the quays and shops, talking with hospitable townspeople curious about their voyage. The weather was superb, brilliant with sunshine, cool airs, and a tranquil sea clear to the horizon. In such benign weather no one could imagine the menacing danger Captain Reynolds feared at sea. So during fourteen days' inspection the colonists enjoyed the company of countrymen who treated them royally, invited them to feast, and marveled at their courage. It was a respite almost heartening enough to sustain their voyage.

Yet one shopkeeper told Catherine Carver, "You are a brave lot, madam, to take off across this sea. It seems a great adventure, but for what, I ask ye? Can there be any land better than England?"

Catherine swallowed, then confided, "No, none. I wish we could stay."

"Then why do ye go?"

Catherine paused. Did she dare tell him the truth, that they were escaping the King's wrath? Colonists were leaving every day for foreign shores. "We have heard wondrous tales of the New World," she said. "We thought our fortunes might be made there." Her cheeks flushed.

"Ha!" he scoffed. "Savages and wild animals more like, so I've heard."

Catherine cringed, needing no reminders of her worst fears.

❧∽❦

The day came at last when Reynolds announced the unthinkable verdict: The *Speedwell* had indeed been overmasted at Leyden and simply was not seaworthy for the long Atlantic crossing. They must leave her behind. The company was confounded. Surely it was not possible to crowd both ships' passengers on the *Mayflower* alone. Yet Reynolds left them no choice.

They consulted Captain Jones, who told them gravely, "He thinks his ship insufficient. No competent captain will take a ship to sea under such conviction."

"Dare I ask a mundane question?" asked Isaac Allerton, who had brought his whole family along—a wife and three children.

"Ask," said Brewster grimly.

"We spent hard money for the *Speedwell.* Is she a complete loss?"

Brewster sighed. "Isaac, bear with us. Whatever Reynolds' motives may be, our dilemma now is not to regret our monies, but how to crowd so many of us on one ship. Either we plunge ahead and make our voyage, or abandon it entirely. How say you, friends?"

The choice proved overwhelming to twenty passengers who decided to abandon the venture and return with the *Speedwell* to London. Among these was miserable Robert Cushman, demoralized by the events of the past weeks. "If ever we make a plantation, God works a miracle," he muttered morosely.

Dorothy Bradford pleaded with William. "Did I not tell ye 'tis hopeless? How much more must we endure?"

"Dorothy, I cannot abandon this voyage."

"Yet you abandon your son."

"You know my heart, wife. May God forgive you those bitter words."

"God knows I speak honestly, Will, as some others do not, for all their noble claims. I would go back myself, if I could live without charity."

"Which ye cannot. You agreed you would come with me, Dorothy, if I left John behind. Must we suffer this schism forever?"

They poised on pinnacles of opposition—she as adamant that the trip would fail as he was convinced it would not. No resolution of their difference was possible except that one submit to the other. And that obligation was Dorothy's. "Aye, we will suffer it," she answered with resignation. "Yet I have promised, and whether we fail or not, I will bear my cross."

Now the company aboard the *Mayflower* numbered 102 passengers, servants and hired men, and a crew of thirty. She was a "sweet ship," having absorbed spillage into her timbers of cargoes of wine and cognac from the French coast, which gave her a pleasant fragrance and probably a hidden benefit no one thought of at the time, an antiseptic barrier against disease. Bradford learned from the crew that she measured ninety feet in length, twenty-one feet across her beam, about seventy-eight feet at her water line, and drafted thirteen feet. She was armed with cannon and steered by a whipstaff attached to her tiller. The crew was housed in the forecastle near the galley, and the captain and mates were quartered in the stern. The poor passengers were confined in the "'tween decks," an area hardly five feet high, where they slept on pallets within their allotted eighteen square feet per person. They were forbidden access to the galley and the crew's sanitary facilities, and certain other ship's quarters restricted to the captain or crew. They must prepare their own food on small portable stoves and manage bodily functions with the traditional bucket.

Their new company of strangers almost exactly matched the number of Leyden saints—seventeen men, nine women (ten from Leyden), and fourteen children. Eighteen servants and five hired men completed their company. One of these was John Alden, a cooper hired in Southampton to maintain the beer and water barrels, who would serve an indenture of one year. Of the original congregation from Scrooby only the Bradfords, the Brewsters with their two sons, and Francis Cooke were undertaking the voyage across the Atlantic. The Carvers had originally come from Sturton le Steeple near Scrooby, and William Butten, servant to Samuel Fuller, came from Austerfield, Bradford's home.

Now at last they were off. The remnant colony leaned on the rails of their newest home, the *Mayflower*, and gazed upon the green shores of Devon until sea mist blotted out their view like a curtain drawn upon their past. What agonies of homesickness roiled in their hearts could only be known by other voyagers leaving home for the last time.

Sixteen

A Weighty Voyage

The first few days past Land's End, Heaven blessed the *Mayflower* with perfect sailing weather, balmy late-summer skies bathed in golden sunlight and fresh with "a fine small gale." Soon drained of tears, the voyagers turned their attention to more pressing needs: the rudiments of daily living aboard ship, gaining "sea legs" on rolling decks, adjusting their bones to each person's tiny allotment of sleeping space 'tween decks, and most trying of all, the misery of relentless seasickness. The crew, a scruffy lot of thirty or more, added their bit to the passengers' discomfort by pouring mocking ridicule on their suffering. They seemed to relish insulting the voyagers' awkward groping about the tossing ship, and with especially malicious glee jeered the saints' prayer sessions.

Captain Christopher Jones, a rough, sea-weathered sailor given more to cool tolerance than cordiality, treated his passengers with constrained sympathy, yet required no such consideration for them from his men. The crew was bossed by an old boatswain whose technique for goading them to work was to spew streams of purient oaths upon them. His performance was matched in colorful variety by a massive young crewman, whose soaring curses burned the ears of saint and worldly stranger alike. Despite this harassment, the colonists tried bravely to accommodate each other, straining for patience and stamina to endure the long voyage ahead.

Nearly spent of her tears for little John, which still brimmed forth at unexpected moments, Dorothy Bradford watched Stephen Hopkins' wife, Elizabeth, swollen with child, and moaned. Judging by the woman's girth, the child would not wait until they reached shore, and Dorothy cringed at the thought of childbirth in such public circumstances. Even worse was the terrifying prospect of such intimate experience in the wilderness surrounded by savages. Yet Elizabeth seemed unperturbed as she busily cared for Giles, Constance, and Damaris, Stephen's three children by his first marriage, and stoically bore her burdens as if she were safely at home in her own house in England.

Dorothy longed to confide her misery to Elizabeth Winslow, or Susanna White, or even Priscilla Mullins, all young women like herself. Yet Elizabeth gaily looked forward to having a family in their new home, and the Whites, also expecting a child, had brought along their son Resolved, born the same year as John. Dorothy thought she might find a confidante in Priscilla, but hesitated to unduly discourage this young girl whose single state had not yet burdened her with the tribulations of wife and motherhood.

Her only consolation was little Resolved White, whom she tended with delight as some compensation for her John. Even Resolved, though, could not dispel her most insidious fear, that John would soon forget her and accept Bridget as his mother. Often she felt desperately alone, betrayed by her husband and abandoned by God.

Mary Brewster found her one day tucked behind a coiled hawser gasping with sobs. Mary said soothingly, "My dear child, what are you doing here on deck? You should be below."

"I canna' stand the stench down there, m'am. It makes me dreadful ill."

"I know, dear, I know. Yet we must be careful not to interfere with the crew's work on deck. It vexes them to have us underfoot."

Dorothy said tartly, "They despise us. They use any excuse to curse us!"

Mary patted Dorothy's head. "Remember, dear, they do manage the ship, which we cannot. We need make it no worse for them than we must."

Dorothy's heart shuddered. Why was she so different from other women who put their best face on all suffering and never complained? She had agreed to come with William, as a good wife should, but she could not be expected to enjoy it.

Mary must have glimpsed the despair on her face. "Dorothy, all of us longed to stay in Leyden, but it is dangerous for us there. Have faith, my child. The Lord will bless our new home."

Dorothy was too dispirited to answer. It seemed to her that the Lord had forgotten the entire company aboard the *Mayflower.*

As the days passed, the passengers tried their best to ignore the mysterious crawlers in their unwashed clothes, weevils in their food, rats skittering about their heads while they tried to sleep, and unmentionable human scents and discharges in the 'tween decks. The women and older girls dutifully trotted often to the rail to dump waste buckets. They could not wash clothes or bodies, and the perpetual seep of seawater down the *Mayflower's* glistening bulkheads, plus the chafing damp woolens against raw skin were poor substitutes for baths.

As the ship sailed westward, the weather grew colder and the sky cloudy, and the constant beating of the sea against her timbers worked open new leaks and heavier seepage. A diet of cold hard tack, wheat and pea-flour biscuits, dried fish pickled in brine, salt horse, Holland cheese, and beer provided little warmth against the north Atlantic's autumnal chill. While the crew were served hot meals from the galley cookstove, such luxury was denied the passengers. Captain Jones took no unncessary risks with fires aboard his ship. Occasionally, when their spirits were as frigid as their stomachs, they contrived a makeshift stove in a "hearth-box" of sand in which they laid an open fire and warmed some pea soup or a lobscouse, a thick stew dotted with chunks of salt meat. Kindly, Captain Jones seemed not to notice this infringement of his rules.

Since the *Speedwell* was abandoned, not least of the Leyden saints' discomforts was that their company was now composed of a majority of strangers, which required the saints to reassess their mission. The strangers recruited by the Adventurers primarily sought economic gain and were members of the Church of England by inheritance or custom rather than by conviction. One stranger, Myles Standish, was a devout Roman Catholic. The saints recognized that their mission to serve their Christian God living by biblical principles would have to accommodate major differences in worldview.

Perceivng that harmony was essential for their survival, Bradford undertook to promote good relations among the colonists. He attended to small comforts, checked stores, made sure rats and vermin did not devour meager supplies, and pressed John Alden, their cooper, to scrupulously monitor their casks of water and most precious beer. At home, Englishmen were well aware that their lakes and streams were conduits of rank sewage, and drank water only as a last resort.

Yet Bradford's vision extended beyond the company's immediate comfort. Mindful of Pastor Robinson's farewell letter advising that they form a "body politic," he knew that when they reached their destination and set up their habitation, the company must adopt some sort of governmental order. Under the terms of the Virginia patent they would be subject to English law, but they must also establish a local civic authority. He began to envision plans for governing their village, which would serve both saints and strangers equally. To his knowledge, this sort of self-government had never been done without inherited authority. Administered by men's selfish nature, was such a government possible? Would even his own godly people accept so radical a concept? Intrigued, he shared with Brewster his concerns for the new dynamics strangers had brought to their venture.

Brewster was pleased. "I commend your thinking, lad. I think you will find that all of us from Leyden are wondering what practical way we can reconcile differences among us, yet maintain control of our mission."

"Sir, we must stress that all opinions are welcome, but that we will not compromise our purpose." He grinned. "And remind them that we hold the patent!"

"I am thinking that we already have our model. We 'take it to the church.' We need to demonstrate this congenial and most practical method of reaching agreement. I cannot think that any stranger would disagree with that concept."

Brewster called a conference on the foredeck with Carver, Winslow, Allerton, Fuller, and Cooke, and allowed young Bradford to sit in. "Because we are now allied with strangers not committed to our mission, we need a system of government which will establish authority in the group rather than the individual."

Fuller said, "Foremost, each man may air his opinion freely without censure."

Winslow added, "We will choose elders and magistrates to represent us, and if we cannot agree, we entrust them to make final decisions."

Allerton asked, "What about Martin? He already considers himself 'governor.' And that chap Billington seems to resent any authority."

Brewster said, "Martin seems to consider the Adventurers our ultimate authority. We must convince him they are not. The body of our colony is our authority."

Bradford interjected with a grin, "And remind them that we hold the patent."

Cooke muttered, "Billington would trouble any authority."

John Carver spoke quietly, "We must ask for grace to hold firm to our purpose without dominating, and strive to create willing cooperation for the good of all."

The men murmured agreement. Carver added, "We beseech the Lord to inspire us."

Bradford eagerly told Dorothy of their plan. "Think of it! We are searching for a way to devise a body politic governed by consent of the people. This may be a milestone in men's, nay perhaps nations' affairs."

Distracted, Dorothy only sighed. "It sounds very noble, William."

Noting her sad face, he felt a rush of affection for this dear girl of whom he asked so much. So young, so vulnerable, so miserable, how could he expect her to share his vision for government when her very womanhood was being drained from her. God forgive him! Gazing into her pale face now, her girlish beauty dulled with sorrow, he realized how dreadful this enterprise was for the women. He put his arms about her. "Dority, my dear one, I know how much you miss John. I vow to make it up to you. Does it not ease your heart a bit to tend little Resolved?"

"I thank God for him, William, but he is not my own. I confess I am selfish. I should be grateful John is in Leyden. These poor little ones are so restricted belowdecks. Squeezed among us all, they cannot run and play freely."

"Ah, but when we do reach shore, they will have a continent to roam!"

Dorothy's face crumpled. How like William to see only the future, rarely the present. Yet she bit back the threatening tears and sighed. "Oh, I do miss him so!"

William took her to their narrow bed provided with a token of privacy by some hanging blankets, hoping for some solace for both of them there. He whispered in her ear, "It will not be long, Dority. He shall join us next year, I promise." *May God help me to keep that vow,* he said to the creaking deck above their heads.

"I pray God so, William. I do pray so."

❧

The gales freshened daily now, sweeping down from the northern seas, tossing waves higher than any land-bound countrymen had yet seen. The *Mayflower's* slippery decks rolled from starboard to port and bow to stern, making footing especially hazardous for children and the two dogs, John Goodman's mastiff and a spaniel allowed on deck only for "necessities." Some blustery days Captain Jones confined everyone belowdecks except the working crew on duty.

Francis Billington, sturdy younger son of John and Ellen Billington, was given the necessary task of "walking" the mastiff under the watchful eye of one of the saints. He relished the chance to go topside for fresh air, and took his task seriously. Mindful of the tilting deck, he held the mastiff's leash tightly as the dog scuffled and sniffed along the deck for a proper spot to relieve itself. But this day Francis was distracted by the lookout descending from the swaying crow's nest far above his head, and paused to admire the sailor's agility on the rigging. The sailor dropped deftly to the deck and eyed Francis watching him. "What ye gawkin' at, boy?" he growled. Francis swallowed, recognizing the sailor who so delighted in cursing the saints whenever possible.

"Yourself, sir," Francis replied politely. "Are ye not skeered way up there?"

"Skeered? Why the crow's the best watch on the ship, lad. Ye can see all the way to Greenland." The boy's frank admiration popped a sudden malicious thought into the sailor's head—how he might give these glib-gabbety, puke-stocking landlubbers a good jolt. He glanced about, noting that the day's watchman, Stephen Hopkins, stood on the poop deck engaged in conversation with the helmsman. He winked at Francis slyly. "Want to try it?"

Francis drew a breath. "We-el..." He eyed the distant lookout stroking the sky. It would be a grand feat if he could climb aloft and see Greenland. He glanced into the sailor's shifty eyes. "Are ye sure 'tis safe?"

"Safe as your mother's lovin' arms, boy. C'mon, I'll take ye up." He clapped a hand on Francis' shoulder and shoved him toward the rigging, figuring if he rushed the boy up quickly, Hopkins could not move fast enough to stop him. That would give the lubbers a start.

But the mastiff caught sight of the sailor's rough gesture and leaped to defend Francis. At that precise moment the deck tilted abruptly to starboard. The dog slammed into both the sailor and the boy, sending all three skittering across the deck. Terrified, the dog bared its teeth at the sailor, who nimbly sprang aside and snatched a belaying pin to ward off attack, cursing the dog in high voice.

Scrambling to regain hold of the dog's leash, Francis cried out, "No! No! Don't hurt him! Don't hurt him!"

Hearing the ruckus, Hopkins leaped down to the main deck, snatched the leash from Francis, and yanked the dog clear of the sailor's slashing weapon. Spewing a volley of curses, the sailor thundered vows to smash the dog, the boy, Stephen, and anyone else his pin might reach. The helmsman, First Mate John Clark, bellowed orders that all interlopers go below—at once.

Thereafter, both dogs and passengers were allowed on deck only under strict watch, and the entire company's isolation belowdecks was enforced. Any colonist allowed on deck with permission still had to withstand not only the resentful eyes of the crew but that sailor's malice loudly voiced. He declared that he hoped to cast half the lot of colonists overboard before they reached shore. The captain made no apparent effort to restrain him, leading the colonists to conclude, generously, that his motive was to insure that no such incident happened again.

Then, soon after this incident, passengers and crew were astonished when that robust young sailor took violently ill and in only a few hours died as he had lived, cursing and raving "in a desperate manner," so Bradford recounted. His companions were shocked by his sudden demise, which defied all logic.

Francis asked his father thoughtfully, "Why did he die so suddenly, him so strong and all?"

"I know not, boy."

"Maybe because he cursed me and the dog?"

"He cursed us all. You no more than others."

"The dog shamed him that day, knocking him down."

"Do not trouble yourself, lad. He is gone, and good riddance."

Bradford put it simply as "the just hand of God upon him," which Francis considered seriously. For a while he mourned the sailor's sudden death, mostly because he did not get to climb to the crow's nest. Yet gradually it dawned on him that perhaps God had intervened and used the dog to save him from the sailor's evil intent, perhaps even his own watery death. Surely the hand of God *was* sometimes a mystery.

But now the company noted that the deeply superstitious crew began to display, if not quite courtesy, some deference to their psalm-singing guests who apparently enjoyed some sort of direct line to the Almighty. Therefore, these lubbers may be deserving of at least a distant but reverent respect.

The days wore on relentlessly with nothing to alter the tedium of cold food, wet clothing, fitful sleep, and indifferent, tossing seas. Then, one gray morning, Francis Billington, bored and restless in confinement, slipped topside, hoping no one would send him below, and was surprised when no one noticed him at all. The crew seemed preoccupied with their work, not shouting and cursing as usual, and, he noted, kept glancing at the dark western horizon. Yet under the ship the sea ran smoothly, quietly rising and falling in long easy swells. Curious, Francis watched awhile, then boldly approached the first mate, John Clark, looking out from the poop deck. Having learned to show proper respect to seaman of rank, Francis asked politely, "Sir, why are the crew so quiet?"

Clark was gazing intently westward, his eyes narrowed, his mouth grim. He did not answer at once, then nodded westward. "Look there, boy."

The dark sky was rapidly deepening to a deep purple hue, almost black, stretching thickly along the length of the horizon. "Look at that sea," Clark muttered, pointing beyond the bow.

The surface of the sea ran toward the ship like molten slate in long, smooth swells steadily rising and falling, lifting the ship's bow, then sliding under her stern in an easy measured motion, more pleasant, Francis thought, than the usual churning chop slapping against the hull. He looked up at Clark's iron face, then back at the purple bank bloated against the horizon. Suddenly he understood. "Bad weather coming, sir?"

Clark bobbed his head in a brisk nod. "It is coming on to blow, lad."

Captain Jones suddenly appeared from his cabin and charged to the poop deck, bellowing orders to the crew. "All hands! All hands! Up, up, you gobbets, you abbey-lubbers! Up, up!"

Francis ducked out of sight so not to miss the show. He would watch until they battened down the hatches, barring all from the deck except the captain and the helmsman. Jones' voice harried the crew scrambling over the decks and swarming up the rigging, their footwork quick and sure as flies' feet walking up a wall. Francis gasped as they spread out along the swinging yardarms to lash the sails, balanced delicately on ropes running the length of the yards. How wonderful, he marveled, if he could do that!

The purple cloud bank seemed to expand as it advanced toward the ship, and now a high keening wind began to shear foam off the tops of looming swells parading higher and steeper toward the bow.

Clark suddenly spied the boy and bellowed, "Get below!" His look was steel, brooking no argument. Francis took one last look at the ship's bow rising up a gray cliff streaming foam, then glanced back to glimpse the poop deep in the trough behind the wave gone before, as if the *Mayflower* stood on her tail.

"Now!" Clark's arm slashed the air downward as his mouth formed the word silently in the wind. Francis shot down the main hatch to the first hold. Someone behind him slammed it shut.

The crowd confined there was packed together like smelt in a barrel, moving with the ship as she pitched and bucked on her course.

Wide-eyed children cowered in their parents' arms, many crying, some vomiting. By now most passengers had overcome their initial seasickness, but this wild motion aroused even seasoned stomachs. The people's faces shone like pale moons in the darkness, stricken mute with stark terror of calamity beyond imagination.

Underneath the keening wind they could hear a deep rumble in the lower holds, more terrifying than the wind's howl. What was it? It sounded as if a sea monster roared in the depths and drummed against the ship's timbers. Francis flung himself into his father's arms, his family and all the others clinging together. Saints and strangers alike cried out for God's mercy. "Save us, Lord! Save us, Lord!" Even the hardened sailors crouching below desks prayed, knowing in their bones that this was no ordinary blow.

Then the clap of doom itself sounded. A loud crack amidships racked the upper hold, sounding as if the ship had broken in two. Men and crew eased out of their niches and crawled up the gangways to see what had happened.

Amidships they found a beam had cracked, and in falling had dislodged the timbers of the upper deck. This break had surely weakened the ship's structure. John Alden and John Howland put their full weight under the beam but could not budge it. Someone was sent to fetch the captain, who sent down John Clark. "Cap'n can't leave the helm," Clark told them. "Takin' two men to hold her. What happened here?"

Half a dozen men strained under the beam trying to lift it back in place. It moved slightly but gave way if anyone moved position. The carpenter announced that the ship carried a spare beam stowed in the lower hold. Sloshing and stumbling, several of the crew plunged into the ship's depths, found it buried under boxes, dragged it up and secured it under the broken one. It too needed support to keep it in place.

The storm raged on, the ship yawed and strained, and each heart beat with the worst fear of all, that so weakened by this break, she might snap in two. Then Edward Winslow remembered that the screw of the colonists' printing press was stowed in the hold. He called out above the howling wind, "Our press screw! We could prop it under the beam and crank it up." The strength in that iron screw might be enough to bridge the break in the wooden beam. All agreed that anything, *anything*, was worth trying now.

Heaving and hauling, they dragged the screw up through two decks and rammed it in position under the two beams. The trick was to place it square on the break and wind it up to hold the beam in place.

It held firm. Everyone sighed with relief. Yet none dared think, let alone voice the scalding question: Would it last?

The crew grudgingly admitted the device was ingenious. What amazing luck these lubbers had brought it along! But some, loath to hazard their lives, did not think the jig would hold, and that the ship was unlikely to reach the New World. They wanted to turn about and return to England. Still others, reluctant to abandon the voyage and thereby forfeit their wages, figured that since it was as far to return as to proceed westward, the repair would hold as well one way as the other. Only the captain could decide.

Brewster and Carver made their way to the captain's cabin to put the matter before him. Carver said, "Sir, the beam holds now. But we are not sailors, and your crew is doubtful it will sustain. We need your opinion whether it can last."

Jones sorted out his options. His immediate priority was to keep his ship afloat. Where she might go from here demanded another decision. Ahead of them more storms like this one were sure to come out of the northern sea. Yet as they were now halfway between the New World and England, turning back was only slightly less perilous than proceeding forward. They could divert from course and seek safe harbor in Africa or the Canary Islands, but that would delay their voyage, perhaps all winter. They had no such provision for a sojourn that long.

Captain Jones looked these Englishmen in the eye. No, they were not sailors inured to the rigors of the sea, but he had noted their physical and spiritual mettle through the endless trials that had delayed this expedition and now exposed them to the grave danger of foundering. Hardworking English countrymen—not a gentleman among them—these people were used to serving authority, and on the *Mayflower* Captain Jones was supreme authority. It was his responsibility to decide their fate.

Since dependable John Clark manned the helm, Jones himself went down to the gun room to study the break. Then he sounded out his carpenter and crew for each man's assessment of the ship's stamina. Jones himself had brought her through other blows when he had had to jettison half her cargo. Now the carpenter vouched for her strength under water despite leaky timbers above and declared that the splintered deck could be caulked as soon as the storm abated. Jones sent for Carver and Brewster and told them the *Mayflower* was sound to proceed.

So they committed themselves to the will of God and resolved to proceed, Bradford would write years later. But now he told Dorothy eagerly, "The captain says we're seaworthy. That means 'tis God's will we go on."

In her secret misery Dorothy gave way to silent groans.

❧

The beam did hold through endless days dragging through howling wind and pounding seas when only crewmen were allowed on deck holding fast to lifelines. Belowdecks the passengers, who could hardly imagine anything worse, now found their situation intolerable. They were not allowed topside for fresh air, seawater ran down their necks and about their feet, their clothing was constantly clammy, and food brought up from sloshing holds was beginning to spoil. Biscuits were brittle as brick, cheese festooned with mold, butter rancid, their slimy water nauseating, their peas and grains littered with multiple unknown critters, and worst of all, their beer going sour.

Truly, had the Lord commanded them to make this voyage? Not only Dorothy Bradford bowed under terrifying doubts. Many others dreaded they had missed the Lord's will. The young were especially frustrated. Little ones dared not venture much beyond parents' arms. Young women, more stout of heart than body, and coping with complete lack of personal privacy, tried to console each other with humor. "Oh, my," moaned Susanna White. "I see now why *women* do not go to sea."

Elizabeth Winslow agreed. "Whose wonderful idea was this anyway? It must have been a man's. *We* must have been mad to agree to this voyage."

Dorothy smiled a wan smile but found no humor in any of it.

∾∾

Yet if misery could be measured, the young vigorous males suffered as much as the women but reacted more explosively. John Howland, servant to John Carver, had not been allowed topside since the midships beam split. One day, overcome with frustration, he burst through a hatch, pulled himself up on deck, and drew in a lungful of glorious fresh air. Heady with such exhilarating liquor, he gulped deep breaths, then suddenly found himself colliding with the rail as the deck lurched to port. He caught a glimpse of the horizon beyond the bow heaving with one gray sea after another rising steadily toward him. He thrust out for a hold somewhere, anywhere, and seized the sailors' lifeline along the gunwale.

John had learned a bit of elementary seamanship on this voyage: In high seas the helmsman must keep the ship headed into the wind to keep her from broaching, or rolled over broadside by a huge sea. He knew that the bow would emerge from under the mountain bearing down to flood her deck, so he need only grasp the line tightly as the water rushed by.

But suddenly a cross-wave rose high just beyond the port rail. His palms burned, grasping the rope while the avalanche smothered him in white water, wrenched his hands from the lifeline, and washed him across the deck and over the starboard rail in a froth of foam.

He thrashed for the lifeline no longer there, reaching for any kind of hold, but there was no deck under him, only roiling sea tumbling him over and over. All his glorious air gone now, he strove for the surface, gulping seawater, striving, driving until at last his head broke water. High above him the ship's main mast swung back and forth across the sky like the hand of a metronome. Impossible to board her! Then, miraculously, a dark line appeared before his eyes, stark, puzzling, what was it? A halyard dangling free from the topsail yard and trailing in the thrashing water!

Sea spray blinded him; the rope disappeared. Yet his groping hands somehow seized it and clung tightly, his palms burning. He hung on and on and on, swallowing seawater and sometimes air, his eyes fixed on the ship's hull yawing from one side to the other.

Dimly he saw crewmen aligned along the rail pulling at something he couldn't see. Then he felt a sharp jerk on his line—the seamen were drawing his halyard closer to the ship. Now he could look straight up at the men's faces looming at the rail. One sailor hung far out brandishing a boat hook. The next moment he felt another jerk, this time on his jacket, and at once he was caught up in the air flailing like a flounder, hauled over the rail, and dropped on the deck. He lay there coughing violently, gasping for that delicious air, too weak to move, all his strength spent holding that rope.

Crewmen swarmed over him, flipped him over, and pounded his back to clear his lungs. He heaved and choked and vomited seawater. When he could take in air, they bore him gently down into the familiar, smelly depths he so wanted to escape. Yet now the feel of solid timber under him was *life*.

He was told later that the sailors had tied a rope about the waist of his brawny rescuer who hooked him and brought him over the rail. Such a daring feat to save this young man's life diminished the hostility between the sailors and the colonists that had tainted the ship since the voyage began. To the saints, and even a few sailors, this was strong evidence that God's merciful hand still lay upon them all.

Thereafter, no one complained of confinement. The people embraced renewed hope that God's grace guided this sturdy ship through the storms that continued to buffet her relentlessly. Captain Jones was sometimes forced to limit sail to catch only enough wind to keep the ship under weigh, and sometimes to "hull," to furl all sails and drift. Many days they made no progress at all, as if the nearer they approached land, the more the hounds of hell roared out to hinder them. The passengers sank into a dull stupor, simply enduring the onslaught, their only solace prayer without ceasing.

Other trials were to come. Dorothy Bradford sat disconsolately by Elizabeth Hopkins' bed as she heaved herself upright, once again needing the waste bucket. Dorothy sprang up to help her. The night before, Elizabeth began to moan at regular intervals, and at daylight, informed of the impending birth, Captain Jones offered her his cabin to provide a measure of privacy. Women took turns sitting by her to offer encouragement and reassurance. As was customary, males kept their distance.

There was little else to be done for her. Since the storms began, cooking fires had been strictly prohibited, and the usual hot water and clean linen required for birthing were forbidden. The best the women could do was to keep Elizabeth reasonably clean and comfortable in the captain's feather bed. A hardy soul, Elizabeth looked about the cabin and quipped, "Well, this is one way to get into the captain's bed."

Dorothy blushed. Nevertheless, she felt a pang with each of Elizabeth's groans, as if she were delivering herself. *I should never have come,* she told herself. *If I had known how it would be, I never would have agreed.* She suspected that she did not suffer alone, and that the other women only buried their fears as she did. It profited no one to add personal complaints to the company's misery. And Dorothy dared not undermine her husband's earnest efforts to build a congenial community. So in her moments of deepest self-pity she complained only to God: *William has no idea how I feel, Lord, and if he did, he could offer nothing more now than sympathy. Committed to this venture we are now trapped in it, and no escape is possible. Help me, Lord, to bear it with grace. Help me, Lord. Help me!*

☙❧

Elizabeth's son was born the morning of her second day of labor, healthy and hearty and welcomed by all the company and crewmen alike. To the sailors he was a good omen, and to the community a sign of God's blessing on their future. His father named him Oceanus, and for a few hours the joy of his arrival lifted every heart. God had provided a new life for a new future.

Yet the days wore on, the monotony broken occasionally only by

217

Myles Standish's frequent military drills teaching the men to handle their cumbersome muskets. Standish saw his primary duty to prepare the people not only for hunting but to withstand the savage natives he was certain awaited them. A soldier to the core, his focus was on the enemy in whatever guise he chose to appear. He and his men would be prepared.

They had been at sea ten weeks when Mary Brewster noticed uneasily that some of the company was listless beyond the usual boredom. She was particularly troubled by young William Butten, servant to Dr. Fuller, a robust lad from Bradford's home in Austerfield, now fallen into a painful lethargy. "What is wrong with him, Samuel? He is not himself."

Fuller's face was grim. "You have a keen eye, Mary. I fear he shows all the signs of scurvy."

"Scurvy! Did he not take his ration of lime juice?"

"I warned him about that, as I have the others, but the young think they will live forever. I will ask Dr. Heale and Cap'n Jones to look at him. They have seen more of this plague at sea than I."

"And I will call William," Mary said. "They came from the same village."

Jones brought the ship's physician, Giles Heale, to find Butten groaning upon his pallet, alternately sweating and shivering, his face contorting as stabbing pains shot through his joints. "Fuller thinks it's scurvy," the captain told Heale. "What say you, Doctor?"

Heale studied the young man's contorted face. "Lad, listen to me. Have you taken your lime juice as you were told?"

Butten shook his head and rasped out, "Can't stand the stuff."

"I'm sorry indeed, lad. You'll stand more than that for your folly." He told the captain, "Have a whole lime brought to him at once. It may not be too late."

They propped him up and put the bitter fruit to his lips. He turned his head away. "Come now, lad, if you value your life, you must take this down."

Bradford appeared with Dorothy, distraught that Butten might be seriously ill. Dorothy stayed by his side, urging little sips of lime upon him as often as he would take it. She prayed fervently: *Oh, dear Lord, please save this lad, William Butten. Anyone of us could be him. He has erred in your sight, Lord, but so simply, not liking the bitter lime. Do not punish him for his ignorance, Lord. I beg You to spare his life. We need him so!*

Yet during the long night Butten's breathing worsened. Terrified, Dorothy summoned Dr. Heale who pronounced, "Not only scurvy, but pneumonia." He shook his head. "Both are too much for him. May God have mercy upon his soul."

Brewster and Bradford led the colonists in prayer throughout the night, pleading against the agonized sound of Butten's rasping breaths. Then, just before dawn, his breathing stopped. Even the wind and sea seemed to pause in the imposing silence.

Dorothy crept away to her pallet and wept as she had for John. She had thought there were no more tears in her. Though she was not old enough to have borne William Butten, she felt she had lost another child. Moreover, she was certain that his death was at least partly her fault. Why had she not thought to urge him to eat his fruit? So simple a thing she might have done, had she not been so immersed in her own selfish misery.

Now, she thought suddenly, what of the others who seemed to be falling ill? *Oh, God, if we do not get off this cursed ship soon, we shall all die!*

She did not admit her guilt to William, knowing that he would say Butten's death was no one's fault. The boy had simply been negligent. Yet her heart was not consoled, and when his shrouded body was tilted over the ship's rail and dropped into the cold sea, grief settled in her breast like a stone.

On deck Bradford listened to the eulogy spoken for William Butten and recalled the green fields and rolling meadows of Yorkshire, their childhood home. *Oh, Lord, take him home and comfort him there. Erase all memory of these desolate days. And give us the courage to go on.*

Butten's death dispelled the brief joy of Oceanus Hopkins' birth. Mary Brewster eyed others slipping into lethargy, and like a good manager, nagged everyone to take his daily ration of dried fruit and lime juice. Yet several more came down with chills and fever like

Butten's. Others suffered swollen legs and extreme weakness, but by now the tedium of the voyage had so worn down their spirits that it was impossible to tell whether their torpor was physical or mental...most likely both. They could only rely on their faith that their God would save them. Surely having brought them so far, He would not let them die one by one at sea!

John Carver asked Captain Jones if they were anywhere near landfall. Whereupon the captain displayed his charts and confirmed his course along the forty-second parallel. Yet he refused to hoist more sail to gain speed lest the press of wind overstrain the weakened ship. His only safe course was to sustain their slow pace and simply plod on as before.

Then, suddenly, Heaven seemed to open a blessing upon them: storms swept the sea less frequently and much less severely, prompting Captain Jones to open hatches to permit pale sunshine and fresh winds to dry out the decks below. Jones himself descended into the passengers' quarters to urge cramped and stiff invalids to rise up and walk the decks. Quietly, he forbade the crew's usual raucous ridicule and ordered them to treat the people respectfully in their weakness. The dogs and children were ecstatic to be allowed on deck even under strict restraint. Altogether the mood aboard the *Mayflower* brightened, and hope sprang afresh that their journey was nearly done.

Yet the leaden sea still stretched endlessly before them.

Then one morning just after dawn, John Clark noted to Captain Jones that the color of the sea was changing from deep indigo to emerald, a sign of shallow water. Soon after, a gull appeared overhead and wheeled about the ship squawking, taken by the crew to be a greeting. The captain sent the leadsman to take soundings, and soon all ears aboard listened for his sing-song cry: "Twenty fathoms, sir! Thirty fathoms! Forty fathoms!" His chant went on, identifying alternating depths. Then he paused a long moment, calling nothing at all. Suddenly he bellowed, "Bottom at eighty fathoms, sir!"

In the next moment the lookout in the crow's nest sang out the blessed words, "Land ho! Land ho!" Everyone, crew and passengers alike, rushed to the rail. No one could quite believe it, not even the crew, that line of brown along the distant horizon. Was it really land or only a cloud bank? No! Unmistakable, that brown line, nothing at sea that color. It had to be land!

November 9, 1620, sixty-five days out from Plimoth, ninety-seven from Southampton, they had arrived in the New World.

Seventeen

Cape Cod

The colonists fell upon their knees on the main deck and thanked the God of Heaven, who had brought them over the vast and furious ocean "...to set their feet on the firm and stable earth, their proper element." Then Brewster led them in singing Psalm 100, a song of praise. The crewmen, as jubilant as the passengers to be ending this voyage, ignored the religious incantations and sent up a cheer to the gods of *terra firma*.

Yet after rejoicing, the colonists paused to ask the pressing question: Where were they? And where should they go from here?

Captain Jones had been studying his charts and now declared that, according to Captain John Smith's maps, they had reached the coastline of Cape Cod, the southeastern tip of New England on the forty-second parallel Jones had followed across the Atlantic.

That news brought Governor Carver up short. His patent gave their company permission to settle in Virginia, whose northern boundary ended at the forty-first parallel. They had no legal right to settle north of that parallel in New England.

Carver called the men together. He reminded them that the patent and letters signed by Sir Edwin Sandys and John Ferrar, Treasurer and Secretary of the Virginia Company, would introduce them to Sir George Yeardley, Governor of Jamestown, to solicit his advice to help them establish a colony near the Hudson River. A settlement at the Hudson would be far enough removed from Jamestown to pose little threat from the Church of England established in Virginia. "Captain Jones tells me that we are not yet in Virginia territory. We must sail farther south to reach the Hudson, where our patent is legal."

The men stood soberly, their faces drawn.

"We can consider landing here on Cape Cod. Sir Ferdinando Gorges promised me in Plimoth that if we chose to settle here, his Council for New England would grant us a patent at some future time. Think hard on this, friends. We face a longer journey to the Hudson, but we have no patent to settle here."

Christopher Martin spoke up promptly. "I am for putting in here on the Cape to see how the land lies. To push on to the Hudson now may be the straw that breaks our backs."

A lively discussion ensued, but the men of Leyden, having fought long and hard for legal sanction in the New World, were of like mind—to go on to Virginia. God's grace had brought them safely across the vast Atlantic and would surely see them through two more days to the Hudson.

Yet most Londoners agreed with Martin. Why tamper with Fate? they argued. Their food stores were dangerously low, and many of their people were ill. Fishing was said to be magnificent in New England, and the official English Church held no jurisdiction there. Once settled, they could request the promised patent.

The men of Leyden glanced among themselves warily, suspecting a hidden motivation behind the Londoners' preference for Cape Cod, perhaps a yearning for freedom from all authority. Yet the Leydeners' experience seeking official permission to settle in Amsterdam and Leyden, had convinced them that a legal patent was essential for their safety. The strangers arguing for New England ignored the fact that without a patent no jurisdiction could restrict individuals within the community or protect the colony from foreign intruders.

Reading his colleagues' faces, Carver said firmly, "We have a bird in hand in Virginia, men. A patent for New England is like two birds still in the bush, possible but not guaranteed."

Martin began, "But if Gorges promised..."

Carver broke in, "With all due respect, sir, may I say that those of you from London have not shared our community's long struggle to gain legal sanction for our settlement. It ensures our safety from rebels within and predators without."

Martin said, "I take your point, sir. Like yourselves, we desire our freedom. Those of us seeking economic prosperity and others indentured to lengthy service would certainly prefer our independence. Why else have we come here?" He extended his hands in a gesture of supplication.

"You mistake our purpose, sir," Carver said. "We seek freedom to worship under proper authority, not freedom from all authority. We have resisted tyranny which denies that freedom, yet all of you know well that without orderly government, even the best men fall into anarchy." He glanced about the group. "I say now that if any of you intend to break your commitment to this venture, I remind you that we face the hard reality of survival here. Do any of you seriously believe you can achieve this without the community?" He paused. "We have already lost one able-bodied man, many more are sick, and we will need every hand to erect adequate shelter to stay alive this winter."

The group murmured among themselves. Stephen Hopkins' servants, Edward Dotey and Edward Leister, inspired by Hopkins' tales of mutinous exploits in Bermuda, glared sourly at each other until Hopkins cast them a warning glance.

Carver went on. "After we have established residence, if any of you want to break your commitment, we will consider that request. But I believe our best choice now is to proceed to Virginia."

No one else spoke. Carver said, "Are we agreed then that, God willing, we will press on to the Hudson?" The men of Leyden nodded agreement. The others remained silent. No one openly objected.

"I will so inform Captain Jones."

But Jones told Carver bluntly, "I understand you value your patent, sir, but I must also advise you that treacherous water lies before us. Old sailors' lore calls this place 'Tucker's Terror,' the sort of tale seamen revere. We may have very slow going, longer than two days."

Carver asked, "But is it passable?"

"Not without risk. Looks like a field of hidden shoals that can rip out the old girl's bottom. We may have to seek deep water, which will delay us longer." He scowled. "'Tis chancey, but 'tis your mission. I'm willing to give it a go if you are."

Bradford spoke up. "Why not sail out to deep water now and come in south of the shoals? Some clear passage must lead to the Hudson."

The captain shook his head. "We have no reliable charts to show us how far these shoals extend. Considering our low stores and the state of your people's health, time is critical."

Carver sighed, then smiled. "Well, then, this day is young yet, Cap'n, and we have wasted enough time. We are desperate to be off."

The leadsman took his station outside the mizzen shrouds. Using a hand lead, a fourteen-pound weight easier to haul up than the hundred pound dipsey he used in deeper water, he called out the soundings routinely. All the countrymen aboard knew by now that the *Mayflower's* thirteen-foot draw safely required at least four or five fathoms' clearance.

For half the day they progressed slowly offshore, eyeing that tantalizing strip of golden land stretching along the western horizon, while the colonists indulged in dreams of firm soil under their feet again: shelter, warmth, hot food, fresh water.

"Breakers ahead!" The lookout called from the crow's nest.

A curt awakening! All eyes peered southward to see a line of churning white water ruffling the horizon well beyond the ship's bow. The leadsman called, "Thirty fathoms, sir!" And soon after, "Nineteen fathoms, sir!" The sea bottom was irregular, unpredictable. They were already in shoal water.

Jones ordered the helm thrown to starboard, and headed for open sea, but as the ship heeled slowly over, the wind suddenly dropped and the sails deflated, while the tide running under the ship continued to carry her straight toward the distant breakers.

The leadsman's next call, "Fifteen fathoms, sir!" struck panic in all hearts.

"Hard over to starboard, men!" the captain bellowed.

Carver asked, "What's happened, Captain?"

"We're running a two-knot tide straight for those breakers. Tell your people to pray for wind to take us seaward!"

With no wind in her sails the ship could make no headway against the tide. Nor could she drop anchor so near the shoals, lest the tide run out and leave her stranded on a rocky bottom. And they must get to deep water quickly, for the sun was low in the west, fast approaching sunset. By dark they could see nothing.

Carver told his colonists, "Pray God for a breeze, good people.

Captain says 'tis our only hope."

Brewster prayed aloud. "Lord God, we have come so far. Do not desert us now. Send us a robust wind, Lord, so desperately do we need it. We bless You for mercy, Lord."

Jones anxiously scanned the roiling water, dismayed that his best hope now was not in his expert seamanship but in the prayers of these unruly saints. For once he could uphold their cause.

The ship wallowed for twenty minutes or more, her sails limp. Then the merest puff of breeze stirred the mainsail, and the leadsman called out, "Eighteen fathoms, sir!" All held their breath, feeling in their bones poor old Tucker's terror indeed!

They were not out of danger. An invisible rock on the uneven sea floor could in a moment pierce the ship's bottom. The leadsman continued sounding while Jones held the helm hard to starboard, and the colonists prayed fervently. The crewmen stood tense at their posts, hearts frozen, tongues for once silent.

At last the leadsman sang out, "Twenty-five fathoms!" An audible sigh of relief swept the ship. Then another call, "Thirty fathoms at bottom, sir!" Applause broke out. The *Mayflower* had survived another ordeal.

Now a new dilemma presented. If Tucker's Terror was typical of waters south to the Hudson, many more days aboard ship might lie before them. Once again the men gathered in the captain's cabin, those from Leyden holding out for Virginia, but now facing the stark possibility that the Hudson was unattainable.

The captain asked his second mate, Robert Coppin, who had sailed to Cape Cod before, to tell them what he knew of the lay of the land there. Coppin told them, "'Tis a fine harbor on the west side of the Cape. I've seen it meself. Deep water and calm surf. The eastern spit of land curls around like an upraised arm bent at the elbow and wrist, and you can slip your shallop ashore there and look about."

Martin and others from London pressed hard for exploring the Cape. Yet the men of Leyden held for Virginia. Then Stephen Hopkins, a stranger from London, asked to speak. Though rumors had circulated earlier of his adventurous past, now he confessed solemnly his ill-fated voyage to Bermuda. "I sailed aboard the *Sea Venture*, Admiral Gates' flagship bound for Bermuda where Gates would be governor. One of those fierce tropical blows scattered the fleet an' wrecked us off the coast of the island. By the grace of Heaven we all survived, but Gates and Sir Somers at once demanded that we build pinnaces to go on to Virginia. Those of us with a brain or two considered that in Virginia we might be indentured for the rest of our natural lives at the whim of those tyrants. It seemed to me that their authority ceased with the *Venture's* loss, and we owed them no more allegiance."

His audience listened raptly.

"The Gov'nor took offense and accused us of mutiny and rebellion, and sentenced the lot of us to hangin.' I pleaded the ruin of my wife and family, and they let me off." He glanced about the group, then added, "But they took the heads of all the others."

The men exchanged uneasy glances. Why was he telling this story now when their course to the Hudson seemed blocked?

Carver said, "So, Mr. Hopkins, you seem to have recovered well from your ordeal. What lesson can we learn from your experience?"

"Sir, a legal patent is worth its weight in gold. Unrestrained men resort to treachery, or worse. Mutiny. We need the law, sir, no less than food and shelter."

Carver nodded. "We have reached a point of grave decision, whether to pursue our patent, or land at Cape Cod without one. I suggest that we all retire to seek our Lord's direction and agreement among ourselves."

As the Leyden men moved closer to pray together, Myles Standish joined their group. He spoke softly. "If there's trouble brewing, you can count on me, brothers. I am with you."

Carver said, "We thank you, sir. If the Lord is indeed directing us to Cape Cod, we may need your help."

Brewster murmured, "Let us go below and pray with our families."

They dispersed to meditate. Single men without families thought long on their futures, wondering how to predict whether one colony or the other offered better opportunity.

Among the women and children huddled together in the 'tween decks, many coughed in their sleep, and some lay quietly awake, as if too exhausted to sleep. In the dim lantern light their faces shone pale and haggard with hunger. As the ship gently rocked on the calm night sea, the continuous whisper of seawater trickling down her bulkheads and the slosh of water along the decks pressed on the men's ears like a prophecy of doom. The rigors of this voyage had so sapped the peoples' strength that they were rapidly succumbing to disease and despair. This stark reality pierced the men's hearts: They were all one step from starvation. Nothing mattered more now than shelter and food.

Husbands whispered urgent prayers for guidance: *Are You still with us, Lord? Where would You have us land, Lord? DARE we go on to the Hudson?*

Bradford lay down beside Dorothy, shivering in her fitful sleep under a chilly blanket impossible to dry out. He pressed her to him for warmth but did not awaken her, knowing full well how desperate she was to abandon this ship. *Lord,* he pleaded, *make our way clear. Deliver us, Lord.*

Brewster spoke softly to Mary. "Are you awake, my love?"

"Um."

"Jones says it may take days to reach the Hudson. Some want to land on the Cape while we still have provision."

After a moment Mary said, "So many are ill, William. One by one they fall."

"I know. Yet if we land here we have no patent."

Mary's answer was brisk. "If we do not land soon, Will, there'll be none left to need a patent."

Brewster groaned. "I wonder sometimes—forgive me, Lord—why does He allow every possible hindrance to block us? What have we done to provoke this?"

Mary turned her head toward him. "Guard our faith well, husband. Without that we are truly lost."

Carver sought out Bradford. "Son, what is left of our water and rations?"

"I check each morning and evening, sir. The cheese is rancid, John Alden tells me the beer is sour, everything edible is mildewed or rotting. I think on half rations we have barely enough to last a week. We desperately need to go ashore and find game, sir."

The two looked into each other's eyes. Bradford burst out, "Mr.

Carver, sir, I think we must give up hope of Virginia."

Carver nodded. "Aye, lad. Methinks the same."

When early that morning the men gathered in the captain's quarters, they stood in somber silence. Carver said, "Men, we have been at sea sixty-five days. Our people are ill, our stores low. Can we withstand another two days' journey to the Hudson?"

The men stirred glumly, wondering if they could withstand another night.

"What say you then?"

No one spoke. Then Bradford said, "I vote for the Cape, sir. 'Tis our best hope."

A pause, then a burst of assent from the men. "Aye, the Cape." "Let's go."

"Anyone object? Speak up now."

Martin bellowed, "The Cape it is. Any fool can see it."

"Then fools we be, lads. Fools for God. The Cape it is!"

Carver told Captain Jones, "Our people are desperate. We are grateful that God has brought us this far, but we must land as soon as possible."

Jones' eyes ranged over the men clustered in his cabin. For himself and his crew, he was relieved. The sooner he disgorged this company the sooner he could return to England before his own ship's stores ran out. These brave and reckless colonists need never know that Dutch adventurers had pressed him to land the *Mayflower* well north of the Hudson so not to interfere with Dutch settlement there. It had not been necessary to tell them. Providence had kindly arranged Tucker's Terror.

Martin grinned. "Let us be off!"

As the men dispersed to their pallets, Myles Standish stopped Carver on the foredeck. "Mr. Carver, sir. May I presume? Now is the time to take your pastor's advice to draw up a body politic. Now, before we set foot on land."

Carver studied Standish's eager face in the starlight, thinking how remarkable it was that this stranger should so fully ally with the saints' venture. "I have been thinking of that. I'll speak with my leaders today as we sail north."

Carver called the entire company together to announce their

decision to land at Cape Cod. "The Almighty has blocked our way to the Hudson but has shown us a good land on this Cape. We must focus now on making ready to disembark as soon as possible."

There was no rejoicing. The weary women accepted this decision as only one more among many faced before. Yet any land now was preferable to this wet and stinking ship. Bradford gazed upon Dorothy with an aching heart. His pretty wife looked gaunt, her once-rosy cheeks pallid, her golden hair wispy. A pang of remorse smote his chest. Had he known how difficult this journey would be, would he have insisted she come with him? He swallowed the bitter taste of doubt, one of those sharp regrets he rarely allowed himself: *What if we've been wrong? What if we missed all the warnings and heard only our own fleshly desires? No*, he rebuked himself. Those committed to this venture had earnestly sought the Lord's will. Some perhaps, but not all, would have been deceived. And surely, surely, the Lord God would honor their forthright and fervent obedience.

During the journey to the harbor's entrance, Carver called men of both Leyden and London together to discuss plans for leaving the ship. His eyes were sunken in his long lean face, yet his carriage was still erect with that innate gentility he bore so easily. He told them, "We are men of common station facing the monumental task of carving a colony in a wilderness indifferent to our welfare. Therefore, we propose a covenant among ourselves for which we beseech each man's congenial support, his best effort, and steadfast loyalty under the authority of God Almighty. We have asked Mr. Brewster and Mr. Hopkins to set forth a compact of agreement to this end, and earnestly solicit your signatures. Please read it carefully before you sign your name, for once signed, it will be binding upon you."

Some murmured, "Amen."

Brewster read the *Compact* aloud to the company. Listening to its hopeful words, Captain Jones and First Mate John Clark observed keenly this process, sometimes glancing at each other and raising their brows, thinking the same thoughts. This disparate group, thrown together by the vagaries of Fate and facing overwhelming odds, were about to devise some form of self-government under their own authority—subject, as they saw it, to the will of God. A noble and idealistic enterprise, but was it even possible? These hardened seamen had seen men of all stripes at sea and ashore but never known men of different class to conspire together without strict authority. They had seen many of this original group withdraw, leaving only these stalwart few to endure the hardships of colonizing a wilderness. The two sailors steeped in a worldly perspective agreed it would be interesting, nay remarkable, to observe how well they succeeded.

Brewster and Hopkins, the best educated of the group, had drafted the document modeled on the form of covenant the Church at Leyden had followed for years. After the oral reading it was placed on the captain's broad table in his cabin for each man to read individually. It read as follows:

IN THE NAME OF GOD, AMEN
We whose names are underwritten, the loyal subjects of our dread sovereign Lord King James by the Grace of God of Great Britain, France, Ireland, King, Defender of the Faith, etc.

Having undertaken, for the Glory of God and advancement of the Christian Faith and Honour of our King and Country, a voyage to plant the First Colony in the Northern Parts of Virginia, do by these presents solemnly and mutually in the presence of God and one of another, covenant and Combine ourselves together into a Civil Body Politic, for our better ordering and preservation and furtherance of the ends aforesaid, and by virtue hereof to enact, constitute and frame such just and equal laws, ordinances, Acts, Constitutions and Offices from time to time, as shall be thought most meet and convenient for the general good of the Colony, unto which we promise all due submission and obedience. In witness whereof we have hereunder subscribed our names at Cape Cod, the 11th of November, in the year of the reign of our Sovereign Lord King James of England, France, and Ireland the eighteenth, and of Scotland the fifty-fourth. Anno Domini 1620.

First the masters—that is, landowners—signed: Carver, Bradford, Winslow, Brewster, Allerton, Standish, Fuller, White. Then the London leaders: Martin, Mullins, Warren, Hopkins. Next came twenty-seven goodmen and four servants, for a total of forty-one males aboard. Thirteen of those who did not sign were sons of signers. Nine servants and two hired sailors did not sign. Women were covered by their husbands or fathers.

One more item of business to decide was the election of a governor. As "governor" of the *Mayflower* during the voyage, John Carver was the obvious choice. He would serve officially as governor of the colony for their first year.

That Saturday, November eleventh, 1620, they sailed slowly into Cape Cod Bay and from the deck gazed upon the low white sandhills and dense forests encircling the bay. The dunes resembled those of Holland, a familiar and somewhat comforting sight. But as the leadsman took soundings on the ship's careful maneuvers through the harbor's entrance, it soon became evident that the bay was strewn with sandbars and not easily navigable. Captain Jones decided to drop anchor about a mile from the tip of the "bent wrist" of the eastern peninsula Coppin had said separated the bay from open ocean.

The passengers stood entranced, gazing at the untamed land that would become their home. How did it appear to them that day? William Bradford's words written years later expressed eloquently their mutual feeling:

> Here I cannot but...stand half amazed at this poor people's present condition...Being thus passed the vast ocean, and a sea of troubles before in their preparation...they had now no friends to welcome them nor inns to entertain or refresh their weatherbeaten bodies, no houses or much less towns to repair to, to seek for succour...Besides, what could they see but a hideous and desolate wilderness, full of wild beasts and wild men...For summer being done, all things stand upon them with a weatherbeaten face, with the whole country, full of woods and thickets, represented a wild and savage hue. If they looked behind them, there was the mighty ocean which they had passed and was now as a main bar and gulf to separate them from all the civil parts of the world...Let it also be considered what weak hopes for supply and succour they left behind them.

The urgent business at hand was to commence the chores necessary to make landfall. The carpenters already knew that the shallop damaged by storms and her use as shelter by the voyagers would require considerable repair to make her seaworthy. What resources the land itself offered, what trees or rocks or thatch were available, would determine their style of housing. At least these necessities focused the colonists on a common cause, and dispelled any thought of independence among would-be rebels.

Bradford asked, "What could now sustain them but the Spirit of God and his Grace?" He answered his own question with a reference to Deuteronomy twenty-six:

"May not and ought not the children of these fathers rightly say; 'Our fathers were Englishmen which came over this great ocean, and were ready to perish in this wilderness, but they cried unto the Lord, and He heard their voice, and looked on their adversity.'"

Eighteen

A Wild and Savage Hue

Their first day at anchor the young men clamored to go ashore to explore the eastern cape, a curving neck of sand running north and south between the ocean and the bay. They sailed the *Mayflower's* longboat as far as the numerous sandbars permitted but were finally forced to wade through the icy water up to their thighs. Ashore, they were delighted to discover underneath the sand a layer of rich black earth, and that the hills were well-wooded with pine, oak, sassafras, juniper, birch, holly, ash and walnut. They found no evidence of any natives or their habitation. Nor did they find fresh water, a necessity for their home site.

Their reward that day was a boatload of juniper, whose sweet fragrance refreshed their ship and provided warmth and the luxury of a hot meal. They accepted this bounty as God's grace and a promise of new life to come.

Although the crew vocally lamented "wasting" a workday in worship, the colonists observed the Sabbath of November twelfth as strictly as any other Sabbath spent in prayer and song preparing for Monday's labors.

On the thirteenth, despite the cold bath they had to endure wading over sandbars to shore, the crew as well as colonists eagerly set foot on land again. The longboat shuttled from ship to shore bearing, besides people, two dogs, the shallop in four pieces to be refitted, and ten weeks of reeking laundry waiting to be washed. Pent-up children, enthralled by flocks of gulls wheeling and crying and whales "blowing" in the bay, bounded happily on the sands. Only a few small fish were found near shore, but abundant mussels proved a "feast" too rich for some shrunken stomachs and brought on a siege of "casting" and "scouring."

Governor Carver was reluctant to send his ablest men ashore afoot to scout for home sites without the protection of the shallop. Beyond the dark forests any sort of unknown creature, man or animal, might await them. Yet finding a site was so urgent a priority that the men pleaded with him to allow a party to explore. Finally convinced, he sent them out under the military direction of Myles Standish and the council of Bradford, Hopkins, and Edward Tilley. They were instructed to stay ashore only two days.

As the *Mayflower* entered the bay they had seen from her decks what appeared to be a river about five miles downshore from the tip of the cape where Jones decided to anchor. Now armed with muskets, swords and corselets, the men charged out, hoping to find fresh water and perhaps a river large enough for ships to navigate.

Since Captain Jones and some of his men went ashore as well that day, the search party was not surprised to see five or six people and a dog some distance away. But when these men suddenly took flight with "might and main" into the woods, whistling their dog after them, the explorers realized they were natives and hastened to track them a good ten miles. Yet somehow the natives vanished. By nightfall the search party decided to lodge for the night, build a fire, and set out three sentinels to watch.

In the morning they took up the trail again, tracking up hills and down valleys braving thickets dense enough to tear their armor. The natives' trail had come to the head of a long creek and then taken off into another wood, which the men followed some distance but found neither native nor sign of habitation. By now the weary party suffered greatly for lack of water, for no one had had the foresight to bring any nourishment but a bottle of brandy, some biscuit, and cheese.

Standish scolded them for this oversight. "This mistake we dare not make again. We search wild territory, my good brothers. Nothing is provided here but raw nature. Henceforth we must foresee our simple needs and prepare ourselves."

"Aye," the men agreed, chagrined at their ignorance.

Pressing on, they found a deep valley full of brush and grass, evidence of deer, and at last, springs of fresh water, as refreshing a drink as any ever had. Farther south they found a clear pond where vines and sassafras, wild fowl and deer abounded. Continuing toward the river, they paused on the shore to build a signal fire to reassure the *Mayflower* of their safety. Bradford hoped someone would tell Dorothy, for she had seemed unusually distressed when he joined the search party that morning, yet she did not protest his joining the party.

They found a field of fifty acres fit for the plow where corn had been planted recently. Soon after that discovery they came upon puzzling mounds of sand. After some discussion they presumed to dig one up and found a pot, a bow, and some rotted arrows, apparently a grave. Reluctant to antagonize the natives, they restored the site and traveled on. Later that day they made another discovery—a large heap of sand containing a kettle of very fair corn, red, yellow and some blue, a "goodly sight." The large round basket narrowed at the top held three or four bushels. Edward Tilley exclaimed happily, "Seed corn for the next planting season!"

"Then we need take as much as we can carry," said Hopkins.

"You mean 'borrow' it?" asked Tilley.

Hopkins nodded. "We can compensate them later when we find the owners."

Tilley asked, "Will they understand that?"

Hopkins chuckled. "'Tis the law of the jungle, mate. You own what you find, leave some for others, and make it right when you can. Nothing is exclusive here."

"What do you say, Mr. Brewster?" asked Tilley doubtfully.

"Methinks our brother is right. No man can hoard the wilderness unless he stands to guard it. We will make every effort to compensate the owners."

Bradford said, "It seems providential for us, just lying here for the taking."

"Indeed," said Hopkins with amusement. "Even if it belongs to the Indians."

Brewster commented, "I'll wager the natives understand such 'theft' perfectly. What may surprise them is our attempt to pay for it. So, when we have use of the shallop we will hope to parley with them, return their kettle, and pay for the corn."

236

The men jammed their pockets with ears and loose kernels and filled the kettle as full as two men could carry on a staff slung over their shoulders.

When they reached the river they had aimed for they found it split into two streams by a hill, one small and one possibly large enough to allow ships. Two canoes lay on either side of the streams. They did not take time to check if the water was fresh because their two-days' allotted time was coming to an end.

That night they camped on the fresh water pond, making a great barricade of stakes, boughs, and logs to their windward. Three sentinels stood watch in turn and kept five or six inches of match cord burning, lest they need to fire their muskets quickly. Yet a soaking rain all night drowned everything, the match-cords as well.

Friday morning, the seventeenth of November, they buried the kettle, then skirted the coast toward the point of rendezvous. While circling about deep in the woods they came to a curious device, a young tree bent over in a bow with acorns strewn beneath it. Hopkins announced with authority, "Beware. 'Tis a deer trap."

As they studied the ingenious contraption, wondering how it worked, Bradford, bringing up the rear of the column, caught up with them. Suddenly he was jerked into the air by one leg and dangled helpless as a fish on a line. He yelped in surprise.

After a stunned moment, all burst into laughter. "Get me down!" Bradford yelled, not nearly so amused. The men studied the snare, marveling at the rope and noose as cunningly made as any English roper could weave.

It was urgent now that they hurry to rendezvous with the *Mayflower*. One bright note in their trek back was the sight of three bucks plunging through the grass within shot of their muskets. But so fleet were these deer that the men could not light their matchlocks before they disappeared. So too did the men's clumsy crashing through woods flush out flocks of geese and ducks too suddenly to shoot. They began to understand the elusive Indians' mastery of stealth.

On the beach they found that Carver and Jones, alarmed by their late arrival, had already led a party ashore to find them. Those waiting aboard ship were greatly relieved by their return and eagerly awaited their news.

Dorothy did not appear on deck with the other women. Bradford found her huddled on her pallet, her eyes glazed and her appearance ashen. "Dority, my dear, did you fear for me? Look, I'm fine."

She gazed at him a moment, then burst into tears.

He did not like the look of her hollow cheeks and the desperation in her eyes, like that of a terrified child. "We had a good time of it, Dority. We found deer and flocks of birds, a field to be plowed, and best of all, a supply of seed corn."

His enthusiasm did not seem to cheer her, and he took her into his arms and pressed her to his chest. "Soon we will be ashore, Dority, with shelter, plenty of food, and blessed warmth. I promise thee, girl. Soon all will be well."

He rocked her awhile to still her violent shuddering. When she quieted, he jumped up and drew her to her feet. "Come up to the cabin and our juniper fire. You must hear all about our discovery."

She followed docilely and sat quietly with the women while the men told each detail of their exciting search. The farmers among them recognized the seed corn as excellent quality and prophetic of fine soil and bountiful crops, welcoming any glimmer of hope that this voyage would someday prove successful.

Someone asked the most pressing question, "Did you see any home sites?"

Brewster answered, "Not yet. The river we sought does not promise depth enough for ships. And the water is in ponds which may dry up in summer. We have much coast yet to explore, but we are encouraged by what we have seen."

As the people returned to their sleeping pallets, Brewster asked Bradford, "How do you find Dorothy?"

Having noted the gaunt faces of the other women, especially the young ones, Elizabeth Winslow, Susanna White, and Patricia Mullins, Bradford, wanting to believe it, answered, "No worse than the others."

"Yet they have not that hopeless look, lad. Keep close to her, and when you go off, make sure someone stays by her."

Despite the cheerful news the men had brought, an insidious sense of desperation was creeping among the people, much enhanced by

238

worsening weather. It rained daily, more often now turning to snow carried on biting northern winds. The shallop was not yet seaworthy and the longboat blocked by sandbars that forced the passengers to wade daily through freezing water knee deep and often thigh deep at high tide. By now almost everyone was coughing and feverish, and many listlessly dragged themselves about.

Someone proposed that they build another shallop, perhaps a quicker solution than repairing the old one. The grim fear gripping each heart was that elusive place for habitation they must find soon, or all would succumb to exposure.

The weather gave no respite but bore down upon them like a jealous monster determined to drive them out. It was dangerous to go ashore some days and impossible on others—either way a dreadful waste of precious time.

Then, on the twenty-seventh of November, the carpenters announced that the shallop could sail, and at once Carver appointed Standish to lead twenty-four men on an extensive exploration of the river site. The longboat would carry the men ashore, who would then march to the river. There they would rendezvous with the smaller shallop to navigate the river and discover its source of fresh water.

Another immediate crisis loomed. The four men the colonists had hired to sail the shallop had all fallen sick. Carver went before Captain Jones. "You see our plight, sir. None of us is competent to handle that boat in this weather."

"Aye," the captain muttered, gazing at Carver from under heavy brows.

"Would you be so good as to lend us some of your men, sir?"

"Indeed, it seems I must. I assure you, Mr. Carver, that it is to our advantage to see you settled soon. Else we cannot hope to return to England this season."

"God bless you, Captain."

Moreover, the captain offered to lead the expedition himself. Reasonably, his own men, seasoned as they were at sea, might fare no better cast on an unknown shore. Yet as they left the *Mayflower*, neither small boat could withstand the tossing seas and vicious crosswinds barreling across the water. Jones declared the bay impassable and commanded both boats to head for the nearest shore and stay there.

Yet once ashore, the men who had planned to march decided to push on to the river site. With little nourishment in their stomachs and wet clothes on their backs, they marched seven miles through six inches of snowdrift. Bradford would later record these poignant words in his History: "Many took the original of their death here."

The next morning the shallop picked up the frigid searchers, debarked them at the river, and followed them along the riverbank. The flow, however, proved to be only twelve feet deep at high water, adequate for small boats like the shallop and the longboat but not deep enough for ships.

At dusk a pall of ominous weather moving out of the north alerted Captain Jones, who had marched with the party, to suggest wearily that they make camp under some pine trees while others went out to find food. The blessing of that day was three fat geese and six ducks, which they ate with "soldiers' stomachs," the first food they had eaten all day.

By morning some of the party questioned the wisdom of going on to the river's mouth to confirm fresh water. Hindrances to making settlement in this place were evident: water too shallow for ships and, some farmers noted, soil too poor for growing crops. In a lively discussion the men finally agreed that this place was not worth further exploration. A keen disappointment! Not only had they not found a good site, but had wasted two precious days searching. What now?

Jones remarked drily, "Well, men, what name would ye give this place?"

Someone called out, "What else but Cold Harbor?"

Edward Winslow suggested they pursue a consolation prize on the other side of the river, more of the corn they had found earlier. They used an Indian canoe lying nearby to shuttle across the water, crossing eight at a time. Someone brought down two geese with one shot, a cause for great rejoicing.

They found the corn, but the ground was frozen so solid that even their mattocks and spades could only penetrate a foot deep. Still, this corn, added to their original find, totaled about ten bushels of seed corn, more than adequate for the planting season. Brewster told them,

"Men, thank God for His blessing. Had we not tramped on foot through these woods our first trip out, we would never have seen the fresh-turned earth now buried under new-fallen snow."

By nightfall the promise of another dismal night in freezing weather sent Captain Jones back to his ship with the newfound corn and those too sick to endure without shelter. Yet the younger men could not give up. Eighteen camped on the beach that night and set out early the next morning.

The next day they followed a wide Indian trail, hoping it would lead to a village. Yet after hours of meandering they were dismayed to discover it was only a deer trail leading nowhere. Discouraged, they turned back by a different route and soon made another discovery, a long, low mound covered with boards. Digging, they found a mat, then a bow, then another board about two feet long, painted and carved on one end with prongs like a crown. Between the mats were a collection of bowls, dishes and trinkets. Under another mat lay two bundles, the larger one holding a packing needle, a knife, and a skull and bones embedded in a fine red powder. The second bundle held a child's skull dusted with the same powder. Parts of the bodies were bound with strings of fine white beads.

Most astonishing was the adult skull adorned with a shock of blond hair. Could it have been an Indian ruler? Stephen Hopkins put that idea down firmly. "No such being as a blond Indian, my friends. Never seen one anywhere."

The bodies seemed to have been buried with honor, a consoling thought, yet offering little reassurance.

Soon afterwards the shallop arrived, and while the men tramped about looking for new mounds to dig for corn, two sailors discovered two Indian houses within a hundred yards of the party. The houses were constructed of saplings, both ends stuck in the ground, rounded on top and covered with thick mats. Another mat formed a door. A hole at the top let out smoke from cooking fires built on a small platform of sticks. Mats laid about the room served as beds.

Various baskets were placed about the room, some patterned in black and white designs and some made of crab shells. The walls were hung with deer feet, eagles' claws, and two deer heads, one fresh. Pieces of fish and a broiled herring indicated the presence of recent inhabitants. While the men considered whether or not to take some of these articles, Brewster suggested, "We brought trinkets in the shallop we can leave here as a sign of friendship."

But as they left the houses the sailors bellowed that the tide was running out and foul weather coming on. If they did not leave at once they would have to spend another night on the freezing beach. The trinkets were forgotten.

Aboard the *Mayflower* happy news greeted them that Susanna White had given birth to a son named Peregrine. Yet that joy only emphasized the plight of the emaciated and malnourished company. Carver decided that they must make a crucial decision about settlement as soon as possible.

Now a brisk discussion followed. Many were in favor of settling on Corn Hill, where they had found the cache of corn. The soil was good there, the harbor was adequate for small boats, and judging by the fat whales in the bay, fishing was bound to be generous. Others disagreed strongly, contending that the site was steep, water must be hauled up, and the ponds might not be reliable in summer. Bradford insisted that lodgings adequate to withstand winter must be permanent, and if this site proved inhospitable, the buildings could not be moved.

Robert Coppin, the second mate, made a heartening suggestion. There was a good harbor at Anguum, he said, sixty miles north, better fishing and probably better soil. To investigate that site would call for a few more days' exploration. But Governor Carver was aghast at the proposal. He dared not sanction more risk to his few able men. To lose even one man or worse, the shallop itself, in these violent winter storms would hazard their entire expedition.

That night, December 4, William White's young servant, Edward Thompson, died.

This somber reality meant that they must reach a compromise. Carver overruled the possibility of Anguum because it was too far north. Their search should be confined within the limits of the bay. So their new advisor, Robert Coppin, recalling his previous visit, told of a bluff across the bay where a navigable river and a good harbor lay. It was within twenty-four miles' journey.

Carver called his closest advisors together, Brewster, Bradford, Winslow, Tilley, Allerton, Fuller. "What think ye of the mate's suggestion, men?"

Winslow said, "Let us make one more search. If this proves futile we will settle for Corn Hill."

"I agree," said Bradford, speaking for those eager to find the best site possible.

Carver sighed. "Now think ye on this, men. We cannot foresee much beyond the season unless we survive it. Perhaps the site at Corn Hill will do well enough through the winter. If it proves poor, we can rebuild in the spring." He raised a hand to still objection. "I know. Our lodging must be substantial. But our need is so desperate, I fear we can afford to wait no longer."

No one spoke for a few moments. Then Allerton said, "I say we make one more effort and try Coppin's site. And pray the Almighty to give us a few days of good weather to search."

A chorus agreed.

Yet Governor Carver was despondent. Looking at the faces of his sick, starving people tore his heart. He could not condemn them all to death on this ship for lack of adequate shelter. If they could weather this winter season, however poorly, the coming of spring might bring new opportunities invisible to them now.

"Sir," Brewster said softly. "Hear me."

Carver, suffering, nodded.

"I think if the young men are game to try again, God will be with them, for He knows that they have the best interests of the people at heart. Have faith, sir. They will do well."

Carver sighed. "I will certainly beseech Him for that blessing."

Carver addressed their physician, Samuel Fuller. "What do you think, Sam? How much longer can we last here?"

Fuller shook his head sadly. "Pneumonia's one thing, Governor. Scurvy's another." He raised stricken eyes to Carver. "'Tis hardest to watch the young ones go."

That night Carver crawled close beside Catherine. "What do you think best, Cat? Should we settle now?"

"Whatever you say, John."

"No, not because I say it. What do you think best?"

She lay awhile silently. "I think our Lord has a place for us here, and when we find it, we will know and be satisfied."

Ahh, he thought. *She is right. Then we have not found it yet.*

Nineteen

Home Site

The last expedition to search for the ideal home site was set for Wednesday, the sixth of December. Yet on the fifth the colonists suffered a grim reminder of the evil forces arrayed against them.

Much of the weaponry the men took ashore was stored for convenience in the captain's cabin rather than among the people crowded belowdecks. A barrel of gunpowder half full sat in the cabin at the ready for expeditions ashore. Young Francis Billington found his father's musket and shot it off within four feet of the barrel. Had the powder ignited, the *Mayflower* and her passengers may well have gone up with it, but miraculously the flash did not even set off the flints and bits of iron nearby. No one was hurt, but the fright startled everyone.

An exasperated John Billington boxed his son's ears. "Dolt!" he roared, "Have I not said never to tamper with shot?"

Francis protested, "I did not know the barrel was there!"

"No matter. I warned you never to play with pieces."

Carver said gently, "Methinks the boy meant no harm, sir, and has learned his lesson."

Billington glowered. "But at what terrible risk, Gov'nor? I'll not have my boy blowin' up this boat."

Francis' escapade confirmed the dire necessity of leaving this ship as soon as possible.

❧❦

On December sixth, eighteen explorers set off for shore, the healthiest of the men not sick enough to take to bed. They included Captain Standish, Governor Carver, Bradford, Winslow, both John and Edward

Tilley, John Howland, Richard Warren, Stephen Hopkins, Edward Dotey, and two seamen, Thomas English and John Allerton. Of the ship's company, went two master's mates, John Clark and Robert Coppin, the master gunner, and three sailors. Edward Tilley and the gunner were weak with illness but determined to go. Tilley nearly fainted with the cold.

The wind blew fiercely from the northeast and greatly hindered their effort to maneuver the shallop around a sandy point to calmer water. The bitterly cold spray froze on their clothes like layers of iron. They sailed seven leagues by the shore but saw neither creek nor river. They did find an inlet about a league at the narrowest and two or three leagues in length. But their search for a home site took priority, and they chose to leave the discovery of the inlet until the next day.

As they approached the shore they saw a dozen Indians busy about a "black thing" they could not identify. Because the sands lay so flat, they had much difficulty beaching the boat, and by that time the natives had disappeared. Finally ashore, the men gathered firewood, built a barricade, and set out sentinels for the night. They saw smoke rising from the Indians' fires some miles downshore.

The next morning, Thursday, they divided their company, eight in the shallop and twelve on shore, and set out to discover the terrain. They found only a bay with neither river nor creek running into it, but it was about five fathoms deep, adequate for small ships. Later, they discovered the first two streams of fresh water in that country, but each one was narrow enough to stride over.

Several "black things," which the sailors identified as grampuses, had apparently cast up at high water and then found themselves helpless on the ice. Each measured about six paces long and two inches thick with fat like swine, a ready source of oil if they had had means to extract it.

This exploration yielded nothing fruitful. In the shallop they followed the shore, hoping to find the river Coppin had seen. Finding no river, they decided to put ashore and set off tramping through the woods. That day they came upon more graves, some set about with saplings like palisades, fields that had once been planted in corn, several empty wigwams, but no signs of natives. By evening, weary with bone-aching cold, they erected their barricade and settled down for the night.

Sudden piercing cries, like the sounds of wild annimals, aroused them from sound sleep. The sentinels shouted, "Arm! Arm!" In the darkness they could see nothing, but seized their muskets and fired off warning shots towards the woods. At once the sounds ceased. One of the sailors said he had heard such sounds in Newfoundland and believed them to be wolves. Unsettled, but somewhat reassured, they sank into fitful sleep.

Then just at dawn as they roused for breakfast, another volley of sound burst from the woods. The sentinels cried, "Indians! Indians!" and each man dashed for his musket.

"Woach! Woach!" the strange voices cried, "Ha! Ha! Hach!"

No one had ever heard such language before.

Captain Standish, with a soldier's caution, had wisely kept his weapons with him, and fired off a blast at the woods. Others hastily loaded their flintlocks. Some who had left their muskets near the shallop ran to retrieve them, then stayed to defend the boat. They called for a firebrand to light their match-cords, and someone at the barricade snatched a log from the fire and carried it to the boat. This maneuver aroused not only the dreaded native cries but a volley of arrows from the woods.

Despite the musket fire, this time the natives stood their ground, and one lusty chap whom the men presumed to be their captain, continued to shoot arrows into the barricade from behind a tree. Standish, taking careful aim, sent a shot into the tree, splattering the native with bark and splinters. The Indian howled and took off into the woods, his comrades quickly following.

The colonists left six men to guard the shallop, then trailed the natives into the woods a quarter of a mile, but as usual the Indians had vanished. Some guessed that thirty or forty Indians had attacked them. When they returned to the barricade, Edward Dotey exclaimed, "Look here! My coat's full of holes!" Several coats hanging on the barricade were shot through, and they found many more arrows on the ground, some headed with brass, some hart's horn, and some with eagles' claws.

John Howland, the lad washed overboard off the *Mayflower,*

announced, "This is my second reprieve. Holes in the coat but, praise God, not one in the flesh."

Despite the barrage of arrows, not one man had been hit. For this the saints and strangers alike praised the providence of God.

They called this episode the First Encounter with the natives. It would prove to be the least terrifying encounter of that day.

As the morning was fair, they hoisted sail and rounded the shoreline, but as the day wore on, the weather clouded. Rain, then snow, and a gale stirred up the sea so fiercely that it broke the hinges of the shallop's rudder. Two seamen took over the oars. As nightfall approached, Coppin strained to see through the gathering dusk and blowing spray for the elusive "Thievish Harbor" he had seen before. Suddenly Coppin cried out, "Be of good cheer, mates! We have found it!"

First Mate Clark ordered, "Press hard for shore!" But the driving wind caught the sail and snapped the mast, tossing the whole rig into the "very grown sea." The shallop was about to capsize. They chopped away at the rig to free it from the boat while Coppin steered them toward a cove foaming with white water. Then, agony upon agony, they heard Coppin's voice cry out, "Lord, be merciful unto us! For mine eyes have never seen this place before!"

The boat was riding a flood tide straight for the cove. One of the sailors at the oars bellowed, "If you are men, about with her, or else we are all cast away!"

The men manning the oars pulled for their lives to swing the boat away from the cove and its wild water. Heaving with all their strength, they slowly turned the boat about until at last they found themselves drifting on a lee shore, which gave them some shelter from the wind. Yet from the bobbing boat, it was now too dark to see land, and dreading another "encounter" with natives, they decided they would be wiser to huddle in the boat until morning.

Yet as they faced a long night, the wind shifted to the north and the temperature plummeted, threatening to freeze their wet clothing to their skins. Clark took stock of their dire situation and announced, "Men, 'tis better to risk the land tonight than freeze in this boat. I am going ashore." He climbed over the shallop's gunwale and dropped into the thrashing surf.

"Aye," his sailor mates agreed. "Better to freeze ashore than drown at sea. At least we can build a barricade to break the wind."

The sailors followed Clark ashore where they found dense woods crowding the shoreline, quickly cut some branches, and struck up a barricade. After intense effort to dry out their flints, they managed to start a meager fire. Its brilliant light, hardly more than a candle in the vast darkness, and its promise of warmth proved irresistible to the men shivering in the boat. They beached the shallop, clustered about the fire within the barricade, and passed the night in relative comfort. No natives appeared.

By morning they saw that they had made landfall on an island in the bay. The weather was clear and cold, good for exploration, but the colonists, exhausted from their labors, elected to rest.

The next day, Sunday, offered another day of rest. Though the sailors reminded them that they would lose two days for exploration, the colonists, ever faithful to observe the Sabbath, gave God thanks for His mercies and their "manifould deliverances," and with clear consciences spent the day drying out their clothing, cleaning their muskets and sleeping, sleeping, sleeping.

They would name the island for the man who saved their lives that night, First Mate John Clark.

ন্ত্র৺৶ঌ

Aboard the *Mayflower,* lookouts now kept anxious watch across the bay, for their expedition had been gone five days with no sign of their return. Voyagers and crew alike understood that this time they must choose a site, however good or ill it might be. The last two days a fierce northern blow had tossed the ship about, straining her anchor and icing her rigging, and all but the lookouts had burrowed below decks. When the storm passed, the new day dawned clear and bitterly cold, and anxious eyes took up the watch again for a small boat crossing the blue water home to their ship.

When the weather cleared, Dorothy Bradford ventured up to the main deck to stretch her limbs and breathe fresh air into her lungs.

Emerging from the gloom below decks, the bright daylight blinded her at first, but the expanse of choppy sky-blue water offered no comfort. William had left—when? Only a day, or perhaps a week ago? Either way an eternity, for the tedious days only varied with the coming and going of the men exploring the shore and the weekly Sabbath. Since William had left this time, the ice storm had driven everyone belowdecks, dreading to think of their men suffering somewhere in the shallop without any shelter. If they never returned, no one would ever know what happened to them.

Dorothy wondered if William were dead.... She shut this thought off. She could not endure another loss. If he were gone... She looked up at the arcing sky, so blue, so pure, like Heaven. *Heaven! What if William looked down upon her now suffering on this ship while he, free from all pain, beckoned her to join him?* She shook her head. She must be careful not to lose her senses, to give way to vain imaginations. She stood awhile at the rail enduring the blustery north wind, yet dreading to go below to the stinking 'tween decks. *William, please come home. I cannot go on without you. I have lost everything— everyone, my family, my son, and now...you?*

She must go below. It was too cold here, yet only a little warmer belowdecks sheltered from the wind. She made her way down the gangway, found her pallet, and lay down. *William, where are you? Come home.*

She slept awhile, stirred, and realized she needed the waste bucket. So much trouble to get up and find it, yet one cannot abandon all civilities. She dragged herself up from the pallet, then up the gangway. Where did they keep the bucket now? She emerged once again on the deck. The sky and the sea were darker now. All was quiet, everyone sleeping, the lookouts down for the night and only the nightwatch strolling the deck. The ship itself seemed to sleep, quietly bobbing on wind-chopped water. She made her way to the rail and raised her eyes to a night sky blazing with stars—layers upon layers stretching away into the heavens. How lovely! How infinite! Even in this wilderness endless stars testified of an endless universe, recalling to men things eternal, of God's eternity, displayed there in the skies for all men to see.

The water below her had turned black now, showing dimly white where it sloshed against the ship's hull. So cold, so...*not of earth, man's natural element, her William had said. And they had "buried" poor William Butten in this unfriendly, inhuman sea.*

She began to weep again—for William Butten, for little John, for all these good people trying to please God in some mysterious way she could not understand. Was He not as well pleased with families at home raising their children to be good citizens as with adventurers crossing freezing seas for...for...what? To build a town for civilized men in a wilderness inhabited by savages? Yes, some were called to that work. Some. Not herself.

She raised her eyes to the glittering sky. Low on the western horizon, where a trace of the sun's afterglow still shimmered, the Evening Star winked at her, as if sending a message. A sudden thought pierced her reverie. If William was gone, he might try to signal her that he was safe at last, *home* at last. *Come home, Dority. Come join me here.* And yes, gladly, *eagerly,* she would join him—not only as a blessed reprieve from this misery, but to prove as well that, despite their differences, she did love and honor him as a proper, dutiful wife.

⁂

The nightwatch pausing at the bow hugged himself to stir up a little warmth in his blood. Thank God his relief would soon free him to go below for warm beer and sleep. If he were a praying man, he would pray that this time the lubbers find their site and begin at last to depart the ship. If they did not leave soon, Cap'n might decide it was too late to cross the sea for England, and they would be stuck on this stinking ship for the winter. Never again would he sign on for a crossing so late in the season. The voyage was perilous enough without winter storms chasing their tail. Yet, much as he disliked the colonists, he felt a twinge of sorrow for these poor blokes facing a bigger struggle ashore building their own houses before the worst of winter to come. Mad men they were! Every one of them *mad!*

A sound caught his ear. A big splash in the sea, like a big fish slapping the water with its tail, maybe a *whale?* Did they do that in the dark? He snickered. Well, did a whale know dark from light? He walked along the starboard rail toward the sound, leaned over the rail, heard nothing more, then cocked his head to listen more closely. *Something* had splashed out there bigger than the contents of a waste bucket, and no cooks were throwing out garbage this late. He stood, puzzled, and moved along the rail, peering down. The choppy water showed no sign of unusual disturbance. He waited. Finally he shivered again, hugged himself. Where *was* his relief?

Then, suddenly, the man opened the hatch and bounded onto the deck. "How goes it, mate?" he bellowed. "Feels like hell froze over up here."

The first sailor shrugged. "Nothing amiss. But *colder* than hell froze over."

He bolted for the hatch. Halfway down he paused. He'd forgotten the splash. Should he tell the new watch to look out for a whale? He shrugged. If it was a whale, it'd likely show itself again. *Get below, dolt. You're off duty.*

Twenty

New Plimoth

On Monday the eleventh, the men set out to inspect the harbor, which they found to be deep enough for ships. The land overlooking the bay on the western shore offered cornfields and running brooks, altogether "fitt for situation" which the "season and their presente necessessitie made them glad to accept." Greatly encouraged, they rowed twenty-five miles straight across the bay to the *Mayflower,* where all aboard could rejoice in their discovery of a home site. And truly overwhelmed with gratitude, the poor people aboard fell upon the explorers with great fervor. They had been gone a week and were feared dead. Husbands, wives, and children, even some sailors, hugged each other and thanked God for their deliverance.

Bradford made his way up the ladder to the *Mayflower's* deck, bursting with happiness. At last he could give Dority some good news. The sight of her sweet face smiling instead of grim would thrill his soul. Yet, glancing over the women, he saw at once that she was not among them. Perhaps she was still belowdecks tending someone ill, or perhaps not well herself. That would not surprise him, so weary had she been...so discouraged. He could hardly wait to tell her.

Brewster laid his hand gently on Bradford's arm. "Son, come with me. I have news for you."

Bradford looked into Brewster's tortured eyes. "What is it, sir?"

"Come with me."

So, Dorothy *was* ill. He almost expected it, so downcast had she been. Yet she was young and strong, as hardy as any woman aboard. His faith would sustain her.

Brewster led him into the captain's vacant cabin. He paused for breath, his eyes glistening with tears. "Dorothy is gone."

Bradford frowned. "Gone? Where?"

"Overboard. We know not how it happened."

For a moment Bradford could not move or think. Yet the despair on Brewster's face told the terrible truth. Dorothy was *gone*. "I don't understand, sir."

"Nor do we, son. She simply disappeared during the night. Of course we did not miss her while we slept. Then in the morning, busy as usual, we did not notice at once. Then someone..." He swallowed. "Someone said she was not on her pallet, and not tending the sick. We asked the nightwatch, then the sailors on duty. No one had seen her."

"Impossible!" Bradford spat out. "She could not simply disappear on this tiny boat."

Brewster shook his head slowly.

Bradford's own throat closed. This tale made no sense. How? Why? Unthinkable! Surely, someone... He stood paralyzed.

Brewster extended a hand toward him. "We have looked everywhere aboard ship. Every nook and crevice, even the bilges. She is not here."

Bradford became aware of a vast silence outside the cabin, yet could hear clearly the resounding slap of sea against the ship's hull. *My God! My God! Why hast Thou forsaken me?*

Brewster said, "Stay here awhile." He moved to the cabin door. "Stay as long as you like. You need the rest." He left the cabin.

Bradford stood awhile, swaying on his feet but unable to move. Then massive weariness overtook him, and he sank down on the captain's bunk. He saw the captain's belongings—his books, his charts, his clothing hung on the bulkhead. Why was he here in the captain's cabin alone? His mind could not answer. He was so weary, bone-weary, empty, yet not hungry. His stomach was as frozen as his coat had been frozen on the shallop's run into the cove. He went limp and fell sideways on the bunk, lost in the sleep of exhaustion.

Sometime later someone opened the cabin door. Bradford heard the creak as if in a dream, but did not open his eyes.

"He's still asleep," a voice said.

"Let him be," another gruff voice commanded.

"No," Bradford croaked out. "I am awake."

Brewster appeared above him. "We have some food for you."

Bradford opened his eyes. The fact that he slept in the captain's bunk and that Brewster stood above him told him something had gone awry. He should be belowdecks with Dority. *Dority!* Yes, something was wrong with Dority. His mind closed down on the memory he could not accept. He glanced up at Brewster. "Food, you say?"

"Aye. You must eat something, son." Behind Brewster, Captain Jones held out a bowl of porridge and a hard biscuit. His weathered face was grim with compassion.

Bradford gazed into the food. "Yes. I do need something." Yet he only stared at the food, trying to summon energy to eat it.

Dorothy's disappearance almost dispelled the good news of the men's return and their discovery of a home site. Of all the desperate moments this colony had shared, this was the most incomprehensible. What great irony, that God would show them their new home while He took Dorothy home to Heaven. Yet the unspoken, unthinkable question hovered in the air: Did she go to Heaven? Suicide was no less heinous than murder. If she had done this thing, had deliberately cast herself overboard, she would not be admitted to the Kingdom.

The people who had known Dorothy best agonized with grief. Who last spoke to her the night she disappeared? Who knew her desperation? Priscilla Mullins had seen her tending the sick as often as Priscilla did herself, but they had not spoken that day. Mary Brewster knew of Dorothy's despair, but she had never suspected that the girl would throw herself overboard. Brewster recalled that he had warned Bradford: "Keep close to her, and when you go off make sure someone stays by," and now he wished he had pressed the lad harder. Yet it would have been unreasonable, nay impossible, for anyone to watch her every moment. Others who were not ill themselves had their own concerns for husbands, wives, children, the sick who could not function.

Some stopped Bradford to lay a hand on his arm and to look soulfully into his eyes, offering their wordless sympathy. He nodded, understanding their effort, but made no attempt to speak, only once finding courage to question the nightwatch on duty, who had seen or heard nothing. When he could think of Dorothy the person, the woman who had been his wife, he could not believe she had done this thing willfully. She had loved life too much, loved her son too much, to cut off all hope of seeing him again. Perhaps she had only been exhausted and fainted. If it had not been an accident, surely she had not been so determined that she dropped over the ship's rail and would not cry out for help. There were no certain answers. Yet the reasonable answer he dreaded most was that their prolonged exploration had convinced her he was dead. Having lost their child, she could not endure losing her husband as well. She must have lost all hope and could not endure. That he could believe. He could almost believe he might have done it himself.

Worst of all for Bradford, God was silent on the matter.

Then one day the eight o'clock watchman approached him on deck. "Mr. Bradford. May I 'ave a word wit' ye, sir?"

Bradford looked into the sailor's seamed face, whose eyes flicked about, not confident enough to meet his own. "Of course."

"One night just before midnight I was awaitin' my relief when I heard a loud splash beside the ship." He swallowed, dropped his eyes. "I din't think much of it, but then I got curious. Whatever...*who*ever made it was bigger than...well, than wot's in a waste bucket. Couldn't make out anything in the water, thought it might be a whale slapping its tail. Forgot about it. But now...your wife missing an' all. I thought I'd tell ye." His pained eyes darted at Bradford, then glanced away.

Bradford stared at the man's grim face. A sudden sharp image of Dorothy climbing over the ship's rail pierced him to the core. So little substance in this message, yet perhaps the resolution of the mystery. For a moment he could not speak. Then, "Something larger than a waste bucket?"

"Aye. Somethin' *solid.* A dolphin leapin' maybe. Hardly see 'em after dark." At once he looked stricken. This bloke had lost a wife and he's saying he heard a *fish!* "I am sorry, mister. I shouldna' mentioned it."

"No, no. I'm glad you did. Thank you."

The sailor touched his cap and backed off.

Bradford gasped. Had the seaman actually heard Dority fall? Was this the answer to his prayer? *Lord! Lord?*

God was still silent on the matter.

It was over. Dority was gone. Bradford recorded her disappearance in his ledger: *Dec. 7. Dorothy, Wife to Mr. William Bradford.*

And never spoke her name again.

***

Now the business at hand was to make settlement on the western shore of Coppin's Thievish Harbor, or Plimoth Bay, according to Captain John Smith. Winter was descending upon them in full force, and they had no more time to waste.

Twenty-one

1621

On Monday, December fifteenth, Captain Jones weighed anchor and sailed the *Mayflower* toward the shore where the explorers had found their "place very good for situation." A seventy to eighty-ton ship could have reached closer to shore, but the *Mayflower's* 180 tons required deeper water. She dared not risk the narrow channel and sandbars near shore. Also, strong northern winds held the ship back two more days, then shifted long enough to allow Captain Jones to maneuver through the channel. Yet not half an hour after the ship anchored a mile and a half offshore, the wind changed again, which, had they not moved, would have blown them back to the Cape. For these "tender mercies," which often came within a hairsbreadth of failure, the colonists thanked God once again.

Now they delighted in the prospect of a home in this "most hopeful place" on the western shores of the bay. Fish, crab, mussels, and fowl were abundant, the soil was darkly rich and produced an array of herbs, fruit trees, vines, onions and leeks, an excellent hemp, and small brooks ran freshly into the bay. A site on the northern shore offered a river navigable by small ships at high tide. At the southern site the land sloped up from the shore to fields already cleared and once planted in corn. Here a fresh brook ran between two high points offering a clear view of the sea and the inland countryside. Some spoke in favor of Clark Island, where First Mate Clark had saved their last expedition. Isolated, it provided the greatest security from native attack.

Each site had its supporters, but also its limitations. The northern site was farthest from the fishing areas, which was expected to be their main source of income. The southern site would require hauling of supplies from the shore up the steep hills, and Clark Island had poor, mostly rocky soil, no reliable water source, and dense woods difficult to clear for farmland. The colonists could not reach agreement that first day and continued vigorous discussion aboard the *Mayflower* that night. Elder Brewster advised the people to rest themselves for tomorrow's work, seek the Lord's direction, and make their witness known the next morning.

The next day the company still did not agree on a final location but did agree to take one more look at their options. Governor Carver solemnly cautioned them. "We cannot now take time for further search or consideration. Our victuals are much spent, especially our beer, which means, as you know, we are soon reduced to drinking ship's water." Moans rippled around the group. "So, God willing, today we will go ashore one more time, then make our final decision."

They surveyed the northern site again, some strong for the advantage of the navigable river, but others wary of easy native attack from surrounding dense woods. At last those who had signed the *Mayflower Compact* voted. The majority chose the southern site, whose worst fault was the distance they must haul supplies. Now committed, they focused on their new home with fresh perspective.

The site offered several landing spots along the shore—one a large flat rock that provided a stepping stone over sandbars. Standish was pleased with a high hill in one field, an ideal vantage point for their cannon. Their first order of business, however, was to build a common house to shelter the workers who would build the families' homes.

Twenty men stayed ashore that night, prompting the fiendish weather to unleash a New England nor'easter which lasted two days. The men ashore had had no time to erect a shelter, and the bay was too rough for the shallop to transport provisions to them. That week, while the twenty shivered ashore in the raging storm, three colonists died aboard ship—Richard Britredge of London, Solomon Prower, servant of Christopher Martin, and Mary Allerton's stillborn child.

The weather cleared briefly on Saturday, allowing the shallop to cross the roiling bay and the men ashore to begin the arduous task of cutting trees and planing boards for their twenty-foot square "rendezvous" to be built on top of the hill. Sunday, while the workers observed the Sabbath, the storm returned, accompanied by raucous shrieks from the woods, the same cries they had heard during the First Encounter. All matchlocks were held at the ready, but no attack came.

Monday, December twenty-fifth, Christmas Day, dawned relatively clear, but the saints who had never found authority for Christ's birthday in the Bible, and therefore never celebrated the holiday, worked strenuously this first fruitful workday since they had chosen their site. Weary men returning to the ship that night found the crew in holiday spirit enjoying the ship's beer, and then unhappily discovered that the last of their own beer was gone. Captain Jones, however, in a generous burst of holiday good will, offered them some of the ship's brew. This was a bounty they could hardly refuse, no matter the reason, and only regretted that the twenty ashore had neither beer nor water, just a heavy downpour.

At last on Thursday, the twenty-eighth, they laid out the plan for their first street. It would run up the hill to the Common House, and a row of houses would be built on either side surrounded by a protective fence of palisades. Plots would be assigned by lot according to each family's size, and single men would lodge with families until their own houses could be built. Slowly, gradually, despite bitter cold and frequent storms cutting their workdays to half the week, the little village began to emerge from the wilderness.

So many were now ill or too weak to work that those able few drove themselves to exhaustion, desperate to provide shelter and warmth for their brethren. Deaths occurred almost daily. These months of January and February were the "starving time."

Mary Brewster said to her husband one morning, "So many are sick of the scurvy and pneumonia, I fear none will be left to inhabit the village."

Brewster replied, "Yet I cannot think that our Lord will take us all. He has brought us too far to let our mission fail now."

Mary sighed. "I do wonder sometimes...did we leave too late? Perhaps we should have waited until spring to cross the sea."

Brewster shook his head. "My dear, have you forgotten how desperate we were to leave? We cannot change the past, Mary. Our mission now is to survive."

Yet the toll mounted. Only seven or eight persons had sufficient strength to work and accomplish necessary duties preparing food, building fires, performing all the loathsome chores required to serve the sick. Two stalwarts were Myles Standish and William Brewster, strong in spirit and apparently immune to the ravages of hunger and cold. By now all persons of the colony, sick or well, were keenly aware that they could depend only on God and each other.

Despite his resolve to forget the past, Bradford thought often of Dorothy, in his heart secretly grateful that she had missed this starving time. However she had died, he would hold fast to the belief that she was safe with the Lord whose mercy was everlasting. It was himself who needed mercy now, not only God's but his own. He doubted he could ever forgive himself for taking Dorothy away from her son.

The ship's company also began to fall ill. Crewmen complained that those who had caroused together in happier times now deserted one another in sickness. One boatswain who had often sneered at the saints' piety, lamented to one of them, "You, I now see, show your love like Christians indeed one to another, but we let one another lie and die like dogs."

The saint could not resist a chance to witness to his faith. "That is because we serve our Lord, and He requires that we serve each other."

The boatswain shook his head skeptically. "Then why does He let you all sicken and die as we do?"

"His ways are higher than our ways. One day in Heaven we shall know."

The boatswain scowled. "A poor bargain, if ye ask me."

"Ah no, my friend. 'Tis the best of bargains. Sooner or later we all die. Yet we are certain to go to Heaven." He smiled. "Are ye certain where ye will go?"

"Dinna' preach to me, man. I've heard it all."

"Then listen, friend, listen and truly hear that word."

The men working ashore occasionally saw smoke from Indian fires, prompting Standish and his men to tromp through the woods, hoping to find some natives in the flesh. They found only deserted wigwams. This enigma had puzzled them since they had landed on Cape Cod. Where did these natives live? How could they simply vanish? Yet their stealthy presence was not reassuring. Every colonist was convinced that natives watched their every move, waiting for a chance to attack, and therefore every instance of mishap aroused dread.

After one foray looking for natives, Standish and his men brought home an eagle for supper. They found it "excellent meat...Hardly to be discerned from mutton," exclaimed Bradford. Fresh food was so urgent a priority that Captain Jones took his ship to sea to fish and brought back three seals and a cod. One of his men found a hearty herring on the beach, which Jones confiscated for his supper. These finds raised hopes among the people of a bountiful future. Yet no one had advised them in England to bring small hooks for fishing. Now they found to their dismay that their hooks were too large for the small cod and herring abundant in the bay. Captain Jones shook his head, not for the first time astonished at these poor people's naivete.

One day Francis Billington, exploring the territory, climbed a tree and sighted a huge "sea" three miles inland, and persuaded one of the master's mates to help him find it. They discovered two large fresh water lakes brimming with fish and waterfowl. From this source ran the fresh water brook that traversed their town. With each such discovery the people's hopes rose. If only...if only they could keep their people alive until all this bounty could be harvested!

Now it appeared that Christopher Martin lay close to death. Since he had jealously guarded the colony's accounts, it was thought appropriate for Governor Carver to inquire about them. But poor Martin was too ill to discuss finances, and soon after Carver's visit he was carried ashore to be buried on the hill where graves mounted day by day. The colonists reasoned that their safety lay in their numbers, and so covered their graves and planted them with corn, hoping the natives would not know how few and how sick their people were.

On January ninth the Common House was complete except for its thatched roof. Plots were laid out and assigned to each family by lot.

Governor Carver and his leaders, Allerton, Bradford, Deacon Fuller, Hopkins, and Winslow, felt that the people would work more diligently on their own homes than working together on one house at a time. Their driving hope was to bring the people still living on the ship to land as soon as possible.

They made slow progress on their village, for even minor mishaps sapped their meager energies. Bradford was thatching the Common House roof when suddenly he collapsed on the ground, grasping his hip. "Father in Heaven!" he cried, "the Devil seizes me!"

Several near him rushed to his side. He gasped, "Searing pain in...my huckle-bone. Like a bolt of lightning down to the ankle."

They laid him down on a bed in the House, but he tossed with such pain that they thought death itself would take him. Francis Cooke ordered, "Someone call the surgeon."

Dr. Samuel Fuller had begun work on his own plot, but he came running. "What devil has got ye, lad?"

"Old Snatch himself, likely," groaned Bradford, grimacing.

"You took a cold a ways back, wading in an' out from the boat, didn't ye?"

"Aye, but no more than the others. No man stays dry in this place."

"I have a balm for you. Lie still, and I will fetch it."

Bradford did not appear to have either scurvy or pneumonia, but lay in misery all that day. After earnest appeals to the Almighty and Fuller's warm compresses, he began to feel better, to everyone's great relief. When their leaders were laid low, the people were especially distressed.

The next day Bradford was not well but enduring tolerably. It did not appear that he would die that day. As his pain eased, his concerns turned to the unfinished roof. John Goodman and Peter Brown told him they would go off to cut more thatch, a tedious work. Rushes and reeds strong enough for thatch were available only along streams and patched across meadows, requiring much labor to cut, bundle and haul.

Four men went off to cut the thatch. Later that day two of them delivered bundles of reeds to the village, then returned to the spot where they and Brown and Goodman had been cutting. The latter two and their dogs had vanished and did not respond to loud halloos and calling of their names. Carver sent out a search party at once, but they found no trace of the men or their dogs. This event aroused anew lurking fears that Indians lay in wait to attack. The men had not returned by the next night when the thatched roof of the Common House burst into flames that could be seen from the *Mayflower*. The fire convinced those aboard grieving for the missing men that Indians had grown bold enough not only to kidnap the men but to attack the House. Actually the thatch had caught fire from a spark and had driven the sick lying abed to flee into the soggy night. But it was quickly quenched and little damage done to the rafters.

The next night Goodman and Brown and their dogs came limping into the village, "readie to faint with travail and wante of victuals, and almost famished with cold." Goodman's mastiff had picked up the scent of deer and bounded after it, the spaniel following, but the deer soon outran the frantic dogs. Goodman and Brown chased them down and were dragging them back when a chilling cry deep in the woods struck panic in their hearts. Evidently the dogs' ruckus had aroused "lions" hidden deep in these woods. Men and dogs hightailed it through the woods helter skelter heading for home but soon found they had lost their way. They hallooed to no avail, then wandered aimlessly all that day and night in freezing rain and snow, afraid to sleep in such "intolerable cold lodging" as a tree. They spent a fitful night in the snow under a tree, ready to spring up the trunk if the "lions" appeared.

The next day the wanderers set off again and finally reached a high point where they could see Clark Island in the bay. From there they reckoned their way back to the village after dark.

Dr. Fuller said grimly, "Your feet are so swole, lad, we'll have to cut off those boots."

"Ah, no," Goodman wailed. "These are my only good boots."

"Must be done. Or you'll die of gangrene."

They cut the boots away to reveal feet so swollen with frostbite that Goodman couldn't walk for days. Nevertheless, the colonists thanked God for his reprieve.

Stephen Hopkins asked with a smile, "'Lions, you say, here on Cape Cod? More likely wolves, I'm thinking."

His insight was prophetic. Some days later, while Goodman took his spaniel walking, out from the woods sprang two actual wolves aiming for the dog. Goodman seized a stick to ward them off, threw it, and struck one. Both wolves turned tail and disappeared but quickly circled back to boldly confront Goodman and his dog. He seized another heavy stake and waved it at the animals, whereupon they "sat both on their tayles, grinning at him a good while." Heart in his mouth, Goodman continued to brandish his stick, and at last the "lions" turned and left.

While not fatal, each of these mishaps drained the colonists of their meager energies, and more and more fell ill. The Common House, jammed to capacity with the sick, was now used as a hospital "as full of beds as they could lie one by another." The loss of each person was grievous to the colony, as if one by one their "family" who had suffered so much together was ebbing away.

Priscilla Mullins and Susanna White were concerned about Elizabeth Winslow, whose energy was so depleted she could not work. "She's too young to be so weak," Priscilla complained to Mary Brewster.

"I think she's lost hope, almost like..."

Priscilla said, "I know. You are thinking of Dorothy."

Mary nodded.

Priscilla protested. "Edward would be devastated to hear that. Elizabeth was eager to come on this voyage, expecting to have her own home and family. We must give her hope."

Mary sighed, and wondered, *Lord, hast Thou abandoned us?*

Then, as often happened at a point of lowest morale, God bestowed another "tender mercy" upon them. For three days, Tuesday through Thursday, January sixteenth through the eighteenth, fair days "like April" shone upon the village, a harbinger of spring to come. These balmy days of renewal took practical form in their resolve to build a shed near the House to store their common goods. The thatch fire had come so close to igniting open barrels of gunpowder and loaded muskets lying about that obviously they needed a storeroom. They built a shed on Saturday, the twentieth, highly motivated by their hope to bring all the people aboard the *Mayflower* ashore to celebrate the Sabbath as one united body the following day.

Brewster preached a sermon, expressing gratitude for their hopes in the Lord God who had sent them here, and their conviction that He would see them through this desperate season. He read from Psalm 103.

"Bless the Lord, O my soul: and all that is within me
bless His holy name.
Bless the Lord, O, my soul, and forget not all his benefits:
Who forgiveth all thine iniquities; who healeth all thy diseases,
Who redeemeth thy life from destruction...."

Yet February, the depth of winter, would seem to fling their gratitude in their faces. So fierce were the storms that month that the daub was washed from the new houses, and the ship, now light of ballast, near foundered in the bay from violent wind and seas. In the midst of such weather the colonists' greatest fears—starvation and Indian attack—converged to torment them unbearably. Rarely could they work for sleet and snow, and Indians sighted on several occasions struck fear of attack in the staunchest heart.

The behavior of the natives continued to perplex them. On an expedition to find fresh meat Jones and his men killed five geese and brought them home for the sick. On the same foray they came upon a deer freshly killed, yet no meat was taken, only its horns removed. In mid-winter it was inconceivable to the Englishmen that the natives did not harvest fresh meat for which the colonists were so desperate.

More worrisome was the tale of a colonist lying among the reeds waiting to shoot waterfowl, who was startled when twelve Indians walked near him on a trail leading toward the village. He lay still as they passed by, but as soon as the way was clear he raced to the village to warn the people. They dropped their tools, hastened to the House to take up their muskets, and waited. Nothing happened. After awhile Standish and Francis Cooke went back for their tools and found them missing.

This thievery called for immediate action. Not satisfied with emergency measures, Standish called the colony together to organize a strategy for defense. Their first order of business was to name Standish Captain-General and give him "authoritie of command in affayrs." But their business was abruptly interrupted when Francis Billington burst into the meeting shouting, "Indians! Indians!" All rushed outside to see two Indians standing on the hill opposite the fort.

The colonists stared at the brightly painted natives just across the brook while Carver and his men stood calmly considering how to address them.

Carver called to them amiably, "We are happy to see you."

The Indians did not speak but made signs indicating they wanted someone to come over to them. Carver nodded that he understood, then replied, "We invite you to come to us."

They continued to make beckoning gestures. Carver returned their signals while speaking to his men, "They cannot understand my words and are wary."

"Aye," Brewster agreed. "We need to show them we are peaceful."

Carver said, "Men, keep your muskets ready, and I will cross the brook to meet them."

"Pardon me, sir," Stephen Hopkins spoke up. "Let me go. Perhaps I can make out some of their language."

Standish, the officer in charge, snapped, "And I will go with him."

Carver hesitated. He did not want to risk two of his best men. Yet neither did he want to waste this opportunity to parley with the only Indians who had contacted them. "All right. You two go. We will stand ready here for any surprises."

Standish said, "We will take only one musket."

Hopkins nodded. "Good idea. And lay it down before them."

The two waded across the brook, moved slowly toward the natives, then paused. Standish laid down the musket at his feet.

Suddenly, the Indians swung about and ran down the hill into the woods. As they disappeared, the colonists heard a clamor of voices, sounding like a sizable crowd of natives awaiting them. The colonists were disappointed while Standish was alarmed. "They can't be trusted," he insisted. "Why were they waiting there?"

Carver reassured him. "We will stay alert, Cap'n. And now I think it is time to mount our cannon on the hill. Our show of force may convince them to try again to meet us."

The following week the sailors and colonists labored to drag their enormous cannon up the hill to the Common House—now become also a fort. The pieces were a minion weighing 1200 pounds and a sacre 1500 pounds. The minion shot 340 yards through a three-and-a-quarter inch bore, and the sacre shot 360 yards through a three-and-a-half-inch bore. They were mounted on a wooden platform atop the hill beside two smaller bases which each shot a half-pound ball. Besides uncertain aim and limited range, the arms were unpredictable, as liable to backfire on their crews as to hit a target. Yet the people sighed with relief, hoping that the skulking enemy who watched their every move might be properly impressed with such formidable armament.

Yet nothing seemed to abate the winter weather with more to come. The awful toll February had taken on their number was seventeen.

ɔ⋆ɕ

The third day of March dawned fair and misty and brought a warm wind from the south. Birds sang "most pleasantly." That afternoon the first thunder rolled across the sky, strong, short claps that brought a gentle rain falling all that day until midnight. The next day the wind shifted to the east, bringing colder but fair weather. On Wednesday, the seventh, the people planted their first garden seeds so carefully brought from Leyden.

Captain Standish waited patiently through this season of sickness and foul weather to resume his military preparations. Finally in mid-March he called the colony together again to finish the business of establishing military order. They had been in session only a short while when an astonishing event again interrupted their discussion.

A tall brown figure strode boldly into the village and up the street to the rendezvous. After all the futile efforts Standish and his men had made trying to engage the natives, now without preamble one simply appeared at their meeting. Some saw him coming and alerted those in the House. They hastened outside to greet him before he could invade their sanctuary. He paused, raised one hand in greeting, and then spoke clearly the English word, "Welcome!"

The colonists were stunned. Carver, ever the perfect gentleman, addressed him. "Friend, we welcome you as well. We are eager to parley with you."

He nodded to Mary Brewster, who sent Priscilla Mullins hastily to get some food. Priscilla brought back biscuit, butter, cheese, pudding, and a piece of mallard, which the Indian accepted readily. Then he astonished them further by asking if they had any beer. Carver shook his head. "Our beer is all gone. We can only offer you some 'strong water.'"

They brought out some brandy, then waited politely while he ate and drank. The people were bursting with questions, all wanting to talk at once.

Carver raised a hand for silence, then addressed the Indian. "Tell us who you are, friend, and where you come from."

He told them his name was Samoset and that he was a sagamore, or chief, of the Abnaki tribe from Monhegan in the territory of Maine. He had been in these parts only the previous eight months as a guest of Ousamequin, also known as Massasoit, sachem of the Pokanoket, their nearest neighbors living forty miles southwest. Northeast of them lived the warlike Nauset, a hundred or so who had probably been the ones who attacked the colonists in their First Encounter on the Cape.

While he spoke in broken but understandable English, the colonists drank in his every feature. He was tall and straight, had black hair, long in back and short in front, and no hair on his face at all. Here in mid-March he wore only a leather belt with a short fringe about his waist. The women modestly averted their eyes from his nakedness and, glancing at each other, suppressed giggles.

Mary Brewster whispered to Priscilla, "The wind is picking up. It's getting quite chilly. Quietly, so no one notices, fetch that horseman's coat of William's. We'll offer it to him for a cover."

Priscilla blushed, then slipped out to Brewster's house to fetch the coat. When she brought it to Governor Carver, he looked puzzled for a moment, then presented it to Samoset as a gesture of good will. Samoset grinned and swung the coat about his shoulders. Brewster gave Mary a startled frown, but when she nodded and smiled back, he realized she had prompted Priscilla to make the gracious gesture. He hoped fervently that they meant it to be a temporary honor, for the coat was one of his prize possessions.

All afternoon they listened raptly to Samoset's imperfect English as if he were a messenger from God sent to answer all their questions. He told them that their land had been inhabited by the Patuxet tribe, all of whom had been struck down with a plague four years ago. Other tribes in the area, fearing evil spirits had caused that disaster, would not inhabit the territory. That explained the cleared fields not recently planted, and also revealed that no claimants remained to contest the colonists' adopted land.

At nightfall, when Samoset showed no sign of leaving, Carver asked politely, "Where is your habitation?"

Samoset gestured as if to say "anywhere convenient." Since he made no move to go, they felt obliged to lodge him for the night. They thought of taking him aboard the *Mayflower*, but the tide was low and the wind high, which meant that the shallop could not return to shore. Finally, Stephen Hopkins offered to keep careful watch over him at his house for the night. Hopkins reported in the morning that although he did not, Samoset slept soundly all night long.

The next day Samoset told them that the Nauset were much vexed with the English and eight months ago had slain three of Sir Fernando Georges' men. Their grudge was retaliation aimed at Captain Thomas Hunt, a ship's master, who had deceived the people under the appearance of bartering, and taken seven Nauset and twenty Patuxet to Spain to be sold as slaves for twenty pounds each. The natives had not forgiven the English. So the colonists' dread of attack had been well founded after all. They further surmised that the plague that eliminated the Patuxet had surely been God's provision of a site cleared and prepared for their settlement.

The next morning Samoset announced he would return to Massasoit. The colonists gave him parting presents—a bracelet, a knife, and a ring, and urged him to return with Massassoit's men bringing beaver skins to trade.

Carver told him, "We are eager to truck with your people. But to guarantee our friendship we ask one condition: that you leave your weapons some distance away. Do you understand?"

Samoset nodded agreement.

Then, smiling at Brewster, Governor Carver said graciously, "And we will be happy to keep the coat for you to wear upon your return."

The next day Samoset returned with five stalwart natives fully dressed in deer skins and long leather leggings covering their ankles to their waists, much like the trousers of the Irish, the colonists noted with amusement. Like Samoset they had black hair worn short in front and long in back, but their hairless faces were painted with various colors and designs. One wore a feather broadwise in his hair like a fan and another a hanging horse's tail. Their skin coloring was dark like that of English gypsies, and like gypsies they entertained with native chants and dances, "after their manner, like Antics," Bradford commented in his notebook.

They had brought five beaver skins, but the colonists could not trade on a Sunday. Carver approached the subject delicately. "We are sorry that we cannot conduct trade today because it is our Sabbath."

Samoset looked blank. "What is sabbat?"

Carver explained. "Our God instructs us to labor six days and to rest from our labors on the seventh day. We observe this strictly, which means we cannot trade today. I am sorry. We are most willing to trade another day. Do you understand?"

Samoset nodded, then explained to the five in their language. They nodded as if they understood.

Carver went on. "Please ask your friends to come back soon with many skins."

Samoset spoke again to the braves who glanced doubtfully at one another. One held out the skins. Samoset said, "We leave skins with you."

"Please do not," Carver objected. "Bring them when you come again."

The Indians disagreed with this, insisting they would leave the skins.

Brewster whispered to Carver, "This may be a matter of honor to them. Let us accept them gracefully. There's no use risking offense in ignorance."

Carver gestured for Alden and Howland to take the skins. "One more thing," he told Samoset. "Our tools were stolen in the woods. We would like them returned. We need them to finish building our houses."

Samoset told this to the Indians who nodded assent.

Carver now asked Captain Standish to escort them to the place where they had left their weapons. But Standish's armed men flanking the Indians seemed to alarm several, who began to slink away. Samoset and the others called them back, reassuring them all was well, and the two parties left each other with smiles and pleasant words.

But Samoset did not leave. He pleaded sickness, or made pretense of sickness, apparently as excuse to stay with the colonists whose food and hospitality he obviously enjoyed. They hosted him until Wednesday and then urged him to leave and return with his trading partners. They outfitted him with a hat, stockings, and shoes, a shirt and a loincloth, and sent him off. Brewster kept his horseman's coat well hidden.

Once again Standish called a meeting to organize military strategy but hardly had they begun when three Indians appeared across the brook wearing war paint and making a show of sharpening and rubbing their arrows. "What do you think of this?" Carver asked Standish.

"Methinks they are letting us know who's in command," replied the Captain.

"Let's call their bluff," said Bradford. He and Standish donned their armor, took up their muskets, and beckoned two sailors with muskets to follow them. As they crossed the brook the Indians suddenly took flight into the woods.

This day was March twenty-first, a memorable day for the colony. They sailed the shallop out to the *Mayflower* and brought back all the colonists still living on the ship. Yet one mournful event marred this accomplishment. Edward Winslow's wife, Elizabeth, died that afternoon. Thirteen had died so far in March. And none of the fragile signs of spring to come could compensate for these lost too soon.

Bradford tried to comfort Winslow. He put a hand on his shoulder and said, "I feel deeply for you, my brother. I know how you suffer."

"The girls were so young. I wonder, should we have brought them?"

"We had to come, Edward. We took a great risk, and some of us lost. I pray God will honor our effort."

272

Winslow said nothing about the manner of their wives' deaths. Their fates lay in the hands of the Almighty.

The next day Standish once again attempted to finalize his plans for order and once again was interrupted by the appearance of two Indians. This time they were Samoset and a friend named Tisquantum, called Squanto, who, Samoset informed them, "had been in England and could speak better English than himself." The colonists could not foresee that this person would prove providential for their colony, for that day a more prominent visitor captured their attention. Squanto told them that the great sachem Massasoit, his brother Quadequina, and a company of their men had come to the village to meet them.

As they stood awaiting this momentous event, the sachem and Quadequina appeared at the top of the hill across the brook flanked by sixty braves. They were a breathtaking sight. Massasoit's face was painted a dark mulberry color gleaming through a film of oil "greasily" spread all over his body. He wore a deerskin over one shoulder, and a chain of white bone beads from which dangled a knife in front and a leather tobacco pouch behind. The sixty warriors were painted a variety of colors and designs. All were tall and powerfully built. Had this bevy of brawn confronted any Englishmen in the woods, their physiques alone would have intimidated the bravest of white men. Moreover, they were sixty strong, three times as many as the surviving colonists.

Squanto informed Carver that the sachem wanted to parley and requested that the governor cross the brook to speak with him. Carver acknowledged the invitation gracefully but countered with one of his own. Squanto relayed the invitation, but Massasoit, majestic in his royal dominance, shook his head no. Squanto prevailed upon Carver to reconsider. "He biggest sachem, chief of many tribes. He want to parley with you."

Carver was willing to go, but Brewster and Standish cautioned him. "He wants to talk with our head man as befits his status as chief. But we can't afford to lose you, John, if this proves to be a trick."

Carver turned to Squanto. "Tell him we come in peace to this place. He has nothing to fear from us."

Standish snorted. "Tell him if he moves a muscle, he'll hear our muskets."

Carver spoke softly. "No, Myles, make no move to alarm them."

"Gov'nor, sir," Winslow spoke up. "Let me go. If they see that you send me as your representative, they'll know I speak for you. And I believe I can reassure them."

Winslow's diplomatic talents had been evident as far back as Leyden. Carver considered a moment, then nodded. "We'll stand behind you, Edward."

Winslow took with him a knife and a jewel for Quadequina's ear, and a pair of knives and a copper chain adorned with a jewel for Massasoit. He also took biscuits, butter, and a pot of brandy. The sachem received the gifts with pleasure, but his eye was taken by Winslow's armor. He asked Squanto to trade for them. Winslow deftly evaded this request with a speech declaring King James' friendly intentions toward the chief, and his offer of love and peace to be expressed by their governor. He told him that Governor Carver was eager to "truck" with the tribe, and to make a lasting peace with the sachem. Through all this Massasoit listened, his eyes flicking from Squanto to Winslow as each spoke, yet his sober face betrayed no sign of reaction.

Although Winslow explained later that Squanto did not express his placating sentiments exactly, the sachem favorably received what he understood. He and Winslow conversed awhile through Squanto, but Winslow, eager to arrange a parley between Massasoit and Carver, finally offered to remain as hostage with Massasoit's men while the sachem crossed the brook to speak directly with the governor.

Massasoit considered this request for some moments, his face impassive. Then he turned to his men and spoke. Twenty of them placed their bows and arrows on the ground and moved forward to flank the chief. He indicated that Winslow should stay with the other forty warriors. With great dignity he walked slowly toward the brook where Standish and his guard of honor waited. Splendid in their best armament, the squad escorted the sachem down the main street to an unfinished house and ushered the party inside.

Standish had staged the conference area with impressive décor. A green rug and several cushions spread on the floor. Shortly after Massasoit and his men sat down, a trumpet blared and drums rolled outside the house. The door opened to admit Governor Carver and his escort. The sachem stood up and kissed Carver on the hand. Carver returned the gesture, and all sat down in a circle around the room.

Carver continued the ritual. He called for a pot of brandy, drank a first draught, then extended the pot to the sachem. Massasoit, befitting his brawny stature, drank a great draught of the "strong water," and, to the guards' amusement, burst into a glistening sweat. The guards nudged one another at the sight, but the sachem and his Indians turned not a hair.

Now Carver called for fresh meat, offering some first to Massasoit who tasted it, nodded agreeably, then passed it on to his men. In turn Massasoit took some tobacco and a pipe from his pouch, lit it, smoked a few puffs, then passed the pipe to Carver, who passed it around the circle.

Then it was time for business. Carver began. "We come in peace to this place and want to be your friends and allies."

Squanto interpreted and Massasoit nodded. "We too come in peace," he told Squanto.

Carver said, "We have drawn terms of agreement that we hope your people and ours may honor in friendship forever."

Massasoit nodded again. Carver brought forth a paper and read it item by item, pausing while Squanto interpreted its meaning to the Indians. The words were gentle and supplicating, and the sound of Carver's sonorous voice seemed to rest upon Indian ears like a soothing melody. Winslow wrote down the terms for posterity:

1. That neither he nor any of his should injure or do hurt to any of our people.
2. And if any of his did hurt to any of ours, he should send the offender (to us) that we might punish him.
3. That if any of our tools were taken away, when our people were at work, he should cause them to be restored; and if ours did any harm to any of his, we would do the like to them.
4. If any did unjustly war against him, we would aid him; if any did war against us, he should aid us.
5. He should send to his neighbor confederates to certify them of

this, that they might not wrong us, but might be likewise comprised in the condition of peace.

6. That when their men came to us, they should leave their bows and arrows behind them, as we should do our pieces, when we came to them.

Lastly, that doing thus, King James would esteem of him as his friend and ally.

Winslow noted that, "All which the king seemed to like well; and it was applauded of his followers."

༶ঔ৵

The meeting was over, the men rose to leave, and Carver walked with Massasoit to the brook. There they embraced, and the sachem left with Squanto. But Standish had taken the precaution of detaining six of the sachem's men until Winslow returned safely. Yet it was Squanto who soon returned to announce that Quadequina was coming, apparently expecting the same royal treatment given Massasoit. Obligingly, Carver observed the same ritual in the same house, offering the brother meat and drink and friendly conversation. Quadequina, however, unlike Massasoit, displayed strong distaste for the English muskets, and waved them away. Captain Standish, with Winslow's finesse, sent them out of sight but kept them handy in case of surprise. Quadequina expressed gratitude and great friendship as he left. Winslow soon returned unharmed, Standish released the hostages, and all seemed well. The colonists relaxed with great relief. They could not have asked for better success.

Squanto and Samoset, however, did not leave with the Indian party who, they said, were camping in the woods near Plimoth. This news prompted the ever-cautious Captain Standish to post extra guards that night, just in case all this folderol had been a cover for some duplicitous action by the natives. But the night passed quietly.

In the morning their new Indian allies, pleased with the transactions of the previous day, arrived for breakfast. Now the colonists, still on short rations, had to decide whether frugality or hospitality should prevail. Ellen Billington told Priscilla sharply, "We treat them too well. They eat as hearty as they look."

Priscilla said thoughtfully, "Perhaps we should let them know how scarce our rations are. Maybe they will bring us some of their food."

Priscilla told Mary Brewster, who presented this very reasonable idea to her husband. "Umm," he mused. "Winslow's the man for that sort of parley. What puzzles me is that these people survive all winter on deer meat. Why do they prefer our poor victuals?"

✍ ✌

The end of March was the beginning of the new calendar year. On the twenty-fifth the colonists held a meeting to establish order and settle daily business, and to elect a governor for the year 1621. John Carver was their unanimous choice.

Some days in late March were fair and warmer, giving the colonists' their first opportunity to plant seeds and establish gardens. Squanto would prove to be "a special instrument of God for their good" in many ways. He told them that when the oak leaves were the size of mouse ears it was time to plant corn. He showed them how to place five corn kernels at the centers of small hills and to lay alongside three whole fish, heads pointed toward the seeds to guarantee a good crop. They must guard against wolves for fourteen days until the fish rotted.

The women watched him demonstrate the technique by setting the kernels and drawing lines in the soil where the fish would go. Elizabeth Hopkins asked, "So where do we get the fish? We've only caught one cod in this place."

"Soon many fish come to spawn in brook. Easy catch." He stood up and gestured toward the brook. "Soon."

The women looked at each other hopefully. Squanto had already demonstrated his unique talent for catching eels. He had come into the village one day carrying an armload of sleek creatures which tasted "fat and sweet." He led the women to the mud flats where he stomped them up with his feet and snatched them as they wriggled free.

Squanto's remarkable journey about the world convinced the colonists that God had sent him across the seas to Spain, thence to

England, and finally back to Plimoth just so he could teach them how to survive in this wilderness. The fact that he learned to speak English on his sojourn was the convincing evidence. And although the Pokanoket had taken him into their society with no apparent discord, Squanto preferred living with the people of New Plimoth and "adopted" them as his own.

The colonists had so fervently anticipated the coming of spring that no one could imagine any possible sorrow this season could bring. But now they faced one more heartbreak. Their mother ship must soon sail home to England.

Governor Carver had prevailed upon Captain Jones to stay while the colony struggled to establish shelter ashore in mid-winter. And for his own practical reasons Jones had dared not sail during storm season while his crew were severely disabled. Nor could he wait for harvest to replenish his diminished stores, for then another winter season would be upon him. The weather was most favorable now, his surviving crew recovered, and the ship's stores barely enough to see them home.

On the appointed day, April 5, 1621, the colony gathered on the shore to bid Jones and his men good-bye. These people from such different backgrounds had endured much misery together, had seen the depths of character, or the lack of it, in each person, had formed human bonds, and now parted as friends. Carver shook Captain Jones' hand. "Sir, I cannot thank you enough except to say that only God knows how much we owe you."

Jones nodded. "It has been a long voyage for all of us. I wish you and your people success, sir. Without a doubt ye are the hardiest passengers this old ship ever carried." He glanced up at the hill to where half his crew was buried. "And I leave them in your good hands."

Carver grasped Jones' hands with both of his. "God bless you, sir. I pray that our grateful prayers carry you safely home."

Colonists and sailors shook hands and embraced all around. Then the crew boarded the longboat and headed across the bay for the *Mayflower*. The women held their aprons to their faces, and the men bit their lips. Their eyes followed the longboat until they could no longer distinguish it bobbing on the bay. Then they watched the

Mayflower's sails unfurl, and the ship turn about to catch the breeze. They made their way up the hill to better watch her head east toward the open sea. There the remnant of the colony, only half its original company, stood weeping, surrounded by the graves of their own lost ones and the ship's crew, and saw their last English home vanish on the horizon.

Not one of the colonists had chosen to go with her.

෫෦ஜ

Now the business at hand was to plow the fields and set in their crops. Since the survival of their colony would depend on a bountiful harvest, all able-bodied persons were called to the work of digging, spading, hoeing, weeding, and hauling thousands of spawning alewives from the brook up the steep hill to the fields. They planted twenty acres in Indian corn, and six in wheat, barley, rye and English peas.

The warmer weather was a boon not only for planting but for building houses. These were simple-framed walls of wooden planks, thatched roofs, and earthen floors, scarcely twenty feet square. A second level across half the lower floor served as a sleeping loft. Yet the hard physical labor of planting crops, cutting wood, planing, and thatching, besides hunting and fishing for fresh food, drained their weakened bodies trying to recover strength from the sickness of January and February. Only twenty-one men and six hefty boys had survived to do the heaviest labor. Thirteen surviving women and girls tended the households and planted family gardens around each house.

Ironically, an added burden was the Pokanoket, who continually drifted in and out of their village, expecting food and entertainment. Exhausted trying to provide for their own company, the colonists had little to share with their persistent visitors. The Indians had become a friendly nuisance.

Governor Carver took no special privilege as magistrate. He served his turn at the fields like all the other men. One day in mid-April, he suddenly dropped his hoe and seized his head. Others nearby called out, "John! What is it?"

"My head," he moaned. "My head...aches so."

They helped him to the nearest house. The weather was unusually warm for April, and his skin was hot to the touch. They bathed his face and stripped off his shirt, trying to cool him. Catherine came running and flung herself down beside him. "John, speak to me. John, please, please do not leave me."

Yet Carver did not awaken. His wife and Priscilla Mullins continued to bathe him all that day, but by nightfall he had lapsed into a coma.

"Oh, my dear God in Heaven," Catherine cried. "Do not take him from me. I cannot live without him. Please, Lord!"

"Hush," Priscilla tried to soothe her. "He's only overtired and needs to rest awhile."

Dr. Fuller took Priscilla aside. "Heat stroke. Keep him cool."

Two days later their beloved Governor John Carver left their company forever.

After all the others, this loss was beyond bearing. Brewster went before the Lord. *This man was our strength, Lord. A good man, our very best. You ask much of us, Lord, to take him now. Sometimes You ask too much. We cannot bear it. God, give us strength to bear this loss.*

They escorted Carver's body to the top of the hill in a formal procession and committed him to the realm of Heaven. Brewster said a prayer of thanksgiving that John was now safely in Heaven. They shot a volley over his grave, and went home to mourn another of their dear brethren.

Two weeks later his widow, Catherine, sister of Bridget, died of "heartbreak," declared Dr. Fuller. She left her estate to their servant, John Howland, who had survived drowning at sea and Indian arrows at the colonists' First Encounter.

Now the colonists faced another critical decision. They must choose another governor. Who could replace John Carver? Only Brewster matched him in piety and seasoned wisdom, but Brewster was Elder of the colony and could not hold a position of civic authority. The people talked among themselves, considering other good men who had shown talent for leadership—Bradford, Winslow, Fuller, Hopkins, Allerton. Any one of these could lead the colony. After much discussion they chose Bradford, who combined an incisive talent for governance with the sensitivity of a cleric. And Bradford, still recovering from his winter illness, chose Isaac Allerton as his assistant. Concerning civic affairs he and Allerton would consult with other men to administer laws. But in matters of public interest they would adapt their long practice of discussion among the congregation to include the entire adult male population in a town meeting. This extension of the biblical mandate to "tell it to the church" instigated the format for democratic government unique to New England, the Town Meeting.

Bradford's leadership would also initiate a new tone of discipline in the colony. Nearing the end of their first year at Plimoth, he and the younger men, Winslow, Hopkins, Allerton, and Standish, were moving into positions of authority held by their older leaders, Clyfton, Robinson, Carver, and Brewster. While no less spiritual than their elders, these "heirs" took a more pragmatic view of their enterprise, realizing that the survival of the community would depend as much on hard practical decisions as by reliance on religious faith. Their first winter on Cape Cod had intensified their reliance on a loving paternal God to lead them through the grim realities of this wilderness. Yet as He had led the Israelites through the desert, He had revealed to the colonists the grim realities of their own "desert" but did not allow them to avoid its trials.

Governor Carver had presided over the first serious violation of civic order in early spring when John Billington had boldly defied Captain Standish's order to take his stand at night watch. Standish had him brought before the Governor and recommended he be bound neck and heels together without food or water. Billington had protested vigorously but soon began to beg for mercy. The brethren, who always preferred mercy to penalty, heaved a sigh of relief when he repented and submitted to Standish's authority. Within an hour Carver let him go.

Soon after Bradford's appointment to office he confronted a more serious offense. Hopkins' two servants, Edward Dotey and Edward Leister, two suspected of inciting mutiny on the *Mayflower*, challenged each other to a duel. At dawn on a strip of quiet beach, each held a sword in one hand and a dagger in the other, and charged each other. By the time Standish discovered the fight and hauled them apart to be disciplined, both were wounded and bleeding. Furious at such folly, Bradford ordered their necks and heels bound together for twenty-four hours. While they pleaded for mercy, their master, Stephen Hopkins, appealed for their release on grounds they were only foolish boys and should be put to hard labor instead. Reluctantly, Bradford relented, lectured them sternly, then let them go. Their punishment had one lasting effect on the community. Theirs was the first and last duel in the colony.

As summer warmed their fields and soothed their bodies, the remnant began to recover from their dreadful winter sickness, and with a resurgence of energy considered more pleasant means of reorganization. Susanna White had been widowed with three children, and Edward Winslow had lost his young wife. What more profitable arrangement for them than to marry and begin a new family? All colonists were well aware that even in England single parents fared poorly in the best of circumstances, and in this wilderness the embrace of family was essential for survival.

Elder Brewster made the suggestion to Winslow. "You've been a devoted husband, Edward, and these little ones need a father. Can ye find it in your heart to love the dear mother?"

Winslow's eyes brimmed with tears. "Elizabeth and I wanted a child of our own. She looked forward to...." He swallowed, unable to go on.

"I know it's only been two months, Edward. I only suggest it now so ye may give it a thought or two."

"Susanna's a fine lass, Elder. And God knows we need to make the best of this venture. Perhaps we can console each other." Winslow's eyes met Brewster's. He sighed. "I'm willing to try."

Mary Brewster spoke to Susanna on the matter. "Is it too soon to think of marrying again, Susanna?"

Susanna said softly, "I do admire Mr. Winslow, m'am. But no, I have not thought to marry yet." She raised wide eyes to Mary. "Except that...my children do sorely miss their father. I must think of them first." She lowered her head to hide her tears.

"Love is a decision, Susanna. Like a flower, it blooms the better it is tended."

Edward and Susanna were married early in May, the first wedding and the first occasion for merriment in New Plimoth. In robust Elizabethan style the people patched up their most colorful clothes and feasted on venison, fish, and waterfowl. Dancing was forbidden to Calvinist believers, but they did joyously sing psalms and folk tunes.

On their spring run to spawn, the herring crowded the brook, and Squanto's trapping devices yielded a bounty of fertilizer for the corn crop. Now the people could turn their attention to building more houses and nurturing their personal gardens.

Bradford's urgent business was to make every effort to maintain amiable connections among the Indians, whose friendship they needed desperately. Massasoit sent another Indian, Hobomok, to the colony to act as liaison from the sachem's tribe. He was a "pinese," a chief, a "man of value," a combination priest, warrior, and statesman. Massasoit, a shrewd ruler, sent him as much to keep himself informed of the colonists' activities as to maintain goodwill with the community.

Bradford decided to send Hopkins, Winslow, and Squanto on an expedition to Massasoit's headquarters at Sowams, about forty miles from Plimoth. Their mission was to explore the territory, taking note of the quickest route to Sowams in case of emergency, and to persuade Massasoit to curtail the flow of Indian visitors who strained the hospitality the colony could ill afford. They took with them as a present for Massasoit the red horseman's coat now trimmed with lace, with which they had adorned Samoset on his first visit, and a copper chain to be used as a talisman. Reluctantly, Bradford agreed to give up the coat as gesture of good will toward Massasoit. Mary chided him about it. "What noble sacrifices we must make for our welfare."

He scowled. "Nothing noble about it. Simply practical good sense."

Mary giggled. "I will bet that he shows it off more proudly than you did."

Their first stop was the village of Namasket, fifteen miles from Plimoth, a wearisome walk and surprising distance considering the Nauset so frequently invaded their village. They arrived late in the afternoon, were warmly received and served *maizium*, or Indian cornbread, and boiled shad-roe and acorns served with wooden spoons. After the first bites of roe, the two envoys glanced at each other doubtfully, then ate sparingly so not to offend their hosts. Of the shad, much more to their taste, they ate heartily.

The Namasket complained that crows were ravaging their corn crop and asked the men to shoot some. Glad to reciprocate for their hospitality, Winslow took out his trusty musket and shot a crow at eighty yards. The natives were astonished at such firepower.

The envoys journeyed on to arrive at another Namasket settlement at sunset where they were as cordially received and treated to a feast of fresh bass. As the Namasket had no wigwams, they slept in the open air that night, and in the morning resumed their travels, accompanied by six natives. Two of these insisted on carrying each of the white men across brooks and waterways while the others relieved them of the burden of carrying their weapons. Such indulgence amazed and amused the humble colonists certainly not used to such gracious service. Chuckled Hopkins, "Shall we tell them we are not really gentry?"

En route Hopkins and Winslow noted sadly the cleared fields and rich soil now lying fallow since the plague had destroyed the Patuxet. The most poignant evidence was fields littered with old bleaching bones never buried. Whether or not this provision was coincidence or God's grace, both men were grateful for the land that lay waiting for them.

The second day they entered Pokanoket territory and by nightfall had reached Sowams, only to find Massasoit not in residence. While a messenger ran off to summon him, Squanto suggested that the two visitors salute the sachem with a discharge of their muskets. The very sight of these pieces so terrified the native women that they ran away and would not be comforted until Squanto explained that the men were going to salute the sachem, not attack the village.

When Massasoit appeared they shot off the guns, then greeted him with gifts and expressions of friendship. Massasoit invited the two visitors into his lodging and seated them beside him while a throng of spectators gathered to watch the parley.

Winslow began his appeal: "Forasmuch as your subjects come often, and without fear, upon all occasions amongst us; so we now come unto you. And in witness of the love and good will the English bear unto you, the Governor hath sent a coat, desiring that the peace and amity that was between you and us might be continued. Not that we feared you, but because we intended not to injure any, desiring to live peaceably and as with all men, so especially with you, our nearest neighbors."

Massasoit listened closely while Squanto translated, then nodded his approval.

Winslow continued. "But whereas your people came very often, and very many together, bringing their wives and children, they were welcome. Yet we being strangers as yet at Patuxet, and not knowing how our corn might prosper, we could no longer give them such entertainment as we had done and as we desired still to do. Yet if you would be pleased to come yourself, or any special friend of yours desired to see us, coming from you, they should be welcome. And to the end we might know them from others, our Governor has sent you a copper chain, desiring if any messenger should come from you to us, we might know him by his bringing it with him, and harken, and give credit to his message accordingly."

Squanto delivered this long statement in much fewer words than Winslow's while Massasoit nodded as he listened. Winslow went on: "Also we request that such as have skins should bring them to us and that you would hinder the multitude from oppressing us with themselves."

Massasoit nodded vigorously, looked about at his people as if to say, "Hear that? This means *you.*"

Some of his people, understanding, nodded assent.

Winslow took a breath. "At our first arrival at Pamet, called by us Cape Cod, we found there corn buried in the ground, and finding no inhabitants but some graves of the dead newly buried, took the corn, resolving if ever we could hear of any that had right thereunto, to make satisfaction to the full for it. Yet since we understand the owners were fled for fear of us, our desire was either to pay them with the like quantity of corn, English meal, or any other commodities we had, to pleasure them withal. We request that some one of your men might signify so much unto them, and we would content him for his pains."

Squanto turned from the sachem to Winslow as if to ask, "Is there more?"

Winslow raised a hand. "And, last of all, our Governor requests one favor of you, which is that he would exchange some of your corn for seed with us, that we might make trial which best agreed with the soil where we live."

Winslow indicated to Squanto that he was finished. Massasoit looked about his people and nodded his satisfaction. They heartily responded.

Now Hopkins brought out the glorious red coat and the copper chain and offered them to the sachem. Massasoit put them on, then strutted about proudly on display for his people who cheered and applauded. After this show the sachem swept the coat about him and with great dignity answered Winslow's requests. "You are welcome. And we would gladly continue that peace and friendship which was between us and you. And for my men, they should no more pester you as they had done. And I would send to Pamet corn for seed, according to your request."

The sachem then stretched to his grandest height and addressed his people. Squanto translated for the two explorers. "Was not he, Massasoit, Commander of the country about them?" The people applauded. "Was not such a town his, and the people of it?" And should they not bring their skins unto the English?" They applauded and cried out that they were his, and would be at peace with the English, and bring their skins to them. He went on to name thirty places, and they answered every one the same. For Hopkins and Winslow it was a "delightful" performance, but after awhile a bit "tedious."

Massasoit then offered the men tobacco and pipes and sat down for a pleasant conversation. He was curious about England, what kind of country it was, and what kind of person was their king. When told that King James lived alone since his wife had died, the sachem expressed surprise. "How is it that a king has no wife?" he asked. "No one to cook and care for him?"

Winslow replied that the King of England had numerous attendants to do these chores, explaining that the Queen was a consort, not a servant. Massasoit thoughtfully puffed on his pipe, considering this novel circumstance. He turned then to the subject of the French and asked Winslow not to allow them to come up the Narraganset to Pokanoket, his territory, for that was now King James' country and the sachem was King James' man. The two colonists smiled and readily agreed, having been long convinced that Massasoit feared the French as well as the Narraganset, a warlike people, and had shrewdly solicited English friendship, and their amazing firepower, as allies.

By now the envoys, their bellies grumbling, glanced about hopefully. They had long ago digested the Namasket bass but saw no sign of preparation of food at Sowans. Hopkins asked Squanto, "When does the sachem eat?"

"Sachem not home long time. No food ready."

"You mean nobody eats when he's away?"

"People feed selves each day."

"Well," murmured Hopkins, "that's a fine community spirit."

Winslow grinned. "Apparently they rely on community for protection, but not sustenance. Perhaps we can teach them some new biblical concepts."

Squanto broke in. "People catch plenty food in season."

The colonists decided that if they could not eat, they had better sleep. They faced a long trip home. They asked Squanto, "When do the people sleep?"

"Soon."

It had grown late, and the Indians were yawning. At last Massasoit lifted his huge frame from the deerskin he sat on and stood up. "Sleep now," he told Squanto and gestured toward the visitors. He turned and left the parley area.

Squanto said, "Come."

They followed him to the sachem's personal lodging. Squanto gestured toward the sachem's bed, a platform of planks split out of trees and raised on stakes about a foot off the ground, then covered with a thin mat. The sachem and his wife lay at one end and Squanto indicated the two men should lie at the other, there being barely enough room for four persons. The "guests" lay down and tried to ignore their empty stomachs.

"Have we anything left in our knapsacks?" Winslow whispered.

"A bite of dried duck," Hopkins grumbled. "Shared most of it with the Namasket, thinking, like a fool, that we'd be replenished here."

Suddenly two burly chiefs lifted the deerskin door, came in, and flopped down on the bed between the two visitors and the sachem couple. Hopkins groaned, sat up, and batted at his shirt. "Methinks the grass outside might make a better bed, were it not for the mosquitoes." He made a grim face. "In here we have only fleas and lice."

They lay still, trying to compose themselves for sleep. Just as they dozed off, the two braves began droning a kind of tuneless chant. "Do they dream?" Hopkins whispered, "or is this prayer?" Then the sachem's voice joined the two chiefs in a chorus of singing, as best the men could tell, a kind of adult lullaby.

"Barbarous," Hopkins growled.

Winslow muttered, "Well, Stephen, look at it this way. We've completed a successful mission, for which our reward for that good cause is no food and no sleep. Pray the good Lord for the grace of sleep, and maybe He will provide some breakfast in the morning."

They slept fitfully, beset by lice and fleas, and awoke famished, dismayed to see no evidence of breakfast then either. Soon a number of lesser chiefs came to pay honor to their English visitors, and among themselves, began to gamble for skins. When the envoys also offered to shoot at a mark for skins, the natives declined, by now well aware of the power of English muskets. But they did want to see the English shoot at a mark without making a wager. Hopkins decided to dazzle them with firepower. He loaded his musket with bird shot and peppered the target with a multitude of holes. Mystified, the natives stared at the holes, wondering at their magic appearance.

By noon without food and little sleep, the travelers were feeling faint. About one in the afternoon Massasoit himself appeared with two large bass he had caught that morning. They looked like bream, only three times larger and of better meat. Winslow's and Hopkins' mouths were watering so, they could hardly wait to bite into that flesh. Yet by the time the fish were boiled and ready to eat, forty more Indians had arrived to share the bounty. Hopkins was aghast. "Forty men for two fish! Impossible!"

"We should tell them about the loaves and fishes," Winslow chuckled. "Perhaps if we had faith enough, the Lord would provide another miracle."

When Massasoit urged them to stay longer, they quickly declined, insisting they must return home in time for their Sabbath. Actually their imposed "fasting" and want of sleep had so weakened them they feared they would not have the strength to finish their journey. Even Massasoit seemed to sense his hospitality had been inadequate. He sent Squanto out to other villages to procure trade for his visitors, then sent Tokamahamon, a trustworthy aide they had met before, to accompany the two travelers on their journey home.

Winslow and Hopkins departed Sowams early the next morning. At the village where they had been feasted with bass they were given only a little fish this time and bought a string of dried oysters to give the six natives accompanying them. For themselves they bought some *nocake,* Indian meal to be mixed with water each time they drank.

They plodded along the return route, noting lush weeds growing in fertile soil along streams. Many fine oak, fir, walnut, beech, and chestnut trees grew on parklike fields where men could have ridden horses under the trees as they did in England. Yet when they came upon those fields of bleaching bones, remnants of the plague, they could only grieve for this great loss of pagan souls.

Their party stopped again at the weir near Titicut which they had passed coming in. To their great delight an abundance of fish was running here, and two of their Indian escorts caught and roasted their first substantial meal in three days. The two exhausted envoys promptly fell fast asleep while the Indians, keen to take advantage of such bounty, stayed up most of the night catching, roasting, and eating. Although a wild thunderstorm descended upon them, and by morning they could keep no fire lit, the extra fish the Indians had cooked provided an ample breakfast.

By daylight the rain continued to fall heavily, but despite the downpour, the two travelers were so eager to return to New Plimoth that they would not stay the night at Namasket, and made their way home quickly "wet, weary, and footsore."

The colonists, ever grateful for the survival of their people in the wilderness, celebrated their return with thanksgiving. Bradford was much pleased that their success with Massasoit forged another solid link in the chain of friendship between the Pokanoket and his community.

Not all the effort that summer involved bonding with the Indians. Some involved bonding among the colonists. John Alden, long admirer of Priscilla Mullins, who now lived with the Brewster family, finally decided to activate his quest. These long months of misery and despair had broken down barriers of social standing, and John, a vigorous young man, expert at carpentry and building houses, was now as highly regarded in the community as any man of status. Priscilla had lost all her family, and John felt she needed a husband to care for her. What better man could speak for her than himself?

He confided in Elder Brewster. "We have talked together now and then, sir, but I have never revealed my feelings for her. We never spoke of marriage."

"D'ye not think it wise in the matter of marriage to approach the lady first?"

"I would first ask permission of her father or brother, but they are gone. You are her proper guardian now."

Brewster considered a few moments. "Methinks you might best begin to beguile the girl as friend and confidant. Her young women friends, Dorothy and Elizabeth, are gone. She may be lonely."

"So I am thinking, sir. But I would not presume upon her."

"We would be pleased to include ye in our family gatherings, John. Be patient, wait upon the Lord. He will provide the proper opportunity."

Twenty-two

Harvest

Through the summer the business of daily living settled into routine, the fields and gardens growing, more houses rising, and the people slowly recovering their strength. Their rations were still meager and their work exhausting, but the expected bounty of summer promised harvest in the fall.

Then in August the Billingtons' younger son, John, disappeared. The colony grieved for him as lost until they heard from natives that he was found at Manomet, a village twenty miles from Plimoth. The sachem there, Canacum, sent him farther out on the Cape to Aspinet, sachem of the Nauset, whose warriors had attacked the colonists in their First Encounter. Why had they not returned him to Plimoth?

Bradford sent a party of ten men in the shallop to rescue the boy. En route they were caught in a heavy thunderstorm and threatened by a waterspout but finally managed to anchor during the night in mid-bay at high tide. By daylight six hours later the tide had run out, and they found themselves stranded on a sandbar far removed from water. The endless cycle of tides in the bay had once again thwarted them as it had done so often since they arrived at Plimoth. There seemed nothing to do but wait for high tide.

Squanto pointed towards shore where a group of natives could be seen digging in the shallow water. "Nauset," Squanto said. "Looking for lobster. We go ask for boy."

Winslow considered this advice. Sooner or later they must face the Nauset for good or ill. "All right. Tell them we mean them no harm, but only search for our lost boy. Take Tokamahamon with you."

Squanto and Tokamahamon waded ashore across the sandy flats and soon returned with news that John was safe at Nauset. The two natives glanced at each other and grinned. Squanto said, "Their sachem Iyanough invites the white men to breakfast with his people. He young man, only twenty-six years old."

"Can we trust him?" Winslow asked.

Squanto nodded. "Iyanough good sachem."

Ever cautious, Captain Standish spoke up. "Mr. Winslow, we cannot be too careful. I suggest we send a few men ashore and keep the others here. Ask them to send us hostages for good measure." He gave Winslow a stern look to emphasize his concern.

"Good thought, Myles. I trust your instincts."

Winslow went ashore with five of their men and Squanto, and the Nauset agreed to send four men to the shallop. Soon Iyanough himself came down to the shore to greet the colonists warmly. He surprised the white men with his gentle, courteous, and very personable demeanor, "indeed not like a savage at all save for his attire," reported Winslow to Bradford. He welcomed them to a luscious breakfast of fresh lobster and assured the men that their boy was safe with Aspinet.

Only one sorrowful note marred this encounter. An elderly woman, who looked to be a hundred years old, fell upon the colonists in passionate grief. Iyanough explained that her three sons had been kidnapped by Captain Hunt seven years before. She had never seen an Englishman, and the sight of them now overwhelmed her with sorrow.

Winslow hastened to agree that the Englishman had committed an unforgivable evil and promised that none of his countrymen would ever repeat such a crime. As Squanto translated, the woman eyed Winslow tearfully. He smiled and took her hands in his. "I promise you, mother," he said. She glanced at Squanto, then back at Winslow, not quite convinced she could believe this white man

"What more can I say?" Winslow asked Squanto, who shrugged, then spoke rapidly to the woman. Suddenly, she beamed a toothless smile upon Winslow. What did you tell her?" he asked the Patuxet.

"I told her you killed the captain."

Winslow's eyes popped. "You what?"

Squanto shrugged. "It pleases her. She will trust you now."

Winslow asked the other men, "What do you think of that?"

"Lying is convenient for natives," Standish replied. "Truth is often inconvenient."

"Why, Myles, I believe you are cynical. Some have good hearts like any men."

Hopkins smirked. "Will you tell her the truth then?"

Winslow quirked his mouth, his eyes twinkling. "Ummm. I think not. What good would it serve? Then she would distrust Squanto as well as me."

"You see? The captain is right. Lying can be very convenient. And so is a sin easily dismissed by earnest men like us trying to be good, honest Christians."

"Hopkins," Winslow scolded. "Sometimes you try us beyond measure."

After breakfast and entertainment by native dancing and singing, Iyanough and two of his men boarded the shallop and sailed on to Nauset with the colonists. There Squanto and Iyanough waded ashore to greet a crowd of Indians who urged the entire party to come ashore and drag the boat with them. Standish frowned on this proposal, and allowed only two Nauset to board the shallop. One of these, remarkably, was the owner of the corn cache the colonists had found on their First Discovery. He agreed to come to Plimoth to receive payment for his corn.

After sunset Aspinet and a hundred of his men appeared with young John festooned with beads and grinning broadly, apparently none the worse for his misadventure. Aspinet left fifty of his men ashore and waded with the other fifty out to the shallop along with the native bearing John on his shoulders. Each colonist in turn embraced the boy while Winslow thanked Aspinet profusely for his return. He told the Nauset sachem, "We are grateful for your kindness, and hope that this will be the beginning of a lasting friendship between us."

Aspinet listened to Squanto's words, then nodded agreeably. He gestured to Squanto, who repeated his message in English. "He say boy wise boy, eat only berries in woods, but eat much fish at Nauset."

Winslow presented Aspinet and the Indian who had cared for John two handsome knives, a small token for their diligence.

Hopkins asked John, "So were you frightened when they first found you?"

"Aye, sir," John admitted. "But they smiled at me, and put me to eat and sleep with their own boys, and treated me the same. The one who carried me here showed me how to shoot his bow."

As they were preparing to return home, Aspinet calmly reported a rumor that the Narraganset had invaded Massasoit's territory and taken him prisoner. This startling news alarmed the colonists, for if it were true, their own village at Plimoth may be in grave danger. Only twenty able men were left there to protect the colony. "Where did you hear this?" Winslow asked Aspinet.

Aspinet told Squanto, "Nauset hunters hear Narraganset say they take Pokanoket land from Massasoit."

The colonists took hasty council and agreed they must return to Plimoth at once. They boarded the shallop and turned west, but a contrary wind prevented their headway. By now their drinking water was nearly gone, so they went ashore again to embark on a lengthy search for water. What they found was brackish and undrinkable, but in the morning Iyanough himself boarded the shallop and sailed with them to his home at Cummaquid, where they found good water. When at last the tide permitted them to leave, Iyanough draped his own necklace of beads about Winslow's neck. "For friend," he said.

The rumor concerning Massasoit's capture had already alerted Plimoth. One of Massasoit's chiefs, Corbitant, sachem of the Pocasset, who had earlier been suspected of collusion with the Narraganset, was at Namasket arousing hostility against Massasoit, Squanto, Hobomok, and Tokamahamon for their friendship with the English colonists. Bradford and his leaders discussed what they should do. "We need to discover if this is fact or only a rumor. We would be foolish to act without certainty."

Hopkins said, "Send the natives to find out. They have proven trustworthy."

Standish scoffed. "This may only be big talk from a little chief."

Bradford summoned Squanto and Hobomok. "We need your help quickly. Will you go to Namasket and discover whether or not this rumor of Massasoit's capture is true?"

Squanto said, "We hide in woods near Namasket, ask hunters."

The two natives left for Namasket but near the village were

promptly discovered and imprisoned. They were taken before Corbitant, who raved at Squanto. "English come to steal land, kill Patuxet! You traitor!" Suddenly he seized Squanto and brandished his knife at his breast. "You voice of English. You die!"

Squanto quailed before the knife. Suddenly, Hobomok burst with superhuman strength, broke free from his captors, and dashed for the woods. He outran his pursuers and arrived at Plimoth to gasp out the news, "Corbitant threaten Squanto with knife, call him 'voice of English.'"

"Did you see him die?" Standish demanded. Hobomok shook his head no. "Then he may still be alive. We may be able to save him."

Bradford said calmly, "We can defend our colony here and await the outcome, or we can take aggressive action against Corbitant at once. Which shall it be?"

Hopkins said, "If we show fear now, we invite attack on ourselves."

"Aye, the best defense is offense," declared Captain Standish. "Let's give them a good show of our strength now."

Dr. Fuller added, "Methinks if we refuse to avenge this action, the natives will lose faith in us. This is a test of our promise to defend Massasoit."

Bradford looked about the group. "Are we agreed?" All heads nodded. "Then tomorrow, Captain Standish, you will take ten men and confront Corbitant. If he has murdered Squanto, you will exact his punishment in kind. You will behead him." He paused while the gravity of his order sank in. "But if Squanto is alive, assure Corbitant that we mean only to make peace here, not war. And, Myles, if you must punish him, take care that no one but the murderers are harmed."

ॐ∽

The next day dawned dreary and rainy, a dismal climate for bold assault on an enemy. Grimly, Standish and his men donned their armor, marched through the rain to Namasket, and camped in the woods outside the village. They decided that their best strategy was to attack at midnight, and Captain Standish gave each man instructions for the plan of battle. They set off bravely determined but soon lost their way in the darkness and plunged futilely through the soggy forest. Just as they were about to give up, Winslow recognized a landmark on the trail he and Hopkins had traveled to Sowams and turned the company toward the village.

Hobomok now led them to Corbitant's house, which they surrounded. Standish called out Corbitant's name, but no one answered. "No one will leave this house until we have searched it!" he roared.

Inside, the terrified Indians cowered as the English burst in, their muskets at the ready. Standish announced, "Do not be afraid, people. We will not hurt women and children. We want only Corbitant."

Hobomok translated his words, and the natives shouted back, "Corbitant not here!"

Some young men pretended to be girls, calling out, "*Neen squaes!*"—"I am a girl!"—while the women hung close to their "*netomp*" (friend) Hobomok, who told Standish, "They say Corbitant not here. He hide in other house."

"Where is Squanto?" Standish demanded. Again all shouted at once. Standish lost patience and roared above the clamor, "Be quiet! Someone tell me where is Squanto?"

Hobomok heard one clear voice: "Squanto not dead. Here in village." He dashed outside and climbed to the roof and called out for Squanto. After a few moments, to everyone's great relief, Squanto came out of a house nearby, grinning from ear to ear, greeting his English friends and inviting all to breakfast.

Many Indians accompanied the colonists home to Plimoth, offering to carry their muskets and knapsacks on the way. Stephen Hopkins was amused. "Having fought no battle, we are treated as victors."

"But we have won a victory, friend," replied Dr. Fuller. "Overcoming Corbitant without violence will encourage other tribes to ally with us. And I have been given an occasion to heal two of Corbitant's wounded people. All the Indian nations will learn of that. I call this a victory."

Reflecting on this expedition, Bradford nevertheless determined to take full advantage of their "victory" to warn Corbitant that the English never had evil intentions against him or his people but would not tolerate any betrayal of Massasoit. Any action taken against the sachem or their Indian friends would prompt immediate retaliation.

Within the next few weeks Fuller's prediction came true. Several sachems of different tribes sent word that they would honor the English king and pledge peace with his English colony. One was the sachem of Capawak, of whom the colonists had heard nothing at all. Others were Aspinet and Canacum of Manomet and even Corbitant, who sought Massasoit's mediation to join with the English. The new reputation of the bold little colony of New Plimoth and their terrifying weapons enhanced their power as a cohesive force among the tribes of Cape Cod. The "little chiefs" of Plimoth had indeed made "big talk," but it was the novel threat of peace—not warfare.

৯৯৯৯

That autumn nine sachems of the Cape signed a document declaring allegiance to the English king. It encouraged Bradford to attempt another such alliance with other Indians whom they had heard were hostile to their settlement. He began with an expedition to Massachusetts Bay.

Bradford appointed Captain Standish to lead a party of nine other colonists to visit the Bay with a threefold purpose: to see the country, to make peace with the natives, and to establish trade routes with the Massachusetts tribes. Sailing across the vast bay, the party was much impressed with its beauty and its islands, idly speculating that had they traveled farther north of Plimoth and found this location, they might have settled there. The distance from Plimoth to the bay was about twenty leagues, farther than they had anticipated, so they arrived much later than expected and spent the night at anchor in the shallop.

The next morning on shore they found many lobsters gathered together, obviously some native's catch. Thankful for this bounty awaiting them, they treated themselves to a hearty breakfast. Captain Standish then set two sentinels on guard to watch the shallop, and with four of their company moved inland to find the natives' habitation.

They soon encountered an Indian woman coming for her lobsters. They thanked her, and she was contented with payment for the food.

She directed them to the village inland. Squanto was sent ahead to engage the natives and to convince them the white men came in peace.

The sachem of this village was Obbatinewat who, although some distance away from the Cape, was submitted to Massasoit's rule. He received them kindly and told them that he could not settle in any one place for fear of the Squaw-Sachem nearby and the Tarentines, a tribe living on the Penobscot River in Maine. Standish informed him of the pact signed in September by many tribes of the Cape who had agreed to submit to King James' authority. "And we of Plimoth pledge ourselves as his agents to protect your people from your enemies."

Obbatinewat, pleased to agree to the pledge, and apparently emboldened by their presence, offered to escort the colonists to the habitation of the Squaw-Sachem across the Bay. They arrived at night, slept again in the shallop, and by daylight set out for the Squaw. They marched three miles and found a cornfield newly harvested, a house pulled down, but nobody living there. A mile away they found the deserted house of the sachem Nanepashemet, a sturdy structure more elaborate than the usual Indian dwelling. It was built on a scaffold of poles and planks six feet off the ground and set on top of a hill. A mile away a fort had been built of thirty to forty-foot poles set close together in the ground and enclosing a ring a hundred and fifty feet round. A breast-high trench was dug around the structure, and entry was made over a bridge. Inside lay the dead sachem.

A mile from this bier sat another similar house atop a hill where no one would live because the sachem had been killed there and the place was sanctified. Standish sent the two Indian interpreters ahead to inform the natives of their coming and to assure them their mission was peaceful. The Indians soon found some women a mile away, hastily stashing their corn in heaps, covering it with mats, and pulling down their houses. Hearing that white men were coming, they were leaving in great fear. Only by lavish reassurance did Standish and the interpreters persuade them they would not be harmed. The explorers' soothing ministrations soon persuaded the frightened women to cook cod and make cakes for them.

In the meantime, Standish sent messengers to look for the men hiding elsewhere, until at last one terrified native appeared and tentatively greeted the Englishmen. Seeing the women were no longer afraid, he agreed to trade for skins. He told the men the Squaw-Sachem had left the area.

Noting that the women wore garments of thick beaver skins, Squanto now surprised Standish with a shocking suggestion that the captain steal the skins the women wore. "These bad people," he said, "often threaten you. Take skins from the women and depart."

Standish was taken aback. "Were they never so bad; we would not wrong them, or give them any just occasion against us. Understand that we would little weigh their words, but if they attempted anything against us, then we would deal far worse with them."

But now another surprise was in store for the colonists. Pleased that the English had come to trade and not attack them, the women stripped off their fur garments and offered them to the visitors. Shyly they covered themselves with branches and boughs. "What are they doing?" asked Francis Cooke, aghast.

Stephen Hopkins laughed. "Trading, friend, trading."

"They are more modest than some English women," said Winslow wryly. "Methinks this is the beginning of a great trading enterprise."

As they left the bay, they passed the mouth of one of two great rivers the natives had described but did not take time to discover it. Another day they would like to traverse the vast harbor and its many deserted islands, a waterway ideal for shipping. But their rations were low, the wind fair, and the harvest moon bright. It was time to depart for Plimoth.

❧◈❧

The journey to Massachusetts Bay was the culmination of a bountiful summer. The people of New Plimoth had not only achieved a comfortable coalition between themselves and the Indian tribes of Cape Cod but had opened an avenue of trade in furs that would make considerable contribution to payment of their debt to the Merchant Adventurers.

New Plimoth now boasted seven houses and four public buildings for storage of provisions, tools, clothing, and the corn crop. Their Common House served as meeting house for worship, public gatherings, and when occasion demanded, a hospital. Summer had given them time to erect sturdier buildings than the first ones thrown up hastily for winter shelter. The newer houses were framed to support walls of planked boards and thatched roofs, a chinked wooden chimney on one wall, and a loft for sleeping. Parchment paper oiled with linseed served as windows. Yet these sturdy houses required more hard labor than had the first ones. All material must be wrested from the surrounding habitat, lumber hewn from tree trunks, clay dug from banks near streams, then carried to house sites, marsh grass gathered for thatch, and stones for foundations and hearths dug from the earth.

Survivors of the first winter had revived in relatively good health, and their corn crop was close to harvest. Winslow wrote home to England of clams, cod, lobsters, eels, and mussels from the sea, and wild fowl, deer, and turkeys in the woods. Spring and summer provided an abundance of "sallet" greens, lettuce, endive, watercress, and leeks, very sweet and strong fruits, red and white grapes for wine, strawberries, gooseberries, raspberries, and three kinds of plums "almost as good as damson."

In gratitude for God's blessings they decided to observe an old Dutch custom and celebrate their harvest of plenty. Bradford sent a hunting party abroad to supply the colony with enough game to last a week, then sent an invitation by Squanto to Massasoit and his people to share in their feast. The women and girls gathered to cook their most delicious fare, and washed and patched up their best clothes for the celebration.

John Alden spied Priscilla laden with baskets of berries gathered to make pies for the feast and hastened to unburden her. "I do thank thee, John," she said, smiling brightly. "'Tis a bounty indeed we can thank God for, though much work for all that."

John held his breath at her smile. He had visited Brewsters' house on every occasion he could manage—to do some work for the Elder or help him improve his house. He spoke to Priscilla as often as possible but hesitated to court her openly, hoping to establish a bond of friendship first. When the time was right, he would make formal request of

Brewster for her hand, as he would have done of her father in England.

John was becoming a leader in the colony, and that gave him new confidence. The two seamen hired to serve aboard the *Mayflower* for one year, William Trevor and John Ely, had told him they planned to return to England on the first ship to put in at Plimoth. John was surprised. "Why will you leave?" he asked them. "We have everything here we could not have in England."

Ely snorted. "We're seamen, not farmers. Besides, the masters run this colony. Not likely they'll accept us as citizens of equal import."

"But they already have," John protested. "All of us have worked together. Every man and woman has borne his neighbor's burden as well as his own. We've made a good start. There's a future for men like us."

Trevor said thoughtfully, "Aye, it has been a hard year, but maybe better to come."

Ely snickered. "I know where your ambition lies, lad. You have your eye on the Mullins' lass."

John nodded. "That I do. What better lass could I choose?"

"None, if she'll have ye. But will she? Ye are only a cooper."

"She will," John said, suddenly confident.

Trevor said, "'And there's younger ones comin' along. Mary, Desire, Elizabeth, Remember, and the Hopkins girls. Young yet, but soon looking to marry."

"All the more reason you should stay. New Plimoth offers you men opportunity beyond anything possible in England." And suddenly without any doubt John Alden knew he had spoken the truth. The colony had gained a toehold on this land, and with God's help could anticipate a future for common men like himself unknown in England. He would be part of that destiny.

ॐ∽ॐ

The day of festival dawned in a splendor of autumn color. Brilliant reds, russets, and golds flashed throughout the woods. The colonists had missed this glory when the *Mayflower* arrived late in November the previous year. Now like treasure hidden within the trees, luminescent leaves burst forth to proclaim the passing of the season, a bounty of beauty and plenty.

A feast of roast venison, duck and goose, shellfish, eels, "salat herbes," and cornbread was spread before the people. A party of ninety natives arrived with Massasoit and shortly went out and shot down five deer to add to the feast. Between bouts of gorging, the people played games and entered contests for strength and skill. Captain Standish and his men presented a military review and shot off a thunderous volley from the astonishing muskets, thrilling the natives with fear and trembling, who then consoled themselves with more food.

Every now and then the colonists sent forth long prayers of thanksgiving to their Christian God. Despite the trials they had suffered, He had brought them through to "harvests" not only of food, but of congenial concourse among their people and the Indian tribes, and hope for future prosperity.

It was a time of peaceful plenty that would be revered in years to come, for it marked a pause in the parade of calamitous events that would continue to plague these indomitable colonists of New Plimoth.

&-<

Now as the leaves fell and the northern winds signaled the advent of winter, the people, keenly mindful of the trials of their first winter, busied themselves preparing for the next one. To their dismay, they soon discovered that their harvest had not been nearly so plentiful as they had calculated. None of their English peas and only a slim portion of barley and wheat matured. Squanto's ministrations had produced a good crop of corn but barely enough to last through the winter. To augment their dwindling stores from the *Mayflower*, they must reduce their ration of a peck of grain a week per person by half. And they had no hope of a ship bringing supplies before spring.

Then one day in November an Indian sighted a ship under full sail moving into Plimoth Bay and hastened to inform the colonists. Bradford at once called his council, alerted Captain Standish, and made ready to greet the ship. If the company were French from Canada come to raid New Plimoth, they would find stiff resistance. "Every man, yea, boy, that could handle a gun was ready" and took his place of defense. Standish shot off the cannon on Fort Hill to warn the ship that someone inhabited this country who would defend it with their lives.

To their amazement the ship raised her colors, a white ensign bearing the red cross of England. It was the *Fortune* from London, under Captain Thomas Barton, bringing thirty-five passengers. Several of these were "saints": Robert Cushman and his son, Thomas, Elder Brewster's son, Jonathan, William Bassett and his wife, Thomas Morton from Harworth on the River Ryton near Scrooby, Winslow's younger brother, John, and two French Walloons, Philippe de la Noye and Moses Symonson from the Green Gate congregation. The rest were strangers recruited by the Merchant Adventurers and sent without so much as a "bisket-cake or any other victuals." They brought no clothing, nor bedding, nor pots or pans "to dress meat in." Moreover, they were a lusty bunch of young males rowdy for adventure and not likely, so it appeared, to dig in to support the colony.

The colonists were overjoyed to see some of their own but dismayed that their sponsors had sent thirty-five empty stomachs to fill without provisions. Yet, gritting their teeth, with as much Christian charity as they could muster, they welcomed the newcomers and found places for them squeezed within the little houses of New Plimoth.

Robert Cushman had left the *Mayflower* at Plimoth, England, in despair that "if ever they make a plantation God works a miracle." Yet since then he had worked fervently in England for the good of New Plimoth. He came ashore with the good news that the colony's application for a patent sent on the *Mayflower* had been granted in June by the Council of New England to one John Pierce, resident of England, and his associates. It bore the seals and signatures of the Duke of Lenox, the Marquis of Hamilton, the Earl of Warwick, and Sir Fernando Gorges. It established no boundaries but gave to Pierce and associates one hundred acres per colonial resident who remained for three years.

During the next four years each immigrant would be allotted one hundred acres. Fifteen hundred acres were set aside for churches, schools, and hospitals. The business of the colony was to engage in planting, selling, and the making and procuring of staples, such as corn, silk-grass, hemp, flax, pitch, tar, soap, ashes, potash, iron, and clapboards.

Cushman also brought two letters. One was from John Robinson, who lamented the loss of so many of their people and promised to come to the village as soon as possible. He exhorted them to "obedience unto those whom God hath set over you, in church and commonwealth."

But the letter Cushman bore from Thomas Weston was a rebuke for their negligence in sending the *Mayflower* home to England empty and showed not the least jot of sympathy for their trials of that terrible first year.

That you sent no lading is...worthily distasted. I know your weakness was the cause of it, and I believe more weakness of judgment than weakness of hands. A quarter of the time you spent in discoursing, arguing and consulting would have done much more; but that is past, etc. If you mean, bona fide, to perform the conditions agreed upon, do us the favor to copy them out fair and subscribe them with the principal of your names. And likewise give us account as particularly as you can, how our moneys were laid out. And then I shall be able to give them some satisfaction, whom I am now forced with good words to shift off. And consider that the life of the business depends on the lading of this ship, which if you do to any good purpose, that I may be freed from the great sums I have disbursed for the former and must do for the latter, I promise you I will never quit the business, though all the other Adventurers should.

We have procured you a charter, the best we could, which is better than your former, and with less limitation. For anything that is else worth writing Mr. Cushman can inform you. I pray write instantly for Mr. Robinson to come to you. And so praying God to bless you with all graces necessary both for this life and that to come, I rest

Your very loving friend,

London, July 6, 1621 Thomas Weston

Bradford read the letter and was struck speechless. Cushman read his face and said, "I know. He's outrageous. But I came to you, William, because you must come to terms with him. You have no choice but to sign the agreement."

Bradford's eyes narrowed. "As God is my witness, I will never sign. Like a leech, he bleeds us to death. His promises have come to nothing."

"And yet he is our only hope. The other investors threaten to abandon the project. Without him you will receive nothing."

Bradford exploded. "He sent us nothing, and leaves us with nothing. We will sign nothing!"

The council agreed vehemently.

"You must face reality," Cushman insisted. "He swore that he never dared tell the other investors you refused to sign the agreement. Otherwise they would not have spent a half-penny on the venture. You have no one else to turn to. If you cannot appease Weston, there is nowhere else to go." He glanced about the council. "And you will all starve."

Hopkins snorted. "Starve, is it? What does he think we are doing now?"

Brewster asked calmly, "What more does he want of us?"

"You must agree to those two items you refused before. The Merchants should have half of men's houses and lands at the seven-year division. And no weekdays for your private use shall be granted."

Bradford said firmly, "We absolutely will not agree to that."

Brewster spoke up. "Now let us consider this soberly." He looked about the group. "I believe that we are all aware that some of our party want to own their own land eventually. They see no personal advantage in sharing all our goods and produce equally with our sponsors. Whether that is wise or not, it poses a threat that if we agree to the Merchants' terms, we may face a crisis within our community."

All nodded agreement.

"So what is our best solution? To accept our sponsors' terms and discharge our obligation to them as we promised…or to stand alone and risk the failure of our enterprise?"

All were silent. Then Hopkins spoke. "I am a 'stranger' among you. Yet I have cast my lot with this colony and want to see it succeed. We have just achieved a pact with the natives of this land which we swore to honor. Are we wise to jeopardize this achievement by breaking the original agreement we made to come here?"

Bradford snapped. "We never agreed to these terms. They were imposed on us after we signed the original contract without them." He glanced at Cushman. "That is no secret. You know that well, Robert."

"Aye, Governor Carver and I agreed to the alterations because we were convinced that if we did not sign, our venture was doomed never to start."

Dr. Fuller said quietly, "Well, perhaps it was."

Allerton said, "What's done is done. We cannot go back and change it. We must move on. Can we survive another year without new provisions?"

Hopkins said, "We have opened beaver trade with the Cape tribes, even the Massachusetts. By next spring we may well discharge much of our obligation to Weston by fur trade alone."

"Yet we must survive another winter before that," murmured Fuller.

Cushman still held the position of deacon in the congregation and requested that he be given permission to preach the sermon on the next Sabbath. Brewster agreed.

☙❧

The congregation took its usual route on Sunday, December 9, 1621, meeting at the foot of the main street, now named Leyden Street, in their Sunday best and marching to drumbeat up the hill to the Common House. Elder Brewster opened the meeting with a prayer of thanks to God for their blessings and protection from their enemies. He asked for wisdom and discernment of their problems, and the congregation joined in singing psalms.

Deacon Cushman took the pulpit. "My subject is The Dangers of Self-Love, from First Corinthians, Chapter 10, verse 24. 'Let no man seek his own, but every man another's wealth.' What does this passage ask us? Why would you have thy particular portion? Because you think to live better than your neighbor and scorn to live as meanly as he? But who, I pray, brought this particularizing into the world? Did not Satan, who was not content to keep that equal state with his fellows, but would set his throne above the stars?"

The congregation shifted on their benches. Cushman went on to extol the virtues of communal living. He spoke of Lucifer's ambition and greed and warned that nothing in the world more resembled heavenly happiness than for men to live as one heart and soul, and that nothing more resembled hellish horror than for every man to shift for himself. If man would live by thine and mine, then God should provide one heaven for one and another for his neighbor.

His sermon silenced for the time the argument against signing the agreement Weston demanded. At last, with great reluctance, Bradford and his council decided to sign as Cushman urged, simply because they had no other option. Then, having made their commitment, energetically they loaded the *Fortune* with sassafras, a profitable crop, hardwood timber, wainscoting, clapboard, and two hogsheads of beaver and otter pelts traded with the Indians. They estimated the value of this cargo at five hundred pounds, nearly half their obligation to the Merchants, a show of industry that should surely dispel any accusation by Weston of negligence.

Home with the *Fortune* went Cushman and the two sailors, Trevor and Ely, their year of indenture finished. Also went an indignant reply from Bradford to Weston's exasperating letter. After an opening defense of Governor Carter, whom Weston's letter addressed, he boldly refuted the charges Weston laid upon them.

You greatly blame us for keeping the ship so long in the country, and then to send her away empty. She lay five weeks at Cape Cod whilst with many a weary step (after a long journey) and the endurance of many a hard brunt, we sought out in the foul winter a place of habitation. Then, we went in so tedious a time to make provision to shelter us and our goods; about which labour, many of our arms and legs can tell us to this day, we were not negligent. But it pleased God to visit us then with death daily, and with so general a disease that the living were scarce able to bury the dead, and the well not in any measure sufficient to tend the sick. And now to be so greatly blamed for not freighting the ship, doth indeed go near us and much discourage us. But you say you know we will pretend weakness; and do you think we had not cause? Yes, you tell us you believe it, but it was more weakness of judgment than of hands. Our weakness herein is great we confess, therefore we will bear this check patiently amongst the rest, till God send us wiser men...Indeed it is our calamity that we are, beyond expectation, yoked with some ill-conditioned people who will never do good, but corrupt and abuse others.

৵৽

The colonists would not learn for months that their hopes for the *Fortune's* cargo would be dashed by a French pirate who took the ship captive off the English coast. She was stripped of her cargo, and even some of her rigging, and her passengers were detained for fourteen days, then released. Cushman managed to preserve Bradford's letter, one from Winslow, and their journal, to be known as *Mourt's Relation*, a detailed account of their first year at Plimoth.

Ignorant of the *Fortune's* fate, the colonists settled into the rigors of winter, ever hopeful of provisions from England to sustain themselves and their new residents.

৵৽

On Christmas Day Bradford called the men of the colony to work as usual, and was confronted with refusals by the rowdy new strangers among them. It was against their consciences, they protested, to work on this holiday. Bradford conceded that he would "force no one's conscience" until they be "better informed." When he returned at noon to find those tender consciences at play at stool-ball and pitching the bar, he coolly observed, "I take it that this play while others work does not offend your consciences."

The men glanced from one to the other and did not reply. Bradford strode toward the stool-ball and picked it up. "Then I must tell you that I find it most offensive to my conscience that you frolic while others work. If you must observe the sanctity of this day, please do so with quiet devotion in your houses."

The young men slunk away in silence.

⁊ↄ⋆ᕲ

Near the end of December Brewster and Bradford sat by Brewster's fire and reminisced of earlier years. Brewster said, "How long has it been, William, since we walked together to Babworth Church?"

"Aye, long years indeed."

Brewster sipped his hot tea. "Have we done well? What do you think?"

"I think we have done our best, sir. Much could have been done better, but given our limits, I have few regrets."

"I regret most the great loss of our people. There's no comfort in that, except that they have gained their reward in Heaven."

"So shall we all someday."

Brewster sat forward to light his pipe. "You are one who has suffered most, William. Have you recovered?"

After a moment Bradford said, "You are speaking of Dorothy."

"Aye."

"No. There is no recovery. Only resignation. I should have left her at Leyden with John. Perhaps she could have come later on the *Fortune.*"

"John will come some day. You are a young man. You should marry again."

"Perhaps later. Not now. I am wedded to New Plimoth. She needs the nurture a wife expects." He grinned. "She is vulnerable and frail, and still faces many hardships."

Mary Brewster served them more sassafras tea. "How nice that you gentlemen can take your ease indoors by the fire while sleet slashes at the windows. You could not do this last year."

Bradford said, "And for that we thank God." He stared into the flames. "What a fearful wilderness I saw from the deck of the *Mayflower*. What desolation! I wondered why God brought us out of Leyden to this."

Brewster raised an eyebrow. "I wondered if He had abandoned us altogether with the *Speedwell.*" He sighed. "I have asked that question many times."

"And did you receive an answer?"

Brewster sat silently several moments. "I believe He sent us out of England to Holland, and then to Plimoth for some purpose we may never know until Heaven." He smiled. "Yet poor as we were, we did our best to obey."

They gazed into the flames, recalling the years since Scrooby when Bradford was only a lonely lad and Brewster a disillusioned seeker of truth. "I think He is telling us now, William, that He has brought us home."

"Aye. Home at last."

Twenty-three

Wessagussett

Yet the "home" that New Plimoth offered these "pilgrims" was not yet the comfortably safe haven they had once known in Leyden. They faced another winter with meager supplies somehow to be stretched among the new strangers whose worldly behavior, as much as their empty bellies, challenged the saints' patience. Confronted with the demands of daily living on quarter-rations, the people's energies barely sustained them through each day. Besides threat of starvation, occasional rumors of hostility from the Massachusetts and the Narragansett hovered over them, but they took comfort in their peaceful relations with the Pokanoket and the Nauset whose friendship they valued as a buffer from enemy attack.

Then one day an Indian arrived in Plimoth with a gift for Squanto from Canonicus, sachem of the Narragansett, traditional enemy of the Pokanoket. When the messenger learned that Squanto was off hunting, he gave the bundle to Bradford and seemed eager to leave. Bradford studied the "gift," a sheaf of arrows wrapped in a rattlesnake skin. Curious, he detained the messenger and sent for Standish, Winslow, Hopkins, and Tokohamanon to question him.

"What does this mean?" Hopkins asked the Indian.

The native's eyes darted evasively from man to man. "For Squanto."

"Squanto is not here. Why would Canonicus send Squanto such a message?"

The native shook his head vigorously.

Winslow persisted. "What of these rumors we hear of the Narragansett wanting war with us? Is it true? If so, why? We have no quarrel with the Narragansett."

Tokohamanon repeated Winslow's question. Whereupon the messenger rambled out a confusing story that a previous messenger sent by Canonicus the summer last distorted the governor's message and gifts to Canonicus and prompted the sachem's displeasure.

Winslow said, "We need to discover what offended your sachem. As soon as you tell us, we will let you go free."

"If he knows, he will not tell us," Hopkins muttered. "Let him go."

They questioned him further, to little avail. The Narragansett departed gratefully in great haste.

Bradford confronted Squanto as soon as he appeared. "What does this mean?"

Squanto peered at the bundle, then paled. "A warning. Narragansett not like white men here."

"We have no quarrel with the Narragansett."

"They not like white men and that Tisquantum is your friend."

Brewster asked, "Is this merely a token or a challenge? Does it mean attack?"

Squanto shook his head. "No better than a challenge. You show fear, they see weakness."

"Then send it back unopened," Captain Standish growled.

Bradford said, "We hoped to trade with the Narragansett, not war with them. Isaac, what do you think our response should be?"

Allerton and the council felt that the Narragansett message was clear: Their intentions were at best unfriendly; at worst, threatening. Unanimously, they agreed with Standish to show no fear and to send the bundle back to its sender. Standish thought that was not enough. "We may get no other warning before they decide to confront us. We must fortify our village against any surprise attack."

"You may be right, Myles," Bradford said. "We've given them no reason to attack and will make every effort to befriend them. But we will stay alert."

Hopkins advised, "I say, send the bundle back packed with musket balls. They should understand that. See how they take it."

They sent off the bundle by a friendly Pokanoket. Yet the incident was unsettling enough that Standish's urgent pleas prompted them to sit down to plan fortification of their village.

The captain's recommendations were strong and concise. He insisted they "inclose their dwellings with a good strong pale, and make flankers in convenient places, with gates to shut, which were every night locked and a watch kept, and when need required there was also warding in the day time."

Brewster cautioned, "The effort to encircle the village will greatly tax our people's strength. Have they the will for that? We would have to finish it before planting season."

Hopkins said, "Well, we cannot do it halfway. We have no defense against a surprise attack unless we surround the village and bar the gates."

As in all matters affecting the entire community, they put the proposal before the men of the colony. John Billington's voice objected most strongly. "I have no love for these crafty savages, but we're half-starved already. Erecting a wall like that will wear us down to our bones. I say, post guards round the clock, day and night, and trust to the Almighty to warn us."

A number of strangers agreed. One asked, "These buggers are more a nuisance than a threat, hanging about and begging our food. Why would they attack us?"

Bradford explained, "The Narragansett, who are not our friends, sent the token to Squanto. He and Hobomok know their people, and they urge us to prepare. Our hope is if the hostiles see our strength, they will be less likely to attack."

So massive an undertaking in mid-winter was indeed formidable, but it consoled the colonists that they had done their best to forestall disaster. So, after more discussion, the council decided to proceed with the palisade "very cheerfully," and with "great vigor." Standish formed four squads of soldiers, one to guard each side of the perimeter. Under attack some men would stand guard and others be alert for fires.

Mary Brewster called the women together in the Common House to advise them of the plan. The image of a rattlesnake skin sent shudders throughout the group, but practical Ellen Billington pronounced, "I'm not surprised. Only a savage would send a snakeskin as warning. Yet I wonder why they bothered to warn us. They would've been smarter to keep us innocent. I do object to using up our strength putting up this wall. We'll have little energy left to plant crops."

The younger women, Susanna Winslow and Priscilla Mullins, seemed relieved. "Once it's up for the natives to see, we may never need it, but we'll feel safer with it there."

Ellen grumbled, "You girls don't have younguns underfoot wearin' you out. 'Tis all I can do now to keep a decent house."

"But the men and boys will build it, Ellen. You only have to feed them."

"Aye, that's already more than I can bear."

The women laughed.

Then Mary said, "We must trust that the wall is safer than doing nothing. We have lost so many friends; we cannot afford to lose more."

Some weeks later a native runner arrived in New Plimoth bearing the rattlesnake bundle still unopened, having circulated the villages where no natives dared touch it.

During the winter months while the wall was built, other mishaps occurred. Once a fire started next to the Common House, where all provisions were stored, and burned four houses nearby. During the melee a strange voice was heard to say, "Look well about you, for all are not friends that are near you." Who had spoken? The saints were convinced it was a warning from their Lord.

After the first fire had been controlled, smoke poured from the lean-to next to the Common House. There they found a "long firebrand of an ell longe, lying under the wall on the inside which could not possibly come there by casualty, but must be laid there by some hand, in the judgment of all that saw it. But God kept them from this danger, whatever was intended."

Undaunted, the colonists labored on the wall. It required digging a trench around the village deep enough to secure the pales, felling and stripping trees, shaping the ends to drive into the ground, and careful fitting one log against another to close gaps. It was finished by March, in time for spring planting. The little colony now resembled a fort.

Since their first expedition to the Massachusetts the previous year, the men had planned to return in the spring to acquire more beaver skins from the native women. Just before the traders were to leave,

Hobomok told Bradford that he should abort the mission because the Massachusetts were in league with the Narragansett to cut off the party, destroy it, and then attack the village. Hobomok further claimed that Squanto was involved in the plot. Bradford called his faithful counselors to discuss this astonishing news. "Do any of you believe this story?"

Hopkins nodded. "Squanto's a sly one, a shrewd conniver not unlike our 'loving friend' Weston. Always looking out for his own."

Bradford frowned. "We could not have survived here without him."

"Indeed. But his bond with us gives him power with his people no other native can claim, except Massasoit. And I suspect that Squanto might conveniently depose that sachem."

"How so, Stephen?" asked Brewster.

"He's conniving for the natives' dependence on him. I've heard that he told the natives we keep the plague under the Common House, to bring out when we will."

A gasp of surprise rounded the room. "The plague? What does he mean?" asked Allerton.

"Hobomok claims he saw us bury our gunpowder and when he asked what it was, was told it was our God's power to use in our defense."

Bradford wagged his head. "What marvelous imagination."

"Skullduggery, ye mean," growled Standish. "Hobomok claims Squanto's been stirring up the natives against Massasoit. To what end, I wonder."

Winslow spoke softly. "Did we not decide to be instruments of good to the heathen about us, rather than to give them the least measure of just offense?"

"All well and good, Edward," said Brewster. "We do our best, but we cannot account for the secret hearts of men."

At last they concluded that whatever plots were afoot, they dare not close themselves off within their walled village, for their rations were so low they must be free to travel and hunt for food. Therefore, they would proceed with the expedition to the Massachusetts, sending Standish and ten armed men and both Hobomok and Squanto, whom they would watch closely.

Hardly had the shallop cleared Gurnet's Nose, a northern point in the bay, than one of Squanto's relatives came howling into the village, his face streaming blood. He claimed he had been mauled at Nemasket where the Massachusetts had joined the Pokanoket in a plot to attack New Plimoth. At once the colonists fired off their cannon on the hill to summon all men in from the fields, hoping that Standish's party might still be within earshot. All came running to man their muskets and stand ready for assault. The trading party, becalmed and preparing to row, did hear the shots, and quickly turned about and returned to the village.

"What has happened?" Standish demanded.

When told Hobomok's story, Standish snarled. "Ye canna' trust these savages. Quick as ye turn your back, they'll knife ye."

"Myles," Bradford scolded, "there are good men among them. Part of our mission here is to bring them out of darkness. They have not yet heard the Gospel."

The most troubling news they heard next was that Massasoit had joined the Massachusetts, his ancient enemy. Yet Hobomok denied this, insisting that the Pokanoket sachem was loyal to the colony, and that the ruse was Squanto's attempt to split their relationship. Hopkins spoke out. "Send an envoy to Sowams. See what brews there. If Massasoit prepares for an attack, it will be evident."

Hobomok declared, "I send my wife. No one suspect her."

Hobomok's wife found all peaceful at Sowams and answered Massasoit's questions truthfully, revealing that the colonists had been told he had joined the Massachusetts and planned to attack their village. Massasoit exploded. "Who has done this thing? I love white brothers. Go back. Tell Gov'ner I am his loyal friend."

When Hobomok's wife returned with news that all was peaceful at Sowams, the mystery deepened. It appeared that Squanto had sent his relative to alarm the colonists while Standish was absent, hoping to prompt Bradford to react violently. Now they saw that the same ruse had aroused Standish to confront Corbitant at Nemasket a year earlier. But why? If this was Squanto's work, what did he hope to gain?

Outraged at Squanto's duplicity, Massasoit himself stormed into Plimoth to demand Squanto's head and hands according to the terms of their treaty. Squanto was too valuable an aide to Bradford to cut off his head, but neither could he break Carver's treaty with Massasoit without risking the goodwill the colony had carefully nurtured between them. He explained to the sachem how desperately the English needed Squanto's voice to interpret for them but did promise that Squanto would be punished. After Massasoit departed, disgruntled, Bradford called for Squanto and asked him bluntly, "Why have you done this thing?"

Squanto turned large eyes on his benefactor. "Me last of Patuxet. This land mine. I make good sachem."

"But you betrayed both me and Massasoit who are your friends. Do you know what 'betray' means?"

Squanto shook his head slowly.

"It means to 'turn against,' that is, to hurt someone you promised to help. It is an evil thing. Our God would be very angry if we did this thing."

Squanto blinked. "God of the English angry at Squanto?"

"Aye. We believe He sent you to help us. And you did, but now you have turned against us and Massasoit, who demands your head. Do you understand what I say?"

Squanto nodded. "How to please English god?" He frowned. "And also...Massasoit?"

Bradford's heart leapt. He had told Squanto the basic tenets of the Christian faith, hoping one day to convert him, but had never pressed him to believe it. "You repent; that means you say you are sorry for what you have done and will not do it again. Then you ask those you have offended to forgive you; that means they will pardon you and not hold the evil against you."

The Indian nodded readily. "Squanto sorry."

Bradford looked upon this native smiling childlike at him, expecting immediate restoration. Did he have any understanding of this explanation? Bradford patted his chest. "Are you truly sorry, in here, in your heart?"

Squanto watched his gesture, then repeated it. "Squanto much sorry."

Bradford sighed. Probably the Patuxet understood that he had displeased both Massasoit and Bradford and was eager to regain their good graces. But what he understood about the English God was inscrutable. Yet this reconciliation was enough for the moment, Bradford mused to himself. Would any colonist in Plimoth, say Captain Standish or Hopkins, believe that Squanto had *repented?* He would confide in the Brewsters, who might believe it.

Unexpectedly, a day later Massasoit's warriors reappeared with Massasoit's knife, intending to separate Squanto's head and hands from his body and take them back as trophies to the sachem. They brought with them beaver skins as an incentive. Bradford again refused, claiming that it "was not the manner of the English to sell men's lives for a price," while insisting he would punish Squanto. Yet he knew that Massasoit would not be satisfied with the fine subtlety of English punishment. *Lord, You know I cannot execute Squanto. How must I resolve this dilemma?*

While the warriors glared at him, impatiently patting the execution knife, a cry resounded from the fort on the hill. "Boat ccoming! Boat coming!"

All attention swung to a small shallop crossing the bay. The men ran for their muskets. Massasoit's warriors stood scowling, wondering at the sudden activity. Bradford told them, "That boat may be an enemy. Tell your sachem we will deal with Squanto later." Bradford gestured for them to go. Behind him, Squanto vehemently waved them on.

The warriors hesitated, watching the men of the colony scurry to man their muskets and take defensive positions at the wall. Whatever the fuss was about, it was clear they were not going to turn over Squanto. The warriors left in "great heat" to report to their sachem.

Muskets ready, Bradford's men watched the shallop make its way to shore, then cautiously went down to meet it. It was from the *Sparrow,* anchored forty leagues from Plimoth off the Maine coast where dozens of ships congregated to fish at the height of the season. To the colonists' amazement, the mother ship, *Sparrow,* bearing sixty new settlers, had been sent by Thomas Weston, intending to start a new settlement for trade near New Plimoth, a virtual rival to the colony!

The shallop brought letters from Weston, demanding that Plimoth "entertain" and outfit these new strangers. Yet he sent no supplies either for Plimoth or the new colony. His letters, still addressed to Governor Carver, delivered his usual harangue on Plimoth's inadequacy, and indignantly declared that if the colony did not comply with his demands it would constitute "extreme barbarism." He had the further audacity to suggest these men were sent for the colony's "good."

What "good"? Bradford wondered. *Shall we all starve congenially together?*

Other "good news," which came on the *Charity*, another of Weston's ships, informed them that Weston and the Adventurers had parted company, and therefore he was "quit" of them and they were "quit" of him. Letters from Edward Pickering and William Greene of the Adventurers warned Bradford of Weston's plan to set up his brother Andrew, "a heady young man and violent, and set against you there and the company here; plotting with Mr. Weston their own ends, which tend to your and our undoing in respect of our estates there."

The Leydeners' old friend and colleague, Robert Cushman, also wrote to Bradford informing him of the capture of the *Fortune* and warning him of Weston's men:

These people which they carry are no men for us; wherefore I pray you entertain them not, neither exchange man for man with them, except it be some of your worst...I pray you therefore signify to Squanto that they are a distinct body from us, and we have nothing to do with them, neither must be blamed for their faults, much less can warrant their fidelity.

On the other side of Cushman's letter was a short note from one John Pierce, in whose name their patent was taken:

As for Mr. Weston's company, I think them so base in condition...as in all appearance not fit for an honest man's company; I wish they prove otherwise.

Bradford and his men pondered these warnings at length, but decided for their consciences' sake to take the strangers in, partly in gratitude for Weston's help to them, such as it was, and partly in compassion for the new strangers "who were now come into a wilderness (as themselves were) and were to be presently put ashore...and they were altogether unacquainted and knew not what to do." None of the colonists had forgotten their first agonized months on Cape Cod.

The onslaught of sixty rowdy men especially disturbed John Alden, who had conducted his suit for Priscilla slowly and deliberately. Now he saw that she, and the younger girls as well, would have to fend off these "rude men," whose intentions were not nearly so honorable as his. One day, observing Priscilla as she hurried, head down, past a group of rowdies shouting vulgar comments while stripping logs, he realized that she needed the protection of a brawny male like himself to keep the wolves at bay. He threw down his adze and hurried to her side, glaring at the men pulling crude faces and snickering. Priscilla glanced up at him and smiled gratefully. He walked by her side toward Brewster's house where she lived, then opened the gate.

She turned to him and said, "Thank you, John. I am grateful."

He muttered, "This is a sorry lot Weston's dumped on us. They infuriate me."

"I know. We are all disturbed. I fear they will bring us trouble."

"Priscilla," he began, "it's time...I mean...you should not be alone."

"Oh, I am well, John. The Brewsters are good to me."

"I mean, you need someone to...look out for you." He blushed. "You need ME."

She looked at him, her eyes bright. "I do appreciate you, John. You are a good friend."

He shook his head. "I mean...you need a...*husband.*" Suddenly he blurted, "Will you marry me, Priscilla?" He stared at her, feeling his face turn crimson.

She returned his look, then said calmly, "Yes, I will, John."

He was dumbfounded. Did his ears deceive him? Then why had he waited so long? They stared at each other, then burst out laughing. "Are you serious, John? I did not mean to embarrass you."

"I...yes, I am serious. I've been waitng a long time to ask you. And now, suddenly...are *you* serious, Priscilla? Will you really marry me?"

320

She smiled. "I've been waiting a long time, too."

They laughed again.

Emboldened, he cried out, "Let's tell the Brewsters!"

Of course the Brewsters were delighted. In the midst of the colony's many troubles, the joy of a wedding, at least for the moment, overcame all sorrow.

"At last." Brewster sighed. "We've all been waiting a long time."

෨෧

The *Charity* sailed on to Virginia while the colony supported Weston's men during the summer. When she returned, the men left for their habitation in Massachusetts Bay, called by the Indian name "Wessagussett," but left their sick behind at Plimoth to be nursed by Dr. Fuller until their settlement was established. The people of New Plimoth sorrowed for these men but were glad to be "disburdened" of them who had stolen their immature green corn and returned their kindness with "backbitings" and "revilings." The colonists feared what would be the outcome of "such raw and unconscionable beginnings."

As the supplies at New Plimoth had dwindled to almost nothing and "famine began now to pinch them sore, they not knowing what to do, the Lord (who never fails His) presents them with an occasion beyond all expectation, this boat which came from the eastward brought them a letter from a stranger of whose name they had never heard before, being a captain of a ship come there a-fishing." The captain was John Huddleston of the ship *Bona Nova*. His letter informed them of the massacre by natives of four hundred settlers at Jamestown, Virginia, that year of 1622, and warned that "happy is he whom other men's harms doth make to beware."

Bradford sent a note of profound gratitude to the captain and sent Winslow along in a boat of their own to procure what provisions might be available among the fishing fleet. Huddleston gave Winslow what he could spare and prompted others to send theirs as well, which proved of double benefit to the colony. They discovered the way to the fishing grounds for future expeditions and gained barely enough sustenance to survive until harvest. Yet this bounty divided among so many allowed only a quarter pound of bread for each person, doled out daily by Bradford, lest the poor colonists eat it up all at once and then starve.

Having now learned of the terrifying massacre at Jamestown, the leaders of the colony were readily persuaded by Captain Standish to add to their palisade a fort of "good timber, both strong and comely," with a flat roof and battlements on which their ordnance were mounted. Yet many doubted the wisdom of more fortification, "accounting it more a work of superfluity and vainglory than of simple necessity." Winslow declared that the Devil caused "reasonable men to reason against their own safety." The Fort would serve more than one purpose, however, as it was already used for meetings and religious worship as well as safety.

Meanwhile, the men at Wessagussett were left well supplied by the *Charity*, and the *Swan* stayed behind to aid them in expedition and trade. Yet the men there seemed to have no sense of stewardship and "made havoc of their provisions." Since it was now October and winter soon to descend upon them, John Sanders, governor of the colony, proposed that both colonies combine expeditions to search for corn. Bradford and Allerton agreed, for they had unhappily discovered not only that Weston's men's thievery had greatly diminished their yield, but that building the Fort had diverted their energies from properly nurturing their crop.

Squanto now proposed that he knew a route through the shoals on the eastern shore of the Cape, which he had sailed on both English and French ships and would lead them through the shoals to shores further south where they might trade. They were immediately beset by obstacles. Weston's brother-in-law died and was buried at Plimoth, and the journey was aborted twice by bad weather and Standish's illness. Bradford finally elected to lead the expedition himself.

৵৽

The shoals proved as formidable an obstacle for the *Swan* as it had the *Mayflower*, and her captain quickly retreated from the treacherous water. Squanto directed them into a harbor at Manamoycke where a narrow channel and turbulent weather churned up violent tides. The hope that this harbor might lie south of the shoals was impossible to determine. The natives here were elusive, obviously suspicious of white men, yet Squanto's peaceful persuasions elicited from them a feast of venison and eventually eight hogsheads of corn and beans.

Now Squanto was eager to try the shoals again. But suddenly he fell ill, bleeding at the nose, a sign considered by natives to be the knell of death. Bradford was especially distraught. It was inconceivable that Squanto, always vibrant with health, should sicken, much less die. Bradford ministered to him as best he could, but the wily native grew weaker, until his voice was almost gone. He gestured for Bradford to come closer, then whispered, "My things give to friends I love."

Bradford gazed into his friend's brown face. "Aye, that I will."

"Then pray for Squanto."

Bradford nodded. "Of course, we always pray for the sick to recover."

Squanto shook his head feebly. "For Heaven. That English God take Squanto to His Heaven."

Bradford/s eyes suddenly blurred. He bent closer. "Do you believe in Him?"

Squanto nodded. "He good to English people. Good to Squanto."

Bradford swallowed. It would not be manly to send Squanto off with tears. "He waits for you there, friend. But I pray it is not yet time for you to go. We need you here."

Squanto shook his head. "'Tis Squanto's time."

He died that night.

Bradford was desolate. Not only had he lost his faithful interpreter but a dear friend whom he loved, despite his duplicitous schemes. That Squanto had asked to go to the English God's Heaven was some consolation for his loss, but left Bradford bereft not only of the irreplaceable "tongue" Squanto had been for the colony, but also an engaging companion whom he would sorely miss.

Lord, how You do test our faith! Is there no end to our keen losses?

The party had no choice but to continue on. Bradford and the *Swan's* captain decided not to risk the shoals to venture farther south. Instead they sailed north to round the tip of the Cape and on to the Massachusetts, where they found the natives beset with a plague-like sickness and, worse, short of corn. They had already traded with the men at Wessagussett, whom the Indians despised for begging corn. So desperate were these men that they had offered for a quart what New Plimoth offered for a beaver's skin. The *Swan* went on to Nauset and Cummaquid, the villages of Aspinet and Iyanough, where they found some provisions.

The winter storms were so fierce by now that the *Swan* could not take on the corn they acquired, and her shallop was too small and leaky. Bradford commissioned the sachems to keep the corn covered in heaps and free of vermin until he could return and claim it. Then he and his men traveled on foot fifty miles across the Cape to Plimoth, arriving weary and footsore three days ahead of the *Swan* coming by water. There the Wessagussett men departed for their colony, directed by Bradford to return soon so they might retrieve their wrecked shallop and collect the corn guarded by the sachems.

Captain Standish made several attempts to retrieve the corn Bradford had purchased but was continually hindered by contrary winds and seas. Almost as troublesome was the natives' behavior, which now seemed strangely demeaning to himself and his men. At Nauset, an Indian stole some trinkets from the colonists' boat, which Standish demanded be returned, and that the thief be punished. Aspinet made earnest attempts to appease the captain by bowing and licking his hand (as Squanto had instructed him in a mockery of the "English" way). But Canacum at Manomet showed greater favor to two Massachusetts natives than to the captain, which confirmed his suspicions of their intentions toward him. He made little attempt to hide his contempt for this duplicity.

❧❦

By February the state of the men at Wessagussett was so severe that Governor John Sanders solicited Bradford's advice on a scheme to steal the Massachusetts' corn and compensate the tribe when their own corn crop harvested, much as the colonists had done themselves their first year on Cape Cod. Bradford and his leaders strongly disapproved of such action, and sent a letter warning that to use such means would "breed a distaste in the savages which would incur much blame thereby," for which they "should expect no better than the Gaol House" when His Majesty's agents called them to account for the same. Moreover, groundnuts, mussels, and clams abounded in nature that would sustain their strength and were easily gotten. The colonists of New Plimoth relied on these themselves.

Yet Weston's men seemed unable to sustain themselves. They had little stability, nor any sense of the responsibility required to manage their crops or to conserve seed corn, or even by the fundamental need to support each other, as did the families of New Plimoth. They had fallen to such a state of despair that some invaded the stores of the Massachusetts at night, convinced that these greedy savages maliciously withheld their abundance. One too weak to extricate himself from mud where he fell, simply died there. Others traded their clothes and their labor for whatever sustenance they could beg from the natives. Despite public whipping and being "stocked," their demeaning behavior continued until the Massachusetts refused to sell or lend them any corn at all.

દ⁀ભ

During March, while Standish was at Manomet, news of a calamity of another sort reached New Plimoth: Massasoit was dying. As it was a "laudable custom" among the natives to visit friends in extremity of illness, especially persons of high estate, Bradford's leaders saw an opportunity to enhance their friendship with Massasoit's people by sending an emissary to visit him. Conveniently, a stranded Dutch vessel had been driven ashore at the sachem's door at Sowams, which offered the colony an opportunity for a conference with the Dutch. Winslow, the colonists' practiced diplomat, was the obvious choice to represent the colony's concern. John Hampden, a gentleman from London wintering at New Plimoth, and Hobomok were chosen to accompany him.

They spent the first night at Namasket, and the second day arrived in Corbitant's territory, where they were told that Massasoit was already dead and that the Dutch ship had hove itself off and departed. Winslow reconsidered their situation. They were within three miles of

Corbitant's dwelling-place, and "although he were a hollow-hearted friend towards us (the English)," he might succeed Massasoit. Winslow thought it might be wise if they entered " into more friendly terms with him and the rest of the sachems round about...hoping, through the blessing of God, it would be a means, in that unsettled state, to settle their affections towards us." It might be a dangerous move for him personally, since a year before Winslow and Hobomok had been employed against Corbitant, and now the sachem might seek revenge. Yet Winslow resolved to proceed, "if Master Hampden and Hobomok durst attempt it with me."

The men agreed to go, but on the way Hobomok, distraught at the thought of Massasoit's demise, broke into wailing lament for the loss of his loving sachem. *"Neen womasu Sagimus!* My loving sachem! Many I have known, but never any like thee!"

Tearfully he told Winslow, "Whilst I lived I should never see the like among the Indians." He launched into a long lamentation, saying that the sachem was no liar, nor bloody and cruel like other Indians. In anger and passion he was easy to be reconciled towards such as offended him, "and that he governed his men better with few strokes than others did with many, truly loving where he loved." Hobomok feared that "we had not a faithful friend left among the Indians: shewing how he, oft times, restrained their malice." The loyal servant's "unfeigned sorrow," declared Winslow, was so touching "as it would have made the hardest heart relent."

At Corbitant's dwelling, they found that he was already at Sowams, and they sent a runner to discover for certain Massasoit's state. The runner returned before sunset to report that Massasoit was not yet dead, but that the visitors could not expect to find him living.

At once Winslow's party set out in the darkness and arrived at Sowams the next afternoon. So many crowded Massasoit's lodging that the white men could scarcely get in amidst their charms and "hellish noise," enough to "distemper" the healthy, and unlikely, Winslow thought, to ease the sick man. The sachem was surrounded by native women who chafed his body to keep heat in him.

At last someone told him that his English friends had come to see him. Massasoit could not see and asked, "Who was come?"

They told him, "Winsnow," pronouncing the l like an n.

He wanted to see Winslow, who went to his side and took his hand. Massasoit whispered, *"Keen Winshow?* Art thou Winsnow?"

"Ahhe," answered Winslow.

"Matta neen wonckanet. Oh, Winslow, I shall never see thee again."

Winslow called Hobomok to tell the sachem that he had come for William Bradford, who was very sorry for his sickness but had sent Winslow with some remedies to do him good if he agreed. Winslow brought forth a preparation of conserves and fed the sachem on the point of a knife, hardly able to get it through his teeth. When dissolved on his tongue, Massasoit swallowed it, to the joy of onlookers who claimed he had not swallowed for two days.

Winslow then inspected his mouth, which was heavily furred and swollen, so that he could not eat nor swallow for such corruption. Winslow scraped his tongue and washed his mouth, then gave him some more conserve in water which he could swallow more easily. Within a half-hour he had so remarkably revived that onlookers were astonished. Soon his sight began to return, a great encouragement. When Winslow asked, he was told that the sachem had not slept in two days and not passed a stool in five.

Winslow gave him more of the conserve and sent two runners to Plimoth with a request for more medicine and two chickens to make a broth. He described the state of Massasoit's health to Dr. Fuller and requested he send other physic that might help the sachem. Yet he confessed to Hampden, "I am unschooled in the arts of healing, John, but feel we must make every effort to save him. I know only how to pray."

"Aye," agreed Hampden. "Ye cannot be more ignorant than myself. Let us brew up a broth of herbs in hopes it will give him strength."

They set about boiling a broth of cornmeal, corn groats, and strawberry leaves, flavored with sassafras root. Winslow strained the concoction through his handkerchief and Massasoit drank at least a pint and liked it well. Soon his sight began to improve. When Massasoit's people exclaimed about their successful "magic," the white men glanced at each other humbly, knowing that only God's merciful providence was the "magic" that wrought this miracle.

Now Massasoit asked Winslow to minister to his people themselves by scraping their tongues, which chore was "much offensive" to him, not being accustomed to such "poisonous savours." More unsavory effects were to come.

Winslow shot a couple of fat ducks to make pottage, instructing Hobomok to skim the fat from the broth, lest it prove too strong for Massasoit's weakened stomach. Despite his urgent cautions against bolting the rich broth, Massasoit downed a "gross" amount of it, enough to satisfy a healthy man. Within an hour he vomited the broth and began bleeding again at the nose. All were in despair, sure now that he would die. But Winslow reassured them. "His case was desperate: yet, it might be it would save his life. For if it ceased in time, he would forethwith sleep, and take rest: which was the principal thing he wanted." Soon afterwards his bleeding stopped, and he slept eight hours.

When Massasoit awakened, Winslow washed his face and beard, but suddenly the sachem dropped his face into the water and snorted with such violence that he began again to bleed. Surely now, his people thought, this was the end. But Winslow was convinced only his nose was tender, and that the bleeding would stop. When the messengers returned from Plimoth with fowl and physic, Massasoit was so much improved that he decided not to kill the birds but to keep them for breeding and refused to take more physic.

So many had come to see the sachem only to find him remarkably restored that the story of his recovery was told over and over. Some of Massasoit's leaders recalled that before the English came another sachem had taunted him in his illness, scoffing that if the hollow-hearted English had been such friends in deed as they were in show, they would have visited him in his sickness. Yet Massasoit had not been persuaded by these arguments against the English. After his recovery he broke forth to say, "Now I see the English are my friends and love me: and whilst I live I will never forget this kindness they have shewed me."

The ministering "angels," Winslow and Hampden, henceforth enjoyed entertainment that exceeded that of all other strangers.

Meanwhile, the tragedy at Wessagussett was relentlessly unfolding.

At Manomet Standish had reflected on his "insult" by Canacum and the two Massachusetts, realizing that he had been quick to take offense. Yet some sixth sense aroused his suspicions beyond mere pique. He recalled, too, the almost fawning behavior of the Indian from Pamet who had been so courteous and affable toward him. The native had asked the captain why he did not sleep that frigid night at Manomet, and Standish could not explain it; he simply had no need for sleep. Why not? he wondered now. Was the Holy Spirit trying to warn him? He confessed his agitation to Brewster. "Canacum was hospitable enough until these two arrived. Then his manner changed abruptly."

"Yet you could not discern what Wituwamat told him?"

"No. Only that it much impressed Canacum, so that he ignored me thereafter."

Brewster thought a moment. "Methinks Canacum may only have deferred to the warriors' dominance to placate them. The Massachusetts relish dominating those they consider inferior, namely us white men." He smiled and raised an eyebrow.

"Aye. Perhaps. Yet that savage flashed that knife he stole from some poor bloke of Weston's—whom he probably killed—as if he could not wait to use it on one of us."

Brewster sighed. "Those men are a pitiable lot. And there seems nothing we can do for them. I would watch, Myles, and mark any other small thing that disturbs you. After our news about Jamestown I fear we cannot be too cautious with the Massachusetts."

Then a crash of thunder descended on the colony, warning of storm to come.

⤛⤜

Enroute home from Sowams Hobomok took Winslow aside and told him startling news. Massasoit had instructed him to tell Winslow that the Massachusetts conspired to destroy Wessagussett and all its inhabitants. They realized they must also destroy Plimoth with the same stroke, lest the English there rush to their countrymen's defense. A number of sachems had agreed to support this move, including Canacum and Iyanough, but Massassoit refused to participate.

Winslow was stunned. He stared at Hobomok, unbelieving. "Why did he not tell me himself?"

Hobomok said, "He want you safely away from Sowams. Ears listen and eyes watch there."

Winslow shook his head. "The Massachusetts have no quarrel with us at Plimoth. But they must assume that we would defend our countrymen, as they would their tribesmen."

Winslow and Hampden hurried home to divulge this news to Bradford, Allerton, and Brewster who heard it calmly. Bradford asked Winslow, "Do you believe this, Edward?"

Winslow nodded yes. "Hobomok is intensely loyal to Massasoit. He would not conjure so cruel a story. I must believe that Massasoit instructed him."

Bradford turned to Allerton. "Isaac, call a meeting of all our men at once. This deed may be executed before we can confirm it."

When the men assembled, Hopkins' first question was, "How can we be sure? Who else has knowledge of this?"

"We do not know yet. Myles has been suspicious of some Indians' behavior lately, but that does not prove treachery."

"What sort of behavior?" asked John Alden.

Standish told them of Canacum's deference to Wituwamat and the warrior's surly manner toward himself.

Brewster said, "We cannot act on hearsay evidence."

"Word directly from Massasoit is hardly hearsay," insisted Hopkins.

"Agreed," said Bradford. "What motive would he have to deceive us? Though his sentiments may be with his people, he *has* warned us. That itself is a testimony to their treachery, which even Massasoit cannot abide."

"So what options do we have?" asked Alden.

"None," snapped Standish, "except to beat them at their own devices."

330

The men sat silently, weighing Standish's words. Their Fort was a haven now, and they could huddle within its walls and await an assault. But their stores were low. Sooner or later, they must leave the compound to hunt for food and plant crops. Would they wait to be picked off one by one by lurking natives?

"Methinks," Hopkins began,"they are gathering enough strength to attack both settlements at once. Wessagussett alone would succumb easily, and they could rush us before we even heard the news and could retaliate."

"Which means?" asked John Alden.

"We attack first."

No one spoke to this galling prospect of decimating the very people they hoped to convert to God's love for all men. Yet one ominous note thrust into each man's thoughts: the massacre at Jamestown. Had anyone warned them?

At last Bradford broke silence. "Has anyone a better strategy?"

John Howland cleared his throat and spoke. "Suppose we take a force and confront them with what we know. Appeal to their human nature as men like ourselves who care for wives and children and their brothers. Some of these are good-hearted, even kind." He looked about at the somber men. "Why not try? If God meant for us to come here to convert them to Christian belief, should we not appeal to the best that God has already placed within them?"

The men gazed upon this generous young man still so optimistic. Did he actually believe that these natives could be dissuaded from destroying the white men of Weston's colony they so despised? Who, in fact, had earned their contempt, and were hardly worthy of Plimoth's defense. Yet Plimoth by association of race and culture may face their same fate.

Bradford said, "We will wait one day, send out loyal scouts to discern their intentions toward us, and reconvene tomorrow to make our decision."

At the meeting next day a chief Wassapinewat, brother to Obtakiest, a sachem of the Massachusetts, confirmed that the conspiracy was indeed planned. So Bradford called a town-meeting of the entire colony and laid before them the dire threat. All were dismayed to confront the dreadful reality: their sufferings on Cape Cod, their longings for peace and security, and the flickering hope that they could establish in this unforgiving wilderness a community of Christians, would only come to violence. They were going to be forced to take the sort of action that only the desperate take, to kill their enemies in self-defense, the only morally justifiable crime among civilized men.

The colony deferred their authority to Bradford and his leaders. Spurred by Captain Standish's practical tactics, they decided to stage a trading voyage to Wessagussett to warn the men there of the conspiracy. Then they would execute only the conspirators. The mind of each colonist strained to accept the necessity of such action to save their English colonies, and each heart pleaded for revelation of a better way. Was violence to be the final fruit of Squanto's help in their survival, the bonding friendship of the tribes of Aspinet and Iyanough, and Governor Carver's remarkable treaty with Massasoit?

God help us, Lord, rang in each heart.

And each heard only silence.

Twenty-four

One Small Candle

S oon after the town-meeting, as Standish and eight men he had chosen prepared for the assault, a bedraggled colonist from Wessagussett named Phineas Pratt stumbled into their village and told a tale more terrible than the one Plimoth already knew. The rapid degeneration of Weston's town and the harassment of its dying inhabitants by the Massachusetts had been fearful enough, but now Pratt embellished the tale with cruel details.

When his weakened compatriots tried to boil a pot of porridge, the natives snatched it from their hands and ate it before their eyes, stroking their glittering knives all the while. And then Pecksuot and his men, infuriated by one colonist's continual stealing of their corn, had demanded that the thief be punished by his own people as was the custom among their tribes. The men of Wessagussett protested that they had soundly punished the thief and even offered him up to the natives for punishment. Pecksuot objected, saying, "All sachems do justice by their own men. If not, we say they are all agreed and then we fight, and now I say you all steal my corn."

Pratt related that they had released the offender because they had no food to give him and charged him to gather ground nuts, clams, and mussels as other men did, and to steal no more. Only two days later the natives brought him back, complaining, "Here is the corn. Come see the place where he stole it." So they bound him again.

Pratt went on. "Two of our company said, 'We have been to the Sachem's house and they have near finished their last canoe that they may encounter with our ship. Their greatest care is how to send their armies to Plimoth because of the snow.' But when we understood that their plot was to kill all English people in one day when the snow was gone, I would have sent a man to Plimoth, but none were willing to go. Then I said if Plimoth men know not of this treacherous plot, they and we are all dead men; therefore, if God willing, tomorrow I will go. That night a young man lacking wit told Pecksuot early in the morning. Pecksuot came to me and said in English, 'Me hear you go to Patuxet; you will lose yourself; the bears and the wolves will eat you; but because I love you, I will send my boy Nahamit with you; and I will give you victuals to eat by the way and to be merry with your friends when you come there.'

"I said, 'Who told you so great a lie, that I may kill him?'"

"He said, 'It is no lie, you shall not know.' Then came five men armed. These attended me seven or eight days and nights. Then, they supposing it was a lie, were careless of their watch near two hours in the morning. Then said I to our company, 'Now is the time to go to Plimoth. Is there any compass to be found?' They said, 'None but them that belong to the ship.' I said, 'They are too big. I have borne no arms of defense this seven or eight days. Now if I take up my arms, they will mistrust me.' They said, 'The savages will pursue after you and kill you and we shall never see you again.' Thus with other words of great lamentation, we parted."

Pratt paused to take a deep breath, obviously in need of rest but determined to finish his tale. Someone offered him another cup of hot tea. The faces of his listeners were grim, for his story confirmed the urgency of their situation.

Pratt went on. "Then I took a hoe and went to the long swamp nearby their houses and dug on the edge thereof as if I had been looking for ground nuts. But, seeing no man, I went in and ran through it. Then looking round about me, I ran southward 'til three o'clock, but the snow being in many places, I was the more distressed because of my footsteps. The sun being clouded, I wandered, not knowing my way, but at the going down of the sun, it appeared red. Then hearing a great howling of wolves, I came to a river; the water being deep and cold and many rocks, I passed through with much ado. Then was I in great distress—faint for want of food, weary with running, fearing to make a fire because of them that pursued me."

Not a murmur came from his audience. Outside the wind whined against the windows of the fort, an ominous keening wail matching the gravity of his story.

"Then I came to a deep dell or hole, there being much wood fallen into it. Then I said in my thought, *This is God's providence that here I may make a fire.* Then having made a fire, the stars began to appear and I saw Ursa Major."

A murmur of relief rounded the room. Ursa Major pointed to the North Star, a God-given compass for him to follow.

"The day following I began to travel but being unable, I went back to the fire that day. The next day the sun shone and passing by the water on my left hand, I came to a brook and there was a path. Having but a short time to consider and fearing to go beyond the plantation I kept running in the path, then passing through James River I said in my thought, *Now am I as a deer chased by wolves. If I perish, what will be the condition of distressed Englishmen?* Finding a piece of carved wood, I took it up and carried it in my hand. Finding a piece of a jerkin, I carried them under my arm. Then said I in my mind, *God has given me these two tokens for my comfort, that now he will give me my life for a prayer.* Running down a hill, I met an Englishman coming in the path before me. I sat down on a tree and, rising up to salute him, I said, 'Mr. Hampden, I am glad to see you alive.' He said, 'I am glad and full of wonder to se you alive. Let us sit down. I see you are weary.'

"I said, 'Let me eat some parched corn.'

"Then he said, 'Come. Massasoit has sent word to the Governor that Aberdikes and his confederates have contrived a plot, hoping to kill all English people in one day here.'"

In the village Pratt's breathless witness to the Indians' torment of the men of Wessagussett and their plot to destroy both colonies reinforced the Plimoth colonists' plan to attack the conspirators. There seemed to be no alternative.

On April fourth they sailed to Wessagussett, where they found the *Swan* anchored with no one aboard her. Ashore, her captain assured Standish that the Indians had shown only friendliness toward them and even shared their lodgings. No one suspected an impending attack, and the men had scattered about looking for food. Outraged, Standish sternly ordered that all be summoned home at once and stay there on pain of death. From Plimoth's precious supply of seed corn he gave each man a pint of corn to keep them from further wandering for food.

The first day proved too stormy for action and the party was forced to wait. Yet, unknown to the English, on the second day an Indian spy reported to Pecksuot, a chief conspirator, that while the English captain spoke smoothly, the spy could see "by his eyes" that he was angry "in his heart." This alerted the conspirators to the probability that the English had discovered their plot. Yet rather than deter them, it emboldened them with an air of defiance. Pecksuot told Hobomok that they knew that the captain had come to kill them, but added, "Tell him that we know it, but fear him not, neither will we shun him. Let him begin when he dare; he shall not take us unawares."

The pretended purpose of Standish's visit was trade, but as negotiations began, the proud Indians kept making insulting remarks and gestures, especially Wituwamat, who bragged of the excellence of his knife adorned on the end of its handle with an image of a woman's face. Declared Wituwamat, "But I have another at home, wherewith I have killed both French and English and that hath a man's face on it; and, by and bye, these two must marry." He taunted further, *"Hinnaim namen, kinnaim michen, matta cuts,"* which in English meant, "By and bye it should see, and by and bye it should eat, but not speak."

Pecksuot added his bit with contempt for Standish's small stature. "Though you be a great Captain, yet you be but a little man. And though I be no Sachem, yet I am a man of great strength and courage."

Standish controlled his temper, though perhaps not so well his ruddy color and "angry eyes," and bore up under their ridicule, biding his time.

The next day, intending to trade, Pecksuot, Wituwamat, Wituwamat's young brother trodding behind him and scoffing at the English, and one other native came together in one room with four of Standish's men. Standish had planned to assemble all his party together for the assault, but now suddenly saw his best chance of taking the leaders by surprise was at that moment in this room. He slammed the door shut and whirled upon Pecksuot, snatched the Indian's own razor-edged knife hung about his neck, and plunged it into his chest. The other three colonists attacked Wituwamat and the two other Indians.

Hobomok stood by, watching the spectacle. When it ended, he told Captain Standish, "Yesterday Pecksuot, bragging of his own strength and stature, said, 'Though you were a great captain, yet you were but a little man.' But today, I see you are big enough to lay him on the ground."

Yet the Indians had resisted bravely. Winslow wrote that the two leaders sustained an "incredible" number of wounds before they died, "not making any fearful noise, but catching at their weapons and striving to the last."

But now the captain's blood was up, and to make certain the plotters were finished, that day they hanged Wituwamat's brother and killed three other Indians. Their mission to abort the plot was done.

Repercussions from this deed circled out across the Cape like ripples from a rock thrown into a lake. Standish and his men skirmished with other Indians in a swamp, gaining the higher ground, and striking such terror in the natives' breasts that many fled into the swamps and hid there, forsaking their homes and exposing themselves to starvation and disease.

The execution party returned to Wessagussett and freed the Indian women, allowing them to keep their beaver coats and treating them courteously. To the Englishmen of Wessagussett Standish offered sanctuary at Plimoth. Some accepted, but most chose to sail to Monhegan, hoping to return to England aboard a fishing vessel. The captain provided these with precious corn from their meager stores to sustain their voyage. At last, when the *Swan* set sail for Monhegan, Standish and his men returned to Plimoth, where they were received joyously. The head of Wituwamat was placed upon a spike, so that his people, who might not believe he had been subdued, would have no doubts. This was the typically English display of the triumph of justice, recalling the many heads of English traitors adorning the bridges of London, left to rot in the wind and rain and sun, grimly attesting to the duplicity of men and the arrogance of their victors.

A young, amiable Indian who had come to Plimoth while the assault was accomplished had been detained by Bradford. Now, seeing Wituwamat's head in bitter defeat, the youth confessed the plot and its three other conpirators, *Powahs* or medicine men, all known to

Plimoth. The young native had followed Pratt, intending to kill him but missed finding him in the gorge where he built his fire. The Indian claimed that the plot awaited only the building of two more canoes by Weston's men, who had already built three, so that the plotters could seize the *Swan*. The youth begged for his life, claiming he was not of the Massachusetts but merely lived with them. Hobomok gave a good report of him, and Bradford assured him he would not be hurt, then instructed him to take a message to Obtakiest:

> For our part, it never entered our hearts to take such a course with you, until your own treachery enforced us to. Yet, since you have begun, if by any like course you do provoke us, you would never be allowed to rest in peace. And therefore you should take this as a warning. Further, you must not destroy the palisades and houses of Wessagussett, must send the three captive Englishmen back to Patuxet, and send the messenger back with our Englishmen and your answer, or both. The messenger will not be harmed.

The Indian, his ankles unshackled, gratefully fled.

That evening Bradford sat alone by his fire, sipping warm ale. After awhile a knock sounded at his door. "Come," he called out.

William Brewster came in and sat down beside Bradford. Gazing into the fire, neither spoke for some time.

At last Bradford said, "You know what this means, William."

"Aye."

"Is it as bad as I think?"

"Worse, probably."

"We have embarked on a new course, have we not?"

Brewster nodded. They sat longer in silence. Then Bradford asked, "What do you think Robinson will say?"

"We will hear of it."

Bradford sat forward in his chair, leaning toward the flames as if to absorb their warmth. "What else could we have done?"

"Nothing. Our way was clear."

Bradford glanced into Brewster's eyes. "Are you convinced of that?"

338

"I am."

"I wonder—what John Howland suggested—could we have tried that? Would they have listened?"

"I much doubt it."

Bradford sat back and sipped his ale. "Then why do I feel so...bereft? No sense of victory, no triumph. Actually, not even relief."

"Because there is no triumph in execution, only hope that you have prevented worse evil. You made a bold decision to save our plantations, which now we know certainly, were severely threatened. As governor, this was your proper responsibility. Yet you also knew that such action risked dire consequences." He paused. "It was never our purpose to conquer, much less destroy the people here. And yet, the world surrounds us, as much in this wilderness as it did in England. Our God knows better than we ourselves the evil we must overcome, and how it must be done."

"Methinks...my greatest dread...is that I submitted to fear, and then deciding to attack, did not hear *His* voice clearly. Was it God, or Fear, driving me to this sad end?"

"You will never know that until Heaven, my dear friend. You have confessed your weakness and God forgives you. Yet think on this. You did not make this decision alone. The entire colony agreed on this action, and our community survives. For the moment evil has been overcome. Rest in peace. You will face agonizing decisions again."

The widening circles of native reaction to the assault at Wessagussett were soon and dreadfully realized. None of the three English captives returned to Patuxet, for Obtakiest had already killed them before Bradford's request. The sachem expressed sorrow and an earnest desire to make peace with the colony, but none of his messengers dared to approach Plimoth. Obtakiest himself, along with many of his people, forsook his home to wander from place to place, fearing English vengeance upon him. Winslow wrote eloquently but sadly of their distress:

Concerning those other people who intended to join with the Massachusetts against us, though we never went against any of them; yet this sudden and unexpected execution, together with the just judgement of God upon their guilty consciences, hath so terrified and amazed them, as, in like manner, they forsook their houses, running to and fro like men distracted, living in swamps and other desert places: and so brought manifold diseases amongst themselves, whereof very many are dead; as Canacum the Sachem of Manomet, Aspinet the Sachem of Nauset, Iyanough the Sachem of Mattachiest. This Sachem (Iyanough), in his life, in the midst of these distractions, said, The God of the English was offended with them; and would destroy them in his anger. And certainly it is strange to hear how many of late have died, and still daily die amongst them. Neither is there any likelihood it will easily cease: because, through fear, they set little or no corn, which is the staff of life; and without which, they cannot long preserve health and strength. From one of these places a boat was sent with presents to the Governor, hoping thereby to work their peace; but the boat was cast away, and three of the persons drowned, not far from our Plantation: only one escaped; who durst not come to us, but returned. So as none of them dare to come amongst us.

I fear I have been too tedious...yet when I considered how necessary a thing it is that the truth and grounds of this action especially, should be made known; and also the several dispositions of that dissolved Colony whose reports undoubtedly will be as various: I could not but enlarge myself, where I thought to be most brief; neither durst I be too brief, lest I should eclipse and rob God of that honour, glory and praise which belongeth to him for preserving us from falling, when we were at the pit's brim; and yet feared not, nor knew that we were in danger.

The following December John Robinson wrote what would be his last letter to Governor Bradford. His words pierced Bradford's heart.

O, how happy a thing had it been if you had converted some, before you had killed any.... Let me be bold to exhort you to seriously consider of the disposition of your captain, whom I love and am persuaded the Lord in great mercy and for much good hath sent you him, if you use him right. He is a man humble and meek

340

amongst you, and towards all in ordinary course. But not if this be merely from a humane spirit, there is cause to fear that by occasion, especially of provocation, there may be wanting that tenderness of the life of man, made after God's image, that is meet.

Bradford lay the letter down on his desk. He was eager to hear Brewster's comment, for he needed his Elder's words of comfort in this most painful distress.

Brewster looked up from the letter and raised an eyebrow. "What did you expect?"

"Just that, though perhaps a more harsh rebuke. Yet I should remember that gentle John Robinson never criticized harshly. His softest rebuke struck the heart."

"Remember, my son, he was not here. He knows nothing of wilderness, nor the darkened hearts of men who have never known grace and forgiveness but only vengeance. One day this land may be peopled by men like Robinson, but not now. Take heart, brother. What's done is done. God will redeem."

Bradford would share the letter with any of the colonists who cared to read it, for their pastor's word was epilogue to the siege at Wessagussett. Yet the people of Plimoth took heart that though they had entered a new phase of relationship with the natives of Cape Cod, one they had desperately hoped to avoid, the candle they had lit on the edge of this wilderness gleamed on.

Author's Note

One Candle's Light portrays the American Pilgrims not as icons but as "common" Englishmen committed to living by Christian principles in an oppressive secular world. Unique among most colonists seeking prosperity, the *Mayflower* voyagers sought to establish a community for families—husbands, wives, children, and indentured servants. I quote Dr. Paul Jehle:

> There is not another attempt at permanent settlement in all of history up to this time period that parallels this migration of families. Spain's attempt at colonization, or Jamestown in 1607, migrated as men only. Twelve years later, women were imported into Jamestown in order to induce men to marry and remain as families. All understood that unless the family was strong, the colony would not survive.

The Pilgrims' willingness to subject their dependents to this "weighty voyage" could only be supported by their comparable devotion to a loving God who would lead them through the unknown wilderness. Though convinced their mandate came from God, the congregation left their homeland reluctantly, beset with very human fears and doubts. Confronted by dire poverty in hedonistic Holland, betrayed by trusted benefactors, and overwhelmed by raw wilderness in the New World, they clung to their belief in God's promise to sustain them. When sickness and starvation felled half the colony that first winter on Cape Cod, the remnant welcomed natives Tisquantum and Massasoit as emissaries of Grace sent to help them.

Massasoit's warning of a native conspiracy to annihilate both New Plimoth and Wessagussett settlements presented their leaders with a worst-case dilemma: How do true Christian believers forestall a deadly enemy they hoped to convert?

Their "answerable courage" to defend their colony left a legacy to Americans best expressed by Governor Bradford in his history, *Of Plymouth Plantation:*

> ...as one small candle may light a thousand, so the light kindled here has shown unto many, yea in some sort to our whole nation...We have noted these things so that you might see their worth and not negligently lose what your fathers have obtained with so much hardship.

Bibliography

One definition of historical fiction is that the raw data of historical events are like pieces of wood lighted with the "fire" of an author's imagination, which illuminates characters and events for modern readers. Yet among the hundreds of articles, books, and speculations written about the English pilgrims of Plimoth Plantation in Massachusetts, most fictional accounts were written for children. I found one novel written in the 1960s and the movie, *Plymouth Adventure,* in the 50s were fictional accounts of their voyage, and both were more fantastic than factual. *One Candle's Light* bases its portrayal of characters on the facts of their story carefully researched and fictionalized only to enlarge the pilgrims as individual personalities.

The select bibliography listed below are those versions of their story that seemed to me most insightful of the yearnings, determination, accomplishments, and failures of that obscure congregation of Christians who first cast their lot together at Scrooby, England.

Arber, Edward. *The Story of the Pilgrim Fathers, 1606-1623, A.D., as told by Themselves, Their Friends, and Their Enemies.* London: Ward and Downey Limited. Boston: Houghton Mifflin, 1897. New York: Kraus Reprint Co., 1969.

Bradford, William. *Of Plymouth Plantation 1620-1647.* Edited by Samuel Eliot Morrison. New York: Knopf, 1982.

Bradford, William. *Governor William Bradford's Letter Book.* Boston: Massachusetts Society of Mayflower Descendants, 1906.

Bridenbaugh, Carl. *Vexed and Troubled Englishmen: 1590-1642.* New York: Oxford University Press, 1968.

Burgess, Walter H. *John Robinson, Pastor of the Pilgrim Fathers.* London: Williams and Norgate, and New York: Harcourt, Brace, and Howe, 1920.

Dexter, the late Henry Martyn, and his son, Morton Dexter. *The England and Holland of the Pilgrims.* Originally published in London,

1906. (No publisher listed.) Reprinted in Baltimore by Geneological Publishing Co., Inc., 1978.

Dillon, Francis. *The Pilgrims: Their Journeys and their Worlds.* Garden City, New York: Doubleday, 1975.

Fleming, Thomas J. *One Small Candle: The Pilgrim's First Year in America.* New York: W.W. Norton & Co., Inc., 1964.

The Geneva Bible: A facsimile of the 1560 edition. Introduction by Lloyd E. Berry. Wisconsin: University of Wisconsin Press, 1969.

George, Timothy. *John Robinson and the English Separatist Tradition.* Macon, Georgia: Mercer University Press, 1982.

Goodwin, John A. *The Pilgrim Republic: An Historical Review of the Colony of New Plimoth, Centenary Edition.* Boston and New York: Houghton Mifflin Company, 1920.

Jehle, Paul. *Plimoth in the Words of Her Founders: Visitors Guide to America's Hometown.* San Antonio, Texas: Vision Forum, 2003.

Pratt, Phineas. *A Declaration of the Affairs of the English People that First Inhabited New England.* Collections of the Massachusetts Historical Society, 4th Series, Volume 4, 1858.

Sherwood, Mary B. *Pilgrim: A Biography of William Brewster.* Virginia: Great Oak Press of Virginia, 1982.

Willison, George F. *Saints and Strangers.* New York: Reynal and Hitchcock, 1945.

Winslow, Edward. *Good Newes from New England, 1624.* Printed in Young's *Chronicles of the Pilgrim Fathers* and Arber's *Story of the Pilgrim Fathers.*

Winslow, Edward. *Mourt's Relation.* Printed in Young's *Chronicles,* 1841.

Young, Alexander. *Chronicles of the Pilgrim Fathers.* Boston: Little and Brown, 1841.

About the Author

FAY ALEXANDER was born and educated in Pennsylvania. On an Open Scholarship at Ursinus College she earned a Bachelor's degree in English. That summer she married William Alexander on duty with the U.S. Navy in San Francisco. Two sons were born in California before the Alexanders returned to Pennsylvania, where William finished a Bachelor's degree in Political Science at Lehigh University.

The family moved to Gainesville, Florida, where a daughter, Beth, was born, and Fay began studying for a Master's degree in English at the University of Florida. "The Fossil," a story included in the author's creative thesis, *In Season, Out of Season*, was published by *Prairie Schooner* and chosen by its editors as best story of that year, 1976. Recent first-place prizes for two novels, *Under Every Green Tree* (2001) and *One Small Candle* (2004, now renamed *One Candle's Light*) were awarded at the Blue Ridge Mountain Christian Writers Conferences at Black Mountain, North Carolina.

Fay's interest in the pilgrim saga began in 1984 as an English teacher at Living Faith Fellowship School when she visited the New Testament Christian School at Cedarville (South Plymouth), Massachusetts to observe its curriculum. A year later she made the first of three trips to England to research the migration of English colonists to America.

The Alexanders' English and Scottish ancestry piques their continual interest in English history, particularly in the Reformation and its profound role in early American colonization. Fay and William, a retired teacher and history buff, live in Gainesville. Their elder son, William III, is a computer technician at UF, and son Jon teaches social studies at Bradford Middle School. Their daughter, Beth, teaches English in China. You may email the author at: **whaf@cox.net.**

www.oaktara.com